THE
FARMERETTES

GISELA TOBIEN SHERMAN

Second Story Press

Library and Archives Canada Cataloguing in Publication

Sherman, Gisela Tobien, 1947-, author
The Farmerettes / Gisela Sherman.

Issued in print and electronic formats.
ISBN 978-1-927583-64-7 (pbk.)—ISBN 978-1-927583-69-2 (epub)

1. Ontario Farm Service Force—Juvenile fiction. I. Title.

PS8587.H3857F37 2015   jC813'.54   C2014-908146-4

C2014-908346-7

Edited by Kelly Jones and Kathryn Cole
Designed by Melissa Kaita
Cover photographs © iStockphoto
Printed and bound in Canada

*Second Story Press gratefully acknowledges the support of the Ontario Arts Council
and the Canada Council for the Arts for our publishing program. We acknowledge
the financial support of the Government of Canada through the Canada Book Fund.*

ONTARIO ARTS COUNCIL
CONSEIL DES ARTS DE L'ONTARIO
an Ontario government agency
un organisme du gouvernement de l'Ontario

Canada Council   Conseil des Arts
for the Arts   du Canada

Published by
SECOND STORY PRESS
20 Maud Street, Suite 401
Toronto, ON M5V 2M5
www.secondstorypress.ca

Dedicated to my children,
Becky, Jainna, and Charlie, and their future children.
May they never have to endure such a war.

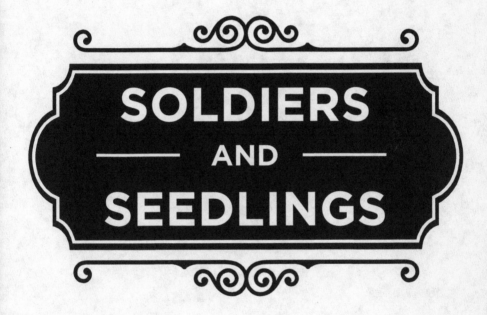

SOLDIERS

AND

SEEDLINGS

SATURDAY, OCTOBER 24, 1942

Helene

Row upon row of men in brown serge uniforms marched, left, right, left, right, heads up, shoulders back, rifles balanced low on their hips. From where Helene Miller and her friend Peggy stood, the line had no beginning and continued forever, though Helene knew they would turn left at the TH&B railway station on Hunter Street. Hundreds of soldiers marched by. They stared straight ahead—each face a proud mask hiding whatever hopes, elation, or fears it felt inside—off to save the world.

The people cheered for their brave boys. Mothers smiled and waved, holding in their tears and terror until they got home. Fathers stood silent, proud, worried. Wives and girlfriends in their prettiest dresses blew kisses. Youngsters ran alongside the columns of marching men, most to revel in the excitement—pretend they too were off to fight this glorious war—and some just to get one last look at Daddy.

"There's the band!" Peggy shouted, dodging a Union Jack waving vigorously beside her. "Wish I could march with them."

Helene smiled at her. Peggy, her freckled face rosy with exhilaration, her smile infectious as always, loved spontaneous fun and drama. She cheered the band and the young enlistees who followed it.

"Isn't that Theo Brock?" Helene pointed at a blond boy with broad shoulders.

Peggy squealed. "Oooh, he looks handsome in khaki." She brushed her auburn hair from her face and waved.

"Hey, Peggy!" Theo called. "Write to me." Without breaking stride, he tossed a piece of paper toward her.

She caught it, read his address. "Camp Borden. I was stuck on him last year. I'll write him every day!" She waved until he paraded from sight.

"There's another swell-looking guy," Peggy said, smiling at a tall, dark enlistee.

Helene wondered if her own father had looked that good when he headed off to the Great War. Had young girls squealed over him? They wouldn't have when he returned.

When the tall enlistee's address fluttered her way, Peggy grabbed it. "Now I have two soldiers to write to."

When a third paper flew their way, Peggy pointed at it. "It's for you, Helene. Catch."

Such a handsome boy would never write to me, thought Helene, shaking her head.

"Take it," Peggy said. "You write better letters than I do."

Helene pocketed the address and looked up at the big Birks clock on the corner just as the four bronze horsemen charged around its base four times. Two-thirty. "I should go home."

"Stay a bit longer, Helene. The parade's almost over." She smiled at another boy and he too tossed an address her way. So did the fellow marching behind him. "Send me your photo," he called.

When the last row had marched past them, the onlookers drifted home to dinner, and the young soldiers boarded the train to uncertain futures.

Peggy proudly clutched four slips of paper. "I knew we'd have fun today." Her cheeks were flushed and her blue eyes shone.

Helene agreed. "I'm glad we came."

"I have an hour before my piano lesson. Want to go for a soda?"

Helene shook her head. "Mama needs me at home." She imagined Peggy going home to play music and sing with her family—they were all so talented—and then sit down to a good meal. Waiting for Helene were three children—one sick, laundry to wash, potatoes and turnips to peel, and a meager supper with six roomers.

Peggy led the way through the crowd. "You want to go write to your soldier," she teased.

A girl in a gray coat, carrying a small cardboard box, stormed down McNab Street toward them.

I'd rather finish my homework, read my new book, and sleep until noon tomorrow, Helene thought.

The girl stopped at a bench, slammed down the box, and stood staring up the street, fists clenched. When a bus pulled up, she glared at the box and rushed onto the bus. As it pulled away, Helene wondered, *What could have upset her so?*

Peggy walked to the bench, studied the box, and gingerly pulled open one corner.

"Peggy, you can't."

"Watch me." Peggy peered into the box and whistled. "Chocolate!" She scooped up the box and brought it to Helene. Lifting the cover, she said, "I've gone to heaven. Ten chocolate brownies. I haven't tasted chocolate for a year." She reached in. "Have one."

"I can't eat someone else's misery."

"Won't help her if they go to waste," Peggy mumbled through a mouthful of brownie.

Reluctantly, Helene took one and bit into it. Her mouth, her whole body sighed with joy. Rich, creamy chocolate. She hadn't eaten anything so heavenly for a long time.

Carrying the box like a trophy, Peggy led the way west. They compared the looks of the boys whose addresses they carried, and made up stories about why the girl in the gray coat was so angry. Twenty minutes later, they turned onto Locke Street. Peggy tore the box in half, divided the brownies equally, and handed one side to Helene. "See you Monday," she said and continued south.

Helene, careful to avoid the broken step, jumped up her front stairs with her treasure.

That night after they'd washed the dishes, and the boarders retired to their rooms, Mama boiled two weak cups of coffee, poured milk for the twins, and the family sat at the kitchen table for their special treat. *It's easy to laugh with chocolate in your mouth,* Helene thought, and silently thanked the unhappy girl in gray.

Once Willy and Peter were in bed, Helene sat at the table to do her homework while her mother ironed sheets nearby. She looked up from her history book and saw her mother's tired face. Her mama put in a full day making tires for army trucks at Firestone, caring for the boys and the house. Mr. Perkins' shirts still needed ironing. And always there was the worry—about bills, the war, Papa. Mama's hair was once light brown like Helene's. Now it was dull, streaked with white, and knotted into a practical bun. Her face was lined, her hands red and rough. Again, Helene wondered if she should leave school like some other girls, work in a factory, and earn more money. But then she'd never escape. She had to do well in school, do better than this life.

Finally, her homework finished, she cleared away her books and folded the sheets and pillowcases her mother was ironing—an endless job when you had to rent out rooms to pay your bills.

"Those brownies were a real treat," said her mother, smiling. "The last time I ate something so delicious was at cousin Anna's wedding. That was some feast. Roast beef, rich gravy on dumplings, fresh peas."

"My favorite meal is roast chicken, stuffing, and a cherry pie," said Helene. "Topped with ice cream and a cup of strong coffee."

"How about a butler to serve it and then wash the dishes?" said her mother. By now they were laughing.

"Why not a chauffeur in a glamorous limousine too? We'd drive all over the countryside, picking up meat, fresh eggs, and fruit."

Her mother pulled the plug on the iron and sighed. "That's

how it used to be—without the car and servants, of course." She folded the ironing board away. "I'll just check the boys' shoes are clean for tomorrow, then turn in. Goodnight, my dear."

"Goodnight, Mama." Helene finished the sheets, then read twenty pages of *Lassie Come Home* before she went to bed. She would have liked a dog, but they could barely afford to feed themselves, let alone a pet.

By midnight, the rest of the house was dark. Down the hall, Mr. Perkins' radio still blared news about the German siege of Stalingrad, and Japanese attacks at Savo Island. He was hard of hearing and obsessed about the latest war news. But the volume forced everyone else to listen too. From the room below her, Helene heard sobbing—muffled but heart-wrenching. She wished she could comfort Alva, but what could she say to a woman with a sick toddler and a husband taken prisoner of war in Hong Kong?

A cool draft chilled the room. An uneven progression of snorts, grunts, and whistles began in the room to the right. Helene wished she could turn on the light and read, but then she'd wake her mother, asleep in the bed along the opposite wall. The boys slept across the hall. The other two bedrooms, the attic, and the dining room were rented out. Times had been tough since Helene could remember. When she was younger, Papa managed odd jobs and day labor between his bouts of anger and listlessness. The Depression meant no work at all, until hitchhiking to Ottawa to build highways became the only answer. This war brought relief of a sort. Women could find employment too. Now her mother brought in enough income to repay their debts and start over.

Someone stepped furtively down the hall, stopped at her door, then continued downstairs. Who? Why? Were they simply trying to be considerate and not wake anyone, or were they sneaking into the supply of food in the cupboard? It seemed everyone in this house held some secret or sorrow.

Binxie

When Binxie Rutherford saw the little yellow coupe parked in her drive, she hurried up Roxborough Street, across her lawn, and yanked open the front door. "Kathryn!" she called as she rushed down the hall.

No answer. Binxie headed for the kitchen, where she found the housekeeper singing "Don't Sit Under the Apple Tree" and peeling potatoes at the sink.

"Hello, Sadie. Is Kathryn home? Where is she?"

"In the study. With your parents."

Sadie's expression told Binxie things weren't good. She went to the study, the thick Persian carpets muffling her steps. Even the solid oak door couldn't block out the emotion in the voices inside the room. She held her ear to the door. What was it this time? She was annoyed. At seventeen, she was old enough to be told things without having to eavesdrop.

One of the voices came closer. Binxie stepped back just as the door flung open and her sister strode into the hall and up the stairs. She caught a quick glimpse of her father—tight-lipped with anger, a comforting arm around her mother—before turning to follow her sister up to a bedroom full of ornate cherrywood furniture. The lone ornament—a gold-framed photo of Kathryn and Binxie perched on a sailboat at the lake—sat on the dresser. Both sisters loved sailing and sports. Now Kathryn slammed clothes into, then out of, and back into her open suitcase.

"Don't go yet."

Kathryn sat on her bed and patted a spot beside her. "How are you?"

"Glad you're home. Why aren't they?"

Kathryn smiled. "Oh, they're happy to see me, just not pleased with my decision."

Binxie grinned nervously. "What is it this time, you rebel?"

"I like your hair that way. Shorter. Very sophisticated."

"Don't try to change the subject. How long can you stay? Can we do something together? *Somewhere I'll Find You* is playing at The Bloor. Clark Gable and Lana Turner."

Kathryn laughed. "Let's walk in the garden. It's been months since I've seen it. Sadie tells me she harvested a record crop of tomatoes and beans in Mother's prize rose garden."

"It's the patriotic thing to do. Wish we could grow sugar and butter too. What are you planning to do that so upsets Mother and Father?"

The girls stepped out the back door, and Kathryn paused to admire a border of yellow chrysanthemums.

"I'll find out anyway, and if you tell me first, I can take your side."

"You know how much I love flying."

Binxie nodded. "You were piloting planes up in the tree house when you were ten."

"I was set to join the women's division of the RCAF so I could do more in this war than cook jam and knit socks."

Binxie rolled her eyes. "But that's what young ladies from good families do," she quoted in a savage imitation of her mother's voice.

"You and I have minds of our own," said Kathryn. "But they won't allow women to fly planes—ever—no matter how skilled they are. I'm an excellent pilot, two hundred and sixty hours flying time and top marks in my class. I'm as able as any man, but they say it's too dangerous for women. They're training us to cook, Binxie. To become chauffeurs, hairdressers, parachute riggers, dental assistants…laundry staff, for Pete's sake. I could do all that at home."

"Actually, Sadie does most of that at home."

Kathryn laughed. "The United States Army Air Forces won't allow women to fly either. Jackie Cochran is campaigning to let women ferry planes, but so far they're just talking."

"So what will you do?" Binxie knew she wouldn't like the answer.

Kathryn studied a maple tree in full crimson splendor. "Do you remember Helen Harrison, my flying instructor from Hamilton?"

Binxie nodded.

"She contacted some of us to come join her in the Air Transport Auxiliary. I'm going to become a ferry pilot in England!"

"England! But that's too far away. And closer to the fighting. I agree with Mother and Father. You can't go."

"None of you objected when our brothers went to war."

"Duncan is sitting in an office in Washington, and Charlie is directing something in Ottawa."

"Binxie, this war must be won. A lot of fine people are working on that. I need to be one of them."

"But flying planes over a country that's being bombed every night. That's dangerous."

"Just as awful for the young men who do it every evening."

"Why fly? Why not help the war effort on land, where the least mistake won't kill you?"

"I've talked to returned soldiers. They fight from trenches full of mud, blood, and rats. I prefer the open sky. Binxie, when I'm up in the air, I feel alive. I'm in control and free. Down here I'm bound by rules that don't make sense. This war will be won in the air. If I'm going to fly, I have to go to England."

Binxie hugged her sister. "I want to sign up too."

"I'm twenty-three. You're seventeen."

"I'll fake it. Lots of boys do."

"Wait a year or two."

Binxie kicked a bush. Kathryn wrapped an arm around her as they headed back into the kitchen. "There is another way to serve."

"Don't you dare tell me to roll more bandages."

"How about the Farm Service Forces? Help feed everyone fighting for us."

"What, the jam isn't enough?"

"Funny. The Farm Service Forces is an army of girls who work on farms for the summer."

"How dull! And what do I know about farming?"

"As much as the other girls who sign up. Our troops need food."

"That's why we have farmers," said Binxie, pouring a glass of water for each of them.

"Most of the able-bodied men have left the farms to fight. The rest are working in factories. There's barely anyone left to tend the crops. Don't you want to break away from our cozy little world, see other places? Or would you rather spend the summer with Mother and her committees?"

"I don't see myself as a farmer. There are pigs and bulls on a farm. And manure."

"Where there's manure, there are horses."

"Hmmm."

"And handsome farm boys."

"Farm boys? *Puhleeze*. I'd never be interested in a farmer. Remember the boys at the stables in Muskoka? Dirty fingernails, dirty mouths, and maybe ten years of education between both of them."

"That's harsh, Binxie. Most aren't like that."

"You're not dating one!"

"Among others."

"You wild woman. Anyone special?"

"No." Kathryn pulled a cookie from the tin on the kitchen counter. "Give the Farm Services some thought. You'd help the war effort and have fun at the same time."

Binxie shrugged. "I'll think about it."

Kathryn clapped Binxie's shoulder. "Want to see that movie before dinner? I hear Clark's a heartbreaker."

Isabel

Isabel Lynch stood across from the Hunter Street train station. She had taken extra care with her blonde curls this morning, and wore her pink blouse and the navy suit that brought out the blue in her eyes. It wasn't warm enough, but it looked smarter than a coat. Now, holding her hand with the small bright diamond over her heart, she scanned the lines of marching soldiers. Where was Billy?

They had said good-bye at home in Guelph two nights ago—a romantic evening of passionate kisses and promises. But she had managed a ride into Hamilton with her uncle today, just to see Billy once more. She had another gift for him. Two nights ago, it had been the photo of them together—to help him remember her and the life they planned after this war. Of course, nothing could compare to the gift he gave her the day he enlisted—an engagement ring. He had taken her for an evening stroll along the Eramosa. At a curve in the river, framed by cascading willows and lit by a full October moon, he said he loved her and on bended knee asked her to become Mrs. Billy Morrison. She cried when he slid the diamond on her finger. It was beautiful. They would spend their lives together. He was going away to war.

Yesterday she'd bought a fine silk handkerchief and spent the night embroidering their intertwined initials on it. Then she'd dabbed a drop of her Chanel N°5 on one corner. She had visions of Billy keeping it in his breast pocket, and when his strength faltered, he would hold it, inhale her scent, and regain his courage.

Isabel moved away from the crowd. The end of the line was

in sight. Had she missed him? As the men reached the station, they milled about in groups, chatting and puffing cigarettes before they embarked.

And there he was. Handsome and tall, he stood out from the crowd. She felt so full of love for him she thought her heart might burst. Pulling the handkerchief wrapped in soft tissue from her pocket, Isabel stepped off the curb. Across the street from her, Billy suddenly threw his head back in laughter. The fellows around him laughed too. In that moment, Isabel hated him. Here she was heartbroken and frightened about him crossing the ocean to fight, maybe to die—and he was joking with his pals. Tears prickled her eyes. She stopped to wipe them away. He mustn't see her like this.

As she pulled herself together, the last group of men surged the platform and she lost sight of Billy. She pushed her way through the noisy throng until at last she saw him—climbing aboard the train several cars down. "Billy!" she called, but he disappeared onto the train. She couldn't bear to stand alone and watch that train leave the station. Isabel tucked the handkerchief into her pocket and walked away. She could always mail it to him.

FRIDAY, NOVEMBER 20, 1942

Jean

Jean McDonnell shut the barn door and brushed bits of chaff from her auburn hair and blue overalls. The animals were fed and settled for the night. She waved at Dad and whistled for Dickens to follow her to the mailbox at the end of the drive.

She felt good. The harvesting, haying, and preparations for winter were finished. Robert couldn't have done better. She thought how wonderful dinner and a hot bath would soon feel. After evening chores, she would spend a delicious hour reading *Out of Africa*.

Maybe today they'd get a letter from Rob. It had been four worrisome months since they'd heard from him. Even then, any mention of where he was posted was blacked out by censors. She had hoped to track his whereabouts on the map posted on her bedroom wall, look up the cities in her atlas.

She opened the mailbox. Rob had painted a cow in a field on it. She pulled out several envelopes and walked back up the drive, leafing through them. Four letters, a farm magazine—an envelope from the government. Jean stopped cold. The telegram shook in her hand. *Was it...please, please, God, no.* She always thought a soldier came to the door to break the dreaded news. Maybe they'd already been there when she was in the back field. She walked to the house dazed by a jumble of thoughts, prayers, and guilt. Rob, her older brother, taught her to swim, shared his paints and treats with her, gave her his travel books before he left. As a farmer and only son, he didn't have to sign up to fight. So why had he enlisted? Because of her.

Her square, gray stone home, its white shutters and delicately carved bargeboard trim, looked so normal, so safe. She opened the screen door to the kitchen. The room was steamy with the aroma of dinner simmering on the stove. Her mother pulled a loaf of bread from the oven, humming along with the radio. In the rocking chair by the window, her grandmother sat knitting socks, with their old collie, Shep, snoozing beside her.

Dad had come in just ahead of her. He took off his boots and headed to the sink to wash his hands. This letter weighing five hundred pounds in her hand was about to shatter their world.

Her mother saw her first. She crossed the room and grabbed the envelope. Jean couldn't breathe as she watched Mum stare at the address. She wanted her to read it—and she didn't.

With shaking hands, her mother tore open the envelope. She read the telegram, then closed her eyes. "Rob is missing in action."

Jean felt like she'd been punched. Her father turned, clutched his chest, and collapsed unconscious to the floor.

X

It was the last dance, and the couples around her had moved closer together, eyes closed, swaying slowly to "Red Sails in the Sunset." They were probably already thinking about the walk home and romance under the moonlight. If only she could be like them. Instead, she dreaded any thought of goodnight kisses with Arthur. He was handsome and fun to be with. She liked playing tennis with him. Any other girl would love him. Any girl but her.

If only there was someone she could talk to. Someone who would explain to her why she wasn't attracted to Arthur—or any boy. Why it was his sister who made her heart race. Was she sick? It was the last dance, and she wanted to cry.

WEDNESDAY, MAY 5, 1943

Peggy

Peggy Pigeon stood in her bedroom holding up the dress she planned to wear tomorrow. It was the perfect shade of red, setting off the warm highlights in her hair. The skirt swung gracefully with her when she moved. She was looking forward to the tea dance after school.

Would Benny be there? She hoped so. Joseph was fun too—knew all the latest dance steps.

"Bang, bang, you're dead!"

"*Ahaht, ahaht, ahaht!* I got you!"

Outside her window, the neighborhood boys ran across lawns, playing war again. A window in the house next door slammed shut. Mrs. Ferguson. Peggy understood. Donny Ferguson had been the best dancer around here—but that hadn't saved him on the rocky beach at Dieppe.

Stop thinking about him, she told herself. *And don't think about Michael. I'm seventeen and I want to care about dresses and dances, not this stupid war.*

From below came the sound of musical instruments warming up. She hung the dress in her closet and hurried downstairs.

"Homework finished?" asked her father. With his dark hair, brown eyes, and tall build, he was more handsome than other fathers, though not as dreamy as Frank Sinatra.

"Most of it."

Her father nodded and adjusted his viola.

Mum stood beside him, adjusting a peg on her violin. Grampa drew a string across his cello, drawing out the first bars of Debussy's "Clair de lune." His wife hummed along with him, resting her violin comfortably on her left shoulder. Both of them were silver haired, but there the resemblance ended. Her grandfather, with his slight accent and rimless glasses, had the stately bearing of a professor, while her grandmother, all jolly laughter, red cheeks, and large chest, looked like an opera singer. But they had made beautiful music together for fifty years.

The cello began playing; the other instruments followed. Peggy sat at the piano and joined in. It felt like old times—before things got tense at home.

Next they played a Dvořák concerto, then Dad segued into the first bars of "Boogie Woogie Bugle Boy of Company B." Peggy snapped her fingers to the beat and everyone sang.

Mum said, "Let's not ignore Frankie."

Dad laughed. "I'll take on that youngster any time." In his rich baritone voice, he crooned and clowned the words: "All or nothin' at all…" Then the others joined him. By the time they reached "Then I'd rather, rather have nothin' at all," they were laughing so hard they could barely finish.

"Could we play something from home now, please?" Peggy's grandmother asked softly. She hummed a few notes, Mum joined in on the violin, and the others followed. Dad's expression became tight and Mum glanced at him several times with an odd look. Warning, defiance, or apology?

Had the mood in the room changed, or was it her? "I better finish my homework now," Peggy excused herself. "I hate this war," she muttered as she climbed upstairs to her room. "I wish it would just end."

She flopped onto her bed and slapped through the pages of

a *Compact* magazine. She stopped at the illustration of three girls in shorts and stylish cotton shirts by a wooded lake. There were no worries in their world. *I'd look good in those shorts,* she thought.

Those suntanned girls made her think of the poster at school: *"The Farm Service Forces Need You."* She remembered the stories the girls in the year ahead of her had told them last fall. They came to school looking spiffy, full of tales about the fun at "farmerette camp."

Peggy sighed and looked at her mathematics book spread open nearby. She'd have to study for exams soon.

Suddenly the answer to everything fell into place. She could skip the final examinations at school. Earn enough money to buy those shorts. Get away from here. Have an interesting summer! All she had to do was sign up for the Farm Service Forces tomorrow. Yes, the summer of 1943 was going to be swell.

TUESDAY, MAY 11, 1943

Helene

Helene watched the greasy water swirl down the drain, then turned on the taps for the next load of dirty dishes stacked on the counter. She looked longingly at her schoolbooks on the kitchen table. She wanted to get at them, lose herself in orderly mathematical equations, biology diagrams; anything but endless plates and pots.

The floor needed sweeping, her school blouse had to be washed and ironed, and lunches made for tomorrow. Luckily the boys were asleep. She hoped the baby's crying didn't disturb them. Or the music and laughter in the sitting room. The merriment was loud, but not pleasant—the kind of guffaws that burst from men sharing crude jokes. Mama should have taken in more female boarders, but they used too much water, cooked in her kitchen, stayed too long in the bathroom. The men paid extra for meals and laundry. But now they lounged in her living room, dropping ashes on the rug, setting glasses on every table, filling the room with smoke and rough words.

Helene scraped oatmeal from the last pot then grabbed a towel to dry. Red and yellow fruits bordered the dinner plate in her hand, making her yearn for ripe cherries or peaches. She knew where to get them—any farm just a few miles away. Peggy was begging her to spend the summer there with her. If only Mama didn't need her at home.

Helene thought of her mother's weary eyes, her job at Firestone, the boarders, her brothers and knew she couldn't leave. Besides, they couldn't afford the clothes she'd need, or the cost of getting there. She rammed the towel into a glass so hard that it broke. She felt a sharp sting. Luckily the towel prevented the glass from cutting too deep, and it soaked up the blood.

Alva entered the kitchen and set the kettle on for tea. "How was your day?" she asked, too tired to notice Helene's bleeding hand. Jake Potter soon followed Alva in. Helene didn't like the way he looked at Alva, as she leaned on the counter, stirring milk into her tea.

"I need a glass of water, sweetheart." He brushed Helene's arm as he reached for the tap. She shuddered. He grinned, showing the ruined teeth that kept him out of the army. He paused as if to chat, but Helene turned away to wipe the counter, and was relieved when he left the room before Alva did.

She had been surprised last night, when her mother brought up the subject of farmerette camp. "I met Miss Landry at the grocer's today," she had begun. "She described the Farm Service Forces project. Suggested you were a perfect candidate. She said the fresh country air, exercise, and companionship of wholesome girls would do you good. And you'd be paid."

Helene had taken a breath and shaken her head. "I'm not interested in going away to farm."

She caught the look of relief on her mother's face just before she could pull it into a neutral expression. Helene had gazed levelly at her mother. "I'll find work around here. May I take the boys to the library after school today? Their books are due, and I need new ones."

"Of course. Pick up a short happy one for me."

I could be a great actress, thought Helene, as she dropped the dishtowel into the laundry basket. *But then, so could Mama.*

By eleven, Helene finished her homework and headed for bed. She was looking forward to her new book, *The Spanish Bride.* It promised adventure and romance in South Africa. She needed that after crying buckets over Jody's fawn in *The Yearling.* What a luxury to read in bed the nights her mother worked the evening shift, when she had her room to herself. But by page nine she was too tired to continue and quickly fell asleep.

She woke up with a start. The wooden floor creaked. She tried to see, to hear more in the dark room. There it was. Another creak. All she could make out were dark shadows. But she heard someone breathing. It wasn't her mother. She willed her heart to slow down. Should she pretend she was asleep, or scream for help? Mr. Perkins' radio still blared. Would anyone hear her?

Then one shadow moved closer. A man. Her heart stopped, and she couldn't breathe. Could she jump out of bed fast enough to reach the door? Not with the large shape blocking her way.

"I won't hurt you," Jake's voice oozed from the dark. "I'm lonely, and you're so pretty."

"Go away!" Helene croaked, pulling the covers tightly around her.

He stepped closer. She smelled his hair cream, oily and pungent. "I know you like me."

Helene screamed and scrunched back to the wall as far as she could. She felt his hand touch the covers over her hip. She kicked with all her might and hit soft flesh. He hesitated. She screamed again, knowing he was too strong to fight off for long.

He touched her side, and the door flew open. Light, her mother and Mr. Perkins burst into the room. Helene thought she might faint.

"I only wanted to talk to her," Jake stammered as he backed away.

"Get out!" shouted her mother in a voice Helene had never heard before. "Pack your bags, and leave this house. Now!" Then she turned to Mr. Perkins. "Please accompany Mr. Potter to the front door."

She shut the door, rushed to Helene, and held her until the shaking slowed down. "You're going to farmerette camp. I don't know how we're doing it, but you're going."

FRIDAY, MAY 14, 1943

Jean

Her back ached, her face burned, and she was damp and dirty with sweat and dust. Jean stopped the tractor and surveyed the field she'd just plowed. The rows of furrowed earth were ready for planting. But that was for tomorrow. Today they were done. Thank goodness Gus, their foreman, had not enlisted. Mum, Uncle Ian, and two cousins would help plant. They'd work with her from dawn to dusk again. Too bad the Farm Service Forces girls weren't due for another week. She could use them today.

Her father was at the mailbox by the road. Although he had survived the heart attack last November, he'd lost weight and tired easily. Forbidden strenuous physical work, he now milked their four cows and looked after the paperwork—ordering, planning, accounting—the details of farm life he hated. Every day, he walked to the mailbox, leaning on it long after he'd found it empty.

She watched him pull out today's mail, sift through it, then stop. He stared at one envelope a long time. Jean knew it was the letter they'd been waiting for. She sat as rigid as he stood, anxious for that news.

He opened the envelope, read its contents, and ran up the driveway to the house. Was that a good sign, or bad? Jean was so tense she could barely steer the tractor across the yard. She jumped off and rushed into the kitchen. Her parents and grandmother stood silent in the room.

Seeing Jean, her mother screeched and danced around the kitchen. "He's alive! Our Robbie's alive!"

The family hugged each other. Even Dickens and Shep nosed into the embrace.

Finally Mum, tears rolling down her cheeks, explained the sober news. "Rob was injured and taken prisoner of war. They don't know where yet, but at least he's alive." She happily bustled off to prepare dinner.

As she carried a bowl of asparagus to the table, Nanny was the first to voice her fears. "How badly is he hurt? I don't trust those Jerries to look after him. Do they even have doctors? Will they feed him?"

Her concerns dampened Jean's euphoria. She tried not to imagine how seriously Rob was hurt. She saw the quiet frowns of worry on her parents' faces. They shared her concern.

But not her extra burden—Rob wouldn't be in that terrible place if she hadn't lied to him.

TUESDAY, MAY 18, 1943

Binxie

"I absolutely forbid it!" Mrs. Rutherford, her salt-and-pepper hair held in place in a smooth victory roll, turned from Binxie to her desk.

"But why not? It's for the war effort." Binxie kept her voice calm. A display of temper never worked with her mother.

"There are dozens of more appropriate ways to help: knitting, filling food packages for our boys in prisoner of war camps, writing letters, selling war savings stamps."

"I've done all that and rather well. I want to do more, and I can't do it at the cottage."

"We have always spent summers in Muskoka. Your cousins and friends will be there. Father had the engine tuned on the Greavette. You'll have a marvelous time."

Binxie sighed. She loved that boat, the lake, and she knew she could win the regatta this year. But it wasn't right. "How can I play at the cottage when so many people, not much older than I am, are out fighting—and dying for us?"

For a moment her mother stood quiet. Then she frowned. "You sold the most war stamps in your school, and helped immeasurably on my committees. You did your bit."

"My *bit*. That's just it. I need to do more."

"Farmwork is not fit for a young lady, and you'll mix with some rough people."

"Well, they won't belong to the golf club, but I hear they're decent, and some may even know which fork to use."

"Sarcasm is a low form of humor, Binxie. I'm concerned for your well-being."

"How much more well could I be than on a farm? Fresh food, healthy outside activity."

"You can get that in Muskoka. Discussion closed. We'll leave for the cottage the day school finishes."

They'd argued all evening. Binxie considered ten weeks of Muskoka lakes, campfires, games, and dances and almost gave in. But there was Kathryn's letter. Binxie folded her arms and stood still—her mother's technique. She spoke in the low steely tone her mother used for effect.

"I'm sorry, but I will not go to Lake Joseph this summer. My duty is with the Farm Service Forces."

Mrs. Rutherford raised an eyebrow. "Kathryn all over again," she muttered. "Tell me the procedure."

First Binxie stood speechless, all the arguments she had planned still whirling in her brain. Then she blurted, "I can sign up tomorrow at school."

"I'll call the director, Mr. McLaren, now. Make sure you're placed properly."

"I'd prefer you didn't," Binxie protested, but her mother had already picked up the telephone.

She always has to be in control, Binxie thought as she left the room. Closing the door, she was surprised to hear her mother grumble, "She always has to get her way."

Binxie rushed up the stairs, two at a time, almost knocking over Sadie, carrying an armload of sheets. She swerved and shouted, "I'm going to be a farmerette!" How she wished Kathryn were here to share her victory. She hurried to her room to start packing. Kathryn's last letter lay on her dresser. Binxie sat on her bed to reread it.

Hi-de-ho, Binxie,

Can't write where I am, censors and all that. Suffice it to say, I can ride my bike to visit Aunt Letitia. Luckily she's far from the bombs that rain down on London. She sends her love to you all and has already mailed Mother a thank-you note for the food package.

I hope you decided to join the farmerettes, and that you'll be as happy as I am now, working for the Air Transport Auxiliary. At last I'm allowed to fly! And oh, Binxie, it is so wonderful! John Magee's poem says it all:

Oh! I have slipped the surly bonds of Earth
And danced the skies on laughter-silvered wings.
Sunward I've climbed, and joined the tumbling mirth
Of sun-split clouds…

I could go on, but one day you'll discover that glorious freedom yourself.

We fly all over the British Isles ferrying new planes from the factories to the squadrons, and damaged aircraft back for repair. We transport military personnel from base to base, and go on medical missions. We're not allowed in combat, but I know each time I fly, I free male pilots to fight.

I began training in an open-cockpit Magister light aircraft, and quickly advanced through Hawker Harts, Miles Masters, and Hurricanes. Every cadet pilot's dream, including mine, is to fly a Spitfire. Since all aircraft are divided into classes, we need only learn one plane per class to be allowed to fly the others in that category. With our trusty ATA handling notebook, we can do it.

My fellow pilots are a fascinating bunch. There's an aviation journalist, a racing driver, company director, antiques dealer, even a magician. Stewart, a veteran of the Great War, flies brilliantly with only one arm and one eye, and he's not the only one-armed pilot in our group. The chaps at the RAF air bases like to tease us that ATA stands for "ancient and tattered airmen," but they know our value.

The other women fliers are skilled and daring pilots who had adventurous lives before the war. Winnifred was a stunt pilot in an air circus. Gloria danced ballet, and Mona played international hockey. They're a jolly lot—dedicated and serious about flying, but lots of laughs off duty.

What binds us all is our love of flight and our desire to win this war. When you realize that, before the war, even the wife of the air minister wasn't allowed to enter an aircraft, we've come a long way.

Let me know all about the farm you're assigned to, and what you do there. You may borrow my Wellington boots to slosh around in, and take some good hand cream with you.

I miss the family, the cottage, and especially you, but what I'm doing is important—and exciting. This summer you too will have new adventures, an important job, and fun. And who knows, perhaps one of the tomatoes or peaches you harvest will end up on my plate!

Love as always,
Kathryn.

Binxie tenderly folded the letter, and tucked it into her dresser drawer. She wouldn't let Kathryn down. She was going to become a farmerette.

SATURDAY, MAY 22, 1943

Isabel

"Has the mail arrived yet?" When Isabel heard a noise at the front door, she dropped her knitting on the couch and hurried to open it.

"Don't look so disappointed." Her sister Gloria waddled in and hugged her.

"It's becoming hard to get near you," Isabel said, affectionately patting her sister's large tummy.

"Only five more weeks." Gloria had gained too much weight, but she glowed with happiness.

"Gloria!" Mrs. Lynch swept into the hallway and embraced her oldest daughter. "Come in, sit down. How are you feeling?"

Once they were seated in the living room, Mrs. Lynch offered tea. "Itsy baked some lovely scones today."

"Mom, I've baked before." *But you did most of it,* Isabel added to herself.

"Oh, honey, of course. It's just so hard to see my girls grown up. Here's Gloria expecting her first baby, Rosemary and her husband moving to Toronto for the duration. And now my baby is engaged and poring over the *Woman's Home Companion.* I have to get used to it all."

Isabel saw the quick roll of her sister's eyes. Gloria had expressed her opinions about Isabel's engagement several times already. "Seventeen is too young to marry. Why, Itsy can't even make her allowance last a week."

"I'll be eighteen in July." Isabel had defended herself. "And we can't marry until this war ends, and who knows how long that will be. You were engaged to Walter at nineteen."

"Walter was twenty-three, finishing university, with an excellent position waiting for him."

"Billy will go back to school to earn his law degree." Isabel hated sounding defensive. She wasn't that young. Besides, this was war, and priorities had changed.

"Don't worry, Mom," said Gloria, patting her tummy. "You'll soon be a busy grandmother."

"I'll make the tea." Isabel excused herself. In the kitchen she set the kettle on the stove and paced back and forth until the water boiled. Then she prepared the tea and scones, and carried them back to the living room.

Gloria and her mother were discussing baby blankets, and while they chatted, Gloria was absentmindedly knitting on Isabel's project. "You dropped some stitches around the thumb," she said, as Isabel handed her a cup. "I'll give it a quick fix."

"Thank you." Isabel forced a smile. She wanted those mitts perfect for Billy.

As her mother and sister talked baby clothes, Isabel nibbled a scone and daydreamed about Billy. She wanted so badly to feel his arms encircle her, press her body into his, soak in his smell. She pictured Billy in his red cashmere sweater, his easy smile, his dark hair neatly combed away from his face. He'd wear sweaters like that when they were married, raising four children—the two boys tall and clever like their dad, her daughters petite, attractive blondes like her. But first this stupid war had to end. Right now she felt like she was in a waiting room. Waiting for the war to end. Waiting for Billy to come home. Waiting to marry him. Waiting.

The sound of the mailbox lid clinking shut broke through her thoughts. Isabel rushed outside. Yes! A small gray envelope with a King George stamp. Tossing the other mail onto the hall table, she clutched Billy's letter and hurried to her room.

It was her ritual—she combed her hair, straightened her dress, sat in her chair by the dormer window with his photo on the table beside her. The extra waiting was delicious agony. She tore open the envelope. First she'd rush through it, devour it. Then she'd reread it slowly, savoring every word, every endearment. Sometimes there'd be pictures of Billy with the fellows. Those were held, stroked, some even kissed and slept with.

Billy wrote how much he missed her, thanked her for her last package. He described the endless drills and marches around the English village where they were posted, but he was not allowed to name it. That gave her a thrill of intrigue—her brave soldier on his heroic mission to fight Nazis and fascists. How proud she had been to walk the streets of Guelph with him in his new uniform, looking taller and more mature than ever. Girls had always eyed Billy and her—the golden couple—all through high school and his college football games. But that day, they had stared with open envy. She was even prouder when he escorted her to Rosemary's house for the engagement dinner. No one called her Itsy then.

This time Billy had included a photo of the Wyecrofts. She was glad many English villagers invited the boys for home-cooked dinners and some family life. She studied the photo. Billy stood in a garden surrounded by a thin older couple, two girls, and a young boy almost dwarfed by the sheepdog beside him. The girls looked about her age, pretty in a dowdy way, but pleasant.

Billy described an amusing incident about the dog and young Cecil, and the inventive recipes Norah and Vera tried out on him. England was rationed far more severely than Canada. He admired the family's spirit, and the hours the women put in volunteering at the hospital. Under all his light news, Isabel sensed a longing to be sent to the front.

Isabel reread the paragraph about the sisters. Billy practically gushed about their courage. They had learned to drive an ambulance. Did he think she wasn't doing enough? He knew she rolled bandages and knit socks. But here in Canada there was no chance for more heroic deeds.

She glared at the photo. Suddenly she didn't like Vera's toothy smile, or Norah's saucy stance. What could she do? Daddy would never let her work in a war factory, and she was too young for nursing. What else was there?

She remembered the announcement about the Farm Service Forces the principal had made last week, and sat up straight. She could pick fruit, do a bit of hoeing. They had to have uniforms. She would send Billy a picture of herself in her smart outfit, ready and able to serve her country.

WEDNESDAY, JUNE 2, 1943

X

She locked the cubicle door and sat on the toilet seat, shaking. What had she done? She'd always been so careful before. But this afternoon, as they changed into their gym wear, it had been too much. Vivian sitting so close to her on the bench—subtle cologne scent, rosy skin. Vivian's mass of long brown curls had touched her arm, and she couldn't resist—she had caressed it. Only for an instant, but long enough to be noticed.

She shut her eyes tight, trying to block the memory of the confusion and horror on their faces. Had the girls guessed her shameful secret? Would they spread it around the school? Around the whole town of Brantford?

Could she move away? Maybe she'd get better in a new place. She had to get away from here, the whispers, the strange looks.

The poster hanging in the hall outside the bathroom all month offered her the chance. Hard physical work on a farm in the wholesome countryside—it would help her make a clean new start. She prayed the Farm Service Forces would cure her.

SUNDAY, JUNE 6, 1943

Helene

"Isn't it swell?" Peggy said as she stretched across Helene's narrow bed. "No more homework, no exams. The girls at school envy us. Wait until they see us in September."

"Your patriotism is truly inspiring," said Helene as she folded a dress into her suitcase. "How many work shirts does the list say?"

"Four. Two with long sleeves."

Helene frowned at the last of the clothes sharing the bed with Peggy. She picked up a plaid shirt her father had left behind, tossed it back, then held up a frayed white one. "Which ones look the least awful?"

Peggy wrinkled her nose. "The white, and that blue one. They're only for working in the fields, anyway. Look at the lovely new things you have."

Helene smiled. "I'm still amazed my teacher was so generous. I love this dress." She held up a flowery cotton frock. On the bed lay various toiletry items, several packages of new underwear, and a crisp white blouse still with that new-clothes scent.

"Miss Landry obviously thinks you deserve it," said Peggy.

"I'll bring her some fresh fruits in the fall."

"Did you hear each camp got a piano and record player this year? Dad is letting me take some records."

"Harry James, I hope." Helene tucked two towels into her bedding and rolled them all up. "That's it. I'm ready."

She checked her dresser top. "Tickets, travel money, the address, and ration coupons." She turned to her friend. "I can't believe we're actually spending summer in the country. It's so exciting."

"Then let's go. Our adventure begins now." Peggy picked up Helene's suitcase and headed into the hall.

Helene held her mother in a long hug, torn between sadness at leaving her stuck in the hot city and joy at her own escape. Everything had already been said over the last few days of preparation and at the special dinner her mother cooked last night. Now her mother simply gazed at Helene and said, "We'll be fine here. You be happy there."

A final hug, and the girls headed off to Peggy's house, where her father would drive them to the one o'clock bus to Niagara Falls.

"I have disappointing news," Mrs. Pigeon greeted them as they rushed into the kitchen. She held up a telegram. "This just arrived from the Farm Service Placement Officer."

Helene set her bedroll down and her hopes plunged with it.

"What's wrong?" demanded Peggy.

"Apparently the farmer in Niagara Falls finished planting early this year, and they have enough girls hoeing. He won't require you for another two weeks."

Peggy gazed at their luggage standing in the hall. "But we're packed and ready to farm. We'll look silly if we go back to school tomorrow—and we'll have to write exams!"

Mrs. Pigeon shrugged her shoulders. "I'm disappointed for you too, and your bus tickets are already paid for."

"Mum, we have to go."

"It's no use ranting," sighed Helene, picking up her bags. "We have to accept this."

Peggy looked at Helene, then at the jaunty red sun hat perched on top of her own bedroll. She turned to her mother. "Gee, that telegram arrived at the very last minute. What if it had come an hour later—after we'd left?"

Her mother grinned. "Telegrams often arrive late." She tucked the note into a drawer. "Don't forget to write, my dear. Now here come your grandparents to see you off."

"Be sure to send their letters inside your envelope, okay, Mum?" said Peggy.

Her mother sighed and nodded, and with a last flurry of hugs, kisses, and advice, the family said good-bye, and the girls rushed out to the car.

MONDAY, JUNE 7, 1943

Binxie

Another lineup! Binxie frowned with annoyance. First the queue for the train from Toronto to Hamilton, then for the old bus that delivered them from Hamilton to this farm, and now they waited to fill out endless registration papers. Her traveling outfit felt sticky under the blazing afternoon sun, and the blonde girl ahead of her whined for water. Two girls at the registration desk held everyone up. The pale nervous one looked ready to flee, and the girl wearing a red sun hat had too much to say—something about a telegram not received and being assigned to a new camp. Would they ever settle it? Binxie smiled at the blonde girl.

Finally the matter at the desk was resolved. The two girls, grinning from ear to ear, ran to the dormitory, and the line moved forward.

Once Binxie had registered and handed in her ration booklet, she hurried to the dormitory too. It was actually a gray barn, its two large doors boarded up, and a regular door open beside them. At the entrance, a middle-aged woman with heavy eyebrows, black hair pulled back in a ponytail, and a strong smell of mints, introduced herself as Miss Stoakley, their camp mother. She welcomed them, and pointed to some stairs to the right of the doorway. As Binxie climbed them, three girls pushed past her. "First ones up get the best beds," one shouted.

Binxie followed them to a large room running the length of the building with about thirty cots lining each of the two long walls. They reminded her of the *Madeline* book her young cousin loved to read. The room was scrubbed spotless and painted fresh white. Next to each narrow bed stood a wooden orange crate. Primitive, but handy. Small windows over every second bed let in light and air. She wondered where the washrooms were—hopefully not outside.

She surveyed the cots and the girls scrambling to claim one next to a friend. No one seemed to want the far end of the room. It was gloomier there and a disadvantage in any race for meals or the washrooms. But she'd have more privacy. Just as she placed her bedroll on the very last cot, another girl plopped her bags onto the bed beside her. Binxie unrolled her bedding as her neighbor opened her suitcase.

When they backed into each other in the narrow space between the cots, they laughed and turned around. The girl looked pleasant—blue eyes, curly brown hair held back with a bobby pin, a pretty smile. Binxie extended her hand. "Hi. I'm Binxie, from Toronto."

"Hi, Binxie, I'm Stella, and that's my friend Grace on the next bed. Isn't this fun?"

Grace waved cheerfully.

Stella continued. "We're from Wiarton. My cousin lives in Toronto. She goes to Bloor Collegiate. Where do you go?"

"Branksome Hall."

Stella's smile fell. She gathered her things and walked away. "Come on, Grace. We don't bunk with private school snobs. We had enough of them last year."

Binxie stood stunned. But before she could reply, another bag flew onto the bed beside her. "Helene, quick! Two beds left together. Grab that one."

It was the loud, red-hatted girl who had held up the line.

Her mousy friend heaved her battered suitcase onto a bed.

At almost the same time, another girl, dressed in blue, plopped her bag onto the same bed as the pale girl—Helene? "This bed's mine. I got here first."

Helene coughed and reached to remove her suitcase. Binxie feared she might collapse.

"No!" her red-hatted friend hissed. "Helene was here first. Go find your own bed."

The girl stood firm, trying to stare them down. The red-hatted girl narrowed her dark blue eyes, pursed her lips, and glared back harder.

Binxie smiled in amusement.

Suddenly the red-hatted girl burst out laughing, a sound that would make a donkey proud. Her opponent shrugged, picked up her bag, and stomped off.

Helene nervously set her old suitcase onto the floor and unrolled her sheets to make her bed. Noting the cheap material, Binxie decided not to mention Branksome Hall again. She smoothed out her own linens, adjusted the blanket, then opened her suitcase.

"Did you notice a piano downstairs, Helene?" asked the red-hatted girl as she fluffed the pillow on her hastily made bed. "As soon as you're finished, let's find it."

Binxie looked in her bags, deciding what could stay in them. There were no closets here, only the orange crates and a row of hooks along the wall.

"Gee, I thought Helene packed neatly, but your suitcase looks military!" exclaimed the girl behind her.

Binxie turned around, paused, and regarded her coolly. "It's organized. Organized people never waste time searching for things."

The girl laughed—another hearty bray. "That sure isn't me."

She stuck out her hand. "Hi. I'm Peggy Pigeon, and that's my friend, Helene Miller. I'm glad to be surrounded by two such tidy people. Maybe it'll rub off on me."

"I doubt it." Helene smiled and waved shyly at Binxie.

"Binxie Rutherford. Pleased to meet you both," she replied stiffly.

"What is she doing?" Peggy pointed at the cot against the wall across from them. The blonde girl who had wanted water in line had arranged a flowery quilt and matching cushions on her cot, a rag rug on the floor. A pink scarf already covered her orange crate. She pulled a gold-framed photo from her purse, stood gazing at it, and stood it tenderly on the nightstand. Next she pulled a stuffed white teddy bear from her bag and placed it on the cushions.

Oh, lucky me, thought Binxie, slapping a comb onto her crate. *I'm rooming with a witch, a mouse, a donkey, and a princess. This could be a long summer.*

Peggy

Peggy ran her fingers along the keys, played the first few notes of "Chopsticks," and remarked that the piano needed tuning.

"We're lucky to have one at all," said Miss Stoakley. She turned to the other girls. "Those shelves to the left hold cards, games, and writing paper."

"Hey! We can play that new card game—Canasta," said

Peggy. She noticed Binxie frowning at her in disapproval. "Wanna join us, Binxie?"

Binxie shook her head, and Miss Stoakley continued the tour of their home for the next three months. They stood on the first floor of the converted barn, in a large room made cozy with comfortable chintz couches and chairs, yellow curtains, several small tables, shelves of games, and, of course, the piano in the corner.

"Is there a record player?" asked a short wiry girl.

"It'll arrive soon," answered Miss Stoakley.

"Will they send records too? I brought a few, but we may get tired of them." Peggy loved this room, and was excited about the fun they would have here. "We can dance in the evenings too."

Several girls nodded, but Binxie rolled her eyes.

"Who knows how to jitterbug?" Peggy did a few fast steps, wiggled her hips, pecked her head, and swirled around.

Miss Stoakley and pointed to a door tucked under the stairs on the right. "There's my office. I share it with the Labour Secretary. You met her at the registration desk today. Every Friday after dinner, you may pick up your paychecks and pay your board there. My door is open whenever you need me. I have a telephone, which you may use for emergencies. Please ask me first, and be prepared to pay for the call when you use it."

"I hope she considers phoning my boyfriend an emergency," whispered a pretty girl in a green dress.

Peggy laughed out loud. "Not an emergency—a necessity."

Looking annoyed, Binxie muttered, "Must you comment on everything?"

"Do you have something against being happy?" Peggy whispered back.

"I'm very happy, thank you, but I don't have to advertise it to the world."

"Well, I like to spread the cheer." Peggy smiled, then followed Miss Stoakley and the others through another door to the back half of the barn. They crossed a hall to a wide arch that opened to a large area lined with wooden tables. "This is the dining room. You'll enjoy nutritious meals here twice a day. Lunches are usually eaten in the fields."

Along the left wall stood two serving tables, and beside them a swinging double door to the kitchen. Peggy could see two large stoves inside, and rubbed her stomach. "Is anyone else as hungry as I am?"

Several girls nodded.

"Our cook will set out sandwiches and lemonade for you when this tour is over," said the camp mother. "The kitchen is off-limits to everyone but staff. We must ration and account for all our food. You may never help yourself."

"No midnight pantry raids," Helene whispered to Peggy.

"It'll make them more challenging."

"Where are the washrooms?" asked the blonde girl who bunked across from them. She looked worried.

Peggy hoped it wasn't an outhouse.

"Just for you." Miss Stoakley opened a door at the end of the hall. "Here it is." She pointed into a large airy room.

Several girls released sighs of relief.

"This was once a storage shed attached to the barn. We installed several toilets, those sinks, and three showers for you.

There are hooks to hang your clothes and a shelf nearby for your toiletries." Miss Stoakley was obviously proud.

"No curtains? We have to shower in front of everyone?" the blonde girl gasped.

"You all have the same parts. There's no need to hide them."

"Where will our laundry be done?" asked Binxie.

"*You* will wash your clothes in those two wringer washers by the back wall. Two large tubs for rinsing are outside. The clothes-line is nearby and there are two irons in the recreation room."

Peggy had to smile at the expression on Binxie's face. Obviously the girl had never washed her own clothes before. *Come to think of it,* she thought, *neither have I. Mum did that. Did Miss Stoakley really say she'd wake us at five-thirty so we can make our beds and wash before breakfast? This summer might be tougher than I expected.*

Jean

"In this field we grow our own food." Jean pointed to a stretch of land to the left of the gray stone farmhouse. The house was fronted by a low rose hedge about three hundred yards away from the girls' quarters. "Everything is sprouting well. If this warm weather continues, we'll have early crops this summer."

The girls gazed dutifully at the rows of seedlings as Jean named them. "Beans and corn here, cabbages, beets, onions, turnips, tomatoes, peas..."

"They all look the same to me," the red-hatted girl—her friend called her Peggy—joked. "They could be poison ivy for all I know."

"Remind me not to eat any vegetables you pick," said a tall

girl with her brown hair held back by a blue scarf. The name on her application said Beatrice, but she introduced herself as Binxie.

Jean wished she owned a stylish scarf like that. Most of these girls wore fashionable clothes. What must their city life be like? In her nineteen years, she had visited the city of Hamilton a few times. On her sixteenth birthday, Mum took her to Toronto for a weekend. What a noisy, busy place! The buildings were so tall she got dizzy looking up. The fancy stores overwhelmed her. Gigantic windows displayed beautiful dresses, coats, and accessories—not practical for farm life, and therefore nothing Jean's mother would ever sew.

And the elegant Imperial Theatre. The magnificent gold leaf and marble pillars, deep carpets, velvet seats, and machines you could actually buy candy from were impressive enough—but then she watched the movie. *Pride and Prejudice* was her favorite book at the time. To see the Bennet family come to life on that huge screen was thrilling. Greer Garson and Laurence Olivier were wonderful as Elizabeth and Mr. Darcy.

Was that how these city girls lived all the time? It seemed glamorous, but also crowded. They lived right beside, and even on top of, total strangers. In Winona, she knew everyone, but there was at least half a mile between neighbors, the way it should be.

"Your dog is so cute." Peggy reached down to pat the golden animal that followed Jean everywhere.

"Dickens," Jean answered and continued toward the barn.

"As in Charles Dickens?" Peggy's thin, pale friend asked.

Jean nodded. "One of my favorite authors."

The pale girl smiled at her. "Mine too. I'm Helene."

As Jean nodded at Helene, she noticed Binxie's raised eyebrow. Did she think farmers didn't read?

"Ew. What's that horrible smell?" A pretty blonde pulled a handkerchief from her pocket and brought it to her nose. She had changed from a navy traveling suit to a white dress with yellow flowers and matching sun hat.

Good Lord, thought Jean. *Does she expect a tea party tonight?*

Someone pointed to an odoriferous pile of manure beside the barn.

"We muck out the barn floor every morning—straw and everything the animals drop during the night. It's good fertilizer." Jean loved telling the city girls, "It'll make your vegetables especially tasty."

The girls wrinkled their faces in disgust. Only Binxie looked straight at her and laughed.

"Come to the barn and meet our animals," Jean invited. "We keep six horses, four cows, and some pigs. The hens have their own coop by the orchard. Our horses work overtime, since tractor fuel is scarce and replacement parts hard to find."

"Don't farmers get more gasoline rations than city people?" asked a tall girl.

A stocky man in muddy blue overalls stepped from the barn. "Never enough gas at plowing and harvest time."

Jean introduced Gus, the foreman. "He'll answer your questions and run the large machinery."

Gus grinned, showing large buckteeth. He grunted, "Hello," and continued across the yard.

All the girls except Helene followed Jean into the barn. Swatting the flies that buzzed at them, they looked around curiously. They crowded around a pen where baby piglets tugged at their mother's teats. Some of the city girls blushed, but most oohed and aahed as the little creatures with curly tails and pink bodies tumbled over each other.

A movement on the floor above made them look up.

"A barn cat. They like the mice in here, but not the people," explained Jean.

"Mice!" someone gasped, and several girls squealed.

Jean sighed. "We store hay for the livestock up there. Mouse food. They won't bother you."

"Animals eat hay?" asked the blonde girl.

Before Jean could think of a withering answer, a small explosion followed by an overpowering stench erupted from one of the stalls.

Jean led the girls out the back door. "Don't mind Oslo. The horse has digestive problems, especially after eating fresh grass."

Peggy gazed around the barnyard and pointed left. "Who lives in that cute little house?" Her hundredth question.

"The chickens." *Where do they find these girls?* wondered Jean. She wished she could fall into her bed, read a chapter, and sleep. But she still needed to feed the hens and tell Dad about the horse's leg. London had favored his front left one this afternoon.

Several hens and their young strutted around the yard, pecking at the ground. The girls gushed over the fuzzy chicks.

"We keep enough chickens for you to have fresh eggs most mornings," said Jean. "And when they stop laying eggs," she couldn't resist adding, "they make a tasty stew. Everyone on a farm has to be useful somehow."

Jean pointed far ahead to a field lined with rows of low green plants. "Tomorrow some of you will—"

"*Eeeeee!*" A terrified screech interrupted her.

She turned to see the blonde girl screaming as she backed away from the rooster. The bird had stretched his wings and puffed his feathers to double his size. With beady eyes glaring, sharp beak stabbing the air aggressively, he charged after her like a bull.

Jean shook her head. Cracker loved to terrify people.

Other girls scattered in all directions. The rooster hissed and pecked menacingly closer. The blonde girl ran, slipped, and landed in a moist lump of manure. Her fancy hat flew off. Cracker pounced and tore it apart.

The farmerettes stood, shocked. Jean grabbed a pitchfork and chased him away. The blonde girl sat in the mess, flushed with mortification. Someone in a white blouse reached to help her up.

The blonde girl pushed away the outstretched arm. "I can get up myself." Awkwardly, she tried to rise without putting her hand on the ground—and slipped again. No one said a word. Finally she stood up. She held her head high, daring anyone to pity her. A clump of cow dung fell off her dress. Its brown stain remained.

Jean turned and walked along a path to the fields. "Our strawberries are ripening early this year—you'll see lots of them soon. You'll pick them here and at neighboring farms. The farmers arrive tomorrow at seven-thirty sharp."

Some girls groaned, though most smiled eagerly, but Jean had focused their attention away from the girl with the ruined dress.

"Our orchards stretch beyond the strawberry fields, right out to the road. We grow strawberries, market vegetables, cherries, and peaches, as well as the food for our own family." Jean waved her arm to take it all in. "And that's Highberry Farm. I hope you all sleep well. Goodnight." She turned back toward the barn, and the girls headed for their dormitory.

Jean yawned. She'd worked since dawn, helping her mother with the new chicks, doing the regular livestock chores, hoeing, and weeding. The questions the farmerettes asked while exploring the farm were almost as exhausting. At least her father had offered to do the five-o'clock milking. She worried about London's leg. Maybe the last field was too hard on him, but the gasket on the tractor had blown again, and they were trying to find a new one. She also wanted to check on Tessie, a nervous young cow, expecting her first calf and overdue.

Jean turned at the sound of a horse trotting up the laneway. A sandy-haired, muscular young man rode into the barnyard and slid off his horse. He led his animal past the girls who were still outside.

As one, the girls sighed. He was very handsome and a bit older than they were—perfect.

Jean smiled at him with welcome relief. Johnny Clifford could soothe an animal better than anyone, even his dad, who had been the local veterinarian forever.

Johnny smiled back at her, an expression that made many girls in Winona dream of a future with him. "How's Tessie?"

"She seemed jittery at noon."

Johnny followed Jean into the barn. He leaned toward the cow, patting her, speaking calmly.

Jean watched his mouth as he comforted Tessie with sweet nothings. She wondered what it would be like to kiss those lips. They were just good friends, but Jean was ready for more. Still, she'd never chase him like the other girls did.

Once Tessie relaxed, Johnny prodded her belly. "Feels like the calf is turned the wrong way. No wonder she's having trouble." He rinsed his hands in a pail and pushed his right arm into her to confirm his diagnosis. Then carefully, firmly, Johnny reached in the other arm too and maneuvered the calf into position.

"That should help," he said, wiping the slime off his hands. "Hopefully tomorrow."

"Thanks." Jean stifled a yawn.

Johnny looked at her with concern. "It should get easier with the farmerettes here."

Jean rolled her eyes. "A few princesses signed in today. One wanted to know where she could take a bubble bath."

Johnny laughed. "She's lucky you didn't send her into the horse trough."

Jean laughed too. "Once they get used to things, they'll be fine."

Johnny patted Tessie again and asked, "Any word from Rob?"

"Finally. A field service postcard arrived Friday with one sentence written in German. *I am a POW in German hands and am well.* He's in Stalag VIII-B. The Red Cross ladies promised to send him a food parcel."

"At least he's alive, hopefully well," he said. "I should get going. Early start tomorrow. Dick Pratt enlisted, and I promised to help him fix his barn roof before he leaves."

Jean couldn't miss the longing in his voice. She knew how badly he wanted to go too. "You're playing baseball Saturday?"

He nodded. "See you there." With a last pat on Tessie's rump, he said goodnight and left.

Jean watched him climb onto his horse and ride down the lane and noticed some farmerettes also eyeing him. She shook her head, yawned, and headed for the chicken coop.

Isabel

Isabel lay in the dark, wishing that the last group of girls would stop giggling and whispering. What could be so funny about these little cots still smelling of disinfectant? She missed her own comfortable bed and pretty room. Some creature was making a chirping racket outside, and the girl beside her snored.

She was tired, but she lay rigid and sleepless. Every time her eyes closed, she saw that vicious rooster again. Why did anyone keep such beasts on a farm? And there was so much excrement here—piled behind the barn in a disgusting heap and lying around the barnyard for anyone to fall into.

She had felt so humiliated, sitting in that reeking mess, everyone thinking she was a baby. She shouldn't have pushed away the offer of help, but for a second, that girl had reminded her of Gloria, always so helpfully superior. Were Mom and her sisters right? Was she not strong enough for this?

If only she could hug Billy, even for a moment, everything would feel better. Where was he now? In some cold, lumpy army cot, wanting her too? Or on a deadly mission, holding brave against the enemy? She had no excuse to feel sorry for herself.

Was that a sob, she heard nearby? Could someone else feel as lonely as she did tonight? Somewhere outside a dog howled. Isabel pulled the covers around her and hugged her teddy bear as if it were Billy. But still sleep eluded her.

X

A few girls still whispered softly, and the spring peepers croaked lustily in the pond outside, but she knew she'd sleep well tonight. Tomorrow was a new start among friendly strangers. She would be normal like these other girls, get rid of her shameful sickness. She breathed in the smell of fresh sheets and clean country air, turned on her side, and fell into a peaceful sleep.

Helene

Helene lay in her bed, too happy to sleep. Inside she was surrounded by the soft, safe sounds of girls settling down for the night, while outside rang the songs of country creatures dining, courting, glad to be alive.

She had followed Jean this evening with awe and joy, taking in everything—the fresh green fields, the pink blossom-clad orchards, the pond full of ducks and geese, the vast blue sky tinged with evening shades of red. She was going to spend a whole summer in this paradise.

When the girls followed Jean into the barn, Helene had stayed back. She turned toward the sun and gazed at the fields stretching to the horizon. Never had she seen so much open space, inhaled air so clean. She flung her arms wide, spun in a circle, and laughed out loud. Then she had slipped into the barn with the others.

Now soft light glowed through the window across from her. How would everything look by moonlight? Helene slipped on shoes, stole to the door halfway down the length of the dorm, and quietly opened it. She tiptoed down the outside stairs, crossed the yard, and watched the moon reflect golden in the pond. She inhaled the scent of grass and newly turned earth. If only her family could enjoy this too.

As she headed back to the stairs, she heard a soft sob over the night noises. Quietly she followed the sound to the back of the barn. There, hunched over a washtub, was her roommate Isabel, scrubbing at her yellow-flowered dress.

Helene stepped forward, but then remembered how Isabel had slapped away the helping hand earlier. She turned, went upstairs, fetched her old white shirt, a bar of laundry soap and came back outside. She rubbed the shirt in the grass and joined Isabel at the washtubs.

Helene nodded at Isabel as if it were quite normal to be washing clothes so late at night. She dampened her shirt and began soaping the grass stain on it.

Ignoring the small glances from Isabel, Helene hummed and rubbed, rinsed, sighed, and scrubbed some more. "That's a lovely dress," she said.

"Thank you. But it's ruined. I hadn't expected a farm to be so filthy."

"Everything is always cleaner and easier in magazines, isn't it?"

Isabel laughed. "Well, look, your stain is gone. You're not using the same soap I am, are you?" She held up her box of

Rinso. "The ad said it would wash away stains just by soaking them for twelve minutes. It lied."

"We make our own soap." Helene blushed. Her family couldn't afford Rinso.

"A secret family ingredient?" Isabel said wistfully, dabbing at her dress again.

"Would you like to try it?"

Isabel hesitated, then took the bar of soap, lathered and rubbed it onto her dress, rinsed, and grinned widely at the clean garment she now held up. "Thank you."

"My mother makes good soap."

Isabel nodded in agreement. "I'm Isabel Lynch, from Guelph."

"Helene Miller, Hamilton. Do you see a clothesline?"

"Right there. And clothes-pegs!"

The girls hung their things on the line. A warm breeze blew them softly.

"Isn't it wonderful here?" said Helene.

"Maybe I'll like it better tomorrow."

"Look up," said Helene. "Have you ever seen so many stars shining as brightly? There's the Milky Way. It's so amazing."

Isabel gazed up at the magnificent celestial display and smiled. "There's the Big Dipper. And Orion, the hunter. I've never seen Sirius so bright."

Helene was impressed. "How do you know so much?"

"Billy used to show me the stars." She spoke softly. "Before he left, he chose our star. Sirius. We find it every night before we go to sleep and think of each other. He could be watching it this very minute."

"Billy?" said Helene.

"Billy Morrison, my fiancé. He's stationed in England." She sighed, and peered up longingly.

Helene wished she missed someone that much. She thought of telling Isabel about the five boys she wrote to every week—she'd taken over Peggy's soldiers when she kept forgetting to write—but she feared Isabel, so beautifully dressed and well-spoken, wouldn't be interested.

Once she had uttered her fiancé's name, words flowed from Isabel. She sat on the steps, motioned Helene to join her, and told her about Billy—how handsome and smart he was, his romantic proposal by the river, their plans for the future.

By the time the moon had traveled high in the sky, Isabel linked arms with Helene as they climbed upstairs to sleep.

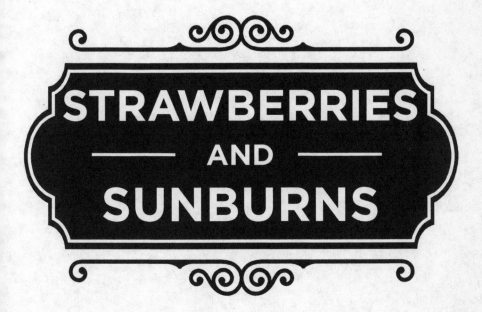

STRAWBERRIES

— AND —

SUNBURNS

TUESDAY, JUNE 8, 1943

Peggy

Peggy stood onstage, Glenn Miller and his band playing behind her, a spotlight above making her white gown shimmer. Glenn smiled at her—his new lead singer—and then at his piano player—Michael. Lights dimmed. She sang "At Last," and when she reached the final notes, her fans stood, shouting "Bravo" and "Encore." Someone whistled.

The whistle shrilled louder. Glenn, Michael, and the adoring audience faded. "Five-thirty. Rise and shine, girls." An overhead light glared through her eyelids. The whistle blasted again.

"Breakfast in thirty minutes," called Miss Stoakley.

The dream totally evaporated. Peggy lay for another minute with her eyes scrunched shut. She wanted that fantasy back. She wanted three hours more sleep until the smell of fresh coffee lured her downstairs to breakfast.

Someone bumped her cot as they thumped by. Girls chattered, and clattered noisily over the wooden floors. Peggy groaned.

"Peggy, wake up. If you don't get to the bathroom soon, you won't have time for breakfast."

Peggy slowly opened her eyes and saw Helene, fully dressed and smiling. "How long have you been up?"

"A while. I'm on my way out to watch the sunrise. Look, the sky is pink already. I'll see you in the dining room."

Peggy watched Helene rush out the side door. It was good to see her so happy, her gray eyes glowing, her pinched expression smoothed into a smile. Peggy was glad they'd fibbed about the telegram to get here. She rolled out of bed, grabbed her toiletry bag, and trudged downstairs to the washrooms.

Hungry and late, Peggy hurried to the dining room, as girls who met only yesterday chatted like old friends. Miss Stoakley stood by the serving table, greeting everyone.

Now that Peggy was washed and fully awake, she was eager to get to the fields. She helped herself to eggs, toast, chunks of cheddar, and milk, then found a seat next to Helene. She introduced herself to her new tablemates and dug into breakfast.

"We're already invited to watch a baseball game this Saturday, the minister asked us to tea, and they're planning a growers' party," said a thin, frizzy-haired girl. "It's going to be a fun summer."

Peggy immediately perked up. "Where's the party? I hope there'll be dancing."

Before the girl could reply, Miss Stoakley announced, "Twenty minutes until the wagons arrive. Time to pack your lunches. Take enough. You'll be hungry."

Still chewing her toast, Peggy joined the others at the serving table, where plates of buttered bread, sliced meats and cheese, carrot sticks, and bowls of fruit were laid out for them. She slapped together a sandwich, wrapped it, and dropped it into a bag along with an apple.

Soon they stood in the barnyard, wearing solid shoes, straw hats, a variety of shorts and trousers, and shirts with the Farm Service Forces badge sewn onto them. Many girls had come here with a friend and were sticking close together to make sure they'd be on the same wagon.

Just as three vehicles drove up the laneway, Jean came from the barn, her brown hair pulled into a messy ponytail, hay and muck stuck to her boots. She wished everyone a good morning, and asked for four girls to stay at Highberry Farm to work.

Binxie stepped forward. Even though she acted stuffy, Peggy admired the tall girl who strode with such confidence—and she enjoyed annoying her. Peggy tapped Helene's arm and they followed. Rita joined them, and the other girls scrambled into trucks of their choice. Soon two groups pulled away, horns tooting, girls waving.

"The strawberries are ripening early this year, not too many yet, but we need to pick them before it gets too hot. The baskets are already out there," said Jean as she led them down the path toward the field. The last thing Peggy saw as they turned a bend was Isabel, running from the dorm. She stopped and stared in dismay at the third vehicle—a beat-up-looking wagon pulled by a muddy tractor.

Binxie

Binxie followed Jean along the path beside a fenced field where two cows and four horses grazed. Wildflowers dotted the grass and the air smelled fresh. The four farmerettes paused to admire the heavy-muscled legs of the Percherons. A beautiful gray one trotted up to Binxie and she stroked its velvety muzzle.

Helene came up timidly behind her. "You're not afraid it'll bite you?"

Binxie smiled. "They're gentle."

"It's ironic," said Helene, standing well back. "This breed was used by the British to fight the Great War, and now their job is farmwork."

"You think humanity is getting wiser?" said Binxie.

Helene sighed. "The horses were replaced by tanks—to do even greater damage."

In the distance an airplane droned. Binxie tracked it for a moment, then said, "Airplanes too. They travel faster and destroy more." It wasn't the first time she wished her sister had become a nurse instead of a pilot. She retrieved an apple from her lunch bag, snapped it into quarters, and fed a piece to each horse.

"You're good with them," said Peggy.

"I love horses. Used to ride them every summer at my cottage." It would be nice to be there now, but she knew she was where she had to be.

A foul odor blew from the back of one horse. Oslo again. Grimacing, the girls backed away.

"Just don't light a match near him," called Jean as she continued on the path to the berry field. The girls hurried after her.

"What a glorious day," Peggy exclaimed. "This will be such fun!"

"Say that again at noon," said Jean.

"Did I hear someone at breakfast mention a baseball game?" Peggy didn't miss a beat.

"Next Saturday," Jean replied. "Local teams. We'll roast wieners afterward."

"Sounds like a blast!" said Peggy. "Wish there was dancing too."

Does this girl ever shut up? wondered Binxie.

"We'll have a square dance soon. Probably at the growers' party in a couple of weeks."

"Oh good. So there are lots of boys around here?"

Jean gazed coolly at Peggy. "Girls too."

Binxie smiled to herself. Were they actually arguing over farm boys?

They had reached the strawberry patch. Jean handed them each a large wooden tray of empty baskets. "When these are full, bring them to the head of a row and get another one."

Jean showed them how to grasp the stem just above the berry, pull with a slight twist, and allow it to roll into their palms. "Pick only the red ones. Green ones won't ripen after they're picked. Pick any rotten or damaged ones too, and toss them into the middle of the aisle."

The girls squatted in the straw-covered earth between the rows of berries and began. Jean watched for awhile, warned them not to injure the plants, then went to work herself. Chatting and joking back and forth to each other over the rows, they started strong, happy in the sunshine.

Two hours later, there was less talk. It was hot. Binxie's back hurt. Her knees ached. She tried crawling from bush to bush, instead of the awkward crab walk, and it helped—a little. Sweat dampened her body. Mosquitoes buzzed and bit. The sun blazed. Oh, for a drink of water.

The others looked equally uncomfortable—Peggy rubbed her legs, Rita scratched mosquito bites, and Helene looked ready to collapse. Only Jean whistled cheerfully as she stacked full wooden carriers of berries on a wagon shaded by an elm tree.

The sun climbed higher. Binxie filled another basket and stood up to stretch.

"Let's take a break," Jean suggested. "There's a pump by the barn and shade under the trees."

The girls hurried to the pump and took turns drinking eagerly. Binxie gulped large mouthfuls of water, splashed some onto her hands and face, laughing with the cool joy.

"Hurry. I want some too." Peggy bumped her from behind.

"Here you go!" Binxie turned and sloshed water at her.

Peggy grabbed the tin cup hanging by the pump and splashed her back. She threw another cupful at the other girls. They screeched with delight. Everyone took turns pumping and spraying each other, ducking, laughing, until finally—soaking wet but cool—they flopped onto the grass to rest.

Too soon it was time to head back to the field.

Binxie's mouth soon felt dry again. Her stomach rumbled. Lunch seemed far away. She watched Peggy twist a large red berry from its stem and pop it into her mouth. Binxie ate one too. It was beyond delicious—sweet, juicy, and warm. She picked another basketful, ate another berry.

Helene also dropped one into her mouth, closed her eyes, and savored it. "So this is how food tastes fresh from the fields."

"Girls, we're trying to make a living here. The berries cost twenty-five cents a basket," Jean called over.

"I'm sorry." Helene blushed. "I'll pay for them on payday."

"Just don't do it again," said Jean. She studied the field. "We'll be finished in time for lunch. Then we'll hoe vegetables."

Feeling guilty, the girls resumed picking, slapping mosquitoes, picking, moving stiffly to the next position, picking.

"Too, too boring," said Peggy. "Are we going to do this another six hours, five days a week for the rest of the summer? How many hours is that?"

"Way too many," answered Rita.

But there was a certain rhythm to this work. Arm out, pick a berry, place in basket, arm out, pick a berry, place in basket. Peggy began to hum. Binxie recognized it as the Hebrew slave chorus from *Nabucco*, which seemed fitting—and surprising. This girl knew opera. When Peggy switched to "Whistle While You Work," the others joined in. Halfway through, a yowl of pain pierced the air. Another cry. A cow! Something was wrong. Jean raced to the pasture.

Binxie ran after her. "Can I help?"

"Find Gus or my father."

Binxie raced back to the farmhouse. Nanny answered the door, her apron and forearms covered with flour. "Mr. and Mrs. McDonnell went to market, won't be back till supper. Gus is plowing at another farm." Seeing how upset Binxie looked, she added, "Jean will manage fine."

Binxie raced back to the pasture where Jean comforted a

distraught young cow. Jean felt her underside with experienced hands as a thin ribbon of thick white mucus and blood oozed from under the tail. Repulsed yet fascinated, the farmerettes watched.

"We're on our own," Binxie panted.

With a bellow, the cow sank to her knees and rolled sideways onto the ground. For an instant, Jean looked as scared as the animal pushing and grunting below her. Then she knelt just behind the cow and cooed, "Good, Tessie. You'll do fine." Jean reached her right arm up into the birth canal.

"The calf is alive. The position feels fine. She should be ready, but it's just not coming." She withdrew her arm, wiped the bloody slime on the grass, and sat back.

Tessie's sides heaved, her eyes looked wild, and at each contraction, her legs jerked up. Between contractions, Jean patted her, crooning words of encouragement.

Suddenly, Tessie bawled a giant grunt of pain.

"Look!" Binxie whispered, and pointed at the cow's rear. A white sac ballooned out of Tessie's enlarged vulva. Inside was a tiny dark hoof. Binxie stood amazed.

The sac and the hoof continued pushing out. A second small hoof appeared and broke the sac. Fluid gushed, then membrane dribbled out in a thin stream of milky white. Tessie heaved herself to a standing position, the two hooves still protruding. She turned her head back and slurped up the fluids on the ground.

The girls stood rigid with revulsion.

Binxie saw the worry in Jean's expression. Something was wrong.

"It has to come out now or it'll die."

"Can we pull it out?" asked Binxie.

"Peggy, run to the truck. Grab a hoe and a rope," said Jean.

Once Peggy handed her the items, Jean quickly tied one end of the rope around the little hooves and the other around the hoe handle.

The girls realized what she was about to do and stepped away. Binxie wanted to stay back, but knew this job needed more strength. She took a deep breath and grabbed the other end of the handle.

"One, two, three." Together, the two girls pulled the handle gently, steadily, with every ounce of strength they had. The forelegs slid out farther. Binxie wanted to rest, but Jean rasped, "Don't stop or it'll drown."

Peggy stepped in and helped too. Now three girls pulled until Tessie moaned and a nose and a red tongue appeared. Jean whooped with relief.

More tugging and the rest of a shiny black-and-white head slid out. Gradually the shoulders, then more and more of the calf emerged. Five minutes later, Tessie gave one final push and the newborn lay sprawled on the grass.

The girls dropped the hoe and hugged each other.

Tessie stretched down to lick her little one clean. The calf shook its head, slapped its still-wet ears back and forth, and ventured a small kick.

Jean untied the rope and tossed it aside. The city girls laughed as tears ran down their cheeks. This was the most amazing miracle they had ever witnessed.

But soon another miracle happened. The calf, not even dry yet, stood up on thin, rubbery legs. It wobbled a moment, took two tentative steps, and fell.

"In another ten minutes it'll walk," said Jean. When it got up again, she leaned over and gently guided the calf's mouth to find its mother's teat. It suckled greedily, its tiny tail switching with contentment. Somewhere across the ocean there was death, terror, and destruction, but in this green field a new life had begun.

Jean sighed with relief. She reached forth her hand to shake Binxie's, stopped, wiped it on her pants, and said, "Thank you."

Binxie grabbed her hand and shook it. Quickly she shook Peggy's too.

"We may as well stop for lunch now," Jean said.

Dickens ran from the barnyard, briefly sniffed the new calf, and joined Tessie in feasting on the afterbirth.

Shuddering in disgust, the girls walked away.

Jean grinned at them. "Welcome to life on a farm."

Peggy stared at the two animals licking up the goo and said, "I'm never going to be a farmer."

Rita added, "I'm never going to have a baby!"

Binxie stayed silent with the wonder of what she had just helped happen.

Isabel

"You gettin' on or not?" a gruff voice scolded Isabel. The man with a battered brown fedora hat, gray beard stained yellow from tobacco, and muddied overalls tapped the steering wheel. "I ain't got till Christmas."

The other trucks were already gone and four girls had disappeared down a path, following Jean. Isabel sighed and climbed onto the wagon strewn with dirty brown straw and who knew what else. The two rows of wooden benches lining the sides were full, so she headed for a seat in the center row. As she crouched to sit, the wagon lurched forward. Isabel crashed into another girl and smacked her funny bone on the hard edge of the bench.

Apologizing, she sat down. Her arm hurt like crazy, but she had to clutch the bench while they bumped along country roads then up a rutted laneway.

As they climbed from the wagon, the farmer, Mr. Scranton, handed each girl a hoe and ordered them to follow him to a field with rows of bushy young plants. He leaned over and gently touched one. "These are potatoes." He spit on two shoots growing next to it, and yanked them from the earth. "And these are bloody weeds. I want you to hack up the damn *weeds*, not the potatoes."

Isabel almost dropped her hoe in shock. No one she knew spoke so coarsely.

"Then hoe up the earth and straw into little hills around the plants. If light hits the potatoes, they turn green and I can't sell 'em." He glared at the girls. "Got that? Now, time's a-wasting. Each of you start on every second row. Begin here, work to the end, then turn and come back up the next row."

Isabel positioned her hoe. The long wooden handle was heavy and awkward, and the blade looked dangerously sharp. *Just like Billy holding a rifle,* she told herself. She watched a sturdy redhead in a green shirt and matching bandana tied stylishly in front—like on the Rosie the Riveter posters—chop at the earth and the weeds. Then cautiously, she began hoeing too. Oops. A tender potato plant toppled over.

"Damn it!" Mr. Scranton bellowed. He grabbed her hoe and demonstrated where to place her hands.

Isabel regarded him coolly. Her dad could have fixed those teeth. She waited until he handed back her hoe, held it almost the way he had demonstrated, said thank you, and daintily resumed her work.

Mr. Scranton watched her like a warden expecting a jail-break. "Never been out of the city, eh, princess?" Then he moved on to the next girl. "Work faster! It'll be August before you finish this row."

Isabel and the girl in green glanced at each other, rolled their eyes, and kept hoeing as the farmer criticized the next girl's efforts.

A minute later, Isabel's hoe slipped again, decapitating another plant.

"I'll deduct ten cents from your pay for every dead plant," Scranton growled.

Isabel was almost too nervous to continue, until he finally stomped to the tractor and drove to another field.

"I hope the old grouch stays there." The green-shirted girl grinned at Isabel. "I'm Kate. I like the way you stood up to him."

"He's vulgar and mean." Isabel smiled at Kate. "Pleased to meet you. I'm Isabel."

The morning stretched on and the sun blazed relentlessly. Flies and other horrid insects buzzed close. Perspiration soaked Isabel's shirt. Mosquito bites itched everywhere.

At last, Mr. Scranton called them for lunch, and pointed

to a wooden picnic table in a grove of maple trees. When the girls noticed the large jug of water and tin cups on the table, they ran. Feeling unbearably hot, Isabel slowly followed them. She felt woozy navigating the uneven ground, and was relieved to sit down.

"I'm starving." Kate sat next to her and tore open her lunch bag.

"I could eat a barn door," said a freckled girl sitting nearby.

"Anything but a potato," added a pretty brunette named Ruth.

Kate snickered, then turned to Isabel. "Are you okay? You look pale."

"I'm fine," whispered Isabel.

"Have some water." Kate handed a cup to Isabel, who drank gratefully. The girls around her chewed and chatted, but the thought of eating made Isabel nauseous. She quietly finished her water and lay down in the cool grass. If only she had slept more last night. She closed her eyes and drifted into a light sleep.

Too soon Mr. Scranton slammed a pitcher of milk onto the table. "Drink up. Five more minutes, then back to the field. You'll have to work a lot harder this afternoon if you want to get paid." He pulled a toolbox from his tractor and headed for a nearby fence.

All through the long hot afternoon Isabel worked, sometimes so dizzy only the hoe kept her from falling. Her arms and lower back were in agony. Blisters formed on her hands. She felt hot, but her skin was clammy. She was hungry, but the idea of food made her feel sick. How would she last the rest of the day, never mind the whole summer? Isabel was disappointed with herself. The others grumbled about the heat and the work, but they were getting it done. By four o'clock, she could barely lift the hoe and had chopped several dollars' worth of seedlings. Would she ever be good at anything?

At long last, Mr. Scranton drove up with his wagon, clouds of brown dust billowing behind like a demon emerging from the mist. He collected the hoes, threw them to the floor of the wagon, and then waited impatiently as the girls climbed in.

"Are you okay?" asked Kate as she helped Isabel up.

Isabel whispered, "I'm fine, thank you," and collapsed onto the wooden bench. With a lurch, the wagon clattered back to Highberry Farm.

As they climbed from the wagon, the girls politely called good-bye to the grizzled farmer. He grunted in reply. But as he watched Kate help Isabel step down, he said, "You're the worst bunch of girls who ever pretended to work for me. Don't come back tomorrow."

For the first time in her life, Isabel wanted to shout something rude. The other girls were angry too. As they stormed across the barnyard, Kate muttered, "How dare he fire us! I wanted to quit first!"

They walked to the lawn in front of the dorm, where some farmerettes sat cheerfully licking ice-cream cones. Isabel sank into a chair beside them.

"Where's ours?" shouted Kate.

"Three miles down the road," a sunburned girl replied. "Mr. Belding stopped at the dairy and bought these on our way home. Said we did a great job thinning his cherries."

"But we're so hot," moaned Ruth. "We hoed a million miles of potatoes today."

The girls looked sympathetic, but no one offered a lick. Peggy pointed to the pump at the side of the barn. "Go get a drink. You look like you could use one."

"And how was your day?" a chubby girl asked Kate, taking a long, slow lick of frosty white ice cream.

Isabel, Kate, and Ruth looked at each other, ready to spew complaints. Isabel surprised herself by answering first. "We had quite a time. Mr. Scranton is unbelievable. Hoeing potatoes is much easier than crouching in the dirt for strawberries or climbing up cherry trees. We want to go there again."

Her coworkers looked at her and quickly nodded in agreement. Tomorrow, let *these* girls hop onto Scranton's wagon first, so they could race to the ice-cream farmer's truck.

Isabel smiled weakly, got up, and went inside. If she could just get to bed and sleep, she'd be fine.

Binxie

When the dinner chime rang, Binxie followed the stampede into the dining room. Girls ladled serving spoons of mashed potatoes, turnips, something green, and slabs of meatloaf onto their plates, then into their mouths faster than they ever did at home.

"I've never been so ravenous," said a slim, pretty girl named Shirley. She mumbled through a mouthful of turnip, "This is yummy."

Binxie noticed the gravy was almost as lumpy as the potatoes, and the vegetables were so mushy it was hard to tell if they were peas or beans.

"I could eat a horse," declared a plump girl, reaching for another slice of meatloaf.

"Good, because I think that's what this is," said Peggy, who always seemed to end up near Binxie. Peggy poked her meatloaf suspiciously, then shrugged and ate a forkful. She smiled at Isabel, across the table from her. "I've been starving since two o'clock. Tomorrow I'll pack a bigger lunch."

Isabel smiled back, but looked pale as she toyed with her potatoes.

Binxie was ravenous too. Not wanting to be seen as "the private school snob," she nibbled at the strangely red meat, then concentrated on the beans or peas.

After dinner, most of the girls headed for the recreation room. Helene found the record player and put on a record. Frank Sinatra crooned to the exhausted girls as they flopped into soft sofas and compared aches and itches.

Peggy told them about the amazing birth she had witnessed, describing the event in detail for her rapt audience. Binxie was glad, for once, to let her chat on. The way she told the story made the other girls share their awe. There was more to Peggy than she had first given her credit for.

A blonde girl with very red skin changed the subject. "Does anyone know how to soothe a sunburn?"

"Butter," replied Isabel.

"Flour," advised Rita.

None of it helped, and soon they were comparing sunburns and who had the most bug bites.

"At least we'll have beautiful tans by September," said Peggy.

"If you think crisp toast is beautiful," Helene muttered.

"The sun is mean to redheads," added Kate. "I'll burn, freckle even more, but stay just as pale as before."

"Will the red be gone in time for the baseball game Saturday?" asked Ruth.

This launched a discussion about the game, the growers' party, and what other events were planned. Binxie lost interest and headed outside. The air was still warm, and the sky was studded with a thousand silver stars.

She gazed at the vast space above her. That was where her sister loved to be, why she'd gone to England. Binxie had flown with Kathryn who once offered her a turn at the controls, but she had chosen to remain an awestruck passenger.

She crossed the yard. A chorus of crickets serenaded her, and the scent of lilacs surrounded her. She turned to see Jean coming from the chicken coop. "You live in paradise."

Jean smiled. "The work is backbreaking, the weather can destroy an entire season's crops, our animals could die from any number of diseases, and the market prices aren't always worth it. But I love every bit of this land and this life."

The two girls fell into step together and walked in companionable silence toward the orchard. "How are Tessie and her calf?"

"Fine. Johnny checked them over while you were at dinner. He's impressed with our work."

Binxie remembered the good-looking fellow who stopped by the farm last night. "He's young to be a vet."

"He's not a vet. His dad is. Johnny's been Dr. Clifford's shadow since he was knee-high to a grasshopper. Has everything but the degree."

"That skill would come in handy overseas," said Binxie.

Jean glared at her, and Binxie realized she had behaved like an outsider judging her host. "I'm sorry," she said. "That was out of line."

As they continued walking between the trees, fragrant with pink blossoms, Jean said, "The day he turned eighteen, he went with my brother to sign up. The army took Rob, but turned Johnny down. My brother got a uniform and headed for Halifax, then overseas. Johnny came home ashamed."

Binxie flushed, and nodded sympathetically. "Your brother's fighting in Europe? My sister, Kathryn, is in England. Flying for the Air Transport Auxiliary. Her dream, my nightmare."

Jean sighed. "Half my nightmare came true. Rob was injured and captured. It took us months to find out he's a prisoner of war in Poland."

Binxie sensed there was more that bothered Jean, but kept quiet. "Poland. It's a beautiful country. Lots of farms. At least he'll get enough food."

"No one in Europe has enough food. I've seen photos of the bombed-out fields." Jean kicked a clump of earth. Then, wistfully, she said, "You've been to Europe?"

"No. When I was twelve, my parents toured the continent. They brought home photos of too many museums and churches. It was their pictures of forests, vineyards, and mountains that took my breath away."

"They saw the canals of Venice? The Alps? Walked the streets of Paris, where Hemingway and Fitzgerald sat and compared ideas?" Jean sighed.

Binxie assessed Jean's muddy work boots, muscled arms, and

intelligent blue eyes. She had underestimated this country girl.

As if she had read her mind, Jean stared straight back at her. "I follow the news on the radio. I've read every novel and magazine the library holds. My favorite Christmas gift is a book."

"Then you know more than I do," answered Binxie. "I don't read much outside of school. I mean to, but there's so much else to do."

The setting sun profiled Jean. "Is it wrong to long for more? For a lot of my neighbors, Winona was the whole world. Then the war came and suddenly Winona shrank. Our fathers, brothers, and sisters went to train in Calgary, Ottawa, Halifax, even Washington. Now they're in England, Italy, Africa, and Asia. I know they face terrible danger, but they're out there, seeing the places I dream of."

"That's why your horses are named Rio, London, Oslo, Cairo, Bombay, and…why Merlin?"

"Berlin until the war started."

Binxie smiled. "Kathryn predicts one day people will fly across the ocean to distant countries quite regularly. Can you imagine?"

Jean shook her head.

Binxie leaned toward a branch to sniff the blossoms. "Africa fascinates me. Deserts and jungles, lions, elephants, and pyramids."

"And Australia," added Jean. "So far away and exotic. Kangaroos, koala bears…"

"And crocodiles lying in wait at every river, not to mention the snakes."

Jean laughed. "Maybe visiting in books is safer."

TUESDAY, JUNE 15, 1943

Helene

"What's wrong with Jean's father?" Rita asked Helene.

Helene watched Mr. McDonnell walk from the field, his head up, fists clenched. "He looks fine to me," she answered. She adjusted her position and resumed hoeing the vegetables. She hated gossip, especially about someone's family. Mr. McDonnell spoke kindly to her. His quiet manner, his large gentle face framed by thinning brown hair, reminded her of her father on the good days long ago.

He had just shown Isabel how to straddle one row of cabbages and hoe the crusty earth on either side of it—for the third time—with no display of impatience or anger. When Isabel smiled, looking helpless in her baby blue shorts and frilly white top, he had hoed the soil for several feet to demonstrate.

Jean had hurried over and curtly warned Isabel, "You need to cope by yourself." She joined her father for a quiet but vehement argument. It ended with Mr. McDonnell leaving the field, head held up in stiff pride, eyes straight ahead.

"Jean sure is bossy," Grace said. "My dad wouldn't put up with that."

Helene knew Jean was worried about her father working in the heat.

Stella snorted in agreement. "My dad keeps us all in line. Says a good swat on the backside builds character. He's already a captain in the navy, and I'll be a WREN in nineteen months."

"I hope the war doesn't last that long," said Helene.

Peggy shuddered. "Every month the war continues, more innocent people die. My cousins in Coventry were bombed out of their home in 1940. They were lucky—their neighbors died. They go to bed every night praying the Luftwaffe won't attack again."

Helene patted Peggy's arm.

When the lunch bell rang, Jean headed for the farmhouse, Dickens close behind. The girls finished their rows and hurried to the shaded tables in the barnyard. Even there it was hot, so they splashed water from the pump over their hair and blouses.

As they sat down, Stella bragged, "My dad helped blow up a Nazi submarine last week."

Helene watched Isabel weave unsteadily across the grass and collapse onto the bench across from her. The other girls were rosy with sunburn, but the flush on Isabel's face looked different. Drops of perspiration beaded her forehead as she absently unpacked her lunch.

"What does your father do in the war?" Stella asked Kate at a volume meant for everyone.

"Army. He took part in both battles of El Alamein," Kate answered proudly.

"And you?" Stella nodded at the next girl.

Lucy shrugged. "He's too old to serve, but he volunteered for the home guard. He does his duty."

Helene chewed nervously hoping Stella would ignore her, as usual.

"How about your family, Isabel?" Stella asked.

Isabel looked dazed. "Um. My Billy is training in England. Ummm. Dad's a dentist," she murmured.

Helene wondered why no one seemed to notice how vague Isabel sounded.

"So your dad's making a profit from the war," Stella shot at her.

Isabel looked confused. "He repairs teeth so men can enlist."

Helene wanted to make sure Isabel was all right, but she couldn't risk drawing attention to herself. She was glad when Peggy moved toward Isabel and spoke quietly. Stella quickly singled Peggy out. "Your dad isn't away fighting."

Peggy looked Stella up and down. "No. He works for the ministry of war—to keep all of your fathers supplied with food and weapons."

Helene admired her friend. No one could tell from her light tone how much tension that had caused in her home.

Isabel got up, staggered from the table to the cool grass under the tree, and lay down. Something was wrong. Helene hurried to her side and felt her forehead. Clammy.

"No sneaking away, Helene. What about your family?" Stella's machine-gun voice zeroed in on her.

Helene's mouth opened like a goldfish, but nothing came out. Answers raced around her brain, tripping over each other. How could she admit she didn't know where her father was? That he had abandoned his family?

An icy voice rescued her. Binxie. "I hardly think we honor our families and their sacrifices by bragging like this."

Shamed into silence, Stella concentrated on her dessert, while Binxie brought a cup of cold water to Isabel. "Drink this," she said gently.

Helene helped Isabel sit up to take a few slow sips. "You shouldn't work this afternoon," she ventured.

"Definitely not," Binxie agreed.

Isabel took another sip. "Let me rest a minute. I'll be fine."

Binxie and Helene gazed at each other doubtfully, but Isabel lay down again and turned her back to them. They stayed beside her, even when some girls got up to toss a ball around. Peggy brought their lunches over and joined them.

Too soon, Jean returned. The girls quickly used the bathroom, washed up at the pump, and trooped back to work.

The midafternoon sun blazed. Helene wished she was as strong as Peggy, leading the girls in a merry medley of songs. But she loved the green fields, the heady smell of earth and leaves, the bright blue sky above. Was there any place on earth this wonderful?

She hoped it wasn't this hot at home. Maybe a breeze from Lake Ontario was cooling Hamilton down a bit. Her brothers wouldn't care, swimming in the bay, playing cowboys or army with their shirts off. But her mother worked in the factory, then cooked, and did other people's laundry. Helene worked faster, trying to hoe away the guilt.

"Isabel!" someone shouted.

Helene looked up as two girls jumped across the rows toward a mound of baby blue and white. She got up and raced toward her friend. "Someone bring water!"

Nancy ran to the pump.

Jean's face scrunched with concern. "Peggy, get salt and some cloths from the house."

While they waited, Helene cradled the crumpled figure who lay with eyes closed, face drained of color. Desperately she fanned the air over Isabel. "They're bringing water. You'll soon feel better," she told her.

Jean barked at the other girls watching them. "Go back to work." Then she softened her tone. "Please."

When Peggy returned, Jean dipped a cloth into the pail and wiped Isabel's forehead, neck, and arms.

Jean's mother hurried toward them with a cup. While Helene propped Isabel up, Mrs. McDonnell gave her a few sips of salted water, which Isabel swallowed with a shudder. Her eyes fluttered shut again.

Mrs. McDonnell soaked two more cloths and rolled them under Isabel's armpits. She lifted her shirt and sponged her back until finally Isabel opened her eyes again, and tried to smile.

"How do you feel?" asked Mrs. McDonnell.

"Dizzy," Isabel whispered weakly.

"Take another sip."

Isabel drank, stopped to rest, tried another mouthful.

"You'll be okay now," said Jean. "I'll get back to work."

Isabel looked stricken. "I'm sorry I held you up."

"It's not your fault. It happens in this heat."

Isabel looked at the other farmerettes working in the field. "But they're all right."

Isabel tried to sit up, but Mrs. McDonnell held her back. "You're not out of the woods yet. I need to keep cooling you down before you can move. How do you feel now?"

Helene heard Isabel whisper, "Like a stupid baby." More loudly, Isabel answered, "I'm fine, ready to work now."

Mrs. McDonnell shook her head. "You've had sunstroke. We need to get you inside."

Isabel began to stand, but swooned back to the ground. Helene let her rest before she tried to help her up again. This would not be easy.

From a nearby row stepped a tall girl with a yellow scarf tied around her hair. She bent down, swooped Isabel into her arms, and carried her from the field.

Mrs. McDonnell followed. "I'll leave the water bucket and salt tablets here for the rest of you," she called back. "If anyone feels the least bit faint or sick, stop right away and get to the shade."

Helene watched them disappear down the lane. She felt slightly woozy herself, but she had a job to do. She finished another row, and then stopped at the water bucket, which now had leaves and an unhappy insect floating in it. She scooped out the bug, filled the tin cup with water to drink, and patted some on her face. She glanced up at the sun, blazing on her right. It was midafternoon. Would she last three more hours?

WEDNESDAY, JUNE 16, 1943

Isabel

Next morning Isabel woke up to weak light wavering through a small window. Her head pounded, every muscle ached. She lay still, trying to place herself. From the bottles and bandages on a shelf nearby, she realized she was in the infirmary. She gazed around the cubicle. Two beds were set apart from the main dormitory by half a wooden wall. The pale light must mean a new day. Then she remembered yesterday.

Miss Stoakley had kept watch over her, bathed her with cool cloths, smoothed lotion on her arms, made her drink too much water and juice. Isabel had slept restlessly, her sunburn stinging, her stomach queasy. Every time she awoke, either Miss Stoakley or Helene was sitting by her side with a smile and a cool drink. Once she had awoken to the laughter of a card game on the bed beside her. Peggy, Helene, and Binxie waved at her cheerfully, and kept on playing.

They cared about her. But no one gushed over her like Mother and Gloria did at home. At first she missed that, then she was grateful. Baby Itsy didn't exist here.

Miss Stoakley entered the silent dorm and whistled. "Time to rise, girls."

Moans and groans emanated from under blankets on the other side of the half-wall. Cots creaked as girls got up to plod downstairs to the washrooms.

Isabel flipped back her covers and tried to sit up. A bolt of pain shot from her forehead to the back of her skull. Gently she eased herself back down. She lay listening to the parade of girls marching downstairs, chatting and giggling, energized for the new day. If they could do it, so could she. She took a deep breath, swung her legs over the edge of the cot, but then a shadow loomed over her.

"Isabel, you stay there." Miss Stoakley looked official this morning in a crisp white blouse, her hair twisted back into a knot. "You're not getting up today."

"I need to work. That was just a silly spell yesterday. I'm fine now."

"No. You had sunstroke. We take that seriously here."

"But I feel better."

The camp mother shook her head. "I'm afraid not, my dear. I'm calling your parents this morning to arrange for them to pick you up."

The horrible events to come flashed through Isabel's mind. Father and Mother rushing her to Dr. Jones, clucking and fussing about her, babying her for the rest of the season. Her sisters barely hiding their I-told-you-so smirks.

And worse, what would Billy think? He and his mates faced terrible danger and hardship. He was watching as the English girls endured bombings, then pulled victims from the rubble. Would he respect a fiancée who couldn't handle strawberry picking?

"I'm not leaving." She sat up. Pain bolted through her head, but she blinked and bore it.

"Yes, you are," Miss Stoakley said gently, but firmly. "We appreciate your dedication, but we won't endanger your health. Sunstroke is dangerous."

"I'll wear a hat and long sleeves. I'll be fine. Please don't call my parents."

"Be reasonable," Miss Stoakley crooned. "Next time it could be worse. You can't risk your health out there."

Isabel looked around her in desperation. She spotted the empty glasses that had been left for her last night. And the dust balls in the corner. "I don't have to work outside," she said. "I could clean. I can cook." Hadn't she read all those magazines for recipes and decorating ideas? Wasn't her cubby the prettiest in the dorm? "Please. I'll peel potatoes, wash floors, anything. Don't make me leave."

"Yes, please, Miss Stoakley." Peggy stood at the entrance of the room. "Let her stay." Helene and Binxie came up behind her to add their support.

Isabel smiled at them gratefully. She noticed Helene leaning against the doorway, looking quite pale. *She feels sick too,* Isabel realized.

Miss Stoakley hesitated. "Well…Cookie's second kitchen assistant wants to transfer to a camp closer to home. But she's a strong girl. It's a big job."

Binxie said, "Isabel has baking experience and she's eager to work."

Helene added, "Isabel's a fast learner. She'll do a good job."

Isabel sensed that Miss Stoakley was ready for that final push to say yes. She regarded her with anxious blue eyes. "Please don't call my parents. Please let me stay."

"I'll need to file a health report. See what the director says."

"Of course that's the right thing to do," agreed Peggy. "But they're so busy there, still placing girls. Maybe we should wait a week or two before we send it—so it doesn't get lost with all their more important mail."

Miss Stoakley raised an eyebrow at Peggy, the girl who had conveniently lost one telegram already. She looked at Isabel, sighed, then nodded. "Rest this morning. Be ready to help prepare dinner tonight. You'll have a lot to learn."

"Thank you, thank you, Miss Stoakley!" Isabel couldn't stop grinning. She flashed a victory sign to the others. She was staying on the farm! And they had stuck up for her! All her strength spent, she lay back on the bed and fell asleep.

SATURDAY, JUNE 19, 1943

Jean

Jean squinted across the strawberry fields into the just-risen sun. It wasn't the glorious display of golden dawn that concerned her. It was the rows of ripening red berries. The day promised to be another scorcher. She could almost see the fruit turning mushy. There was one less girl to help pick—Isabel for sure wouldn't return, and a couple of others looked as if they wouldn't last either. The Women's Institute in Hamilton needed all the berries she had, to make jam for Great Britain. If she couldn't supply enough, they'd find another farm.

She rubbed her eyes, still tired. She and her mum had picked until dark last night, then finished the other chores. Now here she was again. Luckily Gus had asked the farmerettes to start work an hour earlier this morning.

There was a time when June Saturdays meant swimming in the lake, strawberries and cream for dessert, and evenings on the porch swing deep in a book. That seemed so long ago.

Jean crouched and began picking. She hoped to finish several rows before the girls arrived. If only she had slept better last night. But the heat had kept her restless—and the letter.

Rob's note was too short, probably checked by his guards. Did he really think his cheery tone would keep them from worrying? It didn't answer their questions. Was his injured leg healing? Was he hungry? Did her letters telling him they were managing the farm just fine, and that his fiancée was waiting for him, bring him comfort? Did he even receive them? And had he forgiven her?

Jean shook her head. Worries wouldn't pick berries. She filled another box, wiped the sweat from her forehead, and kept picking.

When the farmerettes arrived, they were cheerful and eager. What would she do without them? She was glad to see Binxie in the lead. Binxie worked quickly, quietly, and kept the others working steadily too. And Jean couldn't help but smile at Peggy bouncing along behind Binxie. Her good-natured cheer and her songs kept up everyone's spirits.

Behind the girls came her mother. She looked tired and her hair was hastily held back with bobby pins. "Milking's done. Dad's working on the books today. I had to convince Nanny she's more useful in the kitchen than out here." She picked up a box, and joined the farmerettes in the field.

Binxie

Binxie dreamed she was flying. With arms spread wide, she glided freely through the air, no controls or tail drag to worry about. Her sister smiled and flew beside her.

"I knew it was easy," Binxie said, swooping into a graceful curve.

Suddenly she heard a pop, then another. Gunshots? She panicked and sank.

"Sorry," Kathryn whispered. She faded away and Binxie woke up. Valiantly she tried to get back to sleep, to be with her sister again, but a rustling sound began and she knew she was awake for the day. Across from her, Isabel was shutting her suitcase.

Binxie sat up instantly. "You're not leaving!"

"Shhh." Isabel raised her finger to her lips, then indicated the other girls stirring in their sleep. Binxie glanced at her alarm clock. Five o'clock. "Why are you up so early?"

Isabel bent over to pick up her shoes and tiptoed closer. "I'm on kitchen duty," she whispered proudly. "See you at breakfast."

"Glad you're staying," Binxie mumbled as she scrunched back under her blankets. "Hope you learn to get up more quietly."

An hour later, Binxie munched crisp toast—really crisp— and watched Isabel, a frilly white apron over skirt, her hair tucked into a hairnet, preside over the breakfast table as if she were serving King George himself.

Binxie left the toast, finished her tea, carried her dirty dishes to the counter, and headed outside. They were starting an hour earlier today, but she didn't need to pack a lunch. Saturdays they only worked until one o'clock—even though ripening berries didn't take weekends off.

This afternoon, most of the farmerettes were going to town to watch the baseball game, then find ice-cream sodas some-where. She hummed to herself as she walked to the field, picked up her basket, and crouched down to work.

At one o'clock, the girls headed back toward the dorm, hot and tired of working, but with enough energy left for an afternoon of fun.

As the girls chatted, an ominous hum in the eastern sky grew louder. Binxie shaded her eyes and squinted upward. The others hadn't noticed anything yet.

The low rumble intensified. Soon it echoed across the fields. Even the leaves seemed to tremble at the sound. Flying and turning in unison, four airplanes, wings glinting in the sunlight, flew their way. Binxie stared in awe. How could machines designed to deliver death be so beautiful?

A high-pitched scream pierced their roar. "Nazi bombers! Run for your lives!"

Binxie glanced at the old woman standing on the farmhouse porch as Jean ran to calm her nanny.

The farmerettes stood looking up and around, confused and frightened.

"Head for cover!" Nanny shrieked.

Peggy, ever the showman, dove under a wooden wagon, as though that rickety thing could protect anyone from a bomb. Kate raced for the trees, and most of the others followed. Two girls stood frozen with fear. The roar became deafening.

This didn't make sense. Binxie stayed where she was and studied the planes. She tried to remember what she knew about identifying aircraft, as the other girls screeched for her to run.

Isabel appeared from the kitchen. "What's going on?"

Nanny shouted, "The Nazis are coming to kill us!"

Isabel stood transfixed by the planes. Two of them had broken formation and were flying straight at them. "So this is how I'm going to die. Hot and dusty in a barnyard, never to hold my Billy again," she said sadly.

Peggy climbed out from under the wagon. "Those aren't German planes. They're Canadian Avro Ansons. See? They're painted bright yellow—training planes."

Isabel looked puzzled.

"We learned to identify planes at school last year," Peggy explained. She yelled to the others, "Don't worry. We're safe."

"Not if that plane crashes into us." Binxie pointed up. One machine rejoined the others, but the second one still flew too low.

The other girls came cautiously out from the trees.

Jean called out to them, "There's nothing to worry about. Those are our boys, learning to fly. They're from the training base in Mount Hope."

"But your nanny…," began Isabel.

"Every time she hears a plane, she's convinced the Nazis are attacking us, no matter how often I explain they can't fly this far inland."

"Well, whoever they are, one of them is flying right at us!" shouted Peggy.

The breakaway plane dipped a wing as it rushed past the girls, close enough for Binxie to see a helmeted head inside and an arm waving at them. Then it rose again.

"Stupid show-off." Binxie said. Slowly, the other girls left the safety of the trees, excited about this taste of danger.

Although his mates were rapidly flying west, the rogue pilot circled back.

This time his audience waved and cheered him on. But not Binxie. Kathryn would have been appalled at his reckless behavior. And she was hungry for lunch. Why couldn't this idiot just fly away?

He was flying too low, heading straight for the barn. Too late the plane swerved, cleared it, then grazed the flagpole with a wing tip.

Isabel cried, "He's going to crash!"

Every eye was riveted on the machine. Each heart pounded, every lip prayed.

For a second the plane seemed to hover in midair. Then it wobbled forward, dipped, and landed hard in the field near the road.

The farmerettes raced to the plane, and Helene detoured to the dorm. "I'll phone for help."

As Binxie neared the yellow Avro Anson, she saw the pilot slumped against the side window, eyes closed, sunlight glinting on red blood trickling from his temple.

"Let's pull him out of there!" shouted Peggy, trying to climb onto the wing.

"Stop!" ordered Binxie.

"Why? He needs help."

Binxie pointed at the pilot. "If you open his door, he'll fall over. If his back is injured, he'll end up crippled for life." She ran around to the other side of the plane, climbed onto the wing, careful to step on the marked pad, and wrenched the passenger door open. She crawled in next to the pilot and felt his wrist for a pulse.

"Ummm, that feels nice. You smell good too."

She jerked back, and stared down at the young man now assessing her with saucy blue eyes and a cheeky grin. "Guess I won't try that stunt again. But it sure was worth it to meet such a bevy of beautiful gals."

"I hope your squadron leader feels the same about you ruining a plane," Binxie retorted.

The young pilot lifted his arm, winced in pain, and fainted

onto the control wheel. *Great,* thought Binxie. *Is this another attention grabber or is he really hurt?*

Jean knocked on the window. "Is he dead?"

Binxie shook her head. "Good! You brought water. Come on up. Walk only on the marked mat or you'll step right through the wing. I'll look for a first aid kit."

Binxie rummaged around the back as Jean climbed in and dabbed cool water on the pilot's cut.

A minute later, he came to. He gazed at Jean gratefully. "Another angel. My head and arm hurt like hell, but I'll live."

"Until your flight leader gets hold of you," Jean answered.

"Keep still." Binxie crawled forward and pointed at his left arm wedged against the door at an odd angle. "I'm sure it's broken." She handed Jean a bandage for his head.

"Damn. That grounds me for awhile." The pilot grimaced. "And I was ready to leave for merry old England next week."

A military jeep raced up the road and into the field. Two men in blue uniforms climbed out and approached the plane. One offered to help the girls down.

"We got up on our own." Binxie ignored his arm and jumped to the ground. Jean followed. The medic climbed into the plane, and an officer barked questions at the girls. Soon the medic helped the pilot out of the cockpit to the jeep. A truck pulled up and a mechanic in greasy overalls stepped out.

Once the officer had spoken with the fellow, the jeep pulled away. As he was driven off, the handsome pilot cheerfully saluted the girls.

Binxie shook her head, but the other girls giggled and sighed.

After lunch, the girls left for the baseball game and passed the air force mechanic working on the plane. "He's cute," Peggy declared. "And so was that pilot."

"He was too cheeky for me," Jean retorted. "And he knows he's good-looking."

"If he keeps acting that recklessly, he won't last long," added Binxie.

Jean

By nine-thirty that evening, Jean sat on the front porch to catch her breath before she had to feed the chickens. The first star glowed in a denim sky. Jean loved the evenings, when time stood suspended in that hushed expectant way just before night fell. She was nodding off to sleep when a cheery "Hello" startled her.

Johnny walked up the porch steps. Something about the way his smile reached his brown eyes made Jean's heart lurch. "You heard we had lemonade. I'll get you some."

When he had settled in the chair beside her with his drink, he said, "I missed you at the baseball game today."

"No time. The berries are a nightmare. The faster we pick, the quicker they ripen." She grinned. "But we got them all— until tomorrow. I hear you won the game."

"Six–four. I hear you had some drama here today."

"A training pilot from Mount Hope tried to impress us and ended up crash-landing. I expect he's in a mess of trouble. Did you get your hay cut?"

"Yup. Tomorrow we plant the late corn crop."

They sat sipping lemonade, watching stars appear in the darkening sky. Jean was aware of the girls down by their dorm, craning their necks to see Johnny. She turned away slightly. She preferred having him to herself.

"One of the Beldings' dogs twisted his front leg in barbed wire yesterday."

"Ouch. What did you do?"

"Fed him a handful of aspirin, then untangled it fast."

They fell into comfortable silence as the peepers in the pond began a backup chorus to the song of the crickets in the bushes. Too soon, Johnny left and Jean headed for the chicken coop. Would there ever come a day when they didn't have to part in the evenings?

THURSDAY, JUNE 24, 1943

Isabel

Isabel struggled to carry a heavy pail of water across the kitchen to the stove.

"Try getting that here before July!" Cookie said.

Isabel stopped and regarded the cook, a tall, muscular woman who looked more like she belonged in a munitions factory than a kitchen. "Every time I take a step, it sloshes over the rim. I have to wait until it settles again."

"You can mop up after you finally fill that kettle."

I don't know why she's called Cookie, thought Isabel. *It should be Sourdough.* She set the pail down twice more to give her aching arms a break. She was exhausted. Whoever heard of getting up at five o'clock to make breakfast? And this was the fourth morning in a row.

"Next time fill it halfway and take two trips," Cookie grumbled. "Why have they sent me a princess?" She grabbed the pail handle with one muscled arm and swung it onto the stovetop without spilling a drop.

She could have told me that sooner, Isabel thought as she found the mop and squeezed her trail of puddles into another pail. She stepped outside to toss the water into the yard and saw Jean staggering to the barn with a pail of feed. They nodded at each other in understanding.

"Fetch some apples from the storage shed, and don't drop any this time," Cookie demanded. "We'll serve Salmon Surprise and Apple Brown Betty tonight."

The surprise will be if the salmon is edible, thought Isabel, as she hurried across the barnyard. As always, she was careful to avoid Cracker. He perched on his fence-post throne, glaring at her with beady eyes, deciding whether to attack or merely intimidate.

The storage shed was cool and gloomy. The smell of earth and ripe things was strong. Spiders and bugs scurried into cracks in the wooden walls and floor.

She looked around for the apple bin. She felt greasy, hot, and exhausted. Her hands were nicked in several places where she had cut herself peeling turnips, carrots, endless potatoes. Her thumb blistered where she had scalded herself over the teakettle. Baking at home was never this difficult. But at home she hadn't cooked for seventy people.

It occurred to her how much preparation and cleanup her mother must have done around her. Odd—she never noticed it at the time. Totally discouraged, she sat on a wooden keg and lowered her head to her hands. She couldn't handle farmwork; she couldn't stand the sun. No civilized person should have to get up before dawn. Cooking was hard work. Scrubbing the floors killed her knees, and washing the toilets was disgusting. Tomorrow they would have to spray the kitchen with DDT again—to keep insects away.

Isabel kicked backward at the keg she sat on. She couldn't do anything. She really was an itsy princess.

She couldn't kick a keg either. Her heel throbbed with pain. But it snapped her out of her pity session. "No!" she yelled. "Even princesses are useful. Princess Elizabeth herself drives an ambulance for the war." The girls in England were clearing bomb rubble with their bare hands, nursing broken and dying people. Compared to that, what was peeling a hundred potatoes or scouring a washroom?

"I *can* do this. I'll tell Billy amusing stories about it when he comes home." Isabel stood, squared her shoulders, and stepped outside into a stream of sunlight. It was a sign. She was strong and capable. She ran back to the kitchen, firm with purpose.

It wasn't until Cookie banged a pot lid that she realized she'd forgotten the apples. Sighing, she rushed back to get them.

SUNDAY, JUNE 27, 1943

Helene

Sunday afternoon, Helene felt sticky and tired like the other girls. It had been a blistering hot week of hoeing, weeding, and picking berries. Last night, they stayed up too late dancing to records and raiding the kitchen at midnight.

After church, they had lunch at the rectory with Reverend Ralston and his wife. Helene was stuffed full of dainty sandwiches, polite chatter, and goodwill. Now no one had the energy to do more than lounge around the recreation room, playing cards and listening to the radio.

Helene was glad when *The Army Show* came on. She loved Wayne and Shuster's humor, and hearing the other girls laugh. They were annoyed when the deep voice of the radio announcer interrupted a hilarious skit with a war update.

> *"Operation Pointblank is proving successful. A massive Allied air raid involving eight hundred planes has destroyed the city of Dusseldorf. Twenty-seven Nazi fighters were shot down. In North Africa, intensive naval and air power achieved the surrender of 275,000 Italian and German troops. On the Italian front, Allied..."*

Peggy turned down the radio and asked, "Anyone interested in playing The Landlord's Game? It's fun." She pulled a worn box from the shelf.

"I'll play," Helene offered.

Isabel, from her chair in the farthest corner, shook her head. "I have to start dinner soon." She retreated back into her mail, poring over Billy's old letters, since none had arrived this week.

Kate jumped to join them. "I'm buying George Street and putting houses on all my properties, so everyone will owe me rent."

"Ha, you'll be lucky to get Goat Alley or the Ting-a-Ling Telephone Company, my friend," answered Peggy.

"We'll see," said Kate. "I wish half the cards weren't missing."

"Wait," said Helene, searching the shelves. "Miss Stoakley delivered new games yesterday. Here it is." She pulled out a clean box. "This is the one from the United States. They renamed it Monopoly."

Peggy looked intrigued as Helene unwrapped the game. Lured by the novelty, Irene joined them too, and soon the girls were amicably gouging rents from each other for landing on Park Place and the four railroads.

Isabel tucked her letters into her pocket, and left for the kitchen. "Poor Isabel," whispered Irene. "I heard the real reason the last kitchen assistant left was because she couldn't take Cookie's temper anymore."

Helene worried about that too. How would Isabel last in that kitchen?

Stella passed by, balancing her laundry on one arm and carrying a bar of yellow soap in the other hand.

"Gosh, I should wash my clothes too," said Kate, but she returned to the game instead.

An hour later, Helene excused herself. "I have to write my letters before I'm too tired."

"I should write too," agreed Irene.

"I'm the richest; I win. Just call me the Queen of Monopoly," said Kate, raising her arms in victory before she helped pack away the game.

"Wait till next week," said Peggy, laughing. "I should answer my mail too."

Binxie was already deep into her letters at a round wooden

table. Helene sat beside her to finish the notes to Peggy's soldiers. Only four now. One of them had found a girl in Halifax before he shipped out, and was exchanging letters with her instead.

Then she wrote to her mother.

> Dear Mama,
> It's a relief to know Hamilton is not too hot for you, and the boys are a help. Please hug them for me on their big day. It will be the first family birthday I've missed, and I'll think of you even more that day. I'm enclosing ten dollars to buy them a cake and a gift each and something for you too. I have no use for it here—we're fed well, and I have more clothes than I need. Jean shares her books with me, and there's a library in town.
>
> Life here is wonderful. I'm so grateful you let me come. I've seen animals born and thrive. Every day I admire the sun rising and setting over fields of green and gold. My cough is gone, and I feel strong and full of energy. I only wish you and the boys, and Alva and her baby, were here to share it with me.
>
> Take care of yourself, Mama. I miss you.
>
> All my love,
> Helene.

She saw Peggy looking at her envelopes with a guilty grimace. "Next week I promise I'll write to the boys. I never know what to say."

Helene shrugged. "Everyday things. They want to hear about normal home life and that someone cares about them."

"You always put things so nicely," replied Peggy.

"You play the piano beautifully," said Helene. "We're even."

"Funny, no one ever compliments my singing."

"I wonder why." Helene grinned.

"I better write home too. I just wish there was some way to let them know what I'm doing without having to write a whole letter." Peggy sighed, found paper, and made herself comfortable at the table. Helene slid into a soft chair and read.

Isabel

The pen felt awkward in Isabel's hand as she tried to avoid the bandaged finger she had cut with a paring knife.

> *My Darling Billy,*
> *Thank you for the photos. The army has put extra muscles on you, and it suits you well. England looks lovely. You must send me Mrs. Wyecroft's trifle recipe so I can make it for you when you come home.*
>
> *I'm still doing my part for the war too. I was promoted to camp assistant. The cook and I plan and prepare the meals and oversee the general domestic care of the camp. Tonight we're making Dinner-in-a-Roll. It's excellent training for the day I run our home. I wish I could enclose a strawberry shortcake and a thousand kisses for you, but that must wait. In the meantime, here's a picture of me and my friends in the orchard.*
>
> *My work here is fulfilling, but I long to hold you in*

my arms, to dance with you to our song, to hear you talk
about the beautiful life we'll build together when this war
is over. I look at our star and pray for you every night.

With eternal love and devotion,
Your Isabel.

She knew there was no reason to worry. Since last October, Billy had written at least one letter every week. Sometimes they were delayed and she'd get two or three at a time, but they always came. Lately he had skipped a week here and there, probably too busy training. His last letter said they were preparing to be shipped "somewhere hot."

She tucked the photo into the envelope. She knew she looked good in it. She hoped he'd notice how much slimmer she had become.

After writing to her parents, she added her letters to the basket of outgoing mail, put on her apron, and hurried to the kitchen.

"You're late," said Cookie. "I started the potatoes without you."

Considering all Cookie had to do was light the stove after Freda and I peeled a hundred of them two hours ago, that wasn't so hard, thought Isabel. She didn't apologize.

"Since I'm behind with the ham loaf and you're so anxious to bake, you may make dessert. I left the recipe for Crumb Cake on the counter. It's an easy recipe for beginners. Use the two large pans stacked beside the oven. Call me if you need help.

I've already added salt to the potatoes. Watch they don't burn; Freda will prepare the peas and turnips later. Any questions?"

"I'll manage, thank you," declared Isabel, miffed at the easy-for-beginners comment.

Cookie shrugged, and went to prepare the meat.

Isabel was thrilled. Finally she could show her talents. As soon as she heard Cookie say she could bake, she had been so busy thinking about the cake that she stopped listening.

She scanned the recipe. It wasn't just easy—it was dull. She leafed through the booklet to find something with more zip. Ahh. Coffee Spice Cake. Much better. She gathered the main ingredients, but then remembered Cookie had said something about salt and the potatoes. There were a lot of potatoes, so she sprinkled salt in generously.

She creamed the shortening and sugar, added eggs, measured the flour into another bowl. Golly, there was a lot of it. Sixteen cups. Now for the rest. This cake would be perfect.

She searched the cupboards for the spices. She knew cinnamon, but what did cloves and nutmeg look like? Luckily the bottles were labeled. Carefully she measured the cinnamon and cloves. The nutmeg was weird. Hard brown balls the size of grapes. Oh well, they probably melted as they were baking. She tossed six balls into the mixture.

She heard hissing on the stove. The potato water was boiling over. Quickly she turned the heat down and tossed in more salt before reading the next step of her recipe. Raisins. Fine. Cold coffee? She looked around. Cookie always made coffee at lunch. Luckily the grounds were still in the percolator. Isabel scooped out four spoons. Was that enough? Another two would give it extra flavor. She added the wet mixture with the coffee grounds to the dry ingredients, smoothing out most of the lumps.

She poured the batter into the cake pans. This cake would taste delicious. But there was no icing. Every cake needed icing. She flipped back to the crumb cake recipe.

What was that smell? She looked around, sniffing.

Cookie ran into the room. "The potatoes!" She lifted the lid. "You didn't add more water! You've burned them!"

Isabel was rather annoyed. How could she be expected to do two things at once? "That's all right. I was planning to brown them anyway."

"They're not browned, they're *burned*. And they'll *taste* burned!"

"I'm sorry. I'll throw them out and make something else."

"People are starving in Europe and you want to waste food." Cookie glared at her in disgust. "Get those cakes into the oven and clean up this mess. Then scrape away the burned potatoes and salvage the rest." She stomped off, muttering.

Isabel decided to skip the icing. She slid the cake pans into the oven, carefully noting the time, and headed for the potato pot. She scooped out the potatoes that didn't look burned, and placed them into a new pot. Then she tossed in butter and salt to disguise any burned taste there might be. Once Cookie ate her dessert, she'd be forgiven.

By dinner that evening, Isabel was too exhausted to even look at food, but she wanted to be there when everyone ate her cakes. They had turned out perfectly, if she did say so herself. And sprinkled with fresh parsley and chives from the garden, the potatoes looked lovely.

The girls dug into their food as usual, but when they tasted the potatoes, they grimaced and reached for glasses of water. Isabel was surprised. She took a bite and almost retched. The salt! Awful! Freda must have added more when she wasn't looking. *Too many cooks certainly do spoil the broth,* she thought.

Peggy downed her glass of water and said brightly, "I'm looking forward to that cake of yours."

Maybe she'd talked about it too much. She'd even invited Jean over for some.

When the time came, Isabel proudly set the pans on the serving table. Her cakes were a lovely rich brown color, like chocolate. To make up for the lack of icing, she had sliced strawberries on top. Presentation was important.

"How pretty," said everyone as she handed out slices with a regal smile. She watched eagerly as they ate, and nodded their approval. They liked it!

Then Stella asked, "What are these black specks? They're sticking in my teeth."

"A bit gritty, but I like the flavor," Jean added.

Isabel rolled her eyes at Stella. *She's always critical,* she thought. Then she answered Jean. "It's coffee and cinnamon."

"Coffee?" asked Freda. "How well did you read that recipe?"

Isabel defended herself. "It said cold coffee."

"That's actual coffee, not the grounds."

Isabel gasped. How could she have been so stupid?

"I like it anyway," said Helene, taking another bite.

Suddenly Millie screamed. "Ouch! My tooth!" She spit a brown ball into one hand, and with the other clutched her mouth in pain.

Cookie ran from the kitchen, took one look at Millie's open hand, and shouted to Isabel, "You put a whole nutmeg into the cake! You're supposed to grate it! Come into the kitchen right now."

Isabel was mortified. "I'm sorry, Millie. Are you okay?"

Millie nodded, still holding her mouth.

"If your tooth is damaged, my dad will fix it for free." Isabel was almost in tears. Then she addressed the room. "There are five more nutmegs in the cakes. Please, watch out for them."

With all the dignity she could muster, she turned and followed Cookie to the kitchen, her face white, her hands shaking. This time for sure she'd be sent home.

Binxie

Binxie sat propped up in bed, finished a note to her parents, then reread Kathryn's latest letter.

> Dear Binxie,
> By the time you get this letter, you'll be settled at Highberry Farm. I'm glad you decided to go. You'll like it far more than another season at the cottage. Yes, we had great times growing up there, but suddenly sailing regattas and stuffy cocktail parties seem dull.
> My last two weeks have been wonderful. I am finally allowed to fly a Spitfire. It's a beautiful machine—light, maneuverable—like it's a part of me. On Monday, I ferried a brand-new Tiger Moth north, couldn't catch a flight home, so ended up returning on a dark train crammed with troops. Every sound made

me nervous—was it a V-I rocket hurtling upon us? Too
many railroad lines here are bombed and twisted like
steel spaghetti.

Wednesday I made six flights, on five different
planes. There was barely time to grab my parachute and
maps from one plane, sign my delivery chits, and get
to the next one. The next day I flew a Miles Master to
transport an air commodore from Leeds to Wales, hoping
he'd approve of my flying skills. Saturday I picked up a
damaged Swordfish from Scotland and got lost in some
clouds coming home. Luckily they opened in time for me
to land safely at a little airport north of London. Even
on clear days, it's easy to lose your way—from above,
one town looks like the other, and the airports are cam-
ouflaged against enemy pilots. But thanks to our trusty
maps, our handling notes, and some heavenly help, I
always manage to make it.

Some time ago (can't say when), I delivered a
Spitfire to a small airfield. Two tough, silent men wearing dark coats, low hats, and blackened faces took over.
I'm sure they were headed for some secret mission across
the channel.

Can you believe there are still people who disap-
prove of us—little ladies flying big machines, daring to
wear trousers! I do enjoy landing a heavy plane at a new
airfield and seeing the shocked faces of the other pilots
and ground crew as I emerge from the cockpit. Before I
get out, I comb my hair and put on fresh lipstick, just to
disturb them more.

Last week, my fellow pilot Diana Barnato invited me to spend three days at her father's estate in Surrey. It was such a pleasure to trade in my leather flying jacket, slacks, and serviceable black shoes for pretty dresses and dancing slippers. We dined at the Orchid Room in London one night with the very handsome son of Lord Wexbourne. He taught me what to do next time I fly into clouds, even drawing me a diagram on the white damask tablecloth. He promised to take us dancing next time we're in the city.

There is so much to see and to learn, such fun and adventure, and I know the good I'm doing. There'll be many stories to tell you when I get home.

Meanwhile, keep up your fine work, and let me know all about it.

Love and hugs as always,
Kathryn.

Binxie read the letter twice. Clearly her sister was in her glory. Although Binxie was extremely proud of her, and Kathryn made light of the dangers, she worried. She yearned to be old enough to join her in England, but even more, she wished Kathryn would come home safely.

She picked up her pen and wrote.

Dear Flying Whiz,
Thanks for your letter of June 7. It arrived quickly. What an exciting life you're leading. Who would have guessed

all those years you read about Amelia Earhart, Charles Lindbergh, and Alcock and Brown's flying triumphs with such longing that you'd be a "mighty pilot" one day too.

I can't wait to join you. I'm studying flight manuals to prepare myself, and will sign up for lessons in September.

As you predicted, life on the farm is dandy. It's an interesting assortment of characters—farmers who lift eighty-pound bags of seeds over their shoulders with ease, but can hold a little chick or tender seedling with hands as gentle as a baby's; a cook with arms like ham hocks who yells better than she cooks; a nasty rooster who threatens my dainty friend Isabel whenever he spots her in the barnyard—and a handsome neighbor who has a wonderful way with animals. The farm women toil inside and out, while praying fervently for their sons to return. This area lost too many boys last year at Dieppe.

The other farmerettes are nice. Four of us have become pals. Peggy is a character. She keeps us entertained on the piano and with whatever instrument is handy—last night, she showed us how to make music with a spoon. She gets us singing and laughing in the fields and never runs out of ideas for fun. Helene is smart, thoughtful, and has a dry sense of humor. Isabel is like a porcelain doll. She struggles to cook and clean. She's good at adding flourishes to make our ordinary meals more appealing. Under her pink and fluffy exterior, I sense a tough soul, even if she doesn't.

You'd like Jean, whose family owns Highberry.

When she's not working, we like to walk, or ride the horses together—Merlin for her, Cairo for me. She knows everything about farming, and more geography than our teachers back at good old Branksome. She loves the farm but dreams of travel overseas.

Our "camp mother," Miss Stoakley, is firm but fair. She's a stickler for the rules, but last week, some of us spotted her puffing a cigarette behind the barn! That's definitely against the rules, so we pretended not to see. Now I know why she eats so many mints. We call her Smokey now.

The work here isn't hard—just monotonous—nothing like soaring across the skies to save the world. All but one of the farmers treat us well. I have become used to green stains on my fingers and cow dung on my shoes. I'll never look at a piece of fruit without utmost appreciation again.

Binxie then described how the cocky pilot crash-landed in front of them. The girls had talked about him all week. She saved the best story for last, telling about the birth of Tessie's calf. She hoped she could convey to Kathryn how marvelous it was.

As always, she signed off begging Kathryn to stay safe.

THURSDAY, JULY 1, 1943

Isabel

Isabel watched Freda carry the large cakes into the dining room, a dozen candles sparkled on the biggest one. The lights were dimmed, and seventy people burst into "Happy Birthday."

Isabel and six other girls came to the serving table. Cheers echoed around the room and everyone called, "Make a wish."

Isabel wished for Billy to come home soon, then helped the other girls blow out the candles. Applause filled the room. Isabel smiled and watched as Freda sliced into her beautiful creation. The slab cake had come plain from the bakery but Isabel spent an hour swirling on clouds of pink and white icing. The pink geranium petals scattered artistically over it were a last-minute inspiration.

Once everyone was served, Isabel took her plate to join her friends at their table. She was greeted with warm wishes and hugs. Her actual birthday wasn't until July eighth, but for practical reasons the first of each month was the day chosen to celebrate every birthday.

Each of the seven July birthday girls received a gift—a small jar of lavender-scented hand cream—from Smokey, and various joke gifts from their friends. Tonight they would all head to Romeo's to dance. Peggy and Kate had discovered the restaurant by the lake that not only served hamburgers and sodas, but had a jukebox full of modern hits by Bing Crosby, The Mills Brothers, Harry James, Glenn Miller, and of course, Frank Sinatra. It had been a long time since Isabel had danced, but she planned to tonight.

Her birthday gifts from Billy and her family were already tucked under her bed. She fought the temptation to open them, savoring the anticipation. But she hadn't been able to resist reading Billy's birthday letter. It was so full of love and sweet longing that she almost cried.

Eighteen. She gazed at her diamond ring. Old enough to marry. When this war ended, her life would begin.

SATURDAY, JULY 3, 1943

Binxie

"Could I borrow that silver hair clip?" Kate asked Binxie, pulling a brush through her mass of curly red hair.

Binxie hesitated, then handed it to her.

"Thank you." Kate moved aside so Binxie could see herself in the mirror too. Binxie checked herself over. Chin-length, wavy brown hair, clear skin, a flared red skirt, white blouse with short sleeves that showed her tanned arms, and a simple strand of pearls. She looked good. Maybe too good for a party in a barn. On the other hand, perhaps that Johnny Clifford would be there too.

Millie sprayed liberal amounts of cologne on herself. It drifted over several others too.

Binxie was glad to leave the crowded washroom, but even the dorm was a frenzy of dressing, swapping blouses to match scarves, trading skirts, sharing scents, and fashion advice. Nancy was drawing a black line down the back of Irene's legs. Since silk stockings were impossible to get, painted-on seams and a tan had to do.

"I feel like I've stepped into the giant closet of my dreams," Peggy said, admiring herself in a pair of blue shorts donated by someone in exchange for her red blouse. "If we all keep sharing clothes, we can dress in a different outfit every weekend this summer." She grinned cheerfully at Binxie. "You can borrow anything you like of mine."

I'd never wear someone else's clothes, thought Binxie. "Thank you," she said politely and headed outside, where two wagons waited to transport the girls to the growers' party. She approached the closest horse and patted his soft muzzle. "I'd rather gallop across the fields with you than bump around a barn with a bunch of locals," she whispered to him. Working at Scranton's farm yesterday had left her grouchy about farmers.

Another wagon clattered up the laneway, and girls trickled from the dorm. They clambered into the wagons—freshly swept out for the occasion, with clean blankets spread over the benches. Binxie settled in one.

"Wait!" someone shouted, as they rolled down the drive. She turned to see Isabel, clad in a flowery dress and matching yellow hat, carrying a large box, running across the barnyard. The wagon stopped for her and eager arms pulled her up.

"Thank you," Isabel puffed.

"What took you so long?" Peggy chided. "You nearly missed the party."

"I peeled onions all morning, had to shower twice." Isabel smiled and pointed at the box in her lap. "And I baked tarts for tonight."

"Have some water ready," Stella joked, but only Grace laughed.

Binxie smiled at Isabel. "You look lovely. And I bet the tarts will be delicious." She was as relieved as the other girls that Isabel could stay. In spite of her mistakes, everyone appreciated how hard Isabel tried to make things attractive, and lately, her desserts had become quite tasty.

Even though dark clouds were gathering over the lake to the north, the girls were in a jolly mood as they reached the Beldings' farm. Several farmers and their families were there by the massive brown barn. A WELCOME FARMERETTES banner hung over the wide double doors. The Beldings loved entertaining, and judging by the cheerful talk and the amount of food being loaded onto tables lined up in the barnyard, they did it well.

Mr. and Mrs. Belding were the first to say hello. Their two blonde daughters stood back a bit. *Are they shy,* Binxie wondered, *or just suspicious of us city girls?* Then others made their way over, and greetings and laughter filled the barnyard.

This is pleasant, but a bit sad, thought Binxie. A party full of old people, women, and girls and boys too young to enlist.

"Who's playing volleyball?" Peggy called from behind her.

Evie Belding nodded shyly.

"Are you any good?" Peggy challenged with a devilish grin.

"We sure are," her sister, Alice, shot back. "Evie whacks that ball so fast you won't see it 'til it spits up dirt on your side of the net."

"In that case, I'm on your team," Peggy answered. "I do a mean spike."

"Come meet our cousin. She gives a wicked serve," Evie invited, all shyness gone.

Binxie watched Peggy beckon Helene to join them. She liked the way the two looked after each other. The four girls crossed the yard to meet a tall, brawny girl. Soon all five chatted together like old friends.

"Hello, Miss."

Binxie turned to greet the minister, a salt-and-pepper-haired, stooped man with a solid handshake. She tried to look attentive as he talked about their church choir and the knitting club, but she was more interested in the girls stringing up a net and batting the ball around to warm up. Reverend Ralston introduced her to a group of white-haired choir members. Wondering if you had to be eighty years old to join, she exchanged pleasantries with them.

Soon the volleyball game was in full swing. The players threw good-natured taunts across the net and shrieked in triumph when they hit the ball. Even Isabel removed her hat and joined the game, giggling prettily every time she dropped the ball.

Just as she answered her ninth question about life in Toronto, Binxie heard Peggy call. "Hey, Binx! We need you on our team!"

She looks after me too, Binxie realized as she jumped into the game in time to smack the ball neatly over the net and score a point. Everyone cheered as she got into position for her team's next serve. Then Johnny arrived, looking handsome in blue jeans and a white T-shirt that showed off his muscled arms, and joined the other side. A minute later, Binxie whacked the ball over the net—right into the side of his head. He took it cheerfully, but Binxie, blushing crimson, wanted to run to the barn and hide.

By the time Mrs. Belding called them to dinner, everyone knew each other's name, and no one knew the score. "We may have to eat quickly." She pointed at the dark clouds rolling across the lake.

"Nah. There's lots of time before that storm hits," Mr. Scranton drawled. He wore the same battered fedora, but he had shaved and changed into a clean shirt and overalls. Two of his sons sat next to him. Younger versions of him—short haircuts, large teeth, solid builds—they piled food onto their plates. The third son, finer-featured and thinner, stood behind them. He pulled out a chair for an older woman, and sat beside her.

Binxie helped carry platters of ham and vegetables to the table until Isabel patted the chair next to her. "I saved you a seat."

Binxie headed her way, then realized it was next to Johnny. She hesitated, suddenly feeling shy. He stood up to pull her chair out for her. As she sat down, he introduced himself. His smile was devastating and his eyes as deep and brown as the earth. She could barely stammer her name. Luckily Jean sat to his right and chatted to them both about the volleyball game.

On her left, Isabel was breathless and exhilarated. "I actually knocked the ball over the net! It came at me so fast I shut my eyes and hit. It flew over the net! And we scored a touchdown!"

Binxie didn't have the heart to correct her.

At the head of the table, Mr. Belding stood up and officially welcomed the farmerettes with a short, funny speech. Miss Stoakley spoke a bit longer—not as amusing, though no less sincere. Reverend Ralston said grace, and everyone dug in to the food.

Someone passed a basket of rolls her way.

"Hey, Binxie, throw me one," called Alice from across the table.

Johnny clutched his head and ducked.

Binxie blushed and handed Alice the basket. Johnny grinned at her and waited for her to say something. Binxie, master of polite small talk, sat speechless. What good was all that etiquette training if it failed her when she most wanted it?

Johnny helped himself to potato salad and handed the bowl to Binxie. She served herself and passed it to Isabel, thinking hard. She could talk about the weather—those dark clouds were rolling closer. But when she turned his way, he had already resumed his conversation with Jean. Binxie surveyed the tables, loaded with food. Everyone, including the farmerette camp, had contributed—fried chicken, fresh asparagus, cabbage rolls, pickled pigs' feet, deviled eggs, rhubarb strawberry pies, Isabel's strawberry tarts, and, of course, strawberries. She'd never have guessed there was war rationing. These people had gone all out to welcome them.

She wished she felt as welcome to Johnny and Jean, discussing cows, crops, and people she didn't know, with only a polite comment here and there directed at her. At least Isabel chatted with her.

Just as people were finishing the last pies, a brown Hudson drove up and parked near the stables. Out climbed a man wearing a red-and-white checked shirt and a straw hat with a red hatband to match his bow tie. Evie and her friends cheered, and four choir ladies rushed to greet him.

"That's Seth Rogers. Looks like we'll dance after all," Jean said. She hurried to fill a plate with food for the square dance caller.

Luckily Seth wasn't much of an eater. He soon stood up, requested a glass of cider, and strode to the barn. Everyone followed. Inside, Gus and another man already stood on an improvised stage, tuning their fiddles.

Quickly young and old alike grabbed the hands of eager farmerettes, divided into squares of eight, and tapped their toes to the warm-up notes coming from the stage. Old-timers explained some steps to the visitors, and the music began.

Soon the barn was swinging to music and Seth's calls. "Now the girls lead in and the gents go out, then turn your two stars round about…" Binxie do-si-doed and sashayed with cheerful farmers, happy young people, and nimble choir ladies. She had never laughed so much in her life.

Seth called, "Now the little ladies sashay left, leaving all the men feeling quite bereft," and Binxie swung from a grizzled farmer to the bony arm of a granny who smelled like lavender. Suddenly Johnny stood before her. He held her hands and they promenaded across the square together. Binxie felt his arms and muscled shoulders against hers, his breath against her ear. Too soon the delicious moment ended, and Binxie did feel bereft. Minutes later, the music changed and the dancers formed different squares. Alice grabbed her and they bowed to their new partners. The music sped up and people whirled in a kaleidoscope of arms, smiles, and colorful outfits. Binxie was having so much fun she ignored the rumbling from the northeast. No one else seemed to notice it either.

Seth continued. "Bow to your partner, bow to your corner, allemande left, and roll away."

The joy of music and friendship filled the room. The approaching storm, the crops ripening in the fields, and the war raging across the ocean—were, for one evening, forgotten.

Peggy

Peggy was having the time of her life. First the exhilaration of whacking that volleyball back and forth, then the happy bunch at dinner, and now the fiddle music. She skipped from partner to partner with such joyful exuberance it infected everyone around her. It would have been nice if there were more young men to dance with, but the boys were cute and the old farmers and their wives pleasant.

One really handsome fellow about her age—with broad shoulders and closely cropped dark hair that made him look heroic—had held her a bit closer, a second longer, each time they met in the square.

She noticed Stella eying him too. Stella had positioned herself across from him, and smiled extra sweetly whenever he skipped across the square with her. But on the next set, he deftly switched places with a choir lady so he could dance with Peggy one more turn. Stella glowered at her.

When it was time to break, Peggy was delighted when he crossed the floor with two glasses of cider. He introduced himself as Harry Rayner. "So how do you like working on a farm?"

She liked his deep voice too. He had to be at least eighteen. "It's tough, but good. You farmers work awfully hard."

He grinned proudly. "Sure do. Whose place have you been to?"

"Beldings', Grants', Scrantons', but mostly Highberry Farm. The strawberries ripen faster than we can pick them."

"Too hot, too early. Everything is coming up sooner than usual. Glad you girls are here to help." The way he said that as he gazed into Peggy's eyes seemed to indicate that he meant *her* more than anyone else.

Peggy smiled at him and the music resumed.

"It's cooler outside. Want to sit out the next dance?" he whispered.

Peggy pretended to think for ten seconds—she shouldn't look too eager—then nodded.

Harry offered his arm.

What a gentleman, she thought, as she hooked her arm in his and headed for the doors. *I wonder why he isn't taken?* She glanced at the dancers, and saw not only Stella's frown, but also Evie Belding's glare and the scowls of Evie's sister and friends, and she had her answer. She felt badly. Evie was a nice girl, but Harry was sooo good-looking.

As they reached the barnyard, she heard the low rumble

of thunder. A heavenly warning? Never one to heed signs of caution, Peggy let him hold her closer and continued walking.

A yellow sliver of moon hovered low on the horizon, still at the beginning of its journey across the sky. As they strolled arm in arm across the yard, Harry lightly steered her away from a group of farmers smoking and arguing about battle strategies on the Italian front.

Peggy was glad to walk farther into the field, to talk about the latest music, their favorite movies—anything other than war. She wanted to listen to Harry's deep voice, watch his dark eyes lock onto hers, maybe share some kisses.

In the dusky field, Harry stopped, faced her, and stepped closer. He slid his hand up Peggy's bare arm. She barely breathed. This was the most romantic experience she'd ever had. Somewhere in the back of her mind lurked her mother's warning: "Never walk in the woods with a man." But they hadn't quite reached the trees, and Harry was sweet.

Even this far away, bits of the barnyard battle conversation floated their way. "Our boys really showed them how we win a war. Imagine a bouncing bomb!" The men were talking about the Dambuster Raid in May, when an important dam in the Ruhr Valley was blown up. Peggy's family had talked about that mission too, Dad proud, Mum in tears. But right now she wanted to concentrate on Harry.

He stroked her cheek and gazed into her eyes. "I wish I'd been there," he declared. "Those pilots were amazing. I'd like to have blasted that dam too."

Peggy stepped away from him. *You sure blasted this romantic spell,* she thought, and told him, "The night that dam burst, the flood killed hundreds of innocent people downriver—mostly villagers and Polish mine workers."

He shrugged. "It was a strategic mission. It's too bad extra people died, but that's war. Next month I'll be fighting too. I can't wait."

At that moment, the moon drifted behind the clouds, so she couldn't see his expression, but she felt the sudden pressure of his hand around hers, heard the pride in his voice. "I've signed up. Passed my physical, got my uniform. I'll show you tomorrow."

Damn this war, Peggy thought.

"Yep." He nodded. "I'm gonna bomb me some Krauts."

Peggy dropped his hand. "Those bombs will kill women— and little children too. Doesn't that bother you?"

"They'll just grow up to be Nazis."

Something sour rose from Peggy's stomach to her throat. She brushed away his arm and wondered what he'd say if she told him some of those Krauts were her relatives—her aunts, uncles, and cousins in Hannover. Would he apologize for his remarks? Or would he turn on her? She knew the answer. She wouldn't tell him, and she dared not tell the girls at the farm. They'd hate her, or at least treat her with suspicion, like her neighbors in Greenvale had. "We'd better get back before they miss us." She turned toward the barn.

"Wait." Harry sounded confused, angry. "You can't run off on me like this."

Peggy didn't answer.

"What's the matter with you?" Harry grabbed her arm.

Peggy shook it off and kept walking, Harry close behind.

Helene

Helene stood by a post, tapping her foot to the music, drinking in the happy scene around her. She enjoyed watching the youngsters play tag between the dancers, hiding and seeking in the hay, and running for the sheer joy of it. They sped along the dessert table, snatched a cookie, slid a finger across the icing of a cake, and scurried off. Her brothers would have loved this. And it would have done her mother good to cut loose and dance.

Cut loose and dance? She wanted that too, but how? Where would she barge in and begin? The caller sang so fast she didn't know how anyone could keep up with him. She'd not only trip on her own feet, but stumble over everyone else's too. Peggy signaled her to come join them every time she whizzed by in the maze of dancers, but Helene felt safer on the sidelines.

A snow-haired choir lady swung past her in the arms of Mr. Scranton. Cleaned up and smiling, he didn't look so bad, and he was surprisingly light on his feet. So were his two taller sons. Girls seemed eager to partner with them and smiled blithely in their arms.

The third son stood, painfully thin, with darker brown hair combed neat, fine features, the only young person wearing a long-sleeved shirt on this hot evening. She watched him walk with a slight limp, balancing two cups of coffee and a plate of cake, to the older woman who had sat beside him at dinner. She sat still and regal, her gray hair swept back in an elegant roll, a well-cut dark dress. Every so often she summoned a farmerette to talk with. The rest of the time, the two perched on a bale of hay watching the dancers. At one point she seemed to be urging him to join them, but he shook his head.

Suddenly the woman turned to beckon Helene.

Helene hesitated. Then, not wanting to be rude, she walked over to the woman, who offered her hand. "Hello. I'm Mrs. Agnes Fraser."

Helene curtsied and shook Mrs. Fraser's hand. Although lined, her face had a classic beauty, high cheekbones, and intelligent tawny-colored eyes. She turned to the fellow at her side. "And this is Daniel Scranton, my efficient farmhand, accountant, and friend."

"People call me Dan." He smiled at Helene, but held his right arm protectively at his side so she nodded at him.

Mrs. Fraser continued. "And you are?"

"Helene Miller."

"From?"

Helene decided to answer as briefly as Mrs. Fraser fired her question. "Hamilton."

"In school?"

"Just completed grade twelve."

"Will you continue?"

"Grade thirteen for sure." Helene frowned. Her marks this year would decide whether she could go on after that. She had to get a scholarship.

"Are you clever?"

Helene blushed. "Yes. I am."

"So what will you do with those brains when you graduate?"

"I've always wanted to teach children."

"And what will you teach them?"

Helene paused. How could she turn this interrogation into a conversation? She looked Agnes Fraser in the eyes, and said,

"I'd like to share with them the wonder of books and words and ideas."

"Share something with me."

Helene hesitated, then recited her favorite poem.

"Two roads diverged in a yellow wood,
And sorry I could not travel both
And be one traveler, long I stood…"

Mrs. Fraser joined her for the next line.

"And looked down one as far as I could
To where it bent in the undergrowth…"

They regarded each other and smiled broadly. They had connected.

Dan completed the poem.

"I shall be telling this with a sigh
Somewhere ages and ages hence:
Two roads diverged in a wood and I—
I took the one less traveled by,
And that has made all the difference."

Helene hid her surprise. Who would have expected Mr. Scranton's son to know Robert Frost?

Mrs. Fraser continued. "How do you like farm life?"

Helene grinned from ear to ear. "I believe I was meant to be here."

"Why?"

Helene wondered how to put her feelings into words. Dan nodded encouragement. "Last question," he gently chided Mrs. Fraser, then turned to Helene, waiting for her answer.

"I love the endless green fields, the wide clear sky, the smell of earth and freshly cut hay, the scent of blossoms, fresh milk, the peepers singing in the pond, hearing the cows moo in the evenings." She stopped for breath. "And I like my dorm mates, the people here, this wonderful evening…"

"So why aren't you dancing?"

Helene opened her mouth, hoping an answer would come out. Suddenly someone smacked into her stomach, making her lose her balance. An arm whipped out to keep her from falling.

She looked up into the eyes of Dan Scranton. "Thank you."

"Willy Grant! You stop that tearing around," Mrs. Fraser scolded. "And come apologize to our guest."

A little fellow her brothers' age, straw stuck to his overalls, came shamefaced before her. "I'm sorry, Miss. I was trying to catch my friend."

His name stabbed Helene with homesickness. She nodded at Willy then crouched down to ask him what he was playing. They talked a minute, but sensing his restlessness, she told him to go have fun. She watched him race off again, turned to Agnes, and blurted, "Excuse me." She hurried from the barn.

She stood outside, sucking in deep breaths of air. What were her brothers and her mama doing now? Certainly not gorging on food and dancing. How could she love it here so much and worry about home so terribly too? For once she couldn't take comfort from the farm. No breeze stirred; everything felt heavy, still, waiting for something large. An arrow of lightning shot across the lake.

"No stars out tonight. They usually make a spectacular show," a deep voice behind her said. Dan.

"One more thing to love about the country."

Another streak of light was followed by a thunderous boom seconds later.

Dan surveyed the western horizon. "Dry May. Wet June. We need rain but a storm won't be good for the strawberries."

"They'll spoil?"

"Fast. And E.D. Smith and Sons, as well as the ladies in Hamilton, need all our berries for their jam."

Helene pictured mushy strawberries. "So much of your hard work can be ruined by one storm."

"Or lack of one. Or insects, disease, frost, or too much heat. That's the downside of farming."

"But not down enough to stop."

"Never. The war tried." He raised his right arm slightly. She noticed the red, scarred skin visible under the cuff of his sleeve. She glanced sideways at his profile—erect posture, a good face, kinder than his brothers. They and most of the boys here looked to be in their teens, but Dan seemed older. Fighting age. She wondered about his story.

On the other side of the barnyard a group of men in overalls stood smoking and loudly debating the war. "Why are they bothering with those little Italian islands? They should be blasting the Nazis out of France and Holland!"

"Barnyard generals," said Dan.

"Hey, Scranton! You were there. Come settle this," called an old farmer.

Dan waved him off and turned toward her.

"Aw, come tell us about it," called a young fellow Helene recognized. Hadn't he gone outside with Peggy earlier? Where was she now?

The group advanced toward them. Should she stay with Dan or leave the men to their talk of weapons and strategies? A fat raindrop made her decision. Several more splattered down, then sudden sheets of rain slashed at them. Helene, Dan, and the farmyard generals dashed into the barn. The men aimed for the food tables, pulling Dan along with them. Peggy's fellow strode up to a pretty farmerette in a pale blue dress.

Helene looked for Peggy. She must be dancing at the far side of the room. She certainly wouldn't stay out in that rain. She glanced at Dan, now surrounded by the group of men, picked up two strawberry tarts from the table, and joined Mrs. Fraser to watch the gaiety from the sidelines.

Jean

Jean skipped across the circle on her mother's arm, and watched Peggy leave the barn with Harry Rayner. That would surely annoy Evie and some of the other farm girls. They'd be happy in September when these city girls would leave their boys alone. Quickly she skipped left from her mum, and on to Johnny. He smiled and squeezed her fingers before she whirled over to Mr. Belding's calloused hand. Seth Rogers and the fiddles were at their best. Only the sound of Dan Scranton's fiddle was missing.

Had been since he'd gone to war three years ago and returned last winter with scars on his arm and deep inside.

Johnny allemanded back again and they two-stepped around the square. As she passed Alice Belding, Uncle Ian, then Gus, they smiled at her and she grinned back. These were her people and it was a relief to laugh and dance, without thinking about weather, weeds, and hungry livestock.

Then she spied Fran Murphy do-si-doing in the next square with Lou Puddicombe. Did she have to dance that close to him, giggle so happily? How could she flirt like that when Rob was imprisoned in a POW camp? Jean stared bullets at Fran until the smile left the girl's face.

When Johnny danced toward her again, they skipped to the right together. Suddenly she realized how much she too was enjoying herself, while her brother—whom she had sent away—paid the price. As soon as the set was over, she hurried outside, past the men loudly winning the war in the barnyard. She needed air and quiet. She turned the corner and stopped behind the barn. *Tears won't help Rob,* she scolded herself. She took a deep breath and another; the sounds of music and gaiety throbbed from the barn at her back.

Before her lay silent fields and shadowed trees barely visible under the starless sky. Was it this dark for Rob too? What time was it where he was? She prayed he was peacefully asleep, dreaming of freedom and home.

A small sigh nearby startled her. She walked along the side of the barn until she saw a dark shape huddled into the wall.

"Isabel?"

The shadow quickly stood taller. "Yes?"

Not sure what to say, Jean blurted, "Your strawberry tarts were a hit tonight."

"I couldn't have done them without your nanny."

Jean nodded. After the salty mashed potato and the nutmeg disasters, she had suggested Nanny take Isabel under her wing and teach her to bake. Nanny was delighted to pass on her skills and have company several afternoons a week. "Nanny tried to teach me too."

"You're lucky. Farm women are natural bakers."

Jean laughed. "The first time Reverend Ralston asked me to bring a pie to our Thanksgiving feast, I stayed up half the night. Baked five horrid pies to finally get one decent one. My mother did the same when she was young."

"So maybe someday I'll bake as well as Nanny?"

Jean nodded.

"And you won't tell anyone?"

"They don't need to know."

"Thank you."

Thunder boomed somewhere above them. "We should go inside," Jean said.

Isabel sighed. "I can't see our star—and it's the brightest one." She pointed south. "Sirius. It's usually there."

Jean looked at her. "Billy?"

"We named it our star just before he left. Promised each other we'd look at it every night." Her voice quivered. "I can't see it."

Jean reached tentatively to touch Isabel's shoulder. Isabel flung her arms around her. Jean awkwardly returned the embrace and made comforting sounds like ones she might make to an ailing calf.

Raucous laughter burst from around the corner.

Isabel jumped.

Jean scoffed. "The safe-side soldiers have won another battle." She watched the men standing in their smokers' circle, exhaling tales of daring and glory. She wondered if they ever spoke of pain and brutal death.

"You're out here alone for a reason," Isabel said gently. "Are you thinking of someone over there too?"

"My brother. He's a prisoner of war."

Isabel frowned sympathetically. "Our boys are so brave to face such terrible danger. I guess we need to find the courage to keep going until they come home."

Jean didn't add, *if they come home.*

Two dark shadows emerged from the field. First Peggy, then Harry Rayner. Without glancing at the girls, Harry abruptly turned left toward the men in the barnyard. Peggy joined the two girls. Jean noted she kept her face down.

Sounding as glum as Jean felt, Peggy muttered, "You can dance and sing at the top of your lungs, but you can't escape this damn war!"

Her vehemence surprised Jean. "Are you all right? Did Harry behave badly?"

"Oh. No. He was a gentleman." Under her breath, she added, "But an awful person just the same."

Jean let the comment go. Everyone had their own worries.

Somewhere across the lake, thunder rumbled and lightning flared. "It's on the way," Jean said. "Wish it would wait another week or three."

"It isn't all sunshine and plenty out here, is it?" said Peggy.

Jean shrugged. It had been easier when Rob was here and Dad was well. But there wasn't a thing she could do about it, except pray the rain would end quickly before too many berries were ruined.

Music and laughter erupted from the barn.

"Shall we join them?" said Peggy.

Lightning, then deafening thunder exploded overhead.

"This must be what the war feels like for Billy," Isabel said. "How can I dance when he's out there fighting for us?"

Peggy wrapped her arm around Isabel's slim shoulder, and regarded both girls. "We've all read their letters. They're taking some good times whenever they can too. Don't you think Billy's been to a few parties on his base in England? That Rob and the other prisoners have found ways to cheer each other up?"

Jean and Isabel looked doubtful, so Peggy pushed on. "I think they try to forget the war sometimes too, escape into fun. I'll bet they expect us to do the same. We can't help them by spending these years crying." Another bolt of lightning punctuated her speech. Closer this time.

"Let's go in before the next set begins," said Jean. "We don't want to miss another one."

Binxie

Binxie skipped across the square with Johnny's arm linked to hers, her hand wrapped in his. He smiled down at her. *Did my heart just flutter?* she wondered, then mentally kicked herself. *I'm not in a romance novel. But why does it feel so good?*

A final twirl and the music ended. The dancers stood clapping and puffing for breath. People divided into streams—toward the refreshment tables, and outside for relief. Binxie only half-planned to stand beside Johnny at the table of baked goods.

With a wide white-toothed smile, he passed her a plate of strawberry tarts.

Stop staring at him, she told herself. She took a tart and concentrated on eating it. What was wrong with her? She had been taught how to handle herself in any social situation, say all the appropriate words. Where were they when she needed them?

Johnny turned as if to leave. Binxie blurted, "You'd think I'd be tired of strawberries by now, but these taste so delicious."

He turned back and regarded her. "Do you have the strawberry crouch yet?"

"Is that a disease?"

He demonstrated an exaggerated strawberry-picking position.

Binxie grinned. "My knees may be permanently damaged."

"You did a great job helping Tessie the other day. Jean told me you were a natural."

"It had to be done."

Johnny smiled at her. "Not everyone could do it."

"The calf is so cute. I watched it run across the field today, and thought how lucky we were to save it."

"Farm life suits you."

Binxie realized it was true. "I feel useful here."

"We sure need you farmerettes…"

The rest of his words were drowned out by a barrage of thunder.

Binxie remembered what Jean had told her about his way with animals. "There's more to it than the crops we pick."

"Maintaining the machinery, the buildings, paperwork, planning, purchasing—Jean's dad, my mom, spend hours on that."

"I meant the livestock."

Johnny nodded. "That's the best part. Animals trust us and give back more than we give them."

Binxie thought of the roast chickens and ham they'd eaten earlier. "Some give us everything."

Johnny nodded. "You've square-danced before."

"At our cottage. It's more fun than ballroom dancing."

"You are a farmer at heart," Johnny said with a grin. A few weeks ago, Binxie would have felt insulted, but not now. She relaxed and asked about his work with the animals. She'd hit the right topic. They talked for several minutes.

"But think of Oslo. There's no cure for him," said Johnny.

Binxie laughed. "I've met him. A cure would be sweet."

Another tremendous boom of thunder stopped her. Suddenly Jean, Peggy, and Isabel ran inside the barn and headed their way. The fiddlers tuned their instruments again and everyone hurried to form their squares.

"Come join our set," Johnny invited her, but his eyes were already on Jean as he headed for the dance floor. Binxie sighed and found Isabel and Peggy at another square of dancers.

The music and joy soon took over her mood again, and she danced as happily as the others. Then one deafening crash, like an explosion, burst through the merriment. The music paused. Everyone stopped in mid-step and stared at the open barn doors. Outside, rain slashed down in sheets.

"That hit something mighty close," said Mr. Belding.

"Should we head home?" asked Shirley.

"No sense in that," Dr. Clifford told her. "Rain's pouring, lightning's cracking everywhere. It's smarter to stay put."

The music and the gaiety continued. In the light and warmth of the barn, people celebrated, while the storm outside battered their fields and homes, and soldiers stormed at each other in fields across the sea.

X

The rain had stopped and the night air felt cool, a welcome relief after days of heat. She sat quietly among the other girls, forcing the misery from her face as the wagons rolled home on muddy, puddle-pocked roads. Sitting on damp blankets and splattered by mud flying from the wheels, the girls were too full of music and excitement to be tired.

The only person looking almost as unhappy as she felt was Binxie, wistfully looking ahead at Dr. Clifford's car, where Jean sat in the backseat next to his son, Johnny.

"How did you two manage to walk outside with the cutest fellows?" Beside her, Kate teased Peggy and Helene.

Peggy shrugged. "I noticed you flirting with the boy in the plaid shirt."

"It was such a nice evening," sighed Isabel. "The best time I've had since last October."

She watched Isabel's pretty lips tremble, wishing she could put her arms around her, stroke her hair gently, comfort her. If only Isabel wanted her instead of longing for Billy.

She tried to force away these wicked thoughts. Coming to the country had not cured her; it had made it worse. She was hopelessly in love with this delicate angel. Isabel. Even her name was beautiful.

She'd fought this feeling so hard. Every night, she prayed for it to stop, but the day she carried Isabel from the field, she had to admit it to herself. The light body she held protectively in her arms, the lovely face, the blonde curls draped over her elbow as she carried her to the infirmary and gently deposited her on the bed—she loved this girl. She hated herself, but there was nothing she could do about it.

Tonight when they danced around the circles, their hands had connected for a moment. It had felt like an electric jolt— her whole being had soared to life, throbbing with love, never wanting to let go. Isabel had smiled at her—and skipped merrily on to the next partner, bestowing on him the same happy expression.

She had been aware of Isabel all evening—Isabel hitting the volleyball her way, so she'd purposely missed it; the joy on Isabel's face that she'd earned a point; Isabel laughing; Isabel standing alone and sad, missing someone overseas. She knew she could never comfort her.

Once again she made herself look away. Above her the stars shone extra bright and the silhouettes of the trees stood clear against the dark sky as if the rain had washed everything clean. Everything but her.

SUNDAY, JULY 4, 1943

Binxie

Sunday Binxie and most of the girls slept in. Six days of farm-work, last night's dance, and the drizzly morning kept all but the most devout churchgoers in bed. By afternoon, the weather turned hot and humid again and only a few puddles spotted the farmyard. The girls sprawled around the recreation room, listlessly playing cards, listening to music, mending clothes. No one had the energy to go outside.

As Binxie finished a letter to her sister, Peggy went to the piano and leafed through the sheets of music.

Binxie didn't feel like one of Peggy's jolly sing-alongs today. Time for a walk. She headed upstairs for her rubber boots. She came back down to the strains of a Chopin étude. It was beautiful, but she needed air and movement so she continued outside. The afternoon sun shone on the freshly washed countryside. She stopped by the fence to watch Tessie's calf in the meadow.

"We've named her Tinxie," said a voice behind her.

Binxie turned and smiled proudly at Jean, then at Isabel standing next to her. "Really? I didn't do that much."

"She might not have made it without your help."

"I'm honored. A cow named after me. Kathryn will love this…and so will my mother."

"We're heading to my brother's farm. Want to come along?" Jean offered. The two girls each carried a wicker basket covered with a red-checkered cloth.

Binxie was puzzled. Jean's brother was in Europe. She fell into step between them.

"The tree beside the house was hit by lightning last night, probably that loud crash we heard during the dance," Jean explained. "It knocked down half the chimney. My uncle and his neighbor are repairing the damage."

They walked along the road, avoiding the mud and puddles, listening to Isabel chatter about a sugarless cake recipe she had found.

A dozen shades of green surrounded them. Verdant grass and olive green maple leaves lined the road. A stone wall was covered with a patina of moss, and the corn in the field behind it grew knee-high and emerald. The orchards on the north were clad in a gentle haze of apple green.

There was damage too. Tree limbs small and large littered the ground. Young plants lay flattened in the fields. One farmer was already out repairing a fallen fence, and another hammered at boards on his barn.

Half a mile later, Jean turned right onto another road, and then right again, up a lane leading to a weathered brick farmhouse. It looked forlorn and in need of repairs. Its front porch roof sagged precariously in the middle. A board was nailed over a broken window. Chunks of once-white gingerbread trim work had broken off from the high gable long before this storm.

Suspended between the side of the house and a beech tree hung a large limb. It had smashed into the top half of the chimney and broken it off. The ragged line of gray chimney stones teetered dangerously above, and a pile of gray rubble, broken branches, and leaves lay scattered on the ground below.

"Who lives here?" Binxie asked, wondering why anyone would let a house that must have once been quite pretty fall into such ruin.

"My brother," Jean replied. She waved at a man on a ladder as he hammered boards over a hole in the roof.

Binxie was confused. "Your brother?"

"Six years ago, my parents needed extra acreage, so they bought this farm from Craz...um, Miss Nelly Turner. She sold it to them on the condition she could stay living in her home. Rob planned to fix the house after she passed away, marry Fran Murphy, and they'd raise their family here." She gave a bitter laugh. "Nelly died this February, but Rob was already gone. I ruined his plans."

Binxie sensed no question was welcome. She watched a rabbit hop across the yard into a tangle of wild rosebushes. Just as they reached the house a big man emerged from the front door.

"How's it going, Uncle Ian?" Jean called to him.

"Almost done. It'll hold until young Rob gets home."

"Thanks." She turned to the girls. "Isabel, Binxie, this is my uncle, Ian MacDougall. You'll meet him again when the peaches need thinning. The man on the ladder is his neighbor Lou."

They shook hands with Uncle Ian, and waved at Lou.

Jean turned to her uncle. "Mum sent pies and eggs for you both."

"Thanks kindly." Uncle Ian carried the baskets to his truck, then pulled out a tin of nails and returned to the porch. "By the way, we found something you might be interested in. I'll get it for you." He returned with a cookie tin decorated with brass-colored roses.

That should go to the metal drive, thought Binxie.

"Found this in the attic, stuffed into a hole beside the chimney." He offered the tin to Jean.

She looked puzzled. "Why would I want an old cookie box?"

"Look inside."

She took the tin and cautiously lifted the lid. Inside lay a folded piece of lace, yellowed with time. Whatever was wrapped inside it was held together with a frayed ribbon the color of old straw. Full of curiosity, the girls leaned over the tin.

"That could be lace from a wedding dress," said Isabel.

Jean perched the box on the porch railing. Binxie was afraid she wouldn't open the package, but after a pause, Jean pulled at the ribbon and peeled back the lace. Inside lay a packet of flimsy brown and gray letters, worn and faded with age, no envelopes. Jean picked up the top one and carefully unfolded it. She held it so the girls could read with her.

My Dearest Polly, the note began.

"It's a love letter," said Binxie. "Who's Polly? I thought you said Nelly lived here."

Jean shrugged. "I have no idea." She looked at Ian.

He shook his head. "I'll get back to work now." He left and the girls continued reading.

When they finished the first note, Jean leafed through the rest. "They're all addressed to Polly and signed by James. Mum might know who they belong to."

"Look." Binxie pointed to the top right corner of the letter. "February 1918. The Great War."

Jean flipped through more. "April 1918, August 1918, March 1919. They were written the last year of the war and after. There must be over twenty letters here."

"She kept them all this time, wrapped in lace. How romantic." Binxie was surprised at how much this touched her.

"Why were they hidden in a chimney in the attic?" asked Jean. "Wouldn't they be treasured in a drawer or someplace special?"

"Where they could be read every day," finished Isabel. "I keep Billy's mail in a silk pouch under my pillow."

"We save Rob's in a basket next to the family Bible in the parlor."

Uncle Ian came back outside, carrying his toolbox. "That should hold it until Rob returns. Now I'd best get home to supper." Lou climbed from the ladder, carried it to a rickety shed, and headed for the truck.

"Thanks for your help today," said Jean.

Ian nodded, and they drove off.

Binxie looked at the letters in Jean's hand. "Did he sign any with his last name?"

Jean shook her head. "None. And 'James' is even more common than 'Polly.'" She leafed through the letters again until she found an envelope. Unopened. The writing on it was feminine. *To Cpl. James Earnshaw.* She scrunched her forehead in thought. "Earnshaw? I've never heard that name. Maybe Nanny knows."

Jean held the unopened letter in one hand. The others hovered uncertainly above it. "It's not addressed to me."

"It was written twenty-four years ago. And it's the only way we might identify the owners," Binxie reasoned. She felt like she was in the middle of a Nancy Drew novel.

Jean carefully tore open the envelope. "My Dear James," she read aloud.

*As always, I pray you are safe and well. Before you read
on, please think of our love, for I have surprising news.
I hope you will consider it to be good news.*

    *We are going to have a baby. It will be born in late
October, close to your birthday. Maybe it will be a boy
who is just as handsome, funny, and brave as his papa.
Whatever it is, I already cherish it with all my heart,
just as I love you. Please come home safely, my darling.*

*Forever yours,
Polly.*

All three girls stood silent.

Binxie voiced their thoughts. "This letter was never sent. Does that mean he never knew?"

"How awful," said Isabel. "Maybe she wrote a second one."

Binxie doubted that, and more explanations flitted through her mind. Maybe James had been killed first. Perhaps the baby died—or the mother. "What was the date on that one?"

"April 1918. She must have been two or three months along by then," said Isabel.

Jean gently folded the note back into the envelope, placed all the letters back into their lace-and-tin cocoon, and tucked it under her arm. "These were important to someone. I'll take them home. Find out who we should return them to." She looked around. "Everything else looks all right here. Let's go."

On the way back, Binxie wanted to talk about those letters but Jean stayed quiet. Keeping country affairs private from the city girls? By the time they reached Highberry Farm, the supper bell was ringing, so Jean wished the girls good evening. Binxie shrugged at Isabel. They'd have to wait for the answers.

SATURDAY, JULY 10, 1943

Peggy

Peggy and nine farmerettes returned from lunch at the rectory with Reverend Ralston and his wife. She couldn't put off her laundry any longer. Her overalls were filthy and her sheets needed washing too. Someone had slipped chicken feet into several beds last night, including hers. Once she found out who, she'd smear peanut butter or something silly into their shoes. She stripped her bed and thought how much she liked her cozy little area.

Each girl had decorated her own cubby. Helene's orange crate bedside table was jammed with books, topped always with a jar of wildflowers. Photos of her family hung on her wall, while elegant framed Monet prints graced Binxie's. Isabel rearranged her fluffy pink paradise weekly. Farther along the walls hung movie posters, horse pictures, country sketches. There were embroidered pillow covers, rag rugs, all the personal touches the girls added to the place they called home for the summer.

After hanging her wet things on the line, Peggy headed for the recreation room, hoping to start a card game. Most of the girls were busy writing letters. She thought of the letters Binxie and the others found last Sunday. Now, a week later, Jean still hadn't mentioned them. Why not? Those notes wrapped lovingly in lace were the most romantic, mysterious things this side of a movie screen.

I have adored you since that morning I first saw you walking into Linton's Drug Store, and I will love you after the last star falls from the heavens.

Would anyone ever love her that much?

And the unsent letter. Had the couple ended in tragedy? Or were they enjoying a happily ever after? It was twenty-four years ago. They could still be living nearby. Who were they? What happened to the baby? It would be an adult now.

Peggy had wondered about this mystery as she worked all week. The Tragedy of Polly and James. She had even composed a love song for them. She had the music. All it needed was the story, an ending.

She was tired of waiting. "Okay, Helene, you don't need to write a novel. Finish up. I need to do something."

"You could try washing your shirts instead of borrowing mine."

"Already done." She grinned.

Helene rolled her eyes. A minute later, she put down her pen, slid two bills into the envelope, and sealed it. Peggy knew that left her with barely any money for the following week, but it made Helene feel right about her stay at the farm.

Peggy glanced at Helene's other letters. "You only wrote to three soldiers?"

Helene lowered her eyes. "My last letter to Theo was returned."

Peggy thought of the boy she'd had a crush on and felt sick. Suddenly the recreation room seemed too small. She called out, "Who wants to walk to town?"

"Thank you, no. I need to rest before I start dinner," said Isabel.

A few minutes later, Peggy, Helene, and a group of girls walked down the country lane toward town. It was hard to stay gloomy. The sun beamed brightly above, and its offspring, thousands of golden dandelions, dotted the fields around them. Along the roadside grew a rainbow of wildflowers—orange daylilies, yellow buttercups, blue chicory, dainty white Queen Anne's Lace. The lace reminded Peggy of the letters again, just as they were passing near the dilapidated farm where they had been found. Had Polly lived there? She sensed a tragedy, the pain of it swelling in her heart.

A plane roared overhead, and the girls looked up. "Another training mission," said Kate. "I wonder what happened to that cute pilot?"

"What was his accent? Australian? How exotic," said Helene.

"I liked his dashing moustache," said Irene.

Peggy gazed over the fields. "Is his base far away? How can we manage a visit? There must be more where he came from."

The girls laughed. On this sunny, free day, they laughed at everything.

When they reached town, the girls split up with the promise to meet by the bench in the town square in two hours.

The library was the converted stable behind a white frame house on the corner. Helene asked, "Anyone want to come with me?"

Lucy and Patsy nodded. Peggy thought she might find some information about the letters there, so she followed the three girls to the building at the corner.

Helene

Helene opened the door to the familiar smell of books. She loved this room, the shelves of stories, and felt close to home, to heaven. The massive library in Hamilton, with its tall curved staircases, marble floors, and high ceilings, was more splendid, but this humble space held the same Brontë and Austen novels, Agatha Christie mysteries, and the Whiteoaks sagas as the spectacular building at home.

Helene searched the two aisles, hoping to discover something she hadn't read yet. Lucy and Patsy quickly picked a mystery each—the modern new pocketbooks—signed them out, and with a wave at Helene, headed outside.

Helene took her time choosing three promising novels, and carried them to a corner with two faded chintz chairs facing a fireplace, not necessary on this hot day, except for its cozy appearance. One chair was occupied by someone engrossed in a newspaper. She sat in the other one, and opened a book. "*Last night I dreamt I went to Manderley again.*" From the first line, she was hooked.

Deep into page twenty-four of the story, she heard a faint "Hello." But Maxim de Winter had just invited the heroine to have lunch with him, so she kept reading.

At the end of the scene, she looked up. The man across from her lowered and folded his papers and she realized it was Dan Scranton. "Oh," she said. "Hello. I didn't realize it was you."

He smiled. In spite of the heat, he again wore a long-sleeved white shirt, and dark trousers.

"Good book?"

"Sometimes you know from the first line."

He nodded. "*Of Human Bondage* hooked me on page one."

"I haven't read that yet. How about that opening telegram: 'Better drowned than duffers if not duffers won't drown.'"

He smiled. "*Swallows and Amazons.* I loved those stories… always wished I had a special island too."

She regarded him thoughtfully. "And you know your poetry too."

"You mean, how come a farmer is versed in literature?"

Helene blushed. "No. I've never met any man who quotes poetry."

"Blame my mother. She loved it. Made up tunes to some and sang them to us."

"You're lucky," she said.

Dan answered, "My dad called it nonsense." He paused, then grinned at her. "But it gets you through some tough times."

Was he referring to the war? Or other times? She couldn't ask. She nodded and thought about how often she had escaped into books from her own life—nights when she was too worried to sleep, days when she hid from one of Papa's rampages.

Dan stood, picked up his two books from the table beside him, and returned his newspaper to the rack. "Do you feel like some ice cream? Linton's Drug Store has several new flavors."

Helene tried not to look as happy as she felt. "All right. As long as my friends can find me. They're in Jackman's General Store."

"You'd have to try really hard to lose someone in this town."

They signed out their books, waved good-bye to Peggy, and headed for the drug store. *This is my first date, sort of,* thought

Helene. *And with a handsome, clever older fellow. Farm life just keeps getting better and better.*

Peggy

Peggy entered the library behind Helene and watched her walk to the bookshelves as if she were heading for a banquet. She surveyed the room—four windows full of red geraniums, two aisles of bookshelves, a wooden table, the checkout desk, and a cozy corner with a fireplace and two stuffed chairs. Someone had worked hard to turn a stable into this pleasant place.

A man sat in one of the chairs, a newspaper opened in front of him. It reminded her of her dad, and she felt a pang of homesickness.

At least her dad wasn't away fighting. Mum had made sure of that. "Please don't go over there and kill my family," she'd begged.

"I want to defend my country. Our country. I'm Canadian. You're Canadian now," he'd protested.

"I am, and I want the Allies to win this war." Her mother looked teary-eyed. "But please, I can't stand the thought of my sisters and their families getting killed by you."

"My cousins in Coventry were bombed, lost their homes."

That news had upset Peggy terribly. She worried about them every time the news announced another attack on England.

"Thank God they lived," her mother had said. "But can't you find another way to help?"

And so their battle continued. Peggy hated it. She agreed with them both. Canada had to win this war. Her English cousins had to stay safe. But one person dead in her German family was already too much. Especially Michael.

Finally her father had volunteered for noncombatant duties. They weren't eager to send someone his age overseas anyway. Peace reigned in their home again, but tension remained. Before the war, Peggy hadn't known a happier couple than her parents.

She gazed at the bookshelves. Where could she start her research? Newspapers? No. She was looking for an event that happened nearly a quarter century ago. No one saved papers that long. It might be faster to ask the librarian, a woman with white curls framing a pleasant face, shelving books. Peggy was pleased to recognize Miss Willing, one of the choir ladies who had danced at the growers' party. She held a book, squinted at the numbers on its spine, and searched for its rightful spot, a job that seemed more tedious than picking berries.

"Excuse me, Miss," Peggy whispered.

"Hello, Peggy!" The librarian reached out her arm so enthusiastically Peggy thought she might skip-de-doo with her right here in the library. Instead, she shook hands and asked, "How can I help you?"

"Um. I want to find someone who lived here about twenty-five years ago. Polly. I don't know her last name."

Miss Willing held her finger to her cheek. "Let me see. Old Polly Baxter is long gone. Polly McBride was the smartest girl in my grade. Now she's quite batty and can't remember her own name."

Peggy shook her head. "She wouldn't be older than fifty."

Miss Willing brightened. "Polly Belding. Our hostess at the growers' party."

Peggy shrugged. That Polly didn't look tragic. She seemed happily married to Tom Belding.

The librarian paused. "Well, there was Polly Henson, who moved to Toronto to be with her daughter."

This was going nowhere. Peggy took a chance. "Is there a Polly Earnshaw?" She held her breath until Miss Willing shook her head. "No. Nothing even close to that."

"You're sure?"

Miss Willing regarded her, but refrained from asking the questions in her eyes. "I've lived here sixty-three years and never heard of an Earnshaw family in these parts. There was Polly Neal. She moved west twenty-some years ago."

The timeline fit. Peggy hid her eagerness. "Can you tell me more about her?"

Miss Willing scrunched her nose. "She was an angry young thing. Nobody missed her when she left."

Peggy was disappointed. The Polly she pictured from the letters was a sweet-natured girl, more like Mrs. Belding. "That's all?" she asked.

"I'm afraid so."

"And you haven't heard of a James Earnshaw?"

Miss Willing shook her head, and picked up another book to shelve.

"Well, thanks for your help," said Peggy. At least she had some Pollys to check out.

She glanced at Helene, now chatting and smiling with the man in the other chair. Peggy looked more closely. *Hmmm, I saw them together at the growers' party. Do I sense a romance in the air?*

They stood up and walked her way. Helene's eyes sparkled

as she introduced Peggy to Dan Scranton. "We're heading to Linton's for ice cream."

"Would you like to join us?" Dan gallantly offered.

Peggy knew enough to refuse and watched them leave. They were deep in conversation about some book. Of course. That would be Helene's type.

Peggy turned back to the shelves. There must be some local maps showing who owned which farm—perhaps some Earnshaws, or the previous owner of Nelly's farm. Otherwise, she'd have to wait for Jean to cooperate, and that might take forever.

SUNDAY, JULY 11, 1943

Binxie

Binxie felt restless. What would she do today?

Yesterday had been dull. She had politely refused Peggy's offer to join the expedition to town. How could they be excited about going to that little village? What could they possibly want in some dusty, outdated country stores?

Once the group of girls had disappeared down the road, chatting and laughing, she had taken her flight manuals, a blanket, and a thermos of lemonade to a shady corner of a field. Too many notes and diagrams later, she drifted off to sleep.

Last night, most of them had hitchhiked out to Romeo's again. The city girls were at their sparkling best there. The country girls glared at them, but were learning to compete, and the outnumbered fellows were in their glory.

Binxie ate breakfast quickly. Wanting to avoid the crowd

in the bathroom, she'd dressed for church earlier. Too impatient to stand waiting, she walked to the pasture where Tessie and her calf grazed. She felt a special bond with little Tinxie, and tore up a handful of grass to feed her. If only Jean were around. Walking, or riding the horses, was a habit they had developed on the evenings they weren't exhausted. They didn't talk much, just enjoyed each other's company and the stillness that dusk brings. Jean would sometimes quiz Binxie on life in Toronto, and Binxie found she enjoyed hearing about farming. She wondered about the letters, but Jean never mentioned them. Although happy to explain about milking, raising livestock, and the cycle of growing fruit and vegetables, she kept the privacy of the farm folk. Even though it irritated Binxie, she respected that.

Four horses headed her way, remembering the treats she always brought. She patted their soft muzzles and handed them pieces of apple. She looked at Cairo longingly. "I wish we could gallop together across these fields together."

As if summoned by Binxie's wish, Jean appeared, wearing her dark blue church dress and hat. She joined Binxie at the fence and they stood side by side, enjoying the day.

"Can you go riding after church?" asked Binxie.

"We're skipping services today, going to visit Nanny's sister in Mount Hope. Her eighty-fourth birthday."

"That sounds nice—a chance to get away."

"Cairo needs exercise. You can take her out later."

Binxie grinned at the beautiful brown mare. "Oh. Thank you!"

"Take the roads. No galloping through the fields. They'll either have a crop growing, or holes where horses could break a leg. If you lose your way, stop at any farmhouse. They'll point you back to Highberry."

Jean's mother, wearing a fine-print dress, followed Nanny and Jean's dad to the family car. She waved at Jean.

"I better go. Enjoy the ride." Binxie watched them drive away, wishing she could leave for the day too.

After church, the girls devoured a large lunch—deviled eggs and potato salad over-spiced with curry. Luckily they finished with yummy oatmeal cookies full of nuts and berries—Isabel at her best. They still had to put up with her overboiled vegetables and lumpy gravy, but Isabel had become an excellent baker.

After dessert, Binxie slipped away and saddled Cairo. They trotted along the road, enjoying the movement and the fresh breeze. At the sound of hoofbeats behind her, Binxie turned and her heart smiled. It was Johnny on a tall black horse. She brushed her fingers through her hair.

"Good day for a ride," Johnny greeted her. "Where are you headed?"

Maybe it was her restless energy, or the sun and wind on her face, but today Binxie felt she could say anything to him. "Exploring the countryside. Any recommendations?"

"Want to see my favorite spot?"

Binxie decided she'd follow him anywhere. "Lead the way."

They rode side by side along the gravel concession, then turned into a grove of trees. *All those riding lessons were worth it,* she thought, glancing sideways at her escort.

The woods were dappled and cool. Shrubs, ferns, and wildflowers crowded the trail, forcing them to ride single file, Johnny leading the way. A chipmunk skittered across the path and birds chirped overhead. It was so enchanting she half-expected some Walt Disney animals to perch on a branch and sing to them. Prince Charming was already here.

Abruptly the forest ended and before them stretched a magnificent vista—a green field sloping down to a blue lake, which rolled seamlessly into an azure sky.

Johnny stopped and watched her expectantly.

Binxie was too awed to speak. She smiled at him and they rode on until they reached the beach. There they unsaddled their horses, and led them to the cool water to drink. Then they tied them to two shady maple trees and walked along the shore.

"We usually swim in the inlet east of here, but this is more private because there's no road in."

"But the path to get here is so beautiful."

"Not if you're walking on a hot day." He took off his shoes and waded into the water.

Binxie did the same.

"Watch these rocks. They're slippery."

Even as he said this, Binxie's foot slid out from under her and she landed on her behind. Shocked, she sat in the cool water. Even more shocking, instead of helping her up, Johnny burst out laughing.

She dipped her arm into the lake and swooshed a wave of water at him. Then she laughed too.

Dripping, he finally reached a hand and helped her up. "I'm sorry. If you had seen your face, you wouldn't blame me."

"We're wet now. We may as well swim," Binxie shouted and plunged into the lake.

Johnny followed and the two swam far out. And farther. It became a contest—who would turn back first.

Finally, puffing hard, Binxie realized she would need enough energy to return, so reluctantly she angled toward shore. Johnny followed. As they waded from the water, he looked at her, blushed, and quickly turned to point to a sunlit patch of grass. "Let's dry out there."

She realized how her wet shirt clung to her breasts, and sat with her arms folded in front of her. Their silence was awkward until a formation of yellow planes flew overhead.

Johnny looked up. "I wonder how that pilot is doing, the one who crashed in your field."

"I suspect he talked his way out of trouble."

"And is already on to more escapades, maybe overseas."

"He probably needs to find excitement. There's a lot of drudgery and boredom in between the flights," she said, thinking of Kathryn's countless hours of training. Once last summer she and her friend Marion had taken Binxie out to the airfield in Goderich. They'd talked endlessly about throttle friction, tail wheel locks, and hydraulics, checked over every inch of the plane and its instruments before taking off.

"Jean said your sister flies?"

Jean. Binxie wondered how she would feel about this expedition. Did she care for Johnny or were they just buddies? It was hard to tell. "Yes," she answered. "For the ATA in England."

"England?"

"The Canadian forces won't let women fly."

"Picky bunch," Johnny said ruefully.

Binxie knew from Jean that he had tried to enlist at least

two more times. She looked right at him. "They're missing some good people."

He smiled hopefully. "If this war goes on, they may have to get less choosy."

Binxie shuddered. "I'd rather it ended now."

"We'll fight until we win. Stop that madman Hitler."

"I wish there was a better way to do it." Binxie decided to steer the conversation to him. "What are your plans? Veterinary college? I hear there's an excellent one in Guelph."

"Probably. I have some other ideas too."

Binxie tried to picture him crammed into a suit and tie in an office. She couldn't imagine him anywhere but on a farm.

As if he'd read her mind, he said, "My life is in the country, but I may try something new. Raise beef cattle or try breeding some new stocks. I've heard interesting things about French Limousins or cattle from South America. What about you?"

"Not sure yet. First and foremost, I want to fly like my sister. Come September, I'll sign up."

"You fly already?" He looked at her with such admiration she was tempted to fib.

"As a passenger. Kathryn used to take me up. The view from there is incredible. There's nothing like it."

He nodded, and they sat quietly for awhile, watching the silver-tipped waves sparkle in the sun. Nearby, wild red roses grew thick and lovely. They reminded her of the tin the letters were in.

"Have you ever heard of a James Earnshaw living around here?" It didn't hurt to ask.

"Jean already asked me. No, I don't know him."

Jean again. Just how close were they? And why was he sitting here with her?

Cairo whinnied restlessly. "I guess it's time to go," Binxie said reluctantly. "I promised to exercise the horse."

Johnny led the way back through the woods, Binxie wishing they had walked so they'd be closer together for a longer time. Too soon they reached the road. Then with a wave, they separated, Binxie wondering when she'd see him again.

X

She sat in the meadow, sketching the wildflowers and the cows, content in their grazing. How wonderful that must feel, instead of this turmoil, this guilt. She waved at Binxie riding by with that young fellow who sometimes visited Jean. Why couldn't she be like her? She had wept when she realized she loved Isabel. If this was a sin against God, why did He allow it? Was it punishment? But for what?

She pressed her colored pencil so hard it punctured the paper. It didn't matter. She had a dozen pasture scenes already. She had also drawn over forty pictures of Isabel and destroyed most of them. Much safer to sketch scenery.

Jean
Jean felt good speeding through the countryside at twenty-five miles per hour, windows open, her hair blowing in the breeze. Strawberry season was over, the raspberries were under control, and the cherries were coming along—early this year, but not yet screaming to be picked.

Her parents sat in the front seat of the blue Willys sedan.

She shared the back with Nanny, wearing her best dress and in a cheerful, talkative mood. Mount Hope was a long drive and a lot of precious gas away, so she didn't get to see her remaining sister often.

"That nice young Isabel helped me with Fiona's birthday cake. Her pink icing roses are beautiful."

"You spent a lot of time teaching her to bake. The farmer-ettes sure appreciate her now."

"She learned from the best baker in the county. I won every year at the fall fair—my peach pies were famous," Nanny bragged. "But why does she want to keep our baking lessons a secret? She sneaks into our kitchen before the first crow pees, or she arrives in the afternoon while the girls are away."

"City girls have strange ideas, Nanny, but I know she's grateful."

"Keeps me busy. Not many friends left to come calling anymore."

Jean listened and nodded as Nanny talked about old times. "You can't raise five children and run a farm without friends to help each other along. But I've outlived most of them."

Jean saw an opportunity. "Did you know a Polly?" She hoped Mum hadn't heard. Last week, she asked her mother the same question, but her mother had dismissed it all.

"Strange situations happen during war, Jean. People make rash decisions, then spend the rest of their lives trying to live with them. Don't dredge this up now."

"But I want to help."

"Help? You don't know whose carefully built-up life you may ruin. Leave it be."

It made Jean wonder if her mother was living with a mistake too. She hoped not. It also made her more determined to find the star-crossed lovers. If there was a child born of that love, it might want to know about its parents. Perhaps this was one mistake she could rectify.

"Every Polly is gone too," said Nanny.

"No, mother's age."

"Polly Belding you already know. Polly Henson—prettiest girl around here, stole your Mum's first beau." Nanny stopped to gaze out the window into her past.

Jean had read and reread the letters. The early notes were loving and passionate. Gradually they became more formal, but they never stopped begging for a reply. James described tender times together—picnics, long talks, moonlight strolls—it was obvious they had shared a great love. Polly had saved his letters in lace. She cared. Why did she never answer? Why did she not mail the news about the baby?

And what about the farmerettes? She knew by the searching way they looked at her that they wanted to solve the mystery with her. She couldn't—not yet, maybe never. She liked these girls, especially Binxie and Helene, but they didn't need to know her neighbors' business, pass judgment, turn it into an amusing story to tell the folks back home. First she had to find out more herself.

"Polly Neal," Nanny continued. "Her family helped us the winter our barn burned down, but she was a miserable thing. I much preferred Polly Belding—Campbell then."

Which Polly is it? wondered Jean. *I hope not the miserable one, but I can't imagine Mrs. Belding with anyone but her Tom.*

Maybe the girl who stole boyfriends? Is that how she operated? Make a boy fall in love with her, then don't answer his letters?

"We're here," said Mum as they pulled up to a red brick house large enough to comfortably fit her aunt Morag, uncle Douglas, their daughter, Mary, and her two youngsters while Mary's husband served overseas, and great-aunt Fiona. "You can stop quizzing Nanny now."

Jean grinned at her mother and shrugged.

"I hope you won't regret it," her mother said. She turned to wave at Aunt Fiona standing at the front screen door.

The family walked up the stone path and stepped onto the veranda. Nanny happily greeted her sister, adding, "Sorry we're late. Have you waited long?"

"I'm not waiting for you," Fiona replied. "I'm expecting those good-looking young fellows."

Jean was confused. "We didn't bring any good-looking men. Just Dad."

"Not him. I mean, handsome, dashing airmen."

"Sure, Aunt Fiona. We'll bring a batch next time we visit."

"Don't get cheeky with me, young lady. I'm not off my rocker yet."

Mrs. McDonnell stepped forward. "Happy birthday, Aunt Fiona."

Aunt Morag appeared at the screen door. "Welcome, welcome. I have a cold lunch ready," she said, opening the door.

Lunch passed pleasantly, then Jean's father and uncle left to locate some tractor parts. They were in scarce supply, since the factories were building only war machinery. As the women chatted in the parlor, Fiona glanced anxiously out the window several times.

"Who is she waiting for? Reg?" Jean asked her cousin Mary.

Mary shook her head. "No, she knows he's in Italy. Whenever the children ask about their daddy, she points out Europe on the globe."

So she's not completely batty, thought Jean. She looked at her cousin, noticed how pale and tired she looked. "Have you heard from Reg lately?"

Mary frowned. "Operation Husky. They've invaded Sicily. Three thousand ships. He's with one of the eight divisions of men fighting there—the largest undertaking so far. This may be the beginning of the end, and it will get intense. I try not to let the children see me worry, but I lie awake at night imagining the worst. What would I ever do without him?"

Jean patted her cousin's arm. "We're praying for him."

"And Rob?"

"He gets around on crutches now, says he's fine. They actually have a camp orchestra—he plays the fiddle in it. And he works in their hospital. But we get different stories. Some people mention the choir, theater groups, sports days, how good the hospital is, then others describe the prisoners' work in the coal or salt mines and quarries, getting little to eat but sugar beets. What do I believe?"

Deafening screeches interrupted them. Young Archie was yanking his sister's hair, and Annie had dug her nails into his arm. Archie pointed at a mess of Lincoln Logs on the floor. "She wrecked my tank!" he yelled.

"He wouldn't give me any logs to build my house," she sobbed, and hit him.

As Mary wearily rose to referee, Jean stopped her. "Let me." She called to the children, "Who wants to look for frogs?"

It was fun playing with the youngsters along the nearby creek. When they were tired enough, she brought them home for a nap. At last she had some time alone—a blessed hour to sit on the front porch swing, sip ice tea, and read. She was annoyed when a cheery British-sounding voice interrupted her, twenty pages before the end of her book.

"Well, g'day. What luck meeting you here."

She looked up and was startled to see two men in blue air force uniforms climbing the porch steps. She was surprised to recognize the pilot who landed in their field so recklessly.

"What are you doing here?" she blurted.

"I hoped you'd be as glad to see me as I am you." His effort to seem sad made her smile.

Realizing she had sounded rude, she said, "I didn't expect you." She eyed the sling supporting the cast on his left arm. "How are you?"

He laughed. "That's better. Bruises and cuts long gone. My arm is healing, though much too slowly. Missed my transfer to England with my mates. Stuck here with this bloke." He turned to the man beside him, a tall blond fellow, so wide-eyed and gangly he reminded Jean of a calf. "Dick, this is the fair sheila who came to my rescue at my unfinest hour. I missed her name but I'll never forget that beautiful face."

She shook Dick's hand. "Hello, I'm Jean McDonnell."

With a devilish grin, the pilot grabbed her hand next. "Hugh Redmond, at your service."

She let go as quickly as was polite. He still had those brilliant blue eyes, skillfully combed dark hair, and natty moustache. Too slick.

"You're wondering why we're here?"

Actually, she wondered when she could get back to her book.

The screen door burst open and Fiona appeared, all smiles. "You're here!"

Now Jean realized—Fiona had been waiting for these two. Hugh's charms worked on every age group.

"I wouldn't miss your birthday for anything," said Hugh, pecking the old lady on the cheek. "But how can you be eighty-four when you don't look a day over sixty?" With a bow and a flourish, he handed her a small box. "For you."

Blushing like a teenager, Fiona opened the present. "Whitman's chocolates! Oh my! How did you know? My favorites!" She stood on her toes and kissed him loudly. "Now come in, boys. Dinner's about ready."

The airmen entered the house and Annie and Archie, awake from their naps, rushed to the door, and each latched on to one of Hugh's legs. He laughed, scooped up Archie in one arm, swung him around, and passed him on to Dick. Then he picked up the squint-eyed, gap-toothed little girl. "How's my beautiful princess today?" he asked.

Annie giggled. "I'm gonna marry you next year."

Hugh's smile turned serious. "I certainly hope so. I'm waiting for you."

He was obviously experienced at this, but Jean loved the light shining in the child's eyes.

The dinner table was crowded, but there was plenty of chicken stew, conversation, and laughter for all. *He must be exhausted,* Jean thought as she watched Hugh flirt with Fiona and each woman at the table. But the animated old women giggled like schoolgirls, and even Mary looked heartened. Having managed to sit next to Jean, Hugh directed conversation her way several times, and caught her eye when he could. She couldn't help but smile back.

Today was Fiona's day to celebrate. They carefully avoided talk of war. Jean's father proposed a toast and everyone sang "Happy Birthday" when Morag brought out the birthday cake and homemade ice cream.

As they drove home later that evening, Jean thought about the day. She knew Aunt Morag sometimes invited servicemen from the Mount Hope training base for a good home-cooked dinner. Up to now she'd always considered it an act of kindness, her contribution to the war effort. But the ladies had smiled all evening, Aunt Morag had beamed at the compliments to her cooking, and the children joyfully played ball and wrestled with the pilots, for one afternoon not missing their daddy so much. Even taciturn Uncle Douglas and her father had conversed with the pilots about planes, then tractors.

Hugh with his blatant charm and Dick with his awkward sincerity had called themselves lucky as they thanked Aunt Morag for the hospitality, but Jean could see the family had enjoyed themselves even more than they had—a pleasant break from the usual routine.

She had refused Hugh's offer to stroll along the creek after dinner. She'd heard about his type—a wolf in alluring sheep's clothing.

Jean knew she had to stop thinking about him. The moon drifted high in an inky sky as they drove past the turnoff to

Crazy Nelly's farm. Jean couldn't see the house, but she realized what she had to do. Go back to the source. Check Nelly's place. Why were the letters in her house? She hadn't always lived there alone; had she even known they were there? How was she connected to Polly, or did the letters belong to someone else?

As long as Jean could remember, it had been Crazy Nelly's farm—a woman who kept a light glowing in the front parlor window every night, who stared intensely at young children until their parents pulled them away, who sat in the back pew at every wedding, a picture of doom in a dark dress and veil. She chased away everyone who entered her property, wasn't very pleasant to Jean's mother or to church people checking if she needed help. Rumors said she kept a packed suitcase by the front door. Was she waiting for James? Jean could not imagine the bitter old woman as the girl in those love letters. And as for a baby, there was no way to hide a pregnancy in this close-knit rural community.

Tomorrow she would search Nelly's house. After all, it belonged to her family now. But the raspberries were ripening, the sour cherries would soon need picking, and the weeds had overtaken the kitchen gardens. The cycle of farmwork had been interrupted for one brief lovely day. Tomorrow it would roll on, getting ever more intense until the autumn harvest and celebration. There would be days of canning and preserving before they could rest up to begin again next spring. It was a good way to live. So why did she feel restless?

WEDNESDAY, JULY 14, 1943

Binxie

Binxie marched down the road, sore in every way. Her shoulders ached, and her face stung where a branch had smacked her right on the sunburn she got yesterday hoeing tomato plants at the Grants' farm. But she was mainly sore—no, furious—at her treatment in the Scrantons' orchard. How dare he and his boorish sons order her around like that!

The last straw was when that little snip Matthew rudely refused to let her stop to use the outhouse. "You have no right to order me or anyone else around. And your vulgar profanity doesn't impress me," she'd said in a low, cold tone that carried across several rows of trees. "If you don't know the proper words, ask your grade-school teacher to teach you some in September."

Which was why she was walking the three miles back to Highberry Farm at two o'clock. Before he could fire her, she told him to stuff his cherries into his hat and stormed off. The stunned shock on Matthew's face satisfied her immensely.

She cut across a field and through a peach orchard, branches beginning to hang heavy with green fruit growing larger every day. The long walk through the peaceful countryside calmed her down before she reached the field where Jean hoed vegetables.

"Are you all right?" Jean looked up from her work.

Binxie shrugged. "I am now."

Jean leaned on her hoe. "Scranton at his best?"

Binxie nodded.

"Want to tell me?"

Binxie shook her head. "I'm still too annoyed." Then she

grinned. "I'm sure you'll hear about it from everyone else, though. And I'm glad I said it."

"There's lemonade in the thermos under the elm tree."

Binxie took a drink and marched to the shed, grabbed another hoe, and joined Jean in the field. "I need to get rid of some angry energy. Pretend these cabbages are Matthew's head."

"Just don't chop them off yet."

Binxie hacked the ground, weeds flying, clods of earth crushed small under her weapon. Gradually she slowed down to an efficient, steady pace and the two girls worked in companionable silence.

At four o'clock, Jean suggested a break. They sat under the elm tree, sharing lemonade and a muffin.

Binxie noticed Jean watching her. "Did I commit a terrible sin leaving the Scrantons'?"

Jean chuckled. "No. Someone had to stand up to their bullying."

"It was Matthew."

"He's worse because he's our age."

"How did Mrs. Scranton take it? Or is she the same?"

"No choice. Before Mary passed away four years back, she was cheerful and funny when he wasn't around, but meek when he was. I think her books, her rose garden, and her boys were the main joys in her life."

"*Those* boys?"

"They were always loud and wild, but sweet with her, especially Dan. Actually, Mr. Scranton wasn't as crabby either. After she died, they all fell apart. Fought with each other a lot, let her roses wither. Dan started going to Agnes Fraser's, but the others just got…" Jean stopped. She blushed and busied herself with the thermos.

Without looking at Jean, Binxie said, "Every place has strange people. My neighbor yells if we step on her lawn, and one of my uncles collects raccoon tails. We keep a few secrets about my great-grandmother too."

Jean eyed Binxie a moment. "You respect people's privacy."

Binxie nodded. "I expect them to respect mine too."

"But you're curious about the letters."

"Of course."

"No one else needs to know yet."

"You should be the one to tell them, Jean. When you're ready."

"Where's the logical place to start?"

"Peggy went to the library, didn't get more than a list of Pollys and some maps."

"I'd go to the source. Nelly's house."

"Me too." Binxie waited, hoping.

"You just saved me hours of work…we could go there now."

"Let's go." Binxie grabbed both hoes and propped them in the shed. Minutes later, they crossed the fields to Nelly's neglected house.

"Someone's been here," Jean said as they stepped onto the veranda. It stretched across the front of the house and wrapped around the corner to the kitchen door. Near the railing stood a chipped wicker chair—cobwebs, dried insects, and dust its only occupants.

"Your uncle, and all of us were here," said Binxie.

"No. Look at this window. It's wiped clean. Dusty footprints in and out the door, some furniture moved." Jean frowned. "I hope nothing's damaged."

"Isn't the house locked?"

Jean raised an eyebrow. "No one in the country locks their doors."

"What would they be looking for?"

Jean shrugged. "There are lots of rumors about Crazy Nelly. One is that she stashed a fortune here somewhere."

"That story floats around every dotty old person. They said that about my great-grandmother too. Turned out, her treasure was a box full of hair—one lock from each of her children and grandchildren."

Jean opened the front door and they stepped into a narrow hall. The house smelled like moldy wood and loneliness.

"Well, one of the rumors is true," said Jean, pointing to a cracked brown leather suitcase in a corner.

Binxie looked puzzled.

"They say she kept a packed bag by the door, waiting for her true love to come for her."

"James?"

"He wrote to Polly."

"Maybe he couldn't spell."

Jean rolled her eyes at Binxie, then leaned over to open the suitcase. The rusty clasp was impossible to open, so she got a knife from the kitchen and pried it open.

Both girls gazed at the contents. Two silk dresses, a night-gown, expensive underclothing now yellow with age, toiletries long dried up.

"A honeymoon bag," said Binxie sadly. "She waited forever."

"I hope she's with him now," said Jean.

The girls examined the parlor. Dark furniture, some covered with sheets, crammed the room.

"What are we looking for?"

"Some trace of James and Polly."

"Her sister?"

"No sister. Three brothers who doted on her."

"So James was her brother."

"You think he took his letters back from Polly somehow, even though she never answered him, and then didn't even open her letter addressed to him? Plus her brother's name was Turner, not Earnshaw."

"Sorry, I wasn't thinking. We still don't know why they were hidden in the wall. Someone in the family didn't approve?"

"She lived alone since I was twelve. Plenty of time to bring them out of hiding."

Binxie pointed to a thick black book on the shelf. "May I?"

Jean nodded and stepped closer as Binxie lay the Turner family Bible on a spindle-legged table. She flipped to the family tree and the girls skimmed through three pages of names, beginning with the marriage of Henry Turner and Elizabeth Reiman, in Pennsylvania in 1768, eight years before they fled to Canada. The last name entered was Eleanor Anne Turner.

"I guess that's why she visited Philadelphia sometimes. Apparently she had a cousin there," said Jean.

"No mention of a baby," said Binxie.

"At least not recorded," said Jean. She skimmed some pages, then shook the book upside down. Nothing fell out. She returned it to its place and scanned the other books on the shelf. Finally she said, "We don't have time to search every volume."

They passed through the dining room into the kitchen. Binxie noted the old-fashioned icebox and the pump at the sink instead of taps. They peered into cupboards, but quickly decided they were more likely to find private things upstairs.

A wide upper hall opened up to four bedrooms. Three were obviously long unused—the furniture was layered with dust. The girls opened all the armoire doors and drawers—empty.

The last room, the largest, had to be Nelly's. A heavily curtained bay window overlooked the front lawn, and the bed was covered with a faded floral quilt. Piles of books were stacked on the nightstand and an overstuffed chair.

"Mum told me they found fourteen library books after she died. All overdue."

"She died in here?" Binxie felt cold.

"Mum found her outside by the chicken coop. She came by every week to check on her, sometimes leave a pie or casserole. Nelly always finished the food, but never asked her in."

Binxie examined the night table. "Finding a diary would be handy about now."

Jean laughed. "Only in books. We'll have to work harder than that."

"Corporal James Earnshaw. Does that mean he was in the air force or army?"

"The Great War. There was no Canadian air force yet," said Jean.

"Oh, right. It began in 1918. I wonder how that crazy pilot is doing."

"Very well."

"What?" Binxie looked surprised. She opened a drawer full of underclothes but felt too uncomfortable to search it.

"He was at my aunt's for dinner on Sunday, the life of the party. A cast on his arm, so unable to ship out to England with his crew."

Binxie frowned. "The arm will heal. He'll go by summer's end."

Jean checked under the bed. "Nothing so far."

Binxie stared at the underwear drawer and sighed. The other rooms were almost bare. Any clue had to be here in Nelly's own bedroom. Gingerly she pushed some cotton and lace things aside. Nothing.

"Here's something," called Jean, her voice pitched high with excitement. She held up a slim leather-bound book. "It was under her pillow. A poetry book. Oh my gosh, look."

Binxie crossed the room and checked the page Jean pointed to. There, in the same handwriting she had seen in the letters, was the inscription: *To Polly, October 1917. I love thee with the breath and smiles of all my life. James.*

The two girls stood in awed silence.

Binxie sighed. "Nelly treasured this all these years. Could Nelly and Polly both be short forms for Eleanor?"

Jean shrugged. She flipped through some of the pages, then exclaimed, "They were married?"

Again, Binxie looked at the book. Written in a neat flowery hand was a list—*Mrs. James Earnshaw, Eleanor Anne Earnshaw, Nelly Earnshaw, Mr. and Mrs. James Earnshaw.*

"That's impossible," said Jean. "No one ever called her anything but Miss Turner or Crazy Nelly. I would have heard about a husband." She shook her head. "It doesn't make sense."

Binxie smiled. "She was daydreaming. The girls at school do it every time they meet a terrific fellow." She had never bothered to write out names before, but then she realized with a start that she had already mentally tried the sound of Binxie Clifford.

"But they must have loved each other. His inscription, and she kept the book under her pillow. It's a clue," said Jean.

"We should take it with us."

Jean hesitated, then nodded. "It's Rob's house now, so we can borrow it."

"Everything in this house belongs to him?"

"Yes. Nelly's will specified her jewels to her cousin in Philadelphia, the livestock to my mother, and all her money to 'Baby James, who should have been mine.' But no one ever found either money or that baby."

Both girls looked at each other, their eyes wide. "Polly's baby?" they blurted at the same time.

"We have to find that child," Jean said.

Binxie nodded. "If there is one."

"Maybe it's in Philadelphia?"

Binxie shrugged. "With her cousin. It doesn't make sense."

The girls headed back downstairs.

"No basement?" asked Binxie.

"A crawl space. You don't want to go there."

"And this little room off the kitchen?"

"For the hired girls."

"Let's look."

The room contained one boxy wooden dresser, a small cot, plain cotton curtains aged to a dingy gray color. There were no pictures like in the other rooms, nothing personal or pretty.

"The maids usually stayed a year or two, then got married or found a better position, and moved on," said Jean as she quickly checked the dresser.

"It's after five o'clock. The others will be home for supper soon," said Binxie.

Clutching the poetry book, Jean followed her outside. "Looks like Nelly and James were our star-crossed lovers, but something awful must have happened. No wonder she became Crazy Nelly."

"The name still bothers me," said Binxie. "Maybe it was his pet name for her."

Jean shrugged. "Love is strange. But the baby. Maybe she didn't send that letter because James was killed."

"No. He wrote letters after her unsent one. Perhaps the baby died."

Jean shook her head. "Nelly's will mentioned 'Baby James, who should have been mine.' Could she actually have had one that they made her give up for adoption?"

"Gave him to someone in Philadelphia? Or sent him to an orphanage?" said Binxie. "Maybe the poor mite's had a terrible life without parents. We have to find him."

"And they say I read too many novels," said Jean.

As they reached Highberry, a wagon full of farmerettes rolled up beside them. Binxie said good-bye to Jean and watched her cross the yard toward her house. Then they each stopped and stared. Two men stood knocking at Jean's front door. Even from this distance, Binxie could see the uniforms. Were the McDonnells getting bad news?

Helene

"Reach higher! You won't fall."

Helene felt like a mouse waiting for the hawk to swoop down and grab her in its talons. Except she was high up in a cherry tree and the "hawk" stood below. The raptor in this case was Mr. Scranton, hard eyes glinting up at her.

"Stretch higher, farther" was his refrain to all the girls. "You're missing the good cherries."

Sure, thought Helene. *Better we risk falling than waste precious time getting off the ladder to move it to a safer position.*

Earlier he had stood glaring at them to make sure they picked the fruit properly. Twist, pull, then place, don't drop, the cherries into the baskets hanging from straps around their necks. Now, almost satisfied, he wanted them to speed up.

Even worse than Mr. Scranton's gruff orders and rude vocabulary, were his sons. Matthew and Luke, strong, blond, and sturdy, might look better than their dad, but they were just as nasty. When she showed her filled basket to Matthew, he wouldn't punch her card because the cherries were piled too high. "We'll never make a profit this way. Take some out," he barked. Luke liked to grab the baskets roughly from her hand.

It should have been lovely out here, dappled sunlight between green foliage, a soft breeze cooling her face. But she was scratched from branches smacking her in the face, scraping along her arms. The baskets now weighed heavy on her neck, and she had a splinter in her hand thanks to hurrying up the wooden ladders. Ever since the sour cherries had started ripening, the girls drew straws each evening and the losers worked at the Scrantons'.

Helene was glad no one could stop Peggy from chatting for long. She was busy planning their talent show, only three days away. Peggy had spent the last two weeks finding out who could play the piano, sing, or dance. Amid much laughter, she'd trained four girls to play a pennywhistle. Nancy and Ruth begged to sing a duet. Helene was impressed how beautifully Grace dramatized Shakespeare's sonnets. All the girls looked forward to the show with great excitement.

As her talent, Isabel promised a sweet treat afterward. Ever since Isabel had started in the kitchen, Helene had noticed a change in the camp meals. Isabel had a way of adding garden chives, or sprigs of parsley or rosemary, a drop of maple syrup, lemon juice, or spices to foods to improve them. She put fresh flowers on the tables, folded napkins in different ways. But it was in baking that she shone. A steady, delicious stream of cakes, cookies, tarts, and squares flowed from the kitchen.

"Hey," Peggy called from the next tree. "Should I put my hair up, borrow Kate's long dress, buy dangly earrings from Jackman's, and play an elegant Dvořák piece, or is something light better? Maybe 'Over the Rainbow'? I could sing along with the piano."

Helene smiled at her friend. "What are the others doing? You want variety in the program."

"We're not paying you to plan your social lives. You skipped a branch," Matthew shouted at them.

Helene reached for the cherries she'd missed.

Across from her, Peggy picked a green cherry. With a devilish grin at Helene, she held it between two fingers, aimed, and shot. It bounced neatly off the back of Matthew's head.

He turned, furious, but Peggy had already faced the other way, innocently rolling fruit into her basket.

But if Scranton was bad and his two sons worse, their older brother, Dan, was worst of all. Helene couldn't understand it. What had happened since they last met? He had been so attentive at the growers' party, and genuinely happy to be with her at the library. They had talked for an hour after their ice creams. He had seemed disappointed when the other girls came to say it was time to leave. His good-bye was reluctant, with a promise to see her soon—or had she just imagined that?

She had felt a tingle of joy to see him driving the farm truck into the orchard to unload the baskets, dressed again in a long-sleeved shirt in spite of the heat. She waved, but he didn't see her. He worked, favoring his right arm, never looking her way. It was Matthew or Luke who came down her row collecting baskets. Never Dan.

Watching Binxie storm from the orchard, Helene wished she had the courage to leave with her. Was she being too sensitive? Maybe Dan liked to keep work separate from his personal life. But what did a simple wave or a smile hurt?

Peggy noticed too, gazing from Dan to Helene with a frown on her face and questions in her eyes.

Helene shrugged. This hurt. But then, she was used to it—the men in her life had always let her down.

SATURDAY, JULY 17, 1943

Jean

Jean pulled extra hard at a weed that dared to hide in the tangle of squash vines. She was confused, tired, frustrated. She was glad when the girls left to work on other farms this morning, chattering like starlings over a juicy beetle.

"May I borrow your pink dress?"

"What if I forget the words?"

"What looks best with my white blouse—a necklace or Nancy's striped scarf?"

"How do you like the Tangee lipstick I bought last weekend?"

As though orange lips could make you sing better, thought Jean. Tonight's talent show had been their main focus all week—practising every spare minute, worrying if they had chosen the right song, begging Smokey to tune the piano. They had started loud on Monday, and built steadily up to this frenzy today.

And they still gushed about the fun last night. Oh, why had she gone too?

Because Hugh had invited her.

Last Wednesday evening, Hugh and Dick had stood at her door with eager smiles and an invitation. A dance party at their base in Mount Hope that Friday. "We want all the girls to come," he'd said, but he'd looked directly at her with his piercing blue eyes, "especially you."

"I bet you've said that to a dozen girls already," she replied, but his expression told her he hadn't.

Recognizing the handsome pilot, the farmerettes had

mobbed them then, and she had no chance to refuse the invitation—not that she wanted to.

Smokey allowed the girls to leave early on Friday, on the condition they work later Saturday. Only the girls seventeen or over were allowed to attend, and Smokey insisted on coming with them to make sure the base chaperones did their job in keeping her charges' virtue and reputations intact.

The young men at the base had gone all out for their guests. The mess hall was polished and decorated with pink streamers. They put together a great band, played all the modern hits, and served a delicious supper of sandwiches and sweets. And the charm. Jean told Binxie, "I'm convinced every fellow who trains with the air force takes smooth-talking lessons along with their flight instruction."

"I hope it works better on the Germans than it does on us," laughed Binxie.

But when Jean had said as much to Hugh a few minutes later, he replied seriously. "They're just happy to spend time with some pretty girls. They miss their home and friends."

That left Jean without a smart answer.

"And besides, some of you girls are right skilled at this yourself." Hugh nodded toward Peggy, who was having the time of her life flirting with a steady stream of dance partners.

Isabel too was surrounded by a flock of fellows. It had taken the girls awhile to convince her to come, telling her Billy was probably dancing somewhere too, and he'd want her to have some fun. There was something about her blonde curls and sweet sad expression that drew the men to her like bees to an especially fragrant flower. Isabel was polite to them all, but she danced with them at a proper distance, her whole body saying: *I'm not available*. If only Rob's fiancée, Fran, were that loyal to him.

Jean turned to Hugh. "Where's home? Your accent sounds almost British."

"Nay, girl. I'm an Aussie, from God's country."

"Oh, Australia! Kangaroos, eucalyptus trees, Ayers Rock, and deserts."

Hugh smiled. "You know something about us! We also have majestic mountains, a beaut of a seashore, and miles and miles of good ranch land."

Jean looked at him more closely. "You're homesick!"

Hugh blushed. "It's easier now that I'm stationed here, away from the city. Once you live on the land, every place else feels too crowded."

Jean nodded. "I never pegged you as a farm boy."

"Too debonair, eh? We learn it as we shear the sheep."

"Tell me about it."

And Hugh, the charming rake, described life on his ranch in the outback of New South Wales. "We may as well dance as we talk," he said, offering his hand, and Jean stepped into his arms naturally.

Now, no matter how hard she hacked the earth, she was unable to stop thinking about Hugh, how well they danced together. What about her feelings for Johnny? Hugh's handsome face and smooth words were different from Johnny's solid good looks and direct manner. Perhaps Hugh was too suave, but he would not stay out of her mind. And if he moved over just an inch in her thoughts, there was the mystery of James and Polly and the child they may have had. Binxie had checked the cemetery yesterday. No Earnshaws rested there. Small baby headstones, yes, but all were claimed by grieving parents, named neither Polly nor James.

And like an underwater current running through it all was the constant worry about Rob. His last note was so short, so cheery, she feared something was wrong. Last week, she had seen Fran at Linton's giggling over sodas with a group of friends. Sitting far too close to Alan Goode, she waved at Jean to come join them, but Jean ignored her and left the store without buying what she'd gone in for.

Now Jean stood up, wiped her brow, and stretched her stiff arms. From down the road, she heard girls' voices, saw the chug of truck motors, and the dust cloud. The farmerettes were coming home. She saw Isabel rush from the farmhouse to the kitchen—Nanny had given her last-minute advice about the special butterscotch squares for after the show. Jean guessed that dessert would be the best act of the evening.

The noise grew louder and in no time the girls spilled from the wagons. It was four o'clock. In two hours, the talent show would begin. Jean decided to hoe the field farthest away from the chatter.

Then another cloud of dust rolled up their laneway. A large black car stopped in front of the dorm doors. It stood there a moment like a black ominous box. The girls stopped to stare. Finally the driver's door opened. Out stepped an older man wearing a dark suit and a face heavy with sorrow. "Is Isabel Lynch here?"

Isabel

Humming a tune, Isabel pulled the last batch of butterscotch squares from the oven and placed the pan on a rack to cool. Brushing back a damp curl, she surveyed her work. Several dozen cinnamon crisp cookies were already artfully arranged on platters. When the squares cooled, she would cut them up and spread them on trays covered with lace doilies. She had tied blue ribbons around vases full of white daisies and placed them on the serving table. Betty Crocker couldn't do better.

Now all she had to do was prepare the butter extender and break up bread for tonight's caramel ham loaf. Then she would read her latest letter from Billy. The envelope had been waiting on her nightstand since morning. She loved the anticipation of reading it. After that she would shower and get ready for the talent show.

"Isabel."

Isabel looked up to see Jean enter the kitchen, a strained expression on her face. "Someone is here to see you."

"Not one of those persistent pilots from last night, I hope." Then behind Jean she spotted her father, black suit, ashen face— and she knew. As every one of her dreams shattered into empty shards, Isabel collapsed into her father's arms.

Jean left discreetly. Dr. Lynch stroked his daughter's hair. "He died a hero, honey. Died saving our king and country."

Isabel didn't care. Billy was gone. He would never come home to her. Her life was over.

"Mommy's waiting. Come." Her father led her gently from the kitchen out to the car. The other girls stood silent and shocked in the barnyard.

Her father opened the car door. Isabel climbed inside and her mother crushed her in an embrace, her tears dampening Isabel's face. Almost hysterical, she patted Isabel's back, repeating, "My poor baby. He was a hero, sweetie," over and over.

Isabel turned it off. No sound. No tears. Just numbness and pain. Billy was gone.

"We'll take you home," said her father. "I've asked someone to bring out your belongings."

A minute later, Helene, Peggy, and Binxie carried Isabel's suitcases and bedrolls to her. Peggy reached into the backseat to try to hug Isabel, but the large frame of Mrs. Lynch made it too awkward.

Her father spoke briefly with Smokey, then climbed into the driver's seat, started the motor, and they drove off. Isabel was vaguely aware of a line of sober faces watching her, waving, but she was too dazed to respond.

At home in Guelph, she felt like she was underwater—everything looked unreal, hazy, moved slowly. Sounds were muted and it was hard to breathe.

Her sisters were already there, offering sympathy and sweet tea. Soon neighbors and friends dropped by, murmuring condolences and clichés, but it didn't matter what they said. Speech doesn't register underwater. Just pain.

Next day they visited Billy's home, where neighbors, relatives, and casseroles filled the parlor. In his mother's eyes, Isabel recognized her own sorrow. Mrs. Morrison wrapped her arms around Isabel. They clung to each other but neither cried. Their grief was still too raw for tears. Billy's mother broke the embrace when her sister arrived, and Isabel stood numb where she had left her.

People approached her with hugs and sympathy.

Isabel heard the words from underwater. Somewhere in her sea of grief was the awareness that her Billy had died liberating Sicily. She was the widow—if that was what you called a bereaved fiancée—of a hero.

Her haze was penetrated only by the low urgent voice of Billy's aunt telling his parents, "You've got to think of her too. Help her somehow."

A high school friend hugged Isabel. "I'm so sorry."

It was all too much. Isabel slipped away, walked home along the route she and Billy used to take hand in hand, and sank to her bed.

Sleep wouldn't come to her rescue. She lay staring at the engagement ring on her hand, images of Billy flashing across her mind. When her family returned home, she turned her back to them. It took too much effort to answer, to move, even to think.

Two days later, Isabel let her mother lead her to the bath. Mom and Gloria toweled her dry, helped her dress, combed her hair. Bits of advice floated through. "It's Billy's funeral service… he loved you…it's the last thing you can do for him."

She slid into the hard wooden pew behind the Morrisons— the minister in front, draped in black, talking, praying, too many flowers, perfume too heavy, deep organ music, its sad, somber vibrations jarring her bones. Then to the hall—sandwiches and coffee passing by, too many people saying they're sorry, Gloria offering her a sandwich, a strange glance from Billy's sister, talking, talking, all around her. Isabel stood tall and rigid, giving gracious automatic replies. If being a stoic widow was the last thing she could do for Billy, she would do it well.

Finally she was led home and put to bed. She slept awhile. She awoke in the dark, silent house. Her clock showed four-fifteen.

Glad to be alone, she sat in a chair beside her window, watching their star shine lonely in the sky. It hovered closer to heaven than she was—maybe Billy could see it still.

On the floor beside her dresser lay her closed suitcase. The farm. It seemed so far away. Someone must have packed the bag for her. They surely had cleared everything from the top of her night table too—her pink tablecloth, Billy's photo. His last letter. Could she bear to read it? No.

She went back to bed, but her gaze kept returning to the suitcase. Sleep was gone, and the letter was there. She sat up, turned on her light, and stared at the case.

As if the letter were a magnet, she crossed the room and opened her suitcase. Right on top, wrapped in the pink cloth, lay his photo. She picked it up and looked at his brave, beloved face. Gloria had snapped it at their engagement party—a day of sunshine and plans for their perfect future.

She tenderly kissed the picture, clutched it to her breast, and picked up his letter.

My Dear Isabel.

How strange it felt to read these words. When they were written, he was alive and strong in England. In this letter, her Billy still lived.

You are a wonderful, beautiful woman. I admire what you have accomplished as a farmerette.

Isabel smiled, and stopped to wipe a tear forming in her eye. Billy was always so romantic.

I have loved and adored you for the last six years.

He loved and adored me—past tense?

But several weeks ago, I realized I have fallen in love with Norah Wyecroft. She's an amazing, passionate woman.

Stunned, Isabel couldn't believe the words. Was he joking? She had to read on.

When I received word we were being deployed to Italy, Norah told me she is expecting our baby. We were married before I left England.

Isabel stood up, stupefied. There was more, but she couldn't read it. She had been betrayed. Her stomach heaved and she threw up on the floor.

She wiped her mouth and began to shake. Billy loved someone else. He had married another woman. He was going to be a father.

No. He *would* have been a father.

But he would never see his child. And she would never see him again.

She gazed at his picture for a long time. Now his aunt's words and his sister's strange glance made sense. They knew. They were concerned about helping Norah, not her. Their grief would have some comfort—Billy's child. Isabel had nothing.

How could he do this to her? She flung the photo across the room. The glass shattered against the dresser, but his face still smiled up at her. She yanked the ring off her finger and threw it at the picture.

Full of angry energy, she pulled on some clothes, walked

downstairs and out the back door. The sun had begun to rise—their star no longer glowed in the sky.

Isabel walked. And walked. Her mind teemed with images, all of them ending with a picture of Billy getting married, making love—to someone else.

At the bridge over the river where he had proposed, she stopped. The water bubbled and raced below her. It flowed exactly the same way as the evening Billy asked her to marry him, to share the rest of her life with him. That night, moonlight had gilded the glistening waters. Nothing else had changed. Except Billy was gone.

She sighed and walked on. Every street, their high school, every building held a memory of their life together. She couldn't bear to walk among the memories anymore. When her father's car pulled up beside her, she was relieved. She climbed in, and as they sped home, she closed her eyes to the reminders of a life that was now history.

At home her mother poured her coffee with too much cream and sugar. Gloria brought her toast, cut into four pieces. They spoke to her in kind, careful tones. Isabel finished half the coffee, ignored the toast, and got up to clear the table.

"Oh, leave that, honey. We'll do it. You sit, rest."

"I'm bereaved, Mom, not ill." The last thing she needed was rest and time to think. But her mother shooed her from the kitchen. Isabel headed up to her room. The vomit and the broken glass were already cleaned away, the picture discreetly removed. But her diamond ring lay gleaming on the night table. Defiantly, she slipped it onto her finger. At least that still belonged to her.

How long had Billy's family known about Norah? She washed and dressed and headed for his house. Today they were going to tell her everything.

SUNDAY, JULY 18, 1943

Peggy

Peggy sat staring at the empty bed across the room. She missed its pink frilliness. A faint glow from the rising sun tried to make up for it, but succeeded only in making the space look lonelier.

Poor Isabel. Peggy and many other girls wept yesterday as they watched Isabel drive away. They canceled the talent show. Instead, they sat outside on the lawn, watching Isabel and Billy's star, all the stars. They talked about the boys they knew fighting across the sea, about fear and courage, and about growing up during this awful war. Newscasters predicted victory was in sight, but too much had been lost already.

Of course, Peggy's prayers were for Canadian and Allied boys. But she wondered about German, Italian, and Japanese boys too. Didn't they have parents, sisters and brothers, wives, and children who loved them? Didn't those boys grow up in similar fields, streets, and schools, with the same dreams as Canadian boys?

When her parents took her to visit both sides of her family six years ago, she discovered that her granny from Warwick and her great-aunt from Leipzig loved to solve crossword puzzles. Both walked their dogs through miles of countryside, and fussed over her, their distant granddaughter. All her cousins asked questions about Canada, played soccer with enthusiasm, teased each other and her. The English cousins took her rowing along the River Avon. With her German cousins, she floated on the White Elster River.

The sun had now risen completely. Soon everyone would wake up. They would all attend church this morning, pray for Billy's soul, pray for Isabel, for everyone they loved, and trust it would help. But then what would they do? It would have been easier if it had been a working day, to keep their hands and minds busy.

"Swimming."

Peggy looked left.

On the next cot, Binxie lay propped on one arm, watching her. "Let's all go to the lake after church. It's going to be a scorcher."

Peggy nodded. "Let's pack a picnic. Cookie will be in a terrible mood today with her assistant gone."

Helene yawned and stretched awake on her bed. "We'll make our own sandwiches. That should help."

"Anything to keep busy," Binxie said.

By noon, a large group of girls walked to the lake carrying lunches, towels, and sorrow. Peggy kept thinking of Isabel's face in the car yesterday. She remembered the handsome face of Billy, a man she had never met, but whose photo she saw every day.

He reminded her of Michael. Blond, wavy-haired Michael had taken her for bike rides, paid kind attention to his young cousin visiting from Canada. She'd developed a huge crush on him, later exchanged letters and photos. He was the practical joker in his family; people said the party started when he arrived. Yet he always knew how people were feeling, who needed a gentle word. When her uncle Rudolph took them to hear the famous boys' choir in St. Thomas Church, Michael had confided in her. "One day I'll play the organ for such a choir." The German military had other plans for him. He was killed at Dieppe too. Peggy's neighbors didn't bring casseroles or flowers like they did for Donny Ferguson. Her family grieved in secret.

A cloud of dust appeared on the horizon, coming their way fast. A familiar truck. Peggy glanced at Helene. "You know who that is."

Helene nodded. "Act like we're having such an interesting conversation we don't notice him."

Peggy complied, watching from the corner of her eye as the truck approached on the narrow road. "He's slowed down," she whispered. "The passenger window is opening."

"Keep talking."

Peggy noticed Helene's head was averted from the road but her eyes were full of timid hope as the truck pulled up beside them.

"Hello, girls!" Agnes Fraser called cheerfully. "Where are you headed on such a glorious day?" She seemed ready to chat, but Dan looked down, tapping the steering wheel.

He's hurting my friend. He can't get away with this, thought Peggy. She leaned in and spoke directly to him. "Hello, Dan. How are you today?"

"Fine," he answered gruffly, fidgeting with the gearshift.

Before Peggy could say more, Helene elbowed her into silence.

"We're going swimming, Mrs. Fraser," answered Kate.

"Wise choice on a day like this. Enjoy your day, girls." She waved as the truck sped off.

"You okay?" Peggy asked Helene.

"Of course." Helene shrugged. "I was silly to think he was interested in me."

"He still is. He was blushing."

"Then why is he so rude?"

"He's a Scranton," replied Binxie.

Peggy started to answer, but Helene frowned. "No. He was being polite to me that day, and now he's embarrassed. I'm too young, too plain."

Peggy put her arm around her friend's shoulder. "You're prettier than you think. He'd be lucky to have you."

"Everything looks worse today. We're all sad," Binxie added.

"I don't even want to become involved with such a moody fellow. Too much heartache."

Peggy nodded at her. She knew why.

The noon sun shone down hard, and insects buzzed at them. "That lake will feel so good," said Doris.

In a golden field beside them, a man led a horse and plow to cut the hay. He stopped, wiped his brow, and waved at them. Wasn't this the McDonnells' extra field? Nelly's farm? *The letter*, thought Peggy. *Another tragedy from another war. Would they get a chance to right this one?*

Knowing Jean and Binxie often walked together, Peggy turned to Binxie and asked, "Has Jean mentioned Polly's letters? Surely she has found out who Polly is by now."

"Didn't the librarian tell you there are too many Pollys, including some who moved away?" Binxie replied.

Peggy sighed. Then she glimpsed Lake Ontario between the trees ahead, and forgot everything else. Soon she heard laughter. More young people were already sunning and swimming. Evie Belding called to them, "Come on in. The water's wonderful!"

Peggy recognized Alice Belding and Luke Scranton among them. She was relieved Harry wasn't there. She heard Binxie's sharp intake of breath and followed her glance. Johnny Clifford emerged from the lake like a Greek god, water rolling from his chest. *I knew it*, thought Peggy. *There's something between those two.*

Johnny splashed toward them. He waved to everyone, then asked Binxie, "Ready for a rematch?"

Peggy caught Nancy's glance at Binxie as she dropped her bag, pulled off her shirt and shorts, and ran into the lake in her bathing suit.

The cool, soothing water, jumping into the waves, and swimming hard made it impossible to stay gloomy for long. Being young on a sunny summer day trumped grief.

Sometime during the afternoon, Binxie and Johnny wandered off, walking close together along the shoreline. Peggy knew by their serious faces when they returned that Binxie had told him about Billy. Maybe that was why Johnny had hugged her? At least they weren't as bad as Irene and one of the farm boys, kissing underwater.

But Alice glared at Binxie and asked Johnny, "Where's Jean?"

Johnny answered coolly. "Haying the back field. Two fellows from the air base insisted on helping her today, so she took them up on it. She needs all the assistance she can get."

Stella smirked. "Must be that cute guy she danced with

all Friday evening. What was his name? Hugh? He sure looked good in his uniform."

Peggy glared at Stella. Johnny shouldn't learn about Hugh this way, and the dig about the military was cruel. *That witch will find a toad in her milk tonight,* she fumed.

Johnny opened his mouth to answer, but instead turned and dove into the lake. Binxie shot Stella a look of disgust, then sat with Helene, her back to Stella.

Luke approached Peggy. "Want to walk along the beach with me?"

Not after the way you cursed at us last week, thought Peggy, but she smiled. "Sure." She could find out why Dan had gone from hot to cold with Helene.

"My brother can't take a joke," Luke answered as they sloshed through the water. "He got annoyed with us for teasing him about that skinny girl he likes."

Peggy wished she could put a few toads in his drink too. She had to settle for accidentally tripping him into the Canada goose droppings along the shoreline. As he picked himself up, she turned back to join the others.

"Hey, I thought we were going to have fun," he protested.

"We just did," she called over her shoulder, gratified to see him sulk awhile.

The girls returned to Highberry in time for dinner, a somber meal—blah meatloaf, dull mashed potatoes, pale cauliflower, no flowers on the table. At least there were lots of Isabel's squares and cookies, but they made the girls even sadder.

The only bright moment was when Stella discovered a snail sliming through her salad and gagged. Later, her earsplitting screeches—when her toes touched the chicken foot at the bottom of her sheets—gave Peggy some fleeting satisfaction. Seeing Isabel's empty bed stopped her smile. She had planned to write to Omi and Opa today, but her letter would be too depressing. She retired early, but whenever she closed her eyes, she saw images of Billy's face, Donny's, Theo's, and Michael's—and Isabel heartbroken in the backseat of the car. Her last thought before she fell asleep was how glad she was they could work tomorrow and stay busy.

FRIDAY, JULY 23, 1943

Helene

Helene stepped down from the ladder and handed the full basket of cherries to Matthew Scranton. He squinted at the fruit, searching for flaws. She pulled the picking strap from around her neck and rested it on the ground. She scratched three mosquito bites in a row on her leg and pressed an *X* into each one, hoping it would stop the itch.

"One is split, two are overripe, and this one's too green," declared Matthew, the son who most resembled his father. He looked as satisfied as if he'd nabbed a criminal.

"I'm sorry." Helene climbed back up the tree, found four replacement cherries, and brought them back down to Matthew.

Without a thank you, he punched her card and stomped off to scrutinize Peggy's harvest. When he complained about a cherry, she grabbed the offending fruit, ate it, and said, "Tastes fine to me."

Helene watched them stare each other down. When Matthew retreated, she wished she had Peggy's courage.

At noon, the girls left the orchard to clean up at the pump. Then they carried their lunch bags to a shady tree.

The talk, of course, was about the talent show. They'd decided to hold it this weekend, and the dress rehearsal was tonight.

"I've changed my mind. I'm going to sing 'Over The Rainbow' instead of 'Roses in December,'" said Estelle. "It showcases my voice better."

Most of the girls rehearsed every available minute.

"Are you sure you won't sing with us?" Binxie asked Helene.

Helene shook her head. "I could never sing in front of a room full of people."

Peggy shrugged. "I think you could." But she left it alone, and the girls went on to eat their sandwiches and discuss the outfits for their number.

Helene couldn't think about singing when she was so worried about home. Her mother's last letter sounded too cheery. No one had rented Jake Potter's room yet, and Alva and the baby had returned to Alberta to live with her parents. Mama said that meant less work, but Helene knew it also meant less money to pay the bills.

She stretched out on the grass. If she had a short nap, maybe she wouldn't feel so exhausted, so discouraged. But sleep was as elusive now as it had been last night. Her mind would not rest. The money she was sending home wasn't enough. She should go home, take a well-paying factory job. School could wait a year or two.

But she had seen too many girls in her neighborhood leave school "for awhile" and never return. She couldn't do that. She was determined to accomplish something with her life. Besides, she loved it here. Tonight she would ask Smokey to arrange for her to work overtime.

And she grieved for poor Isabel's Billy, for Peggy's cousin, for the boys she no longer wrote to—and for her own father, wherever he was.

More terrible thoughts crowded her mind. She hated working at the Scrantons'. There was no kindness on this farm. Matthew and Luke went out of their way to be unpleasant to her. They gave her the oldest ladders, brought her water last, and fussed over the cherries she picked.

But what bothered her most was Dan. The orchard was not large enough to keep her from seeing him. He would drive by in a truck, work in a nearby field, collect baskets in a distant row of trees. Once he passed her in the barnyard. He stopped as if to speak, then with a grudging hello, moved on. Helene couldn't understand it, but Peggy kept insisting, "He likes you. He stares at you when he thinks no one's looking."

Helene had shaken her head. "Then he has an eight-year-old's way of showing it."

Now Helene shifted into a more comfortable position on the grass. Tonight she would ask Smokey to move her to another farm. But she already intended to request additional hours of work. Afraid if she asked too much that Smokey would say no to everything, she decided the extra pay was more important. She finally fell asleep.

Helene dreamed she was in a lovely meadow. Her mother

and brothers were there. All was carefree, joyful. Why had she ever worried? Helene handed her brothers a bowl of cherries. They laughed, red juice dribbling from their lips. Her mother smiled.

Distant voices called her name, but her mother shook her head. "It's not for you. Stay here with us."

Helene wanted to remain in this peaceful place.

The voices became louder, more insistent. But the twins beckoned her to come swim in a sunny pond that had suddenly appeared. She stepped into the water. It was so warm, so wonderful, she felt released.

Then the laughter broke through. Helene woke up. She stared into the grinning face of Matthew Scranton, who was holding a glass of water to her hand. Beyond him, the horrified expressions of the farmerettes. What had happened?

Helene's hand was wet and she felt uncomfortably damp below. She bolted upright, her face hot with shame.

"I told you we had a cure for layabouts who sleep instead of work," Matthew gloated. He poured the rest of the water onto the grass.

"You swine!" Peggy shouted at him. She helped Helene up, and tried to hug her.

Helene pushed her away. She turned and ran from the orchard. Only when she was on the road, out of earshot, did she let herself sob. She had never felt so humiliated in her life. How could she ever face the girls, Matthew, again? Seventeen years old and she had wet herself. Her shorts, her underpants felt cold and shameful. She had never disliked anyone in her life, but now hatred of the Scranton boys pulsed through her body.

All she wanted was to go back to the dorm, shower for a long time, then pack up and return to Hamilton, where she belonged.

When she heard the truck behind her, she didn't turn. Hopefully it was only a stranger driving by. But the truck slowed down. Could she run into the field? No—a stone wall blocked her way. Keeping her face turned away, she walked faster.

"Helene."

Dan. The last person she wanted to see in this condition. She sped up.

"Helene, please. This shouldn't have happened. I'm sorry."

So am I, she thought bitterly. *I thought I belonged here. I liked you.*

She heard the motor stop, the truck door slam, the crunch of boots on gravel. She ran.

Dan quickly caught up and ran beside her, but he didn't touch her. "Let me drive you home. Please."

Without looking at him, she spat, "Why?"

"You didn't deserve this. It's my fault."

The words came out so broken. She glanced at him, saw his bloody nose and swollen eye. She stopped.

"Matt's sorry now too."

Without a word, she followed him back to the truck. He handed her a towel to wrap around herself, and she climbed in.

In silence, they drove along the bumpy road, then turned onto the lane to Highberry Farm. Dan pulled up at the dorm, got out of the truck, and opened the passenger door for her. She climbed down without looking at him. "Thank you."

"Helene. Can we talk?"

She shook her head.

"Please."

"Not now."

"When?"

She wanted to say never, and she wanted to bury her head in his chest and cry. Instead she shrugged.

"That was a cruel thing Matthew did. He was wrong, not you. Please, when can we talk?"

"I have to wash."

"How about Monday?"

"I don't know." Helene still couldn't face him.

"After your dinner. Seven?"

"All right." Without looking back, Helene hurried into the dorm, grabbed her soap and clean clothes, and headed for the bathroom. In the shower she cried. And dreaded Monday at seven.

SATURDAY, JULY 24, 1943

Binxie

Binxie washed her hands for the third time, trying to scrub the green stain from her fingers, without total success. At least she liked the musky, pungent scent of tomato plants. Her back was sore from hunching over to snip off the suckers all morning, but her mind was on the talent show. Some friends from school were coming to watch, then take her out for dinner. Tomorrow she could sleep in and relax. Girls hurried each other out of the showers, borrowed outfits, tuned instruments, and practiced one last time. The atmosphere was electric.

Binxie hoped the fun and excitement would distract

Helene. Ever since the incident with Matthew on Thursday, the poor girl had avoided everyone. Binxie wished fervently she had been there. She would have stopped the lout before he could hold that glass of warm water to Helene's hand. She couldn't understand why the other girls had just stood by. Of course, Peggy blamed herself for not seeing what he was doing until too late, and had apologized to Helene several times.

Nevertheless, Helene went about her work silently, head down. Any confidence she had gained here vanished. She barely ate, and spent her time off lying on her bed, reading.

"Come outside. We're doing a quick run-through of our song," Patsy called. Binxie followed her to a spot past the chicken coop, hoping Cracker wasn't feeling aggressive today.

"We'll sound better if we look good," Kate had suggested earlier in the week, so they'd rounded up matching checkered red-and-white shirts and denim overalls. Helene had sewn a jaunty red bandana for each girl. Now with some straw in their hats, they did look dandy.

By two-thirty, the excitement was at fever pitch. Friends, neighbors, and girls not taking part in the show milled around the farmyard, sipping lemonade and eating squares—Freda's best efforts to imitate Isabel. Binxie waved at Jean, who had come with her parents and Nanny.

The Belding family, the Smiths, and the Grants took seats near the front. Agnes Fraser arrived with Reverend and Mrs. Ralston. Of course, Miss Willing and her choir ladies were there. Binxie half-expected them to jump up and perform too.

The surprise visitors were Peggy's parents, who drove up in a noisy old Dodge. Peggy screeched with joy and hugged them repeatedly. Then two blond boys bounced out of the backseat, followed by a thin woman who resembled Helene. Helene ran to embrace her mother and held her like a life preserver. Her brothers—identical fellows with freckles and short uneven haircuts—ran around them gleefully.

Watching the joyful reunions, Binxie wished for a moment that her parents had come to watch her, but, the train ride down from Muskoka was too lengthy and strenuous. Then, watching Helene lead her family to the refreshment table, Binxie worried—would Helene return home with them? One friend gone was already too many.

Helene

By the time Helene and the rest of the audience finished the last lines of "The White Cliffs of Dover," tears and happiness mingled on their faces. The talent show had been a success, and this song brought everyone together in a perfect finale.

Helene exchanged smiles with her mother. How good it felt to see her again. But when her mother stopped smiling, the lines remained on her face. Next to the robust farmers and farmerettes, she looked pale and weary.

People rose in their chairs, clapping, cheering, whistling. Finally the performers ran from the stage to greet their guests. Peggy, out of breath and beaming, hugged her parents and shook hands with Mrs. Miller. "A standing ovation! They loved us!"

Helene smiled at her. Peggy would cherish this day for a long time—and she deserved the glory. She had worked hard to put this show together, get everyone involved, give their best. And she'd perfected her performance of Dvořák's boisterous

"Festival March." Helene knew she too would treasure this memory.

Now others came to congratulate Peggy, and meet her parents. Helene and her mother drifted away to watch her brothers tearing around the barn with the other youngsters, climbing the bales of hay, running, stopping only long enough to grab sweets from the refreshment table.

"You look lovely, Helene," said Mrs. Miller. "I've never seen you healthier."

Helene wished she could say the same to her. "I'm glad you came. I've missed you."

Her mother looked at her a moment. "Something's wrong. What's troubling you?"

"I should come home. Give you a hand."

"Don't be silly! Several people are coming to look at the rooms, and until they decide to rent them, I have less work—a little holiday."

Peter ran between them. "Mama, I brought you a cherry tart." He handed her a slightly smushed pastry.

"Thank you, son." She rolled her eyes in exaggerated joy. "Mmm, delicious."

He ran off again.

Mrs. Miller regarded her daughter closely. "There's more."

Does she have to know me so well? Helene looked down at Mama's worn shoes, polished to a proud shine. She wouldn't burden her with the story of her humiliation in the orchard. "It's nothing really. I'm just disappointed in someone I thought might like me."

Her mother nodded sympathetically. "That hurts."

Helene was glad she didn't offer platitudes about getting over it, or say that someone better would come along.

"Hello. You must be Mrs. Miller."

Helene and her mother turned to face Agnes Fraser, who smiled warmly and offered her hand. "You have a charming, bright daughter. She knows how to work too."

Now where did she hear that? wondered Helene, even as she tried not to blush. She introduced the two women and stood by while they talked. When Peter ran up with another tart, Mrs. Fraser stopped him before he could escape, and quizzed him as she had done with the farmerettes at the growers' party. Helene was relieved that he answered politely, in spite of his obvious wish to get back to playing with the others. Finally Mrs. Fraser excused him. She watched him run to the field and said softly, "My little brother was just like him once."

When Mrs. Ralston waved to her, Mrs. Fraser said her good-byes and left.

"She's quite assertive, but I like her. I'm glad she thinks so highly of you, Helene," said Mrs. Miller. Before she could say more, Mr. Pigeon strode over and said, "I'm hungry. Let's eat."

Helene looked confused until Mrs. Pigeon pointed at the car. "We packed a picnic."

The girls helped unload the hamper of food and Peggy led the way to a wooden table near the apple orchard.

It was a cheerful meal with jokes and laughter between mouthfuls of food. Helene thought it was a treat to eat the sausages and salads she was used to at home. How nice it would be to go back with her family. But until this week, she'd been happy here. And Dan wanted to speak with her on Monday. What could he possibly have to say?

Too soon the meal was over and Mr. Pigeon announced it was time to leave. "We need to go before it gets dark on these unfamiliar roads."

Peggy hugged her parents. "Thank you for coming. Give Oma and Opa hugs and kisses from me."

Her mother shot her a strange glance. "They would have come, if you'd let them."

Peggy looked away, and Helene felt bad for her—if her grandparents came, their German accents would tell everyone her secret.

Peter tossed a ball back to one of the farm boys and told Helene, "I want to stay here."

"I wish you could."

He looked up at Helene with big brown eyes. "Come home with us. We miss you."

"We want to hear *Treasure Island* again," added Willy.

Helene realized how much she missed their evening routine of snuggling into bed and reading a chapter. She was ready to agree, but her mother interrupted.

"No, boys. Helene will come home later. She has an important job here. Without her and the other girls, our soldiers would not get enough food. We can't let them down."

Both boys regarded their sister with respect. "Okay," said Willy. "But promise you'll be back at the end of the summer." He climbed into the car behind his brother.

"I want to come home now," Helene whispered to her mother.

"No, dear," her mother said gently. "Your duty is here. Your letters glow with happiness about the farm and the friendships you've made. Don't let one setback change that."

As their families drove off, Peggy and Helene waved until the car disappeared over the horizon. Arm in arm they returned to the dorm. Peggy went to the recreation room, and Helene headed for bed. She tried to read another chapter of *Gone with the Wind* instead of thinking about Monday at seven.

MONDAY, JULY 26, 1943

X

"Ooops! Catch it!"

She stretched her arms farther left, and a head of lettuce flew into her hands, splashing cool water over her chest and face, a welcome shower on this hot day. She placed the lettuce in a crate with the others and stood up in time to catch the next one.

"Sorry, bad aim," called Kate.

"Loved the refreshing shower," she called back, laughing. *And I love everything else about this place too,* she thought as she caught another wet lettuce. The crate was full. Mr. Grant picked it up and left an empty one in its place.

She called to Kate. "New crate. My turn to cut and toss you a bath." She hopped over the row of green heads and Kate handed her the knife. The air was fragrant with the scent of fresh hay. She felt strong, healthy, content. She loved the steady routine of farmwork, long walks through the countryside finding places to sketch, and the companionship of the girls. Sure, she missed Isabel a lot, but everyone did. She enjoyed the banter, the crazy songs they made up as they worked, the tricks they played on each other. Life here was clean, simple, good. Maybe she was finally cured. Maybe she'd even go to Romeo's with the girls this weekend.

Helene

Helene filled her last basket of cherries, handed her card to Mr. Belding, and hopped on the wagon to go home. All the girls were hot, exhausted, and wondering what might be served for supper tonight.

Lost in her own apprehension, Helene sat quietly on the wagon. What would Dan say tonight? *Sorry if you thought there was anything to our conversation, but I'm not interested in you, you're too young, too thin, too boring, too…*Or, *I already have a fiancée.* Or maybe, *I'm too messed up from the war to care for you or anyone else.*

Even though dinner was Swiss steak, she couldn't eat a bite. Canned prunes for dessert made everyone miss Isabel even more. Helene left the dining room early, took special care to shower, comb her hair, and borrow Peggy's best blouse.

"You look lovely," said Peggy.

"Yes, I do," Helene had answered with some amazement. "At least I'll make him regret turning me down."

"If he does, he's an idiot," said Peggy. "You're by far the best person I know. Remember that when you talk to him."

Helene took her book outside, and settled in a chair where she pretended to read. She wanted to be ready, but appear busy, unconcerned, when he came—if he came. *Gone with the Wind* could have been written in Greek for all she comprehended as she sat, staring at her book, calm on the outside, stomach churning, heart beating too fast.

And then he stood before her.

Her surprise was real. "I didn't hear you drive up."

"This month's gas used up. Had to ride the bike." He looked embarrassed, boyish. The hero, galloping in on a bicycle. Not the image he probably wanted, but it helped Helene relax.

She hesitated. "There are bikes in the barn," she said softly. "Do you want to go for a ride?" When he nodded, she felt better. He wasn't in a hurry to run away.

Soon they pedaled along the road, side by side. Helene felt glad to be with him and not to have to talk yet.

They reached the lake, leaned their bikes against a tree, and stood, looking at the waves charging the land and retreating again.

Dan skipped stones across the water and finally spoke. "First of all, I apologize for my rude brother. He was wrong. You didn't deserve such a mean trick, and I told him so."

She looked at his battered eye, now faded to green, and the small bruise on his jaw. "I'm sorry you had to do that."

He shrugged. "I'm not."

The humiliation and anger Helene had felt since Thursday began to seep away. "Let's forget it happened. I'm okay now."

Dan took a breath and cleared his throat. "And I'm sorry for my dismal behavior too."

Helene was about to meekly accept that, but then she blurted, "Why?"

Embarrassment and doubt crossed Dan's face. His eyes were dark with regret. "It wouldn't work, Helene. I'm trying to spare you."

"Shouldn't I have a say in that decision?"

"You're so young, so kind. You don't know how rough it can be. War does things to people. We may have survived, but there's still damage. You shouldn't have to deal with that."

Helene took his hand—the one with the scar reaching just far enough below the cuff to show the world that it was there. "I have lived with it." She closed her eyes a moment. "My father. He survived the Great War, Vimy Ridge. No scars on the outside, but such damage inside. Shell shock. His moods ranged from depression to gentleness to angry outbursts. I never knew how he'd greet me when I came home."

He looked at her with sympathy. "You don't have to tell me this."

"I want to." His warm hand in hers made her feel strong.

"Mama told me he was once a quiet, thoughtful man— worked in the lab at Proctor and Gamble. He loved research, his garden, and her. Before the war, he wanted a big family; afterward, the noise of a crying baby—his crying baby—could set him off. I learned to stay very quiet."

Dan squeezed her hand gently.

"On his good days he read to me, took me for walks in the woods to identify plants, pick mushrooms—as long as it was peaceful. Then the Depression hit Hamilton hard and my dad harder. He lost his job, tried day labor here and there, but he wasn't suited for that. He borrowed money. When my brothers came along—twins—it was too much for him. They rarely saw his kind side, and only remember his silent moods, the horrible shaking, sudden rages. When he finally headed for Kingston to work building highways, we were relieved."

Helene had just spilled the story she never shared. She paused to inhale deeply. "Sorry, that was too much about me." She tried to release her hand.

But Dan held on. "I underestimated you."

"People usually do."

"Not if they know you." He gazed at her, his eyes full of admiration. He let go of her hand and frowned. "Helene, I'm much older than you, in many ways. The war does that too. I saw dead and bloodied French babies, and German children burned to a crisp. I met people at their best and their worst. Their very worst."

He took a deep breath. "My farming ability is limited—this arm, my leg—are scarred, weak. I'll never earn the income to buy my own farm, to support a family properly."

"We don't have to think that far ahead."

"It's unfair for me to even start with someone."

A small song began in Helene's mind. He wasn't rejecting her. He was rejecting himself. "Are you sure you have no temper?" She remembered seeing him argue with his father and brothers, the fight he must have had with Matthew on Friday, her own father's outbursts.

He nodded, puzzled. "Helene, I have sad moments, some nightmares, disagreements with my family, but I don't get melancholy or violent. I promise you that."

"And that black eye?"

"Any man would have done that for you."

Only someone gallant. She was aware of his breath, his scent of clean soap and masculinity. "Then there's really only one thing that matters, Dan." She looked directly at him. "How we feel about each other. Everything else will fall into place."

"Dear, innocent Helene…"

"Don't tell me I've read too many novels. I watch people and listen too." She paused, then blurted, "Dan, do you care for me?"

"From the minute you whizzed through Agnes Fraser's interrogation. She likes you too."

"I fell for you as you quoted Robert Frost. Harder when we talked outside, and completely when we shared the ice cream."

"It tasted that good?" He grinned at her, his whole face changed.

She nodded.

He stopped smiling and asked seriously, "Is it that easy?"

She regarded the arm dangling at his side. "Roll up your sleeve."

He hesitated, then slowly undid the button and pulled up his sleeve.

Helene gazed at the long, ugly burn scar, the skin puckered and mottled red, pale yellow, with shiny ridges. It looked horrible. But it was a part of him. She took his arm, stroked it gently. On sheer impulse, she lifted it to her lips and kissed it.

Dan put his other arm around her, drew her close, and held her tight. She felt his heart beating against her cheek. This felt so right. She wanted to stay there, holding him forever.

After a moment, Dan backed away some. He cupped her chin with his strong hand, leaned in, and kissed her. If she had ever worried how to kiss a man, she now realized it was the most natural, wonderful thing to do.

The two walked hand in hand along the shore. For now, no more words were needed.

When they finally pedaled home, the colors of the evening sky glowed more vivid than ever. They rode past orchards bursting with fruit and birdsong, Helene's heart singing right along.

At the spreading elm tree just before the dorm, they stopped, dropped their bikes, and embraced.

"Do you want to see me again?"

Dan's question was answered by her broad smile.

"Is tomorrow too soon? We could buy ice cream in town."

Standing with him in a wet ditch would have sounded fine to Helene. "I'll see you after dinner. Seven o'clock?"

Their kiss was cut short by the slam of a screen door. Peggy ran past them, toward the darkening orchard, head down and sobbing.

Dan and Helene quickly said goodnight, and Helene hurried after her friend.

Peggy

Peggy watched Helene pedal down the lane with Dan. Not as romantic as a horse-drawn carriage, but she felt hopeful about this.

She headed back inside, humming a tune. A card game would be fun. First she'd go upstairs for her Count Basie record—pleasant background music—then she'd find some partners.

As soon as she reached the top of the stairs, she knew something was amiss. Stella and a group of girls stood around her bed, deep in conversation. When they saw her, they stopped dead.

Peggy tried a smile. "Anyone for euchre?"

"Not with you." Nancy tossed back her head and marched past Peggy to the stairs.

Puzzled, Peggy looked at Millie. The girl glanced away, but not before Peggy caught the fear in her eyes.

What have I done? Peggy turned to Stella, who waved an envelope at her. Then she knew. This was the moment she'd dreaded all summer.

"You thought you could sneak in here, pretend you're one of us," said Stella, her cheeks red with self-righteous indignation. She shook the envelope at her. "You left this on your nightstand."

It was the letter from Oma. The gothic script was the first clue. The address to Margarete Pigeon was the second. The return address, Mrs. Otto Reichholtz, made it certain.

Stella narrowed her eyes at Peggy. "You're German—a Nazi." She almost spat the words.

Peggy stood tall. "I was born in Canada. My father is Canadian…with English parents."

"Ha! I see German names!"

"Yes. My mother was born there. She came to Canada when she was twenty, became a citizen, and her parents followed. We're all loyal, proud Canadians."

"You've been very sneaky about this, hiding behind your Canadian name. Why should we believe you?" Stella was in her glory. This was about more than patriotism for her. This was revenge for Harry. "Our fathers and brothers are overseas risking their lives to stop your people, and all the while we're facing danger in our own beds."

"Don't be ridiculous. My dad works for the war office. I buy war bonds and work here as hard as any of you," Peggy defended herself to the suspicious faces.

"Really? Then how do you explain this? Once we suspected you, I searched for more evidence." With a look of triumph, Stella reached into the top shelf of Peggy's orange crate and pulled out the photo of Michael. "You keep a picture of a Nazi soldier! Even now he could be shooting at my dad."

Suddenly Peggy had to blink back tears. "He isn't shooting anyone. He's dead. Put that picture back, please."

"Don't you people belong in a camp somewhere?" said Grace. "How do we know you aren't spies or saboteurs?"

Two girls nodded.

Peggy looked at the girls facing her. They were her friends. But Millie frowned in confusion. Ruth stared at her, open-mouthed. The others watched her with cold, appraising eyes.

It was the same as when they left Greenvale four years ago. In Hamilton no one knew. They thought Oma and Opa were Swiss. It was no use reasoning with these girls. Stella had done her work well. Soon everyone at the farm would hear about her. She would have to endure suspicion and hostility—or slink home in disgrace.

Peggy glared at Stella until she put Michael's picture back onto the orange crate. Holding back tears, Peggy fled the room. She rushed downstairs, out across the barnyard to the far orchard, and, finally exhausted, she stopped and slid down a gnarled old peach tree. There she sat with her head in her arms, and cried, the ugly word *Nazi* ringing in her ears.

She had been so careful, telling her mother to make sure her grandparents' letters were enclosed with hers, not letting them and their German accents come to the talent show, even though she wanted to see them. It had all been for naught.

The deep blues of evening sky set in. The trees silhouetted against it stood ancient and peaceful, not caring where anyone came from. She loved being here with the other farmerettes, working and playing side by side every day—sharing meals, laughter, clothing, and secrets. But even now she heard their voices in the barnyard, discussing her. How could friends turn against her so quickly? Not one of them came out to support her. She hated this war with all her being.

Then through the dusk walked Helene. She sat beside Peggy and touched her arm. Once Peggy told her what had happened, Helene said, "It'll blow over. They know you."

Peggy shook her head. "You didn't see how the girls looked at me. They hate me."

"That's how they feel about the enemy. We all do. Give them time to think. They'll understand you're on our side."

"I am, Helene. I'm Canadian and proud of it. I have cousins in England I care about, but I like my relatives in Germany too. I worry about all of them."

Helene nodded. "Of course. Look, you're here—working to feed our soldiers."

"And we're not Nazis. My mum's German."

"Right now they don't see a difference," said Helene.

"No. If you had heard what Stella said to me…"

"Stella's jealous of you. She's never forgiven you for being more popular. She's just nasty. Running you down makes her feel good."

"But they believe her. They've heard so many stories about German atrocities, about bombs on England, dead women and children. I've seen posters so awful I believe them."

"Every country does that in war. No one advertises what damage their own side does."

"There's more," Peggy whispered. "The ugly posters, the goose-stepping sadists on the newsreels, the horrible stories. Mum and I spent a summer in Germany six years ago. My aunts, uncles and cousins, the villagers were kind, ordinary people. They wouldn't do those things."

"I'm sure they don't," Helene said soothingly. "But obviously some people do."

"And the rest of us get tarred with the same brush."

Helene nodded. "You and your family have always been kind to me."

"Thank you." Peggy sat silent for a moment, then looked up. "I didn't even ask about you. How did it go?"

Now Helene broke into a wide smile. "Beyond my craziest dreams. Oh, Peggy, he cares for me."

Peggy clasped her friend's hands. "I knew it! I saw how he watched you. What did he say? Did he explain himself?"

"He's worried he'll be bad for me. Says he can't farm well enough to make a decent living."

"You don't care about that," said Peggy. "Tell me more." She wanted to hear something pleasant, anything to mask the hateful words still echoing in her mind.

Even in the twilight, Peggy saw Helene's flaming cheeks. "He kissed you?"

Helene smiled.

"You devil!" Peggy punched her arm. "How was it?"

"I've wondered if anyone would ever want to kiss me. And if they did, how it would feel. Well, it was glorious. My heart, my whole body felt unbearably light and joyful."

"I'm so happy for you. When will you see him again?"

"Tomorrow night—going to Linton's for ice cream." Helene smiled. "And now, dear friend, it's getting dark and damp out here. It's time to go back."

"I can't face them."

"I'll be beside you."

"I'd rather go home."

"You love it here."

"Not if everyone hates me."

"They don't."

"They did just now."

"Wait until morning before you decide. You can't leave tonight anyway."

"And you can't leave me in the lurch," said a voice from the dark. Both girls jumped up. Jean stepped close, Binxie right behind her.

"What on earth is going on?" asked Binxie. "We're out in the stable unsaddling our horses and everyone's gone crazy."

Peggy stood and brushed bits of grass and soil from her clothes while Helene explained. "Stella found out about Peggy's German relatives, and accused her of being a dangerous alien."

Binxie took one look at Peggy's face and stepped over to hug her. "You're no more alien or dangerous than these trees," she stated. "What's wrong with that twit?"

"You're a good worker and a fine person—even though you

eat as much as you pick," said Jean. "Give them a day or two. They'll be fine."

"How can I go back there?" asked Peggy.

"The same way you do everything else—with lots of spirit and a joke," said Binxie.

Jean began to walk.

Helene reached for Peggy's hand. "Come on."

Together the four friends headed back to the barnyard, where several girls sat chatting on the lawn. They stopped as the four approached, then quickly glanced away. Stella glared.

Peggy's knees felt weak, her heart pounded, but she held her head high and walked toward the dorm, eyes focused on the door ahead. She knew the second she passed them that every girl would stare at her. She felt like a criminal.

At the crunch of gravel in the lane, all eyes turned in that direction. Even Peggy glanced at the familiar truck rolling closer. Had Mr. Belding heard about her already? Was he coming to tell her to stay away from his farm?

But Tom Belding waved cheerfully as he pulled to a stop. He climbed from the truck and walked around to the passenger door. He opened it and out stepped Isabel.

Binxie

Binxie stared at Isabel, pale and delicate in her black dress. She looked more ethereal, more lovely—grief suited her.

Peggy and Helene ran to Isabel. Hugs, tears, and laughter, words of surprise and sympathy followed, while Mr. Belding stood by, smiling. Finally he swung a suitcase and a bag from the back of the truck to the ground.

Isabel threw her arms around him and thanked him for the ride.

His face flushed. "You're welcome, Miss," he stammered. "I'm glad I could help." He climbed back into his truck, waved, and drove off. He was such a kind man; Binxie hoped it wasn't his wife who once loved James Earnshaw and carried his baby.

Now the questions began.

"How did you get here?"

"Are you back to stay? We missed you."

In reply, Isabel reached for her luggage. Peggy picked up the suitcase, but Isabel insisted on carrying a small bag herself. "Is my bed still free?"

"So you're staying?" asked Binxie.

Isabel nodded. "Billy would have wanted me to continue my work for our country."

It sounded stiff, rehearsed, to Binxie, but who knew how grief made people act.

As they walked inside and up the stairs, other girls welcomed Isabel and expressed their sympathy. She handled them with perfect grace and the occasional brave sigh.

Binxie watched Peggy, well behind Isabel, carrying the suitcase like a shield. Isabel couldn't have timed her entrance any better—all attention was on her, not Peggy.

They dropped the bags by the bed, and Isabel got busy smoothing her sheets and blanket onto her cot. Smokey arrived, puffing minty gasps from her run up the stairs. She welcomed Isabel back and asked her to come down to the office. That suddenly left a large group of girls standing around, staring awkwardly at each other. Most turned back to what they had been doing. Some seemed puzzled or curious about Peggy's new identity, a few looked at her with disdain.

Peggy turned to fluff Isabel's pillow. She stayed busy until most of the others left. Binxie was relieved for her when Kate called out, "Hey, Peggy. We're setting up a Monopoly game if you want to join us."

"I'll be there in a sec," Peggy called back. She stood still a moment, then turned around. In a chirpy voice, she called Helene and Binxie to come too.

Helene nodded, but Binxie declined. "I want to read my sister's letter." Seeing Peggy's disappointment, she changed her mind. "I'll read it downstairs."

The recreation room was abuzz with news of Isabel's return. If they spoke about Peggy too, it was hard to tell. Binxie chose a chair near the Monopoly game and opened her letter. She'd read it already, but she loved rereading the details. It felt like Kathryn was with her—almost.

Next year I'll be flying with her, thought Binxie, *soaring through the skies. Free. Fast. In control. Not like home, where my parents and "being a lady" limit me. Or here, where the YWCA makes the rules, the farmers choose the jobs, and a bell tells us when to wake up and when to eat.*

She skipped descriptions of each plane Kathryn flew and went to the interesting part.

I delivered a Spitfire to London, and Lord Wexbourne's son took me dancing as promised. His name is Alastair. Binxie, I'm in love. We're in love. Deeply, madly in love. I have never been so happy. Yes, five weeks sounds crazy, but things happen fast in wartime. Everything is more intense, urgent—much more delicious. I feel like I've already lived a lifetime here.

Anyway, aside from being devastatingly hand-some, Alastair is funny, smart, and full of plans for the future. He wants to form an airline after the war—to fly freight and passengers all over the world. He asked me to join him! Now that we know so much more about the capabilities and advantages of flight, the sky's the limit—pardon the pun. Once this war ends, it will be such an exciting world…

Binxie could feel Kathryn's enthusiasm jumping off the page and into her veins. She was in love. Alastair had to be special. Men had fallen for her beautiful, spirited sister before, but they soon either bored her, or they couldn't cope with a woman smarter and more outspoken than they were.

Binxie folded the letter away. What she would give to have Kathryn here now. Kathryn would listen thoughtfully and tell her what to do about Johnny. Every time Binxie saw him, she tingled. She wanted to be with him. But what about Jean? Was there anything between her and Johnny?

She looked up as Isabel came from the office. "Smokey says I can start back in the kitchen tomorrow morning. I should phone my parents, let them know I'm here."

"You didn't tell them you were leaving?"

"They would have said no."

Binxie tucked Kathryn's letter into her pocket. She had predicted this war would soon be over. The enemy was being pushed back on several fronts. If only Kathryn was right. Binxie wanted her home safely. But if the war ended tomorrow, would she leave the farm? No. She needed to stay. There were fields to hoe, crops to be picked—and there was Johnny.

FRIDAY, JULY 30, 1943

Jean

Jean had no stomach for dessert tonight. Dad looked pale. He had spent the afternoon on the couch, angry about his weakness, agitated by the news.

Mussolini was ousted and jailed, and Italy stood close to defeat. The Allies could now focus on destroying Germany's industrial areas and ports. Lorne Greene's Voice of Doom doled out more details of bombings and battles by the hour. They were tidied up for family audiences, but Jean could imagine some of the horror.

Mum turned off the radio at dinner. "We don't need that to spoil our appetites." It may as well have been left on, for the worries stayed with them like unwelcome guests.

Before Nanny even cleared away the unfinished cherry cobbler, Dad spread a map on the table. Stalag VIII-B was somewhere in Silesia, Poland. How close to it were the Allies bombing? Could a stray bomb hit the camp? Rob would be powerless to escape.

Jean's guilt lay like a rock in her chest. She had to step outside to breathe. The heavy heat of July was finally subsiding. A light breeze fanned her face, swayed the young corn in the fields. The sun clung stubbornly to the lower western sky, reminding her there was still time to work.

The last eggs had to be gathered. The hole where a skunk could enter the chicken coop needed to be sealed. She could even pick a few baskets of young cucumbers before they grew too large for Nanny and Mum to make pickles. Feeling weary of it all, she decided if her chores were always waiting, they could wait a bit longer. She'd collect the eggs then stop.

She heard the crack of a bat, and shouting, as a baseball arced far over the nearby field and three girls ran their bases. Binxie at bat. Saturday night, they were invited for a game and cookout with the farmerettes at the nearby Smith farm, and they planned to win. Jean smiled. Even after working all day, they found the energy to play.

Fifteen minutes later, she left the eggs in the kitchen and headed for the far orchard, where the silence could soothe her. *Surely the Allies wouldn't bomb their own men below. Surely this war would end soon. Rob would come home, set up his own house, ready for the family he wanted. Would Fran share it with him?* All Jean could envisage was the girl dancing and flirting with the boys here.

After another turn around the orchard, she headed back home, her soul somewhat lighter. Twilight had ended the game and all was peaceful in the yard. She passed the elm tree and saw Binxie, Peggy, and Helene sprawled in the grass, listening to Isabel. As Jean got closer, she heard Isabel explaining how Billy's unit had been chosen to fight in Sicily. Jean sighed. In spite of his death, Billy was still Isabel's main topic. Her dark clothes, her diamond ring still sparkling on her finger, her sad blue eyes, the certain proud way she held herself—made Isabel the perfect widow, or whatever one called a bereaved fiancée. How ironic. Isabel couldn't let go of her dead Billy, while Fran seemed to have forgotten her living Rob altogether.

Jean was about to pass by, but Binxie called her over. She sat on the grass.

"You were right," Helene said. "*Gone with the Wind* was an incredible story. I must have cried at least three times. Do you think Rhett and Scarlett will get back together?"

"Probably not," Jean replied.

"Oh, a romance," said Peggy. "What's it about?"

"The American Civil War, but enough about battles. Who's reading something cheerful?" asked Jean.

"An article about Roy Rogers. He's so dreamy, and Trigger is such a smart horse," said Peggy, holding up her *Life* magazine.

Binxie grinned. "A flight manual. Fascinating plot."

Isabel whispered, "I can't concentrate on reading anymore."

"I'm out of books," said Helene. "I can't get to the library until Saturday. Dan's taking me. But I need something now. Last night, I was so desperate I read our farmerette handbook."

Jean knew that feeling. "You've gone through almost every book I own, unless you want to read an atlas."

Helene smiled. "Maybe another time."

Jean hesitated. "I have one other book…*Sonnets from the Portuguese*." She caught Binxie's slight movement of surprise. "Are you interested?"

"Poetry! Yes."

"Follow me to the house after, and I'll give it to you."

"I'd like to read that too, sometime," Binxie said quietly.

"Oh—" Jean began.

But Isabel softly recited, "'How do I love thee? Let me count the ways. I love thee to the depth and breadth and height my soul can reach.' Billy once read that to me."

They all needed a distraction. Jean took a deep breath and provided it. "My book belonged to Polly. James gave it to her."

Peggy and Helene sat up, stared at Jean, eager for more information. Binxie said what they all wondered. "You've found out more?"

Jean shook her head. "Only that neither James Earnshaw nor any other Earnshaw ever lived around here. He must have been passing through, visiting."

"Maybe he was stationed at the air base," said Isabel.

"It wasn't there in the Great War," said Jean.

"James is a dead end." Peggy sighed. "If only there were some giant telephone directory where we could just look him up. It's the same with Polly. I've quizzed everyone about all the Pollys around here, but none of them fits. How do two people just disappear like that?"

"We're back to Nelly. Can we find that cousin in Philadelphia she visited?" Binxie suggested.

"Even if someone knew her name and address, and even if she still lived there, what would we write? 'You don't know me, but did your cousin have a baby a quarter century ago?' Not likely," said Jean.

"Then what's next?" Binxie asked cautiously.

Jean smiled at her. "It's okay. It's going to take all of us to solve this."

"Where did you find the first clue?" asked Helene.

"In Nelly's house," answered Peggy.

"Then that's where we need to go for our next clue," said Helene.

"Actually, that's where we discovered our second one too," said Binxie. "The poetry book."

"This weekend..." Jean spoke louder as the sound of a car coming down the lane dulled her words. "...let's go to Nelly's. We can say we're cleaning the house, getting it ready for Rob. It needs to be done anyway."

A car door slammed nearby and a cheery Australian voice shouted, "Hallo! Anybody here?"

Several other farmerettes answered him as they appeared from various directions. Hugh's charm and dark good looks were irresistible.

"Is Jean here?"

She couldn't help it—her heart actually fluttered.

The five girls stood up and approached Hugh.

"You're still here, soldier?" teased Binxie.

"Navigator. Air force. Not for long. We get orders next week."

A chill stabbed Jean's spine like a bayonet. How many more people could she stand to worry about? Especially this one, with his blue, blue eyes and saucy grin, eagerly regarding her.

"Care to step into my coach and ride to the lake to watch the sunset, m'lady?" He bowed and swept his arm toward his dusty jeep.

"How did you get that jeep?"

Hugh winked.

"If I drive with you, is some MP going to arrest us for stealing it?" Jean tried to sound severe, but she couldn't help smiling.

Hugh looked wounded. "I do like your loving ways. But, this is legit. My flight officer owes me a favor. Coming?" He opened the passenger door.

"Helene, if you want that book, go to the house and ask Dad to give it to you." Jean stepped into the jeep. As Hugh circled to the driver's side, a truck chugged into the yard. *This place is becoming a highway,* she thought, and turned to see Johnny.

She stiffened as he climbed from his truck. Why did people drop in without warning?

As Johnny crossed the yard, he noticed Hugh and Jean in the car. He paused a second, then waved at her as cheerfully as always. Jean waved back and watched him continue walking toward Binxie.

Hugh hopped into the jeep, started the engine, and steered down the lane. Behind them, Jean saw Binxie and Johnny climb into his truck.

Hugh chatted while Jean wondered—*did Johnny come to visit me or Binxie?* If he had come first, for her, which boy would she have chosen?

Isabel

Isabel watched the vehicles carrying the two couples down the road, twisted her ring, and sighed. She had so loved being half of the golden pair in Guelph. She and Billy had done almost everything together. But Billy was gone. Twice gone. Had he lived, he would have shared his life with Norah and their child.

She gazed at her ring, once so full of promise. She touched its hard, sharp surface. Was it foolish to still wear it? No. It had been put on her finger with love and hope. She couldn't forget that day, the joy in Billy's brown eyes. She'd try to forget his betrayal—it was this stupid war's fault—and remember only their love. His ring was the only connection she still had with him, and she would treasure it for the rest of her life.

Isabel felt Peggy touch her arm. "Let's go in and play cards. I have a new Perry Como record to listen to."

Isabel was glad to be back. The girls were concerned but not smothering. At home one more careful word, one more look of sympathy would have driven her crazy. She hated being dishonest with her friends, acting as if Billy had been faithful, but she couldn't bear to tell them of his betrayal, her shame.

Helpless Itsy didn't exist here. She had worked hard to learn how to bake in Nanny's kitchen. So many girls welcomed her back, told her how much they missed her and her meals. Cookie yelled at her for peeling too much skin off the potatoes yesterday, and for spilling flour this morning. It felt good.

"Can the cards wait a minute?" asked Helene. "I want to fetch that book first."

"Sure. I'll check if my clothes are dry," said Peggy.

"I'll come with you," Isabel told Helene. "I haven't said hello to Nanny yet."

The two walked to the farmhouse while Peggy headed for the clothesline.

"Can we go this way?" Isabel pointed at the route farthest from the chicken area. Cracker had already welcomed her back yesterday, flapping his wings at her, screeching hideously until Gus drove him away with a shovel.

Mr. McDonnell invited them in. "Jean's out and Mrs. McDonnell and my mother are at their ladies' group, knitting for the boys. You'll do a better job finding that book than I will. It's likely in the parlor."

They found it easily, and said good-bye.

"We sure were sorry to hear about your young man," said Mr. McDonnell at the door. "Too much of that has happened around here already. Such a waste." He shook his head.

"Thank you." Isabel clenched her face into a smile.

"Nanny's looking forward to continuing the baking lessons."

From the corner of her eye, Isabel caught Helene's quick glance her way. But she knew her secret was safe with Helene.

"Well, goodnight, girls. Hope you enjoy the book."

As they crossed the farmyard, they saw Peggy waiting for them outside the dorm. She was still nervous about facing the others alone.

It dawned on Isabel that she wasn't the only one hurting. Peggy had lost some of her spontaneous sense of fun. Jean's family worried about Rob; Mr. McDonnell would never completely recover from his heart attack. The Grants had lost two nephews at Dieppe. Binxie and most of the girls here prayed every day for someone fighting overseas. What would they say if they knew how Billy had really died?

Jean

Jean strolled beside Hugh, intensely aware of everything about him—his masculine scent of soap and spicy aftershave, that flashing smile, his way of guiding her over rough spots along the beach. The setting sun reflected in the lake might have been beautiful to see, but she noticed only his blue eyes intent upon her. He was an excellent listener as they compared stories about their lives.

"Then there's Cracker, the nastiest rooster in the land," she said. "We got him after our last rooster, a gentle old fellow, was taken by a hawk. Nothing would dare tangle with Cracker. He actually lies in wait for victims. Once he's terrified them into running, he jumps up and catapults himself at them, so his spurs can take a chunk from their leg."

Hugh replied, "He must be related to a cat we once had. Slashed whatever annoyed her, man or beast. Scared us all."

Jean talked about Rob. He spoke about his three sisters and young brother with such affection she wondered how she could ever have thought him a dandy.

She could have listened all night to his descriptions of life on their sheep station in Australia, the animals, the plants, with his irreverent wit and Aussie accent. "Australia," she sighed. "It sounds so exciting, so beautiful."

He took her hand to help her over a fallen log, and she let him, even though she'd hopped over logs all her life. She was so aware of her hand still in his that the lake could have disappeared and she wouldn't have noticed.

But Hugh stopped to gaze at the rose-tinted heaven above, then at the golden fields behind them.

Jean smiled. "Not as exotic as Australia, but it is lovely."

Hugh faced her. "Beauty around me, beauty in front of me."

"Now, that's corny," said Jean, embarrassed.

"But true." Hugh touched her cheek. She lifted her face and his lips met hers, the first touch electric, then delicious.

They wrapped their arms around each other and kept kissing. Her mouth, her arms, her entire body wanted him—to stay connected, desired and desiring, intensely alive. They kissed for a minute, an hour, a day—she had no idea how long, but she wanted it to go on forever.

He stopped, leaned back, and regarded her with warm indigo eyes. "We better go before it's too dark to see," he said reluctantly.

Hand in hand, they retraced their steps. She had always assumed her first kiss would be with Johnny, though none of her dreams had warned her how amazing a kiss really is.

Hugh squeezed her hand and said something funny, and all her thoughts flashed back to him like a magnet.

At the jeep, they kissed again for a long wonderful moment before they turned into the laneway at Highberry Farm. Jean would have stayed there all night, but Hugh put the car back into gear.

"I have to have the jeep back by midnight."

"Oh."

"You look disappointed," he said with a broad smile, and reached for her again. Finally, reluctantly he let her go and continued driving to the house.

The yard was deserted as Hugh opened the car door for her. A quick peck on the cheek, the promise of more, then he sped away.

Not ready for sleep, Jean sat on the front porch swing. The warm night embraced her as she savored the memory of the evening, waiting for her heart and mind to slow down. Both the moon and stars hid behind clouds, leaving the night velvety black, but she was sure the glow she felt inside could light up the whole farm.

Just as she considered going to bed, she heard the truck squelching up the driveway. It parked in front of the dorm. No one could see her here on the dark porch. She watched Binxie and Johnny climb out and kiss goodnight. Knowing how she had felt with Hugh earlier, Jean wanted her friends to be happy too. So why was she shifting uncomfortably in her seat?

SATURDAY, AUGUST 7, 1943

Peggy

Peggy straightened the newspaper, but before she could hang it back onto its dowel, a young farmer took it from her. The little library was full of people looking for the latest reports from the front.

He skimmed the headlines and whistled softly. "Good news, eh?"

Peggy nodded. The articles were jubilant—Soviet forces had recently repulsed the German army near Kursk. It was the first battle in which a blitzkrieg was defeated before it could break through enemy defenses.

Operation Gomorrah had just destroyed Hamburg, city of many industries, oil refineries, shipyards, and U-boat pens. The bombs created the greatest firestorm in history, a 1,500-foot-high tornado of fire that incinerated German armament production. It also killed thousands of civilians. The Battle of the

Ruhr had begun—British bombers conducted night bombings over Germany, and American squadrons flew daylight attacks.

Let that end this horrible war, Peggy prayed. *Let the Allies win fast and let this killing stop.* She thought again of Michael and Donny, both determined to fight for their country, leaving their families broken with grief, of Billy snuffed out before he and Isabel could begin their life together.

She even felt bad for Harry Rayner, about to join it all. He'd been at Romeo's last night, the first time she'd had the courage to go there again. He arrived looking taller, more important in his smartly pressed brown uniform. "I leave for Camp Borden in the morning," he announced.

The girls flocked around him with admiration and good wishes. He managed a dance with most of them, but as the evening neared its end, he and Stella clutched each other ever more tightly on the dance floor, then slipped outside for air. On his way out, he'd told Peggy, "I'll show your buddies what we do to Nazis."

She turned her back on him, relieved when another fellow pulled her away to dance.

"Don't mind him," he said. "We all know you're not one of those people."

Peggy had smiled at him gratefully; he meant well.

Now Peggy reached for a *Ladies' Home Journal*. She tried to read, but couldn't concentrate, and was relieved when Helene finally checked out her books.

"Ready for ice cream? The others should be there by now. Dan's joining us."

Peggy smiled at her friend. Lately Helene had a radiance

about her. Her quiet competence now included more confidence. Jean, Binxie, Doris, and Ruth had each coupled up too. Funny, she'd always thought Jean and Johnny belonged together, but Hugh was a sweetheart, and this war changed the paths of so many lives.

Isabel followed them outside, clutching a bulky cookbook.

"Another glorious, sunny day," said Helene.

"All the more glorious because we're not picking anything," answered Peggy.

"I just found some wonderful recipes," said Isabel. "I think I'll try a trifle for Binxie's birthday on Thursday."

"Mmm, delicious," Helene said. "She'll turn eighteen. Old enough to go."

Peggy nodded. *Another friend to worry about.*

Isabel looked sad. "It's the seventh today? We have only four weeks left, and then…"

She stopped talking, but Peggy guessed she was wondering what to do with her life after she got home.

Although Peggy would be sorry to leave here too, she looked forward to her last year in high school. She'd be a senior, with new clothes and a pretty tan. She was sure she'd grown an inch taller too.

Helene was telling Isabel, "You're such a good cook. Your family will appreciate that when you get home."

Isabel sighed and shook her head. "My mother will never share her kitchen."

"There must be somewhere else you can use your talent. I think there's a school in Guelph that teaches cooking and homemaking."

Typical Helene, thought Peggy. Always seeing education as the answer. It worried her. She knew how desperately Helene wanted to finish grade thirteen. She wanted to spend their last year of high school with her best friend, but the news from home wasn't getting better. Helene's mother had a new boarder, more rent. But then a water pipe burst and the plumber's bill had used up most of August's bank payment. Helene's mother was working extra shifts at Firestone. Ever since she'd found out, Helene filled baskets of fruit at a ferocious rate.

"You're looking too serious today," said Helene as they neared Linton's Drug Store. "Are you all right?"

Peggy smiled. "I'm fine, just thinking too much."

Helene avoided an obvious joke, and squeezed Peggy's hand instead. She paused, then opened the door to the drug store. Dan waited, a silly grin on his face.

The seats were filled with Saturday shoppers, and a table of farmerettes. Kate waved and Binxie moved over to make room. Peggy and Isabel slid in beside her and Helene joined Dan at the counter.

Soon everyone was savoring cold, sweet sundaes and talking.

In a brief lull in the conversation, the words behind them sounded loud. "Why, that's crazier than Old Nelly!"

Peggy and Binxie looked at each other, then turned to see two old women—Granny Grant and a farmwife with fluffy white hair—gossiping over ice cream.

"You knew Nelly?" asked Peggy. Excitement raised her voice a pitch.

Granny Grant squinted at her through thick glasses and spoke in a hoarse voice. "You're the girls who work for my son?"

"Yes," answered Binxie. "He's kind to us."

"You're hard workers. He likes the lot of you." She faced her companion. "Irma, these are Hiram's farmerettes."

Irma smiled at them through a mouthful of ice cream.

"Thank you. Pleased to meet you both," said Peggy. Did you say you knew Miss Nelly Turner?" Maybe, finally, they'd get a clue.

"Sat behind her in church for years," Mrs. Grant said. "Her family always sat in the second row. She never said more than a frosty hello to me." She ate another spoonful of ice cream and continued. "Too snooty to talk to us farm girls."

Irma added, "Lot of good those airs did her. She ended her life bitter and alone, her suitcase packed for a beau who never came."

Irma seemed to enjoy giving information to fresh ears. "Her best friend was that white horse she rode everywhere. Her brothers married and moved away, her parents passed on, even the horse eventually died. She lived alone for the rest of her days."

Not to be outdone, Mrs. Grant added, "She was friendly with a hired girl awhile, until they had a falling out and she fired her. Nelly went to Philadelphia after that and came back more stuck-up than ever."

Philadelphia! Peggy almost jumped out of her seat. "When did she go there?"

Irma and Mrs. Grant looked at each other, their eyes squinted in calculations.

"She wasn't here when the Great War ended. Must have been around then," said Irma.

"She was back here for the Christmas service. Wore a fancy blue dress and a new hairstyle," said Mrs. Grant.

Irma continued, "She got crankier and crazier every year—stopped going to church, wouldn't take help from anyone except Mrs. McDonnell and Reverend Ralston."

"That's sad," said Binxie. "Who was the hired girl?"

Mrs. Grant shrugged. "Her family had so many over the years. Girls from away, or sometimes the orphanage. They'd stay a year or two, then move on to better jobs in the city. A couple of them married local boys. Oh, who were they, Irma?"

"I think there was a Hetty, an Annie, a Mary or two, that saucy little Vaunie. Oh, and Jane Freeman, lives in Beamsville now. Can't remember any more. My mind's still sharp but my memory's faded some."

Peggy was disappointed. She'd so hoped to hear Polly.

"Why are you interested?" asked Mrs. Grant.

"Oh, we love local history," said Binxie. "We've heard some Nelly stories and we wondered how true they were."

"Well, some have gotten out of hand, but you can believe a lot of them. I know the one about the tablecloths is true. I was in Jackman's one January when she stood there, insisting on a round one, the exact same size as last year's. It had to be dark. She kicked up a real fuss to get what she wanted. Whoever heard of buying a new tablecloth every year?"

"If you like our history," interrupted Mrs. Grant, "you should learn about the Smiths, the Beldings, and the Puddicombes. Now, they're interesting. So's the story of how our town was named for Winona, the Indian Princess. She jumped over the falls rather than marry a suitor she didn't love."

For the next half hour the women told stories of local history in minute detail. When Helene finally came over to say it was time to go, the girls smiled with relief and thanked the two old women.

"That was fun," said Irma. "Next time we see you, we'll tell you more."

You're sweet, thought Peggy, *but next time I see you, I'll hide.* She was frustrated. Somewhere in all those tales was a clue. They just had to figure out what it was.

"I'm sure one of the hired girls was Polly," said Peggy as they headed out of town.

"But a hired girl wouldn't have left her love letters in her old employer's home," said Binxie. "That Philadelphia visit. It still looks like those letters, that poor baby, were Nelly's."

"How could they be? You read the letters, saw the love poems—Polly sounded sweet."

The girls debated until they ran out of theories. Then they moved on to other topics, enjoying the sunshine and each other's company. Life was good on a farm in Canada.

TUESDAY, AUGUST 10, 1943

Helene

Helene smiled at Mrs. Fraser. "Thank you again," she said. "Those fruits and vegetables will mean everything to my family. I don't know how to ever repay you."

"Nonsense. It's a plentiful harvest this year—more than I need. I'm driving into Hamilton tomorrow anyway."

Helene said good-bye and climbed into Dan's truck. As they

drove away, she waved at the proud silver-haired woman standing in her yard. She turned to Dan and said, "She's wonderful."

"That's Mrs. Fraser. Mind bright as a diamond, tongue
sharp as steel, and a heart of gold."

"A jewel. You really care for her."

"She's looked out for me ever since I fell through the ice
on her pond when I was nine. After my mom died, she became
my second family, even wrote to me overseas. I'd rather be with
her than at home."

Helene thought how much she enjoyed spending time with
Willy and Peter, of her mother's quiet love and support. She
couldn't imagine not wanting to be with family, and her heart
ached for Dan.

He continued, "My mother was gentle, kind. She taught
us to read and sing and appreciate nature. When she died, the
light left our house. Dad got grumpier; eventually both Paul
and I enlisted."

"Paul?"

"My other brother. He's fighting in Africa. There are four
of us."

"You're all as gruff at home as in the fields?"

Dan tried to smile but his lips pinched into a line. "Dad's
lonely, unhappy. My brothers are decent fellows. They went
overboard teasing you when they knew I was soft on you."

Helene couldn't help smiling inside. His words took the
pain out of the water incident in the orchard. "Both our fathers
have disappointed us," she said wistfully.

"At least yours left," Dan said. His low tone couldn't mask
the bitterness. "Mine stayed, criticizing every little mistake,

beating me for big ones, until I grew too tall. Since Mom died, I'm not comfortable at the farm, but where do I go? Who'll hire a limping man whose right arm is close to useless?"

"What about something else?"

"Leave the farm? It's in my blood." He thought a moment. "Actually, it's the land I love. I plan to own some one day. But I don't want to farm full time. I'm saving for university. When I heard you talk to Mrs. Fraser about teaching young people, I realized I'd like that too—if I had the education, the money." Dan stepped on the brake as a rabbit hopped across the road. He shook his head as if he had just woken up. "I'm sorry. That was a pathetic display of self-pity."

Helene stayed quiet. She'd never heard him so discouraged.

"I'll take you home, Helene. I'm not pleasant company today."

"Why today?" she asked gently.

He hesitated. "August tenth. Four years since my mother passed away."

His melancholy left no space in the truck for words, so she held his hand. After a silent mile, she suggested, "Do you want to visit her?"

"Will you come with me?"

She nodded.

Soon Dan turned down a narrow gravel road. On the left stood orchards full of goldenrod and ripening peach trees. On the right a low stone wall enclosed a "stone orchard" lined with graves. He parked the truck by the side of the road. Without a word, Helene slid from the seat, picked some wildflowers, and joined Dan through the wooden gates. He took her hand as they walked along the rows. They stopped at a small granite stone marked simply *Mary Patience Scranton, beloved wife and mother. February 8, 1895–August 10, 1939.* Underneath that, Alfred Scranton's name was already engraved, ready to join his wife.

Dan knelt to lay the flowers on his mother's grave, then stood upright, head bowed, deep in memories.

Helene looked at his mother's name again. Something about the "M" and the "P" so close together made her think of Peggy or Margarete, as the other girls had discovered recently. Margarete to Peggy—*M* to *P.* Weren't girls named Mary sometimes called Polly? So far all their Pollys had come to a dead end. Should they be looking for a Mary?

The thought almost overwhelmed her. The search had widened—perhaps too far—Mary was a common name. But maybe now they'd find the girl who owned those long-lost letters.

THURSDAY, AUGUST 12, 1943

Binxie

"Happy birthday!"

Binxie woke up to Helene's cheery greeting. Then Peggy and Isabel chimed in. Bright beams of sunlight streamed through the windows. It was going to be a glorious day.

She grinned at her friends. "I'm eighteen! I can sign up!"

"Not today," said Peggy. "We have plans for you."

"You're not leaving!" gasped Isabel.

"Not yet," Binxie reassured her. "But come September, I'm off to the skies."

"You can't even fly yet," said Isabel.

Binxie frowned. It was high time to organize all that, but this summer was so busy. "Once I get back to Toronto, I'll sign up for lessons," she vowed. "By spring I'll be in England."

Helene shuddered. "I pray the war's over before that."

"Then I'll work for Kathryn and Alastair's air transport company."

"You've mapped out your life already," said Isabel wistfully.

"We should control our lives, Isabel. I'll live my own goals, not my parents' plan for me to attend college to marry well, so I can spend my days chairing committees and social events."

Peggy laughed. "A rich husband sounds okay to me. Now get up. I know we celebrated your birthday on August 1st with the rest of the farmerettes, but today we'll have our own celebration. Isabel made your favorite breakfast—pancakes with blueberries. See you downstairs in twenty minutes."

It was the beginning of a perfect day. The sun shone kindly on them as they picked peaches at the Beldings' orchards. The girls were especially jolly, and on the way home, Mr. Belding stopped to buy ice cream for all.

Back at the dorm, Binxie opened her presents. Her parents sent clothes, toiletries, and a camera with several rolls of film. Binxie read Kathryn's birthday card, wishing she were here to say the words in person. Her gift was a white woolen scarf. *A racy flying scarf—it gets blooming cold up there*, Kathryn had written. *I knit it myself, as you'll quickly see by the uneven rows.* Binxie wrapped it around her neck. Knowing how much Kathryn disliked domestic activities, she understood this was a labor of love.

She took her camera outside and snapped her friends posing and clowning for her. She'd send Kathryn those pictures and some of the farm, Cairo, Tinxie, and, of course, Johnny.

Somehow Isabel had persuaded Cookie to prepare Binxie's favorite meal tonight—roast beef with browned potatoes, baby peas, and a delicious trifle for dessert.

Right after dinner, she showered, put on the new blue dress from her mother, styled her hair for tonight's date with Johnny, and went downstairs to wait.

Jean knocked at the screen door, carrying a magazine. "Happy birthday, Binxie. This is just a small gift. There's a story about Amelia Earhart in it."

Binxie swallowed hard. "Thank you. That was really thoughtful." She hadn't seen much of Jean lately—between work, and Hugh and Johnny's visits, it was awkward to find the time. "Can we walk tomorrow? I miss our excursions."

Jean nodded. "I'd like that."

Johnny drove up. Jean waved at him cheerfully, and headed for the barn.

"Happy birthday." Johnny kissed her. "I wangled a car for tonight. We can go dancing in Stoney Creek. There's a great place by the lake."

"That sounds wonderful."

And it was. They laughed as they stepped and swung to the jazzy music, and held each other tight for the slow songs. At the first notes of "Stardust," Johnny led her out to the terrace, where they danced under stars shimmering in a sable sky. Johnny gazed at her, his brown eyes tender, and he leaned in and kissed her. She pressed closer, felt her breasts crush against the heat of his body, her hips move with his. Later, they walked along the beach arm in arm, the bright moon reflected in the velvet water beside them. She was intensely aware of Johnny's arm around her, his deep voice humming the "Stardust" melody.

One more dance and it was time to head home. Along the lane to Highberry Farm, Johnny stopped the car and took her in his arms. His lips touched hers, gently at first then more urgently, and Binxie answered with a passion she didn't know she possessed. A minute later she pulled back.

Johnny smiled, stroked her hair, and asked, "Did you enjoy your day?"

"It was perfect," she answered and kissed him again.

Finally they said goodnight, and she went inside still feeling his lips, his arms, his body. As she slipped into bed, Binxie wondered how it would feel to lie next to him. Finally she reached for her flying scarf, hugged it to her heart, and thought about her lovely day. It was the best birthday of her life.

SATURDAY, AUGUST 14, 1943

Jean

Jean carried a bushel basket of early tomatoes from the family garden, thinking of the delicious sauce her mother would make with them.

"Need some help?" Johnny came up behind her and took the basket.

"Thanks. I didn't see you coming."

"You were concentrating on the tomatoes. I had some time off and thought I'd see if Binxie's around."

"She walked to town after lunch but she should be back soon."

"May I wait? It's been awhile since I've talked with you," he said, carrying the basket into the kitchen, where Isabel and Nanny were pulling cinnamon rolls from the oven.

"Hmmm, they smell terrific," said Johnny, smiling at the two women.

Nanny flushed with pleasure. "You may try one when they cool."

Jean poured two glasses of milk, gingerly pushed four hot cinnamon rolls onto a plate, and led the way to the porch.

When they sat, Johnny bit into a roll and rolled his eyes in mock ecstasy. "No one beats Nanny's cinnamon rolls."

"Isabel made these."

"She learned well. How's she doing?"

Jean shook her head. "Sad, brave, but something else too. She's holding something back."

"And Rob?"

"He writes he's fine, that everything is fine, but that's likely all he can say. I wish I really knew."

"He'll be home soon. We just sent the Germans and Italians running across the Messina Strait to Italy. Rome is on the verge of defeat. It's the beginning of the end."

"Oh, I hope so," answered Jean. "Prime Minister Mackenzie King is meeting with Winston Churchill and President Roosevelt in Quebec City this week. The faster they figure out how to win this war, bring Rob and our boys home, the better."

"You're smart to get Rob's house ready for him."

"His house ready?"

"Crazy Nelly's place."

"Uncle Ian repaired the chimney after the storm. We haven't done anything since."

"Oh? I saw a bike parked there last week, and the door wide open yesterday. Figured you were fixing the place up."

Jean looked puzzled. "It's odd, I noticed someone was there a few weeks ago. Why? And who?"

"Someone searching for the rumored treasure?" Johnny laughed.

"They better not." But it made Jean wonder. No one really believed Nelly had a fortune hidden, but maybe someone was searching for a different treasure—old love letters. Could James or Polly have returned? "We'll keep an eye on the place. What's new with you?"

"I bought my first two calves yesterday. Aberdeen Angus."

"Good start. They're supposed to have excellent meat."

Isabel stepped out onto the porch, said good-bye to Jean, scowled at Johnny, then walked across the barnyard.

"Have I offended her?" Johnny asked.

Jean shrugged. "She's grieving."

When Johnny talked about his plans for his cows, Jean didn't mention that Hugh had hundreds of Black Angus on his ranch. Instead, she told him Dad had finally received the part for the tractor. Now the horses could have a break. She finished her cinnamon roll, and turned her face to the sun. How comfortable it felt to chat here on the porch with Johnny.

Before either one could say more, a high-pitched scream of terror rose from the barnyard.

Isabel

Isabel took off her apron, brushed white flour from her skirt, and smiled at Nanny. "Thanks again for your help with the cinnamon rolls. I'll bake more in the kitchen tomorrow, and the girls will love them."

Billy would have loved them too, she thought. But then she wondered, *Why am I still learning to cook like this? Billy's gone.*

The answer swooped upon her. *Because I love doing this. I like sliding a perfect pie from the oven. Watching everyone enjoy my food makes me happy.*

Nanny interrupted her thoughts. "I was named best baker at the county fall fair for ten years."

"I'm sure that's true," Isabel agreed.

Nanny looked pleased. "It's good to have someone appreciate my work. Someone worthy of learning my skills and secrets."

"Mother, we appreciate it," said Mrs. McDonnell, entering the kitchen. "I have neither the time nor the talent to bake like you do, so I'm grateful." She dropped some muddy new potatoes on the counter, washed her hands, and picked up a hot roll to nibble. "Mmm, perfect."

"They'll taste better after the war, when we get decent flour again," grumbled Nanny.

"Hello, Isabel," said Mrs. McDonnell. "These are delicious."

"Thank you. I'll know so much when I get home." Isabel sighed.

Mrs. McDonnell nodded kindly and washed the potatoes at the sink.

"Would you like a hand with those?" Isabel wanted to keep busy.

"Everything's almost ready, thank you," said Mrs. McDonnell. "Go enjoy your time off."

With a last wipe of the counter, Isabel said good-bye and left. The day was bright, but Isabel felt dark. No dinner duty today, no letters to read, none to write. Most of the girls were in town, or had gone to play baseball at a neighboring farm. This evening they'd go to Romeo's.

They had invited her but she wasn't going. "I can't dance when Billy lies buried in Italy," she'd replied.

"I don't want you to spend the evening alone," Peggy had said.

"I'll be fine." Isabel touched her friend's arm. "I'll finish knitting some socks and get to bed early. Breakfast shift at the crack of dawn tomorrow." Isabel sighed. Being the brave widow of a man who betrayed her was exhausting and dull.

Now Isabel blinked in the sunlight, then crossed the porch, where Johnny and Jean sat munching her rolls and discussing cows.

Isabel said good-bye to Jean but scowled at Johnny. *He's as bad as Billy,* she thought. *Carrying on with two girls. Except, of course, he didn't promised to marry one of them.* She rubbed her diamond against her apron to make it gleam. Billy had meant it when he gave her that ring, and he would have kept his promise—it was the war that broke it. She'd never tell anyone here about Billy's deceit.

Across the barnyard she saw Binxie coming up the driveway, carrying a bag, heading for the dorm. When Binxie saw the couple on the porch, her gait slowed only a second.

Isabel took her usual long route to avoid Cracker and

wondered, *Is this what war does to men? Johnny wasn't away fighting, but everyone knew he went back to the registration office every month, hoping they would accept him one day.* Did war make boys greedy to taste as much life as possible while they could, no matter whom they hurt?

A horrendous screech burst Isabel's thoughts. Giant flapping wings rushed from behind the tractor, where he had lain in wait for her. The rooster's sharp beak stabbed forward as he shrieked threats at her. Isabel backed away. Cracker's chest puffed out, his wings spread even wider, to double his size, his red wattle shook.

Terrified, Isabel ran.

The rooster launched himself into the air. His legs thrust toward Isabel at an angle, his claws ready to rip and maim.

Isabel dodged. The rooster missed by an inch. Hissing and pecking furiously, he chased her even faster.

Suddenly Mrs. McDonnell raced toward them. She grabbed the ax from the woodpile, seized Cracker by the neck, and in one clean stroke, she chopped off his head. His headless body dropped, then strutted in circles around the yard, blood soaking his feathers.

Isabel stood paralyzed as Mrs. McDonnell tossed the head aside and found a piece of rope. When Cracker finally collapsed, she grabbed him by the legs, looped the rope around them, and hung him from the branch of a tree to drain. He dangled there, suddenly small, his wings drooping lifeless, his blood dripping and forming a pool on the ground below.

Mrs. McDonnell tossed the ax onto the woodpile and looked at Isabel, whose eyes were wide in horror, mouth agape.

"I've had enough of his nonsense," she said. "He'll be stew tomorrow night. You're all right now." She headed back inside.

The terror, the blood, the body dangling from the tree—Isabel sank to the ground and sobbed hysterically.

Binxie ran to her, with Jean and Johnny close behind. Binxie held her, murmuring comforting words. When Isabel had calmed down, Binxie helped her up and led her inside to a chair. She brought a damp, cool cloth and gently wiped her face.

"I can't stand it anymore," Isabel sobbed. "It's not fair," she moaned over and over again.

"You're bearing too much," Binxie cooed. "Billy should never have been killed."

"Billy!" Isabel spat out the name.

Binxie looked shocked.

"Billy, my faithful love? My hero? You think he died courageously fighting the enemy, true to his fiancée?"

Looking confused, Binxie tried to soothe her.

"No. He was splashing in the warm waters of the Adriatic Sea. Got caught in the undertow and drowned. My hero died playing water polo with his buddies." She sobbed again while Binxie stroked her head helplessly.

Isabel sat up, her face stony. "There's more." She blurted out the words. "He met another woman in England. Norah. Married her before he went to Italy. She's expecting his baby." Out loud, it sounded worse.

Binxie sat in stunned silence.

After awhile, Isabel spoke. "Will you tell Peggy and Helene for me? And Jean. They should know, and I can't say it again. But please don't tell the other girls. It's too humiliating."

Binxie nodded and looked down at Isabel's finger.

"You're wondering why I still wear his ring."

Binxie shrugged. "It comforts you."

"When Billy gave it to me, we loved each other. That's what I want to remember. I've belonged with Billy so long I don't know how else to live. This ring keeps me joined to him. It's all I have left, and it means everything."

Binxie looked at her friend. "It's better to remember him with love, but…"

"It wasn't his fault. It was this war. I'll never love anyone but him."

Binxie nodded, stood up, and put away the damp cloth.

X

She couldn't bear to see Isabel in pain any longer. She had come home from the baseball game to see the hanging rooster and hear the story. She wished she could be the one to console Isabel.

Frustrated, she took her sketchbook to the orchard to get the images of the rooster and Isabel's sad, red eyes from her mind. Would anyone ever love her as Isabel loved Billy? Jean and Hugh, Binxie and Johnny, Helene and Dan, Stella and Harry, Doris and Jack. Girls and boys paired off together, the way it was supposed to be. Why not her?

She drew lacy wildflowers and peaches hanging fat and ripe from the trees. The sumacs were turning red, and here and there a yellow leaf drifted to the ground. Signs of autumn. In three weeks she would have to go home. Life on the farm had been good—but it hadn't cured her. What would greet her when she returned to school? Suspicious looks? Shame? She couldn't face it all again.

SUNDAY, AUGUST 15, 1943

Jean

Jean stretched her legs on the blanket and sighed. A blue sky streaked with rose glowed above her, the waves on the deep aqua lake rolled in nearby. Golden fields, peace, and beauty surrounded her.

"Are you happy, darling?" Hugh asked.

She smiled at him, his arm warm around her, the taste of his kisses still on her mouth. She loved being with Hugh. She loved his laugh, his charm, the way he missed his family, his unpredictability. One day he brought her flowers, the next he took her rowing on the lake, singing silly songs. Yesterday he snuck her onto the base to see the planes. They sat in one, pretended to take flight, ducked when a guard passed by, then cuddled and necked awhile.

Now he pulled her closer. Kissed her nose, her cheek, her ear. She giggled and wrapped her arms around him again. His body felt firm, his mouth soft. He stroked her back, slowly lowered her onto the blanket. His hand slid to her front.

Her entire being focused on that hand and how good it felt. She yearned for more. When he reached lower, nothing existed but his hand.

But Polly flashed through her mind. Reluctantly she sat up.

Hugh gazed at her, hunger, love, frustration in his eyes. "I love you."

"I can't. It's not right."

Hugh collected himself. "I'm sorry. It's just that I'm leaving Wednesday for England."

It felt like a slap. Wednesday. Only three more days. How would she ever let him go? How could she stand him going—to war, then back to Australia. She'd never see him again. The thought was too terrible. Her lip quivered.

His sincere eyes, bluer than the sky, held hers. She so wanted to give him his loving farewell, to complete their love. But she knew what could happen. Afterward he'd be far away, and she'd be here, trying to cope. She shook her head. "I can't."

"I've never met a girl like you, Jean. You make me a better person."

She crushed him to her. "I'll miss you every minute."

"When this war ends, I'll come back for you."

Her heart lurched with hope. "Come back here?"

"Yes. To take you home with me."

She was too stunned to talk. Finally she croaked, "To Australia?"

"Yes. Marry me. We'll run the best ranch in New South Wales, have beautiful children, a wonderful life together. Jean, I love you so much."

"I love you too, Hugh," she whispered.

He drew her to him and they kissed again. The knowledge that they planned a future together but would soon be apart made them more passionate than tender.

But something, perhaps the thought of Polly and James, kept her upright. There would be time later—in Australia.

Helene

Helene and Isabel walked down the aisle and out of the church, the final verse of "Abide with Me" and the deep tones of the organ surrounding them with majesty and comfort. She was grateful there had been no sad names read out before the service today— for the sakes of the young men, their families, and for Isabel, who was so near the edge that another dead boy might push her over.

"Let's take the long way home," she suggested. "It's so lovely out."

Isabel's smile looked forced, but she was trying.

"May we escort you ladies home today?" The offer came from a boy with the shadow of a mustache, advertising he was almost ready to begin shaving. The boy beside him gazed at Isabel.

"That's kind of you, but we have lots of girls to walk with." Helene tried to let them down gently. Two local girls were glaring at them. *They'll be so happy when we leave in September,* she thought. That made her sad. Home in September. No more Dan, no more farm life, no funds to finish school, just a bleak future of drudgery in some factory.

"Why would they ask us?" asked Isabel as the boys left, defeated. "Do I act like I'd want to meet a fellow?"

"They were only being boys," Helene reassured her. "Everyone knows you're loyal to Billy." She'd said the wrong thing. Isabel twisted her ring and her lips quivered. They both knew she hadn't been the unfaithful one. It was hard to see Isabel so miserable when a whole glorious day with Dan lay ahead of her. He was picking her up after lunch.

Other girls joined them. As they walked home, Peggy entertained them with an imitation of Reverend Ralston, and a story about last night at Romeo's until finally even Isabel chuckled. Helene was glad Peggy was regaining her old exuberance.

Back at Highberry Farm, Helene had just changed into shorts and a blue shirt and was clattering down the stairs for lunch when Dan appeared at the screen door.

"You're early!" she said, delighted.

"Hoped you'd prefer a picnic," Dan said, smiling sheepishly.

Twenty minutes later, as he shook out a blanket beside a creek, he confessed, "Actually, I couldn't wait any longer to see you."

Helene helped him unpack the picnic hamper—two baloney sandwiches, some peaches, and a jug of apple cider. She decided next time she'd pack the meal. But it was lovely to eat in this peaceful grove alone with Dan, instead of with seventy chattering girls. They passed the cider jug back and forth.

"I should have packed cups," Dan apologized.

Helene refused the peaches. "I've picked too many of these furry little creatures. I itch just thinking about the fuzz on my hands, arms, and neck."

Dan laughed. "It was all I could find. I've had enough of them too, though I'll eat a peach pie any day."

"It's so beautiful here." Helene gazed at the water and the woods. "Can we take a walk?"

They followed the stream, talking about the new lighter ladders the Beldings used at their farm. "They're easier to move. It makes picking faster," said Helene.

"It's a bumper crop this year, in spite of the heat," said Dan. "We hope to buy another tractor—if we can find a decent used one."

"Who, your family, or Mrs. Fraser?"

"The Scrantons. Mrs. Fraser borrows her neighbor's."

"That's a big farm for her to look after."

"She rents most of her acreage to her neighbors on either side. Keeps just enough for a ring of privacy around her."

"She likes being alone?"

"She has plenty of church and choir friends, her quilting guild, and book club."

"No children?"

"No. She doesn't talk about that."

"What happened to her husband?"

Dan smiled. "You picked up her cross-examination skills. He was sick for a long time. Died two years ago."

"Sad. Wouldn't it be easier for her in the city?"

"She loves Winona. During most of their marriage they lived in other countries—her husband worked for the government—so they were happy to retire here. She taught at our local school a few years until Warren got sick, then stayed home to nurse him. He didn't know her near the end, but I think her voice reading to him soothed him."

Helene watched his tender expression as he spoke. "She's lucky she has you now."

He shrugged. "She's good to me."

"I like her too."

"You're her favorite. She admires your mother too. They and your brothers had a nice visit when she dropped off the vegetables."

The valley opened up before them and the sparkling stream meandered through the woods in glorious late-summer foliage. "I can see why she won't leave here," Helene sighed.

Dan took her hand as they turned to go back to the grove.

As they reached the blanket, he said, "You look exhausted. Sit down while I clear up our picnic things."

Before Helene could object, Dan kissed her into silence. "There isn't much to do."

"I don't know why I'm so tired."

"Could it be you're working like a demon, racing up and down ladders trying to out-pick everyone? You worry about everyone but yourself. Sit. Rest a minute."

Helene felt grateful that someone was looking after her for a change. As she sat, her eyes felt heavy.

When she awoke, Dan sat beside her, lost in a book.

She rubbed her eyes sleepily. "I'm sorry."

"You're beautiful asleep," he answered. "Except maybe when you're snoring."

"I wasn't!"

"I wanted to finish this chapter."

She squinted at the title of his book. *The Great Gatsby.* "You like it?"

"It's brilliant. I wish Matt and Luke would read it. They're missing so much."

"You're the only reader in your family?"

"My brother Paul too. He recommended this one. Says that's the only trouble with the army. No good books. So he writes letters the length of one."

"You miss him."

Dan nodded. "He's not a soldier. He's a poet. I'm saving all his letters for him. He'll write a great book about the war one day."

Helene sat up. "Maybe being creative is the way to cope

with the horrible things that happen in life. Maybe if my papa had that, he'd be okay now."

Dan shook his head. "Shell shock can't be cured with a story. When those bombs blast close to you, they jolt every cell in your body. You may look fine on the outside, but on the inside, your brains are scrambled."

Helene shuddered. "Papa still looked so handsome, so kind…" She thought about the last time she saw her father. He had been extra gentle that night to make up for his outburst at the twins that rainy morning. He told them a story and tucked them in with a kiss. After, he shared a cup of tea with her and encouraged her to follow her dream to become a teacher. Had he known then he wouldn't return? Had she told him she loved him?

Dan rubbed her shoulders. "What are you reading nowadays?"

She looked at his hazel eyes, felt his work-roughened hands so soft on her shoulders. Whatever Dan had experienced in the war may have scarred him horribly, but it hadn't taken away his kind nature. She smiled at him and quoted, "'How do I love thee? Let me count the ways. I love thee to the depth and breadth and height my soul can reach.'"

Dan looked at her and continued, "'I love thee with a love I seemed to lose with my lost saints. I love thee with the breath, smiles, tears, of all my life.'"

"Of course, you know it too," Helene teased.

"Why did you pick that one?" he asked.

"It touches me."

Seeing the expression on his face made her wish she hadn't quoted it. Did this remind him of an old girlfriend? Had he shared a blanket and poetry with her too?

He stayed silent a moment, then explained, "That was my mother's favorite poem. She recited it so often Paul and I wrote a melody for it. She hummed it sometimes while she worked in the garden." Dan looked at her so tenderly she thought her heart would melt. "I should have known you'd love it too."

Their kiss was gentle, then hungry, and lasted a long time. Finally, reluctantly, Dan leaned back. "Mrs. Fraser is waiting for us."

Helene stood up a little unsteadily. She shook out and folded the blanket, and carried it to the truck. They drove in contented silence.

As they approached the Fraser farm, Dan said, "I'd like to see that poem again. Is your book from the library?"

"No, it's Jean's."

"Would you, would she, mind if I borrowed it?"

Helene paused. That was the book Jean had found at Crazy Nelly's. Did she have the right to lend it? "Take it," she answered. How could she refuse when it meant so much to him?

Jean

Jean crossed the barnyard, deep in thought. When she saw Binxie coming her way, she lowered her gaze and walked faster. Binxie turned back and Jean hoped she hadn't hurt her feelings. She was so confused about everything—she had to think it through alone.

She headed for the orchard, the late afternoon sun casting

a warm glow on the peaches. It was peaceful here, and quiet. Only the empty ladders propped against the trees indicated the frenzy of activity here during the day.

There was so much to decide. First there was Hugh's proposal. Her pulse raced when she thought of him, of their kisses. Life with him would be exciting and she knew the warmth he was capable of. She loved him.

And Australia! She'd read everything about the continent down under, studied every map. His cattle station was located just outside Mandurah, close to the Indian Ocean. For so long she'd yearned to travel. Now her dream could come true. She was living a fairy tale. Hugh was certainly her Prince Charming. She looked at her dry, rough hands. She was no princess, but he made her feel like one.

But her fantasies of travel to distant places had never included leaving for good. She'd always assumed she'd return home. This was her land—had been since her great-grandfather Gordon McDonnell came here from Scotland and cleared it. Did she have the courage to begin brand-new in a strange place with other people, other customs? Hugh would be with her—and their children, eventually. They would forge a new life, a new heritage together, just like her great-grandparents had. She knew crops, cattle, the rhythm of the seasons. It wouldn't be that different.

Underneath that decision was the unceasing worry about Rob. She had heard about life in POW camps—the shortages, the brutality. It was every prisoner's duty to escape. If they were caught, they were shot. Would Rob try anything so brave and foolish? Was his leg really healing? Or was it festering untended, draining the life from him? Why, oh why had she lied to him about Fran?

Because he had annoyed her. He had been primping to go out with Fran on a Friday night while she sat reading a book.

"Why aren't you going out? There are lots of fellows at Romeo's tonight."

"Not interested," she said. "I've known them since they were runny-nosed kids."

"No, it's because you like Johnny," he'd teased. "Why don't you just tell him? Stop him from seeing other girls?"

She threw the lie at him playfully. "I hear Fran sees others too."

He laughed. "Not my Fran. She's crazy about me."

He was so smug, so sure, admiring himself in the mirror, she said more. "I'm sure she said that to the cute soldier I saw her with last night."

Rob snorted.

Jean wanted to wipe the smirk from his face. She tossed her book aside and said the worst thing she could think of. "I wonder if she told him that while his arm was wrapped around her at Linton's. He looked so good in that uniform."

Rob swore and stormed off. Jean's satisfaction ended when she heard the truck motor roar, the gravel spew, as he charged down the laneway. *I shouldn't have said that,* she thought when she heard him come home unusually early that night, *but it'll blow over by tomorrow.*

When she got up next morning, he was already gone. That afternoon, he arrived home tall with pride. "I've enlisted."

Jean begged him not to go. Told him she had never seen

Fran with anyone else, but Rob merely nodded and soon left for Camp Borden.

She thought of Fran—full of life, full of laughter. She should have been at the train station kissing Rob good-bye, waving and weeping like the other girls, as the train disappeared down the track. But she wasn't. Since then, Fran had been out flirting with other fellows. Perhaps her fib had been true after all.

But she should never have thrown that at her brother, should never have made him go off to war, get injured, be taken prisoner. *Your fault, your fault, your fault*—the words pounded into her with every step she took.

Now someone was breaking into Rob's place. Perhaps stealing from the house he planned to repair and turn into a home for the family he hoped to raise there. Was that dream about to vanish too?

Jean found herself walking to Crazy Nelly's. No, not Nelly's—Rob's. *He will come home,* she told herself. He will make this place beautiful again. If not with Fran, then someone else.

Ahead stood the neglected building. Even from here she noted the sagging roof, the hastily repaired chimney…the wide-open windows and door!

Someone was there.

She walked faster. How dare someone enter that house! What for? As she crossed the yard, she picked up a sturdy stick, then climbed the porch steps cautiously. At the door, she hesitated. From inside came the sound of something heavy scraping along the wooden floor. A grunt, a pause, and the sound continued. Was someone stealing furniture?

Jean took a deep breath and stepped in. She crossed the hall into the parlor. A figure in dark pants and shirt, head covered with a scarf, was hunched over, pushing a chesterfield.

The figure straightened up to reach for a nearby mop and pail, turned, and gasped. "Jean! You surprised me."

"What are you doing here?" Jean demanded.

"What does it look like? I'm cleaning my house." Fran began vigorously mopping the floor in the space just occupied by the sofa.

"Your house? Cleaning?"

Fran squeezed the mop and dirty water drizzled into the pail. "Yes, the home Rob and I will share."

"He told you to do this?"

"Of course not." Fran tucked a strand of hair back under her scarf. "But he'll want to start our life together as soon as he gets home. Everyone says the war is nearly over."

Jean was dumbfounded. Why hadn't she started cleaning the place? Why had it been this flighty, flirty girl? "Are you sure he wants you to do this?"

"Yes, Jean. I'm certain." Fran stood tall, the mop in her hand like a rifle at ease. "In spite of the little story you told him about me, Rob and I write to each other every week—well, him not so often since he was captured."

"You have?"

"Of course. We love each other. As soon as he gets home, we'll marry."

"Rob wasn't angry at…my story?"

"Not at me."

Jean knew she deserved that, as well as the scowl Fran aimed at her.

"Then why did he rush off to enlist?"

Fran rolled her eyes. "Because he'd planned it for weeks. I couldn't talk him out of it."

"You knew."

"We discussed everything."

So Rob had not enlisted because of her lie. Jean felt a giant weight lift from her heart. The guilt was gone. She had not made Rob go to war.

She looked at Fran. "I'm sorry." She saw Fran's red hands, her damp pant knees, and her shirt streaked with grime. She said it louder. "I'm really sorry, Fran."

"You have no reason to dislike me." Fran sounded angry. "I've never harmed you, and I'd never hurt Rob."

"I know. I lied because I was mad at my brother. It was stupid and I've regretted it every day since."

"And all the dirty looks? Leaving the drug store the minute you saw me?"

Jean decided to be honest. "If you're engaged to Rob, why do you flirt with other men?"

Fran dropped her mop and sank onto the arm of the chesterfield. Her face crumpled. "Because I miss Rob so much. I'm terrified he won't come home to me. And if I laugh with friends—I'm always with a group of people, never alone with a fellow—why would I even want to be when I love Rob? When I'm laughing with my friends, I can pretend everything is normal, that nothing bad will happen."

She looked at the floor she was washing. "And if I make this house clean and ready, I can convince myself Rob will come home safely." She turned to face the window, shoulders heaving.

Jean picked up the mop and dipped it in the pail. "Let's do this together."

MONDAY, AUGUST 16, 1943

Binxie

Binxie moved the ladder over three feet, adjusted the strap on her neck, climbed back up the tree, and continued picking. *Darn this peach fuzz,* she thought, brushing off her arms and neck. "I'd rather pick anything but these hairy monsters," she called to Peggy in the next row.

"But they taste good." Peggy held up a half-eaten peach like a trophy. "Is it time for lunch yet?"

"I hope so," said Binxie. When her basket was full, she climbed down again and handed it to Mr. Grant.

"Good work." He smiled at her, punched her card, and carried the basket to the wagon.

Binxie dragged her ladder to the next tree. As she climbed it, a truck swerved into the orchard. Mrs. Grant jumped out.

"Are we eating early?" Peggy called.

But Mrs. Grant was empty-handed and breathless. "Binxie," she said, "there's a phone call for you at the farm. I'll drive you there now."

Binxie sighed. *Mother's really overdoing it,* she thought. *That's a letter and two calls this week, all to convince me to take a place at Mount Holyoke College in September.* "I'll call her after supper tonight," she said.

"No. She wants you by the phone at noon. That's in ten minutes. We better hurry."

At Highberry Farm, Smokey let her into the office just as the phone rang shrilly. Binxie rolled her eyes and Smokey left the room.

Binxie picked it up. "Hello, Mother."

Her mother sounded hoarse, her words broken, hard to understand at first, then unbelievable.

"What did you say?" Binxie asked. As it sank in, everything went black.

She revived with her head on Smokey's shoulder, the woman's arms around her. The phone dangled from its cord like a noose.

Her mother's words screamed and echoed in her head. "Kathryn's plane crashed. Kathryn is dead." Binxie wanted to pass out again, to make those awful words stop.

Smokey pointed at the phone.

Binxie shook her head. She couldn't hear that again.

Smokey held the phone to her own ear and spoke to Mrs. Rutherford—first the condolences, then a series of yeses.

By the time Smokey hung up, Binxie had sat in the chair like a statue, numb. She ignored the offer of a glass of water.

"There's a driver on his way to take you home to your parents," said Smokey.

When Binxie didn't react, Smokey led her to the dorm, sat her on the bed, and pulled her suitcase from under it.

Binxie would never recall the drive home that day. All she remembered was sitting in Kathryn's room, staring at the photo of her sister, alive and vital, laughing by the lake. How could the person she loved most in the world, a woman who filled a room with her presence—how could she be no more?

Her parents had greeted her, ashen-faced, red-eyed. Her mother spread her arms to her remaining daughter and Binxie stepped into them like a child. She felt her mother's salty tears touch her cheek, but her own tears stayed inside her in a heavy ball of grief.

Her father, gray hair, gray face, looked twenty years older. "She was delivering a new plane across the channel to Ireland. Something malfunctioned and she crashed. Alastair has sent a letter with more details." He wrung his hands in despair.

"Are they sure?" asked Binxie. "Maybe she bailed out over the water, made an emergency landing somewhere. She'll arrive back on base any minute."

"The plane disappeared four days ago. They found her yesterday." Her father sobbed at the last word.

The tall, strong-jawed owner of a small steel company was a commanding person. When he gave orders, people jumped. Her mother headed every committee she joined because she got things done. Now both stood helpless. For once their determination or a well-placed phone call made no difference. They could mail a check to God, and Kathryn would still be dead.

Then it hit her. Four days ago? Her birthday. She had been so happy that day. She had no inkling about her sister. When did Kathryn take her final breath? Was it while Binxie laughed with her friends as she took silly photos—or as she was dancing and kissing Johnny? She and Kathryn had been so close—why had she not felt something at that terrible moment?

Binxie couldn't stand it. She wanted to scream, kick, smash her head against the wall.

After her brothers, Duncan and Charlie, arrived, the family

sat at the dining room table, picking at food that Sadie served. Tears streamed down Sadie's face. Kathryn's empty chair stood too large at the table. They moved to the parlor and talked through most of the awful night, sharing stories about Kathryn, united in grief.

Late next morning, Binxie awoke with a heavy weight crushing her chest. Why? Then, it walloped her all over again. Kathryn was gone. What was the sense of getting up? What was the point of anything? When Sadie came in with coffee, Binxie closed her eyes.

An hour later, the door flew open and her mother charged in. She was pale, new lines had developed overnight, but her hair was immaculate as usual, her dress impeccable. "We have arrangements to make. I expect you downstairs ready to go in thirty minutes."

She stroked Binxie's shoulder, then strode from the room. Binxie wanted to throw something at the door as it shut, but she knew this was the only way her mother could deal with her loss.

And her? How would she manage? She didn't even want to. Slowly Binxie got up, bathed, and dressed. Like her mother, she'd get through the next few days because things had to be done. Rites and duties performed. People to speak to in hushed, gracious tones. During that time, their words and reminiscences would keep Kathryn alive for her. But when it was all over, Kathryn would be completely gone.

Three days after the memorial service, Binxie sat on a bench in the garden, too numb to notice any beauty or birdsong. Her mother joined her. She patted her daughter's arm, but remained silent for some time. Then she asked Binxie about her plans.

Plans? Life without her sister loomed as a hopeless empty expanse. She wished she'd been in that plane with Kathryn.

"Come to the cottage with us."

Binxie bounced her leg in frustration. How would that help? The beach, the sailboat, the cottage swing—would all remind her of Kathryn. There would be no solace, only memories that stabbed. Every childhood story she ever had was now changed—tainted by the new ending—Kathryn was dead.

"You can't stay here alone until September. You'll need the people you love around you," Mrs. Rutherford pleaded.

Binxie didn't care where she was. The pain would follow her.

"You can recuperate at the cottage. I promise not to mention college or your future."

Binxie smiled weakly. *But you will,* she thought. *You can't help it.* She took her mother's hand gently. "I can't face the cottage yet, and I can't stay here."

Her mother opened her mouth to interrupt, but Binxie continued. "I'm going back to the farm. They need me there and I have to keep busy."

"I need you in Muskoka," her mother said softly. She waited, then stood up. "Perhaps the farm is best for you right now. It's only three more weeks. We'll spend time together in September."

SUNDAY, AUGUST 22, 1943

Peggy

Peggy pulled her last shirt from the rinse water, wrung it out, and hastily carried her wet laundry to the clothesline. She couldn't leave the wash area fast enough. Behind her she felt Stella's and Grace's eyes boring into her back.

"Forget those two. Most of the girls don't care where your mother came from. They like you," Helene had told her yesterday. But it was the others, those who looked at her with uneasy glances or who acted friendly but made little comments, that upset Peggy.

Three days ago, August nineteenth, had been hard for her. One year since Michael and Donny died at Dieppe. The Grants looked sad that day too, remembering their nephews and neighbors killed or captured on that terrible beach. Everyone on their farm was extra kind to them. Only Helene understood why Peggy didn't sing in the orchard that day.

Peggy hung her clothes on the line, then went back inside to put away her soap. An overpowering smell of bleach filled the building, making her eyes smart. Binxie was furiously scrubbing the washroom. She hadn't stopped moving since she arrived back at the farm yesterday.

Peggy decided to soothe both Binxie and her own restlessness with a gentle Debussy piano recording.

"That's lovely," said Helene, stepping in the door, brushing peach fuzz from her arms.

She looks exhausted, thought Peggy. She can't keep working these extra hours forever. "I saved you some lunch," Peggy offered. "Come join me after you wash up."

Helene nodded gratefully and plodded upstairs to change. When she hadn't come down after twenty minutes, Peggy went upstairs and found her asleep on her cot. She hadn't even removed her shoes.

Binxie came up and tiptoed across the floor, avoiding the squeaky boards.

"I'm awake," Helene said, stretching sleepily.

"Me too," Isabel said from her cot. "I have an hour before I need to go back to the kitchen. Come sit with me, Binxie. You'll exhaust yourself."

Peggy knew that was her aim, but Binxie sat beside Isabel, united in sorrow.

"I'm starving. Let's go eat that lunch you saved me, Peggy," Helene said, tactful as always.

"Any news from home?" Peggy asked her friend as they sat at a table munching sandwiches and pickles.

Helene shook her head. "Mama decided to sell the house. She thinks a small apartment will be easier, but who wants to buy a house in these times?"

"Someone will come along. Everything will turn out all right." Peggy knew she sounded too chipper.

"I'll collect a good paycheck this week to help out," Helene said, but she looked miserable.

Peggy's heart ached for her. And for Isabel and Binxie upstairs. She had to find a way to cheer them all up.

TUESDAY, AUGUST 24, 1943

Jean

Jean took extra care putting on her prettiest dress and brushed her auburn hair to a shine. When Hugh knocked at the front door, she took a last glance at the mirror and pinched her cheeks to make them rosy. She had to look her best. It was their last evening together for a long time—Hugh was leaving for England tomorrow.

She tried not to think about the dangers he'd face and how much she would miss him. Tonight Hugh expected the answer she had put off too long already. Not because she hadn't thought about it every minute since he'd asked her. She had pored over books about Australia, cattle, and sheep. She talked to her parents, Reverend Ralston, Fran. They had, each in their own way, said, "Do you love him? Then follow your heart. Everything else will fall into place." It was usually Johnny she went to for advice but this was one question she couldn't ask him.

She opened the front door and glowed at the sight of him. How did she get so lucky? Hugh! Australia!

He whistled. "You're beautiful."

She hugged him. How good he looked, standing tall and expectant in her front hallway.

Mum invited him into the parlor, but he offered to help her in the kitchen. "I make great coffee…and your kitchen reminds me of ours," he said. He needed this taste of home before he left for battle.

Dinner was jolly for everyone as Hugh and her parents compared funny farm-disaster stories. Nanny topped them both with her tale about the day their outhouse tipped in the wind with her fat uncle Egbert still sitting in it. Jean had to force her laughter. Tomorrow Hugh would go to war.

After dinner, Hugh suggested a walk. "I need to say goodbye to the horses and the farm." He had already romped with Dickens and scratched Shep's favorite spot behind the ears. The dogs followed them to the pasture, sticking to Hugh's side, somehow sensing he was leaving.

Jean breathed deeply. How she loved this place. Could she leave it? Her great-grandparents had come here from a home they loved in Scotland, had set new roots into this fertile earth, turned it into home. She could do no less.

So why did she hesitate?

The sun sank lower, draining away the gold and leaving shadows in its wake. "Shall we have our peach pie outside?" Jean suggested when they returned to the house.

They sat on the dim front porch eating pie and sipping hot coffee. She wiped a dab of whipped cream from the side of Hugh's mouth, and he kissed her. She loved the intimacy. She wanted to savor every second with him before he left, but she was too tense.

"Let's take a drive," suggested Hugh.

"You got the Jeep again," Jean said. "Someday I'll find out how you manage that."

"I have my ways," he answered, "but they're classified."

She smiled. Life with Hugh would never be dull. But what if he was too daring once too often when he went to war? She could not imagine this vital, wonderful man ever ceasing to exist.

Beyond the Jeep she saw Johnny leading Binxie to the pasture fence. He came every night to comfort her. She walked with him like a girl in a trance. Jean had watched how gently, how patiently he treated her. It wasn't easy for him to find the time to come; there was so much work to do at the farm this time of year, but he did.

Johnny called Cairo and handed Binxie an apple to feed her favorite horse. Jean remembered how calmly he had comforted her after the first bad news about Rob, and how he could make her laugh in the good times.

As she watched him profiled against the twilight sky, she realized she could never leave this land, or Johnny. Yes, he was with Binxie, but she knew that she had loved him since forever and could never totally stop. If she felt this strongly about Johnny, was it fair to marry Hugh? He deserved better than half a love.

She gripped Hugh's hand more tightly. It would be so hard to let him go.

"Are you ready to take a drive?" Hugh asked her.

"Let's stay here and talk," she suggested, an ache already beginning in her heart.

FRIDAY, AUGUST 27, 1943

Isabel

Isabel toweled her hair dry and put on her favorite flowery blouse and blue shorts. All week she had worked hard—setting tables for seventy people, starting breakfast before dawn, washing dishes, peeling and chopping endless quantities of vegetables. At least she didn't have to do the bathroom this week. Binxie had scrubbed it beyond spotless, then cleaned the entire recreation room.

Isabel baked every day too, but that wasn't a chore—she loved creating cookies, tarts, and pies. She felt special with every smile and compliment she received. Several girls joked about taking Isabel home so they could keep enjoying her delicious desserts.

It was Friday night—date night. She stroked her ring wistfully. Last year at this time, she would have been getting ready to see Billy. Tonight, although she wasn't interested in any other man, she itched to go out, do something besides work and grieve.

She pulled her curls back with a blue ribbon, then ran downstairs to join the other girls, scattered around the recreation room. She hoped someone might offer something more exciting than another game of cards or Monopoly. But everyone looked tired, and complained about scratches, aches, and peeling sunburns.

She sat beside Helene, whose face was lined with exhaustion. Binxie slumped in a chair across from them, deep in her own world of sorrow. Several times a day, she went from that melancholy state to rushing around in a frenzy of action.

Lucy entered the room. "Anyone want to go to Romeo's?"

Several girls ran upstairs to change their clothes. *That leaves only us gloomy ones,* thought Isabel. *Is that girl in the corner staring at me again?* She turned her head quickly to see, but the girl was sketching something in her book.

In a clatter of laughter and chatter, the farmerettes left for Romeo's. Peggy stopped in front of Binxie and asked, "You're sure you don't want me to stay?"

Binxie shook her head and smiled weakly. "No. I need some quiet time to study my manuals. Please, go."

"I'll be here with her," Isabel reassured Peggy. Relieved, Peggy followed the others.

Isabel watched them leave, half-wanting to join them. She looked at Binxie staring glassy-eyed at a manual, and Helene holding a novel. Every sound outside made Helene look up at the screen door. *Waiting for Dan. He looks nice enough,* thought Isabel, *but that scar showing under his shirtsleeve is hideous.* From the expectant glow on Helene's face, he obviously made her happy.

Binxie's manual sat open in her lap. The left page was full of dense script, and the right side some complicated diagram. "That looks hard," Isabel said, just to start a conversation. "But I guess it makes sense to you."

Binxie looked up, her eyes vague and lost. "I must learn it," she whispered, "and become a pilot. Kathryn would want me to finish what she started."

Isabel didn't know what to say, so she murmured, "You'll feel better in time."

Dan knocked at the screen door. "Are you ready?" he asked Helene. "I have something to show you."

Helene

Helene watched Dan's profile as they sped down the country roads. She was worried. "Is something wrong?"

"Everything's fine." His face, intent on the road, gave nothing away.

Through all her worries about home, Dan was the bright spot that kept her going. *And,* she thought with some guilt, *perhaps the reason I'm still here. Is he about to end it?*

They turned onto Mrs. Fraser's drive and approached the red brick farmhouse with its tidy garden of vivid flowers. Why were they here?

Mrs. Fraser welcomed them inside. In her formal way she offered them a seat in the parlor and served crystal glasses of elderberry cordial and slices of cake.

"This is so pleasant," said Mrs. Fraser, sipping her drink. She leisurely questioned Helene about the work at the farm, her family. Helene was confused. Apparently there was nothing urgent after all.

When Mrs. Fraser walked to the piano, sat down, and played "Cabri Waltz," Helene noticed Dan knotting his napkin into a wrinkled ball. Why was he so nervous?

Mrs. Fraser finished the first verse. "Dan?" she said, beginning the verse again.

Dan stood up and retrieved a fiddle from a shelf by the piano. He positioned it awkwardly in his weak right arm, lifted the bow with his left one, and accompanied Mrs. Fraser. His bow danced across the strings with spirit and joy.

Helene was astonished and delighted. Watching the two make music together warmed her heart.

"Helene," said Mrs. Fraser when they finished the waltz.

"I can't play anything."

"Then sing." The older woman patted the piano bench beside her.

Reluctantly Helene went to the bench. Dan segued into "Buffalo Girls." The catchy tune, silly words, and Dan's grin made it easy to join in.

I danced with the dolly with a hole in her stocking
And her heels kept a-rockin'
And her toes kept a-knockin'!
So I danced with the dolly with a hole in her stocking
And we danced by the light of the moon.

They sang it twice, then stopped for breath. Dan looked at her shyly. Helene jumped up, ready to throw her arms around him until she realized she might crush the fiddle. "You're wonderful," she said.

"Thanks to you, Helene." He turned to Mrs. Fraser. "And to this tough taskmaster."

The rest of the evening flew by as they played music, sang, and laughed at off-key notes and words they had forgotten. To see Dan so loose and happy was a joy.

Finally Mrs. Fraser stopped and got up to clear the dishes, waving away offers of help. They picked up the glasses anyway. As they walked to the kitchen, Helene told Dan, "You play so beautifully. I bet the square dancers will be glad to hear you again."

"It'll be good to go back. How did you know about that?"

"Someone at the growers' party told me. I could listen to you all night."

Dan hugged her, then returned to the piano and played a short tune.

"That's pretty. What is it?" asked Helene.

"You like it? It's the music for my mother's favorite poem."

Helene was amazed how the simple haunting melody reflected the spirit of the sonnet.

Dan started again and softly sang, "How do I love thee? Let me count the ways."

Helene timidly joined in. Before they reached the end, Dan stopped. "It needs more work. Should I continue?"

"Nothing else could do proper justice to that poem. Finish it," said Helene. She turned to see Mrs. Fraser watching them, tears glistening in her eyes.

The older woman collected herself. "Thank you. That poem is special to me. It's been a long time since I heard it."

She must have shared that with her husband, thought Helene as Dan wrapped an arm around her.

Mrs. Fraser recited the first lines of the poem, then added, "I would love to read the entire sonnet again."

"We have a copy. Dan can bring it next time he visits."

"I would dearly like that." Helene had never heard Mrs. Fraser sound so wistful.

"I'll bring it in now," said Dan. "It's in the truck. I was planning to return it to Helene tonight." He hurried outside and came back with the slim volume.

Mrs. Fraser's hand reached for the worn book, then it flew to her heart. She grabbed the book, opened the front flap to read the inscription. Helene already knew what it said. *To Polly, October 1917. I love thee with the breath and smiles of all my life. James.*

"Where did you find this?" Mrs. Fraser rasped.

Hesitantly, Helene answered. "Jean found it at Nelly's place."

"Nelly Turner's?"

Dan nodded. "Do you want to sit down?" He reached an arm out to her.

"No. Thank you." She stood taller. "But please bring me another glass of cordial."

Even as she drank, Mrs. Fraser clutched the leather-bound book tightly in her other hand. "I never thought I'd see this book again." Then she regarded the young people staring at her with concern. "You need an explanation." She took a deep breath. "It was my brother's. We bought it together in a bookstore in Halifax."

"James Earnshaw is your brother?" Helene blurted.

"Yes. My maiden name is Earnshaw. Jamie was my little brother—your Willy and Peter so remind me of him." She stroked the book tenderly. "He wanted this for his sweetheart. How he loved that girl. Polly. He met her when he was visiting us here in Winona."

Helene stifled a gasp. Dan glanced at her. He knew what this meant to her and her friends.

Mrs. Fraser shook her head sadly. "We were worried about Jamie loving an unknown servant girl, but he reassured us she was a gentle, sweet daughter of a minister. She worked for a respectable old family who trusted her completely. Jamie planned to marry her when the war ended…but she broke his heart. Never answered a single letter he wrote to her."

She sighed and regarded her guests. "How could she do

that? He was so sure she loved him. But even if she didn't, could she not have done the decent thing and written back to a lonely soldier in a strange land?" Mrs. Fraser clenched her jaw. "How could she have been so heartless?"

Only one answer made sense to Helene. "Maybe she never got those letters," she said quietly.

Mrs. Fraser stared at her, puzzled.

Helene took a deep breath. "We found a packet of letters—written to Polly by James Earnshaw—lovingly wrapped in lace. Someone treasured those letters, but I don't believe it was Polly."

Dan's eyes grew wide. "You found them at Crazy Nelly's!"

"And the poetry book was there too?" asked Mrs. Fraser. "You think Nelly stole them? Why would she do such a thing?"

Helene remembered the story about the packed suitcase. "Wasn't there a rumor about Nelly waiting for a lover who never came? Maybe she loved James too. She thought he cared for her, but when she realized it was Polly he loved, this was her way to keep them apart, to get James for herself."

"In a twisted way, that makes sense," said Mrs. Fraser. "But how did she get letters addressed to Polly?"

"If Polly was Nelly's maid, she could easily intercept her mail. Polly never answered your brother's letters because she didn't receive them!"

"My poor brother. I wonder why Polly didn't write to him?"

"Nelly probably stole those letters too, maybe even offered to mail them for her. Then Polly assumed he wasn't interested in her after all, and gave up." Suddenly Helene gasped. "Oh my Lord. There was another letter."

"What other letter?" Mrs. Fraser asked.

"The package included an unsent letter from Polly to James." Its full impact hit Helene like a bullet. She breathed deeply, then continued. "Polly wrote to James, telling him how much she loved him, how she hoped he would write to her… and that…she was expecting his baby."

Mrs. Fraser sat down. "My brother's baby?"

"Nelly must have stolen that letter before it was ever sent. When Polly didn't get an answer, she stopped writing, thinking he didn't want her or their child." Helene ached with pity for the girl.

Mrs. Fraser grew so agitated Dan fetched her a glass of water. She took a sip. "My poor brother. He almost made it to the end of the war. He was killed crossing the Sambre-Oise Canal. November 4, 1918. Almost the last battle of the Great War. He died never knowing he had a child at home. It breaks my heart."

"Mine too," said Helene sadly.

Mrs. Fraser sipped her water and asked softly. "Would you like to see some photographs of Jamie?"

Helene nodded and Mrs. Fraser pulled a faded album from a drawer and carried it to the sofa. Helene and Dan sat on either side of her as she opened the book to sepia pictures of two youngsters in various poses and places. Young Agnes's face, framed by long, curly hair, was strong and determined. James looked like a saucy, happy little guy. He resembled his sister, but he reminded Helene of someone else too—although she couldn't put her finger on it.

Mrs. Fraser flipped through the childhood photos, then reached pictures of them as adults. James had grown into a handsome fellow, the mischief still in his eyes.

His sister touched the photos gently. "My husband worked for the government, so we spent most of the war in Halifax. We visited Warren's parents here twice. Jamie came with us the second time and met Polly. He made a few trips back before he enlisted. The last time I saw my brother was in Halifax, before he shipped out. He was happy, in love, full of plans for the future." She took another sip of water. "For so long I've hated that Polly, but now I realize how horrible it must have been for her too. To be an unwed mother with no support—her father was a rigid Baptist minister from a small town near Lake Erie. He would never have accepted Polly in his house again. Obviously Nelly wouldn't have helped—indeed that's probably why she fired her."

Dan suddenly paled. "I know that story. A girl with a Baptist father who came here from Lake Erie to work for a family that suddenly let her go." He began to shake. "That sounds like my mother."

Helene gasped. "Polly? Mary!"

Dan's brow furrowed in thought. "But she married my dad. It doesn't make sense. She never spoke about her past. Nor about James. We only met her father—a harsh old man who didn't like noisy boys—twice before he passed away."

Mrs. Fraser looked at him with awe. "This is impossible. But if it's true...you could be Jamie's son."

Dan stood up. The muscles in his face, his hands, everything seemed to move at once in agitation. "We need to find out for sure."

"But who would know?" asked Helene.

"My dad," said Dan. "Mrs. Fraser, I'm sorry. We have to leave."

Barely waiting for Helene to follow, he hurried from the room. The second she shut the truck door, they sped down the lane, gravel spewing behind them.

Dan dropped her off at Highberry, and Helene watched him race home. What would he discover there?

SATURDAY, AUGUST 28, 1943

Helene

Helene barely slept that night and dragged herself to the Beldings' orchard the next morning. Although she was bursting to tell the girls the news, she decided to wait until she had the whole story. As she picked, her mind kept racing back to the possibility. She almost fell off the ladder she was so preoccupied.

At one o'clock, as they arrived back at Highberry for the day, she heard Dan's truck. She raced for it and jumped into the passenger seat.

Unshaven and wearing the same clothes he had on yesterday, Dan looked at her, his face full of emotion.

"It's true?" Helene whispered.

He nodded. "He didn't want to tell me, and we have more to talk about—" He hesitated, then continued. "When Nelly fired her, and James didn't write back, my mother was lost. Dad was sweet on her, so he offered to marry her. I was born five months later."

Helene reached for Dan's hand. Several farmerettes came out to the barnyard, glancing curiously their way.

"Mrs. Fraser will be anxious to know."

"I'm on my way. Will you come?"

Mrs. Fraser stood at her door when they arrived. When Dan told her, she made no effort to stem her tears. She stretched her arms out to him.

Dan, quickly wiping at his own eyes, embraced her. "I'm honored."

Mrs. Fraser finally pulled back and beamed at him. "Ever since I first pulled you from that pond when you were nine, I knew you were special, that we had a bond between us. If only Jamie had known."

"If only he had," said Helene, full of emotion herself. "And Polly too. How awful it must have been for her. Unmarried with a child on the way, so desperate she had to marry Mr. Scranton."

"My father loved her," Dan answered quietly. "And they did share some good times. After she died, he was never the same."

"I'm sorry," said Helene. "I didn't mean to be so unkind."

Dan nodded. "We're all emotional right now. I should head home."

"Please don't go yet," Mrs. Fraser said. "Stay for a cup of tea. I need to let this sink in."

"I'll make it," Helene offered and hurried to the kitchen.

As she handed a steaming cup to Mrs. Fraser, then Dan, she realized who else James looked like.

"Jamie's son. My nephew," Mrs. Fraser repeated with wonder. She looked at Dan. "I thank God for this," she said, then turned to Helene. "And I thank you, dear girl. You've brought part of my Jamie back to me."

Helene smiled modestly. At least this one tragedy of war was made a little better. Although James and Polly had not ended happily ever after, at least their son might.

SUNDAY, AUGUST 29, 1943

Isabel

Isabel woke up disappointed again. She'd been dreaming—not the dream she'd hoped for. Even in sleep Billy slipped away from her.

At least she didn't have to get up at five today to begin breakfast. After Helene had shared her amazing news last evening, the girls were too excited to sleep. Even Jean and Binxie stayed in the yard talking.

"We'll never know exactly what happened," Helene had said, "but my guess is, Nelly had a crush on James. He must have chatted with her when he came to see Polly, maybe they even invited her along on some outings, and she read too much into that. She picked up James's letters from the post office before Polly ever saw them."

"Poor trusting Polly," said Isabel. "All those years, she thought James abandoned her. It's so tragic I could cry."

"When Nelly found out Polly was expecting his baby, she fired her," Peggy finished. "Polly had no choice but to marry that awful Scranton."

"To be fair, he gave her a home when most men wouldn't have. They had three more children together. He wasn't always so gruff," said Jean. Quickly she added, "I'm glad you found the rightful owners of the letters. I'm tired. Goodnight." With that she left. She'd been cranky since Hugh shipped out Wednesday.

The girls had discussed Polly's tragedy late into the night. Now they were happy to have slept in until eight o'clock.

They were dressing for church when Peggy said, "Let's do

something spectacular today! We need a grand adventure before
we go back to home and school routines again."

"Like what?" Isabel asked.

"Niagara Falls," said Helene. "It's one of the wonders of the
world and I've never seen it."

Isabel thought of the dreary months ahead of her in
Guelph. "We may never be this close again."

The girls stared at each other. The idea was enormous,
crazy—perfect. Even Binxie was easy to persuade. "It's a long
trip. We need to leave now."

They hurried through breakfast and packed a lunch. When
the others left for church, the girls slipped off to the main road.

Mrs. Belding picked them up and drove them as far as
Grimsby. Then they stood nervously at the side of the new highway, facing oncoming traffic. Cars flashed by, faster and more
often than Isabel was used to on the streets of Guelph and certainly more than the quiet roads of Winona.

Peggy held out her arm, thumb up, but Isabel kept back
with Helene and Binxie, not entirely comfortable. "We do this
all the time at the farm," Peggy reassured them. But in Winona
they knew everyone, and the neighbors were kind about giving
farmerettes a lift.

Soon a red Chrysler stopped. Two young fellows smiled
at them. "Where are you headed?" asked the handsome blond
passenger with a crew cut.

"Niagara Falls," Peggy answered.

"So are we," the passenger said. "I'm Bob and he's Butch.
Hop in." All four girls wedged into the backseat.

As they sped along the highway, Bob and Butch claimed they attended McMaster University in Hamilton. Peggy made up some good stories about their lives back home. In no time they reached Niagara Falls. The girls looked out the car windows almost bouncing with anticipation. Peggy asked Butch to let them off.

"We'll come with you," he offered.

"No, thank you," Isabel replied firmly.

"If you're at this corner around five o'clock, we'll drive you home," said Bob.

With many thanks, the girls hurried down Clifton Hill toward the Niagara River. As the sound of the waterfalls grew, so did their excitement. First they saw the American Falls across the river and stood marveling at the massive amount of water cascading over the cliff.

"There's more," said Binxie, urging them on. The thundering grew louder. Ahead, an even more tremendous wall of foaming waters crashed to the rocks below. As they approached, a cool mist sprayed them. Dozens of people leaned against the iron fence, gazing at the Horseshoe Falls.

They stood awestruck above the crest of the Falls as torrents of water surged downriver, then plummeted over the edge. It was mesmerizing. Under its spell, they watched for a long time. Even when they finally wanted to move on, Binxie stood transfixed, holding onto the iron fence so tightly her knuckles turned white.

"It doesn't care if we stay or go, or die—it still rolls on, day or night, summer or winter, peace or war." She shook her head. "What happens to us seems so small, so unimportant beside this."

Helene put her arm around Binxie. "It's magnificent and eternal, but it doesn't feel."

"I wish I didn't," said Binxie.

"You will again, one day," said Peggy.

"I'll never get over losing Kathryn. I don't want to."

"My neighbor's son died of polio when he was twelve," said Isabel. "She was the only one who made sense to me after Billy drowned. She told me that you never get over losing someone you love. You learn to live with it."

"Hey! There's a boat down there, heading right for the Falls!" exclaimed Peggy.

A nearby tourist told them it was the *Maid of the Mist*. He pointed to where they could line up to get on. They hurried down the hill to the dock, bought tickets, and soon climbed aboard.

The ride was thrilling. In the bulky raincoats they were given at the beginning of the trip, the girls stood at the front of the boat and watched the seething waters below and the immense rush of water ahead—first the falls on the American side, then the mighty Horseshoe Falls of Canada. They loomed even larger, louder, more impressive down here.

Isabel felt excited and a little nervous as the small ship moved closer to the falls, its waters spraying her face, dripping down her raincoat. Would they stop before they were swept into the turbulence? "Is there a point where it's too late to turn back?" she shouted above the roar.

"No!" Peggy called back. "That's only on top, where the current grabs you."

As the spray showered their upturned faces, the girls

laughed from sheer exhilaration. Even Binxie turned her face toward it. The boat stopped awhile in front of the thunderous cascade. Then too soon, it turned and chugged away.

"That was the most amazing thing I've ever done," said Isabel.

"Me too. Now let's eat. I'm starving," said Peggy.

They found a spot on a grassy hill where they had a good view of both waterfalls and the Rainbow Bridge spanning the river to the United States. The tall buildings of the powerful nation to the south fascinated them. Beckoned them.

"I've never been there," said a wide-eyed Helene.

"We're so close," added Isabel.

"What a lark that'll be," said Peggy. "Let's go."

They wolfed down their peanut butter sandwiches. With growing excitement, they walked across the magnificent bridge, stopping several times to gaze at the river far below.

When they stepped onto the soil of the United States, they looked around expectantly.

"It looks like Canada," said Helene. "I expected more."

"Such as?" asked Isabel.

"I don't know."

"You're thinking of New York City," said Binxie. "The energy there jumps right into your blood."

"Let's walk around," said Peggy.

Isabel was aware they looked like gawking tourists, but this was fun. The rhythm of a Tommy Dorsey number drew them to the entrance of a small establishment.

"I think it's called a speakeasy," Peggy whispered. A flick of danger quivered deliciously down Isabel's spine.

The girls stepped into a dimly lit, smoky room and a waiter showed them to a table. Tommy Dorsey's music on the jukebox smoothly segued into Count Basie's blues. Isabel and Peggy ordered a Pink Lady each. When Helene shook her head, Binxie asked for two and pushed one in front of her. "We have to toast the discovery of James and Polly and their baby. You're the one who found them; you should lead it."

Too happy to argue, Helene complied.

"Aren't we sophisticated," said Isabel, sipping her drink daintily and beaming at the others. They giggled. She'd had gin once before, at Gloria's wedding, so she knew there wasn't much in this glass, but it looked pink and pretty, and it felt so very mature. She looked around the room. At midafternoon, it was almost empty except for a group hunched in a corner and a young couple dancing—he in a navy uniform, she in a flared white dress—oblivious to everyone but each other.

Finally, Binxie tapped her wristwatch. "Time to leave. We shouldn't get caught on the highway in the dark."

Reluctantly they finished their drinks and headed back toward the bridge.

"Hey, girls!"

Isabel smiled at the familiar red car.

"Hop in. We'll drive you home," offered Butch. The jolly group sped across the bridge and back to Winona. It was quite dark by the time they approached the entrance to Highberry Farm. As they turned onto the lane, Bob pulled a brown paper bag from under his seat. "It's not even eleven o'clock. Why don't we have a party at your place?"

Peggy

"Sure," Peggy agreed, thinking how much she liked Butch's smile. "We have a recreation room, great music."

Binxie rolled her eyes. "And an vigilant camp mother. You'll never step past the front door."

"She won't hear us if we're quiet," said Peggy.

Butch parked the car partway down the laneway. Everyone tumbled out and crept across the barnyard. Under a sliver of moon, all was dark and silent. Only a light shining over the dormitory door guided them. Peggy tingled with excitement. The day's adventures were not yet over.

She saw Bob hand Isabel the brown bag. "Hide this until we get in," he whispered.

Isabel giggled and tucked it into her purse.

Just as they reached the door, it flung open. Cookie filled the entrance, the light from inside making her appear even larger. She glared at them, muscled arms akimbo, a kitchen knife in her hand. "Thanks for driving the ladies home, but this is as far as you get, boys. Goodnight."

Bob stepped toward Isabel, reaching for her purse.

"I said go!" Cookie's military voice was probably enough, but when she brandished the knife, the boys scooted to their car and raced off.

Frowning, the cook stepped aside for the girls. Each one said, "Goodnight, Cookie," and hurried past her. They rushed upstairs then collapsed onto their beds, smothering their laughter into their pillows.

Peggy looked around the empty room. "Everyone's still at Romeo's."

Binxie shrugged, changed into her nightgown. "Good-night." She crawled into her bed and pulled the covers over her head.

Helene giggled. "I'm too excited to sleep."

"It's too early," said Peggy. "What's in the bag, Isabel?"

Isabel opened her purse, pulled out the paper bag, and took a small bottle of clear liquid from it. "Bob won't be back for this. We can have our own party right here."

Peggy read the label. "Smirnoff Vodka!"

"I don't know…," said Helene.

"We have to celebrate," said Peggy.

"What are we celebrating?" asked Isabel.

"Our trip to Niagara Falls, solving the letter mystery, being a farmerette, friendship." Peggy felt daring. She opened the bottle, drank a mouthful…and gagged. The bitter liquid burned all the way down. This was no gentle Pink Lady. She almost threw the bottle to Helene.

Helene hesitated, then sat tall. "To life and love," she toasted. With a flourish, she took a sip—gasped, and passed the bottle to Isabel.

Isabel sipped, looked like she might spit it out, then swallowed. The second time it reached her, she shook her head. The third time it came her way, she declared, "I'm not Itsy anymore," and drank.

"Binxie, come join us." Peggy hated to leave her out.

Binxie sat up. She reached for the vodka and downed a mouthful. "Horrid," she said, handed it to Helene, and rolled back into her covers.

After two more swigs each, the girls sang "Chattanooga

Choo Choo" in three-part off-key harmony. Helene stood up, chugging like a train. Peggy and Isabel joined her, dancing in a wobbly track around the dorm.

Helene conducted the train to the outside stairs.

"Shhh." Peggy stopped the train. "We can't wake up Smokey." It felt so pleasant outside they continued quietly down the stairs.

"I love this farm," said Helene. "It's the most beautiful, wonderful place in the world. And I love all of yo-uuh," she hiccuped. "But most of all, I love Dan." She stood quietly for a moment. "I want to see him."

"Tomorrow," said Peggy.

"Tonight," insisted Helene. "I don't want this lovely day to be over."

Peggy wasn't ready to end the day either. "Let's raid the kitchen. There's bread pudding left."

"I'm not hungry," said Helene. She smiled wistfully. "You should have seen Dan's face when he played the fiddle for me. Like an angel. And when he found out about his parents…" She wiped her eye.

"He's too far away," said Isabel nervously. "We can't wander the countryside at night."

"I need to hold him." Helene began walking. "Who's coming with me?"

"We'll never find his farm in the dark," Peggy said.

"I know the way." Helene crossed the yard. She spotted the McDonnells' truck parked beside the barn, and smiled. "I'll drive us there!"

"You can't drive," said Peggy with a giggle.

"Of course I can. I've watched Dan do it. Twelve-year-old farm boys drive around here."

Peggy felt a bit dizzy, but Helene sounded so sure of herself she was willing to try.

Isabel squirmed. "Maybe we should go to bed."

Helene opened the truck door and studied the dashboard. "Oops. No key."

"That's a sign," said Isabel. "Let's go back inside. I'll get the pudding from the pantry. We'll have a feast."

Helene shook her head. "No. After next week, I may never see Dan again. I must go to him now." She stood swaying, her brow wrinkled in thought. "We can't drive…" She pointed at the stable. "Horses! We'll ride there." Dramatically she waved her arm at the moon. "I will ride a ribbon of moonlight over the purple moor. I'll go riding, riding, riding up to my dear Dan's door." She galloped to the stable. Peggy and Isabel trotted after her.

"What's gotten into her?" puffed Isabel as Helene stood looking up at Merlin, then Cairo.

"A bit too much vodka. And, she's been working too hard," said Peggy.

"They're bigger than I thought," Helene whispered, backing away from the horse stalls. Slowly she turned and headed for the door. On the wall by the entrance, a familiar set of keys hung on a hook. Helene grabbed them. "The tractor!"

The girls followed her outside. "I've always wanted to ride this," said Helene as she clambered onto the machine. "Who's coming with me?"

At first Peggy wasn't sure, but then she figured it would be one more adventure before the summer ended. "I am. Isabel?"

Isabel whispered. "Oh, I don't know."

"Just one little ride. He doesn't live far. Come on," begged Helene. "For once in my life I want to do something daring."

"You're right," said Isabel. "We can do this. Let's go!"

What harm could it do? It'll be fun, thought Peggy. She stepped up onto the back of the tractor. Giggling and grunting, she tried to climb onto the seat. It was a tight squeeze to fit into a space meant for one, but finally she perched beside Helene.

Isabel tried next, slipped off, and tried again.

"You take the seat," Peggy offered. "I'll stand back here and lean on you."

Helene turned the ignition key, and the tractor rattled to life. She revved the motor.

"Here we go," shouted Peggy, and Isabel cheered, one hand up in a victory sign.

Helene stepped on the gas and off the clutch. The tractor jerked forward. Peggy flew off backward, Isabel sideways. Luckily they fell onto soft ground. The tractor sped away, careening wildly around the barnyard.

"Watch out!" Isabel yelled at Helene as the tractor headed for the woodpile. Helene swerved too late. The sound of metal and wood colliding was sickening. Several logs crashed onto the ground and rolled across the yard.

Lights flashed on in the farmhouse and the dorm.

"Stop!" screeched Isabel, but Helene had panicked. Foot frozen to the gas pedal, she clung rigid to the steering wheel. The tractor raced circles around the yard.

"What's going on out here?" Mr. McDonnell and Smokey each called from the dark. Behind them Jean shouted, "Stop! Use the brakes!"

Helene stepped down harder on the gas pedal. The old machine roared faster than it had ever been asked to do. Smoke poured from under the bashed-in hood.

Helene noticed some of the loose logs on the ground in front of her. She yanked the steering wheel sharply right, and the tractor raced straight at the pond. Helene wailed. With a giant splash, the tractor charged into the water, where it finally stopped.

Helene sat glued to the seat, in muddy water up to her thighs, yelling, "The frogs! The frogs!" A dozen of them surrounded her, croaking displeasure at the intrusion.

Everyone ran to the edge of the pond. Jean and Smokey waded into the water and pulled Helene off the tractor and back through the muck to shore.

"I'm sorry. So sorry," Helene sobbed. She stood on the shore, dripping, shivering, shaking, while Smokey checked her for cuts or broken bones.

Peggy winced at the anger and disappointment on Jean's face. The tractor, so recently repaired, would be out of commission again.

"Get her inside. All of you, inside," Mr. McDonnell ordered. "There's nothing we can do now. We'll deal with this in the morning."

Peggy turned to Jean to apologize, but Jean glared stone-faced, turned, and followed her father back to the house. The three farmerettes slowly followed Smokey to the dorm. How had this wonderful day ended in such disaster?

X

She trod up the stairs behind the other girls, tired and discouraged. Romeo's was exhausting. She liked the music and sitting with her friends to laugh and talk. But they chatted mostly about boys—how spiffy they were, who they'd like to kiss.

The boys had kept them busy dancing. Of course she said yes to any fellow who asked. She wanted so badly to be like the other girls. And she tried. But the eager smiles of the boys who held her, their sweaty palms, their breath in her ear, left her feeling uncomfortable.

Now, as she wearily entered the dorm, the first sight she saw was Isabel, sitting on the edge of her bed, her face streaked with tears. Then she noticed Helene, sobbing, hiccuping, and wiping her nose, and Peggy trying to comfort her.

"What happened?"

The farmerettes gasped in horror as they heard the awful story. Everyone knew how important that tractor was.

"I've hurt Jean and her family," Helene sobbed. "How will I ever repay them?"

There was much sympathetic clucking. Even Stella hugged Helene.

"I have to get that tractor fixed," was the last thing Helene said as they all crawled into their beds and lay in the dark.

FAREWELLS
— AND —
FUTURES

MONDAY, AUGUST 30, 1943

Helene

Helene woke up with a pounding headache and a queasy stomach. She got up quietly and tiptoed down the outside stairs. Maybe the tractor disaster had just been a nightmare. She crossed the yard and saw it still half-submerged in the pond. Oh God, it was true. Helene threw up.

She took a shower, wishing she could wash away last night. While she dried and dressed, she heard the rumble of a large machine entering the yard. Its engine groaned and men cursed as they struggled to pull the tractor to land. How badly was it damaged? She dreaded the answer.

"Coming to breakfast?" Peggy asked carefully.

"I can't eat." Helene gathered her towel and toiletries and headed upstairs.

"I'll bring you something for later." Peggy followed the other girls to the dining room. A minute later, she returned to say they were wanted in the office.

Helene dreaded this, but she was relieved Smokey hadn't interviewed them last night when she would have been able to smell their breath. She followed Peggy downstairs, where Isabel, then Binxie, joined them.

"You don't need to do this," Helene told Binxie. "You were asleep."

"We're together," Binxie answered and led the way to the office.

Through the window Helene saw the muddy tractor, several large dents in the front, slime oozing from its fenders.

"We're all to blame," Peggy told Smokey as they stood repentant in her office.

"Yes," Smokey agreed, regarding them sternly. "Helene may have driven the tractor into the pond, but you two were out there with her. You could have stopped her. Perhaps you planned to drive it next."

No one answered that. Nor did they mention the vodka. On the way over, Isabel had persuaded Helene it would only make matters worse. When Peggy had asked what happened to the rest of the bottle, Binxie eyed her steadily and asked, "What bottle?"

Now Smokey stood before them, her face crinkled with anger and disappointment, the mints unable to mask the tobacco odor. "Why would you, of all people, do such a stupid thing, Helene? This seems completely out of character."

Helene shrugged miserably. Isabel fidgeted and Peggy stood silent, guilt written all over her face. She'd hurt her friends too.

Binxie looked Smokey in the eyes, and spoke in her most

contrite tone. "We were celebrating, Miss Stoakley. Helene got good news and the girls were trying to cheer me up."

"It seemed like harmless fun last night. We were feeling sad and silly that summer is almost over," added Peggy.

Smokey stared at each of them, then at the wall, as if it would display a wise decision. "Well, I should send you home… but I won't. The farmers are desperate to harvest as much as possible before everyone leaves." She shook her head. "And you girls are my best workers."

Helene's tight shoulders dropped with relief. "Thank you," she said. At least she could keep working.

"But you need to discuss this with the McDonnells first. See if they want you to stay, find out how much damage you've done."

Helene shook inside.

After more apologies and copious thank yous, the girls left the office. Helene felt no joy. She still had to face Jean and her parents.

They paused in front of the kitchen door to the farmhouse. Finally Helene knocked and they were let in. The kitchen was warm and savory with the aroma of fresh bread and coffee, but their reception was chilly. Mr. McDonnell looked pale, Jean angry, and her mother discouraged. Nanny glowered at them from her chair. Even the dogs ignored them. Helene felt like a monster.

The tractor's front wheel shaft was bent, something broken. The engine, the fuel tank, the cylinders would have to be completely drained and dried before they could be refilled and used. Gus could do most of that, but it would take too long to find and replace the broken parts, and the wheel shaft repair would cost more than they had. If they couldn't harvest the fall hay crop in time, it would rot in the fields, leaving them without enough grain to get their livestock through the winter.

Helene had never felt so terrible in her life. "I'll pay for those repairs if it takes me ten years," she vowed.

"We need the tractor a lot sooner than that," snapped Jean.

"We'll all help pay," said Peggy, ignoring Helene's startled look. "And we'll work after dinner every night this week, without pay."

With a sigh, Mrs. McDonnell nodded. "The other farmers have arrived. You'd best get out to your wagons."

As the girls left, Helene shivered with relief. They could stay. She turned to Peggy. "I can't let you pay for this. I drove that tractor."

"But we—"

Helene cut her off. "It's my fault, my debt. I have to settle it."

Binxie

Binxie smacked her ladder against the tree. The jolt vibrated through her arms to her body and set her headache throbbing again. In a way she welcomed it. It was the first time since the terrible news she'd felt anything.

She climbed the ladder and started picking. The act had become automatic. Even the insect bites and scratches were routine. She smashed a mosquito on her arm harder than she needed to, and realized she was feeling something else. Anger.

Life wasn't what she'd expected. Until two weeks ago, she

thought she was in control. Any problem could be solved with determination, charm, hard work, and the right connections. Now she knew that death didn't give a hoot about those things. War leveled everyone.

She was angry at this war that destroyed so many lives. And she couldn't help it—right now she felt angry with Kathryn. Why did she have to fly for the ATA when she could have been useful here in Canada? Why did she have to be the noble and headstrong hero? She could have lived a long, safe, and productive life here, instead of causing this unbearable heartache.

Binxie glared across the row at Helene, red-eyed and somber, picking fruit at a frantic rate. She was angry with her and her stupid stunt too. And at Peggy working quietly—no songs or jokes from her today. Why wasn't she responsible last night? Isabel had barely raised her head as she served breakfast this morning. Yet she had cheerfully drunk that vodka last night. Binxie sighed. They all had.

Binxie was even more furious with herself. Could she have tried harder to keep Kathryn in Canada? Why didn't she stop the girls last night, instead of rolling over in bed, wallowing in sorrow. Those stupid boys and their bottle. Everyone was at fault; but Helene, who had never hurt anyone, was paying the price.

Was it always the good ones who paid?

Helene

As the other girls headed for the wagon back to Highberry Farm, Helene approached Mr. Belding. "Please, could I stay over dinner and keep working until dark?"

The old farmer gazed at her kindly. "Go home, Helene.

You need to break for supper too. I could use you for the rest of September if you'd like to earn the money then."

The news must have already spread across the county. When would it reach Dan? How disappointed he would be in her? Mr. Belding's offer was kind, but she couldn't stay. She had to find work to repay the McDonnells. Factories paid the most. She would leave this place in disgrace, forever remembered as the girl who destroyed the tractor. There would be no more school, no more learning—just a lifetime of drudgery—without Dan.

She was surprised to see him at the door after dinner. "Let's take a walk," he said somberly.

"I can't. I promised to pick more peaches for the McDonnells."

"I'll walk you to the orchard."

Birds sang and wildflowers bloomed with extra beauty, as if to defy the misery Helene felt. Dan touched her arm. "What happened?"

Helene told him, finishing with her head bowed in shame. "I've never done anything so stupid in my life." She braced herself for his disapproval.

"Then maybe it's time you did."

"What?" Helene looked up at him.

He grinned. "Helene, this is bad, that tractor is crucial, especially at this time of year, but it's not the worst thing that ever happened. We'll all share our tractors with the McDonnells. Their crops won't go unharvested." He paused to look at her. "You've been worried and overworked for so long something had to burst. So for once in your life you cut up a bit."

"And see what happened when I did," she said bitterly.

"Every farm kid sneaks a ride on a tractor. I did when I was eight. You had the bad luck to end up in the pond."

"There's more to it," she said so softly she wasn't sure he heard. "I think I was drunk."

Dan looked at her in shock. "You?"

"It seemed like a bright idea at the time."

"What did you have?"

"Vodka. It didn't even taste good. We took about six turns drinking it. I don't know what happened to the rest of the bottle."

Dan laughed out loud—a jolly belly laugh.

"Six sips? That's not enough to get drunk—just silly."

"More like stupid."

"Okay, stupid—but not the end of the world. What will you do now?"

"Pay for the repairs, of course. The girls offered to help, but I don't take charity." She told him her plan to work in a factory.

"School means so much to you. There's no other way?"

She shook her head. "Mama has put the house up for sale. She can't keep up with both the mortgage and the repairs. I'd be selfish to add to her worries, not to help out."

His eyes darkened and his lips set into a scowl.

"I'm sorry," she said and turned to leave.

"No." Gently he reached for her arm. "I'm annoyed with myself, not you. That I don't have enough money to help you."

"This was my wrongdoing. It's my debt. You're saving for a farm of your own, for university."

"I want you to be able to finish school," said Dan.

"Maybe in a few years. Right now I can't."

"And I don't want you to leave."

He looked so forlorn she tried to soften her answer. "We can write. You could visit if you're ever in the city. Maybe I'll be back next summer." But she knew she wouldn't. Even if by some miracle she could, by then Dan would have forgotten her.

X

She stood in the doorway, watching Helene walk with Dan, defeat and guilt in every slow step. She had carried that feeling herself for four years. About herself, she felt hopeless, but an idea for Helene formed in her mind.

Peggy and Binxie waved at her on their way to their extra farmwork. Isabel had to finish her kitchen chores before she could join them.

"Wait," she stopped them. "I know Helene insists on paying for the repairs."

Peggy nodded glumly. "She doesn't have a penny to spare."

"Then let's all pitch in and help."

Peggy frowned. "She won't let us."

"She wasn't alone out there last night."

Peggy winced. "We should have stopped her."

"Then remind Helene of that. Don't let her shoulder all the blame." She looked at both girls. "Come upstairs with me." She led them to her cot, reached under it, and pulled out a wooden box painted with flowers and birds in vivid colors.

"You did that? It's beautiful!" Peggy exclaimed.

She felt embarrassed and pleased at the same time. She pulled a two-dollar bill from her knapsack, and dropped it into the box. "This will be our treasury. Helene has been so kind to everyone. They'll pitch in."

"It's a wonderful idea, but I doubt she'll take it," said Peggy.

"She will," said Binxie. She hurried to her cot and returned with a five-dollar bill, which she dropped into the box. "Let's spread the word."

Peggy rifled through her things and pulled out a lone quarter. "I spent too much yesterday," she apologized. "I'll have more Friday. Thanks for thinking of this."

She smiled, happy to help Helene. Then she worried. How much did it actually cost to repair a tractor, and could they raise enough in the one week left?

TUESDAY, AUGUST 31, 1943

Binxie

Binxie watched Helene pull her pictures off her wall and slide them into a notebook. Then she reached for her suitcase under the bed.

Binxie was surprised. "You're not leaving yet?"

"No. I'll finish my commitment." Helene looked pale and determined. "But I need to be ready to go right away, get a job."

Binxie felt badly for Helene—and annoyed. Why was she such a martyr? "For Pete's sake, stop being so noble. We all drank some vodka. Peggy and Isabel would have been on that tractor with you if they hadn't fallen off. We were together then, and we should be together now. Everyone wants to help."

"They can't…"

"Stop," said Binxie. "Come with me." She led Helene to a cot farther down the row and slid a brightly colored box from under the bed. "You can't refuse—we've already begun." She lifted the lid and showed Helene the bills and coins inside.

Helene gasped.

"There's more coming," said Irene from the doorway. "You sewed my torn blouse in the washroom at Romeo's once, saved me from embarrassment. The Highberry farmerettes stick together."

"Thank you, but I—"

"Thank you, Irene," Binxie interrupted. She held out the box for Irene to drop in her money. Then she looked at Helene. "We're not doing this just for you. The McDonnells need their tractor, and this will make it happen."

"Everyone's pitching in. Helene, your job is to find out how much we need." With that, Binxie slapped the lid shut.

Meekly, Helene nodded.

Binxie put the box back and left the dorm. Watching her mother organize committees all these years hadn't been time wasted.

She headed downstairs to wash her face. Johnny would be here soon. As she brushed her hair, the mirror showed her the same brown curls and tanned face as Kathryn's, and she started to cry. In a few years she would look like Kathryn's last photo, then eventually like their mother. But Kathryn would never grow older. The pain felt too big to bear.

Raising money for Helene helped her focus on something else. Even so, the tears would start without warning. Only when she was alone did she allow them to fall.

After awhile, she splashed cold water on her face. Johnny's calm understanding these last two weeks was a comfort, but sometimes, like today, she preferred to be alone. She'd take a quick walk around the orchard with him, then bid him goodnight.

His truck stood in its usual spot, but she didn't see him anywhere. She pulled a tuft of grass, walked to the pasture fence, and waited for Tinxie to scamper over. She found peace in the calf's brown trusting eyes.

She turned when she heard their voices—Johnny and Jean, crossing the barnyard. There was something intimate in the comfortable way they walked and talked together. She and the other farmerettes were shocked when Jean turned down Hugh, so dashing and madly in love with her. Watching the two old friends now, Binxie suddenly understood why.

"Hello," Johnny greeted.

"Tinxie and Cairo will miss you," Jean said softly.

"I'll miss them too…and our walks," Binxie answered, even though she hadn't seen much of Jean lately.

They stood quietly watching the cows for a while, then Jean said, "I'd better go. We're finishing the last bedroom at Rob's."

"Do you need help?" asked Binxie.

"Fran's already waiting for me." Jean smiled at Binxie. "But thank you. Let's take a long ride before you leave." With a wave she headed across the fields.

Johnny, watching her, said, "You girls did a fine thing with those letters."

"How could Nelly have been so selfish?" That bothered Binxie. Because of Nelly, the lovers had died never knowing they were loved. Polly and James. Isabel and Billy. Kathryn and Alastair. How many couples had been ripped apart by war?

"It's good to see Fran and Jean friends again. I wish I'd realized how guilty Jean felt. I could have told her Rob always planned to enlist." Johnny looked directly at her. "How are you, Binxie? Sunday night must be upsetting you too."

"Just one time trying to forget this damn war, and everybody suffers."

Johnny put his arm around her. "It doesn't seem like it now, but you will feel better with time, Binxie. This war will end and we will all get back to living normally."

"Kathryn would have done amazing things."

"She already did. She lived and died knowing she was helping to win."

"But why did she have to die?" Binxie whispered. She quickly turned to pat the calf. "My life was perfectly planned. I'd learn to fly, follow Kathryn to England. Everything seemed so exciting, full of possibilities. Now I don't care about anything."

"You don't need to make any decisions yet," Johnny said.

"I have come to one decision." She couldn't look at him. "I'm going home in six days. You're staying here…"

"Toronto isn't impossible to reach," he began.

"It's better we remember the beautiful part of this summer…then go our separate…" She couldn't finish the sentence.

Johnny stood still, watching her with sad confusion.

"I'm a mess. I can't think about you or anything else." Her eyes pleaded with him to understand.

"What will you do?" he said hoarsely.

She shook her head. "Aside from becoming a pilot, I don't care."

"Do you ever wonder if you really want to fly?"

"No. I need to finish Kathryn's work."

He regarded her a moment. "You did so well helping Jean birth Tinxie. I saw how it affected you. You took command when Hugh was hurt in his plane. Maybe that's where your future lies."

"No," she repeated. "I'll be a pilot like Kathryn."

They stood quietly looking at each other. For once Binxie didn't know how to exit.

Johnny stepped closer, stroked her cheek. "Good luck, Binxie. I'll miss you."

She threw her arms around his waist, curled into his shoulder, until—afraid she'd change her mind—she let go. "I'll never forget you."

She let him walk away first, head held high as he climbed into his truck and drove out of her life. It hurt to watch him go, but her sorrow for her sister was so immense she couldn't tell if the pain was any worse now.

WEDNESDAY, SEPTEMBER 1, 1943

X

She decided the nursery rhyme was wrong. Yes, sticks and stones hurt for awhile, but names stung forever. This time it was worse. The names had been spoken by Isabel.

It was her own fault. She had carelessly left her sketch pad on her chair while she went to the washroom. As she reentered

the recreation room, some girls were admiring her sketch of
Cairo galloping through the field. Betty flipped the page and
there were two portraits of Isabel. On some level the girls must
have understood the love that went into those drawings, and
each one stood staring at it.

"You don't think she could be one of *those* people?" asked
Grace.

"No!" Doris sounded appalled. "Not her. That kind are an
abomination against God."

Isabel asked what they meant. When Doris explained,
Isabel was shocked. "Ew! No one would do something so disgusting! I'd die if I met someone like that."

At that moment, she wanted to die too. She stood in the
doorway, not sure whether to run away from the shame or pull
her sketches away from cruel hands and eyes.

Suddenly Binxie stood up from her chair, grabbed the
sketchbook from Betty, and slapped it shut. "Don't be ridiculous. If you looked at the rest of this, you'd see pictures of all
of us, plus the animals and trees. That's what artists do. They
sketch all the time, drawing everything around them. I wish I
had her talent." Binxie rolled her eyes at the girls and left the
room with the book.

Confused, she followed Binxie. Halfway up the stairs
Binxie stopped, handed her the sketchbook, said, "Beautiful
work," and continued up.

Tucking her sketchbook under her arm, she turned and
went outside, trying to calm down. Binxie had saved her, but
Isabel's words twisted into her soul. Somehow she had hoped
against hope that Isabel would understand.

But no one did. Not even her.

For two days she had felt good, working with the others to help Helene. But how quickly that would stop if they found out about her. Next week she would return to Brantford, where people already eyed her suspiciously. If she stayed at the farm any longer, it would happen here too. No matter where she went, this curse would follow her.

She looked down at the lake. There was one way out.

Isabel

Isabel swiped the potato peels into the slop pail. Time to wash the beets. Soon she'd frost the Raspberry Matrimonial Cake. Normally Cookie insisted raspberry jam was enough—but tonight was their last birthday party. Isabel planned to decorate it with pink icing roses.

As she quickly washed the peeling knife, she nicked her index finger. Ouch. She hadn't done that in a long time. But she was worrying about Helene, about the McDonnells' tractor, and about the huge amount of money it would take to repair it.

Almost every girl at Highberry Farm had contributed to the fund. Even Smokey, Cookie, Dan, and Johnny pitched in. It was nowhere near enough. This weekend they'd all go home. Helene would have to work in a factory. She remembered how thin Helene had looked when she arrived here last June.

She checked on the potatoes, then picked up the basket of beets. She cleaned the mud from them and wished she could wash off her guilt as easily. Although Helene shouldered all the blame, Isabel felt just as responsible. She had climbed on that tractor too, ready to ride with Helene. She'd given all her money. How could she help more?

She rolled the clean beets into a pot of water and lit the stove. Then she turned on the tap to rinse the grit from her hands. A glint of light from overhead made her diamond sparkle at her.

She stared at the ring.

It would pay to repair the tractor.

She swallowed hard. This ring was the symbol of everlasting love, proof to everyone that she had been half of a devoted couple ripped apart by war. It gave her a role in this confusing world—tragic fiancée, loving to the end. Though she hated Billy's betrayal, she didn't know how to stop loving him. She had been Billy's girl for so long. Who else was she?

Billy's eyes had shone with love as he slipped the ring on her finger. They must have shone with love when he proposed to Norah too. She likely treasured some cheap hastily bought band.

Maybe it was time to become Isabel Lynch, her own woman. Let Billy stay in the hearts of Norah and their child. One day she would recover, and the ring would end up, useless, at the back of her jewelry box. Years from now her grandchildren might use the ring to play dress-up.

It was time to let it go. Tenderly she stroked the ring. "I loved you, Billy. Good-bye."

Helene

Helene stared at the empty wall above her bed. She had hoped seeing her space empty and impersonal would make it easier to leave, but every step outside proved her wrong. She loved this place of light and plenty, being part of the cycle of life, the farm families she had befriended—and Dan. He was everything she wanted. How could she bear to leave?

She would always look back on this summer as the most beautiful, idyllic one of her life. In time the summer would fade into warm sepia memories but her passion for Dan would never be tucked away as some pleasant interlude.

Tomorrow she would say good-bye to Mrs. Fraser. Friday the farmerettes at the Smith farm in Vineland had invited them for one final baseball game and corn roast. Saturday was the farewell evening at Romeo's. On Sunday, she and Peggy would take a bus to Hamilton.

But how would she say good-bye to the love of her life?

She picked up her laundry hamper, her soap, and carried it downstairs. Better to arrive home with clean clothes. As she pulled the last pair of underwear from the rinse water, she heard his voice behind her. "You don't think I'll let you go so easily, do you?"

She turned to see Dan, wearing a short-sleeved shirt and a hopeful grin on his face. She stood awkwardly, holding her wet underwear, glad they weren't the ripped ones.

He picked up the laundry basket and led the way to the clothesline. Without a word, the two pegged damp clothes onto the line. Sometimes their hands touched as they reached into the basket for another item at the same time. Helene wished she had washed a hundred things.

"Look how beautiful it is. You can't leave," Dan said.

She pointed at her shirts billowing on the line. "What, this?"

He laughed. "No, that." And he pointed at the sunlight streaming into the orchard.

She shrugged. She didn't want an argument.

"What about us?" Dan said.

"We're all I've thought about this week."

"I have an answer."

Helene looked into his eyes.

"Mrs. Fras...Aunt Agnes is getting on. The house and land are becoming harder to manage. She wants someone to help her."

"I can't—" Helene began.

But Dan talked faster. "Not only you. Your mother, the boys. They need a home and Aunt Agnes needs help. It's perfect."

Helene stood stunned. She felt a moment of hope and joy, then all the obstacles crowded in.

"Do you like the idea?" Dan studied her face. "That's the only question. Everything else can be worked out."

Helene wondered if she was dreaming. "You talked to Mrs. Fraser?"

"It was her idea. She likes your mother and would love to see little boys playing in that house again."

Helene dared a smile.

"She's already composed a telegram to your mother. She's waiting for your permission to send it."

Her brothers playing free in the fields, her mother relieved of excess work and worry, enough food for all...it was too perfect to be true.

"I still owe the McDonnells."

"The farmers need help until October. You can work weekends and after school."

"School?"

"We have a good high school here in Winona."

Tears stung Helene's eyes. Holding them back, she asked, "What about you?"

"My dad needs me at the farm. Matthew signed up."

"But you want more than that."

"I'm working on it." He grinned. "Eventually I'll save enough. Then I'll attend university in Hamilton."

She didn't know what to say.

"Helene. I'm not going to lose you. Consider this offer. You belong here…and in school."

Helene wanted this so badly. Did she dare hope?

THURSDAY, SEPTEMBER 2, 1943

Binxie

Binxie stood up to rub her back, then knelt in the warm earth again to cut another broccoli stem. She tossed it to Peggy, who placed it into the crate. The vegetables filled the crates rapidly, but there were many rows to go.

"We've come full circle," she said to Peggy as she tossed the next broccoli head. "It seems like yesterday we were hoeing these as seedlings." She expected the usual joke in reply, but Peggy stayed sober-faced.

Binxie realized she had come full circle with Peggy too. Last June, she dismissed Peggy as loud and annoying. She was happy to change her first impression. Peggy's volume covered a warm heart, sense of fun, and talent. "Are you okay?"

"It's just my monthly."

It was more than that. Last night, when the radio announced five thousand killed as eighteen hundred tons of bombs leveled Berlin, the room erupted into cheers. Stella taunted her. "We're blasting your Nazis off the planet."

Binxie tossed another broccoli. "It's Stella, isn't it."

Peggy bit her lip.

"Don't let her bother you. She has a nasty streak—you've seen it before."

Peggy clamped the crate shut. "At least she says it out loud. Others are more subtle."

"They're scared for their brothers and fathers."

"I'm not the one trying to kill them. I'm not the enemy." Peggy caught another head of broccoli, then placed it into a new crate. "I pray Canada wins. But I can't help worrying about my relatives in Germany, just as I'm scared for my English cousins."

"Of course."

Mr. Grant came to pick up the crates. "Good work, girls. I'm sure gonna miss you."

Binxie smiled at him. "Me too." She tried to erase thoughts of home. What would she do there? Without her parents' permission, she had enrolled in flying lessons on Toronto Island. Maybe in the cockpit of a plane, up in the sky, she would find her sister's spirit and make sense of her loss.

"Ready?"

She looked up to see Peggy waiting for the next broccoli.

"Sorry." She sliced off another plant. Peggy looked so pretty.

She had the tan she'd wanted and her hair was streaked with sunshine. What a shame she looked so sad. "Peggy, it's just talk. Your friends are all still with you. You know who you are."

"That's just it." She sniffed back hard. "The films, the posters, the awful news stories are even convincing me. Maybe it's in our blood. Maybe I really am evil." She reached to squash a cabbage looper, then pulled her hand back.

Binxie crushed it instead. "Peggy! Don't be crazy. There isn't enough evil in you to fill a thimble."

"I used to believe that."

"Well don't stop now. You're a good person."

"You really think so?" Peggy stood, cradling the broccoli.

"I know so. I also know you can't color a whole race with one brush. There are decent and bad people everywhere—German, English, African, Chinese."

Peggy sighed. She placed the broccoli into the crate.

Binxie cut the next stalk, tossed it to Peggy, and said, "Isabel sold her ring in Hamilton yesterday afternoon."

"I know. It was an amazing thing for her to do. That should pay for the tractor. Helene is over the moon with relief. Of course, she's vowed to repay Isabel."

"The money isn't important to Isabel," said Binxie. "She said it was the best thing she could have done with it. Now Helene can go back to school."

Peggy shook her head. "Her family can't afford it."

"That's sad." She paused. "Will you go?"

"Yes, though it won't be the same without Helene."

"You'll see her on the weekends."

"I hope so. What about you?"

"Learn to fly, then off to England to the ATA."

"Like Kathryn?"

"Like Kathryn."

"I'm curious. Why didn't you learn to fly sooner?"

Binxie worked silently. That bothered her too. Why had she never taken up Kathryn's invitations to fly, or at least hold the controls? Finally she answered Peggy. "I don't know."

The girls finished the row, stretched, then started the next one. This time Peggy cut and Binxie caught. "At least you've read all those manuals."

Binxie glared at Peggy. Did she know how few she had actually read? Peggy had surely seen her nodding off over them. The biographies Jean gave her were more interesting, but even there, she had skimmed over the Amelia Earhart article—she knew the story—and instead found herself enjoying one about Elizabeth Blackwell, who began as a farm girl and now directed a clinic in Hamilton.

Peggy asked carefully, "Do you ever wonder if flying isn't for you?"

"Do you ever mind your own business?" Binxie immediately regretted her outburst. "Sorry, I was rude."

"I was too." Peggy tossed her a stalk.

Although they worked quietly for awhile, Binxie's mind raced with thoughts until one burst from her. "I have to fly."

"Why?" Peggy said.

"I have to finish Kathryn's job. She wanted me to."

"Want to know what I think?"

"No! Yes."

"You don't really want to fly."

Binxie hesitated a second too long. "Yes I do."

"No." Peggy stopped cutting and faced Binxie. "You want to be like your sister."

Binxie stood firm. "I have to live up to what she'd want."

"You've told me Kathryn was independent and questioned things."

"And took time to teach me so much."

"Like having a mind of your own?"

"I need to live up to her legacy. It's the only thing I can still do for her."

"You won't honor her by becoming a pilot. Your sister wanted you to be your own person and think for yourself. If you blindly follow her footsteps, do something you don't even like…you're not doing that, are you?"

Binxie stared at her.

"I think Kathryn wanted you to do what's right for you, the same way she followed her own dream." Peggy turned and gazed at the field, counting how many rows were left.

The giant clamp squeezing Binxie's heart loosened a bit. She took a deep breath. "Throw me another broccoli, will you?"

X

Her work as a farmerette was almost done. Gossip and shame waited for her at home. She couldn't go back.

As the other girls made plans for the evening, she slipped away. The days darkened earlier now, and autumn flowers blazed defiantly before winter frosts killed them. She needed to walk these beautiful fields, feel the fresh breeze in her hair, see the lake at sunset once more—before she was gone.

FRIDAY, SEPTEMBER 3, 1943

Isabel

Isabel finished stirring the custard into the butter, scraped it into molds, and set them into the refrigerator. She filled the salt and pepper shakers. With no dinner to prepare she had extra time. Tonight was the baseball game and corn roast at the Smith farm.

Freda dried the last of the lunch dishes and hung up her towel. "You bought three pounds of flour yesterday?"

"Yes. Cookie gave me permission to bake apple muffins for everyone when they leave Sunday morning."

"They're going to follow you home." Freda smiled at her.

Isabel had enjoyed working side by side with Freda this summer. She'd miss their easy cooperation, and this kitchen with all its modern equipment. She looked at Freda. "You're staying until October? Then what?"

"I'll find some other place to cook, at least until my husband comes home from Africa. He loves my meals as much as I enjoy preparing…" She smacked her hand to her mouth.

"It's okay." Isabel smiled. "That's what I want too—I mean, to keep cooking, learn more about it. Be taken seriously."

"Then you're in luck," said Freda.

"Why?"

"You have a school right in Guelph that teaches cooking and all the domestic sciences."

"Where?"

"The MacDonald Institute."

MacDonald Institute! Maybe there was a place for her after all. She had often passed the big red brick building, but never wondered about it. For the first time in a long while, Isabel felt a glimmer of hope.

The next morning Isabel rushed to the library. Miss Willing helped her find information about the school and its founder, Adelaide Hoodless. "Amazing woman, passionate about the importance of a healthy, efficient home. I was fortunate to hear her speak once and I'll never forget her."

Isabel read an article about the MacDonald Institute with growing excitement. Daddy wouldn't say no—he wanted her to be happy. She belonged there. She felt it in her bones.

The last paragraph smashed her dream. Two years ago, the MacDonald Institute closed to make room for an RCAF training facility. "Damn," Isabel swore—for the first time in her life.

SATURDAY, SEPTEMBER 4, 1943

Peggy

Peggy watched the solemn faces in the McDonnells' parlor. If only the farmerettes could relive last Sunday evening—undo the damage done in those few foolish minutes.

The McDonnells listened politely to Helene's heartfelt apology.

"It's done," Jean's mother finally interrupted. "You're here to repay us."

Helene handed her an envelope of money.

"Thank you," said Mrs. McDonnell, and her husband nodded.

Nanny wasn't satisfied. "And will you send us money for the hours wasted working without the tractor, the time spent looking for the new parts, the back pain—"

Peggy faced the old woman. "We are sorry, and we're trying to make up for it. We worked extra hours all week, and we'll pick your peaches this afternoon too."

"Your time off. That's kind of you," said Mrs. McDonnell. "We really can use your help." Her graciousness made Peggy feel worse than Nanny's outburst.

The girls excused themselves and headed across the barnyard. Mr. Grant's wagon would be here soon to pick them up for a morning of tomato harvest.

"I'm glad that's over with," said Isabel. "I don't know how much sorrier I could feel."

Helene laughed shrill and sharp. Peggy worried her friend would reach a breaking point. Helene had worked too hard, worried so much lately. Now she was afraid Mrs. Fraser's offer was too good to be true.

Peggy wondered if she'd ever love someone as much as Helene did Dan. She preferred someone more dashing, like Hugh—devilishly handsome, daring—and who could sing and play music with her family. But not yet. There'd be some interesting fellows at school next week—if they hadn't enlisted. She'd be a senior, in the school band, and head of the social committee.

One quick trip to the washroom first. She whistled "Oh, What a Beautiful Morning" as she washed her hands. Now that they had settled with the McDonnells, she looked forward to Romeo's tonight.

When Stella and Grace joined her at the sink, Peggy stopped whistling and braced herself for a comment. Peggy glanced in the mirror at her, then Grace. No words, just a smirk and a lifted eyebrow. It was enough to make Peggy cringe.

Angry at them, and at herself, Peggy stormed out to Mr. Grant's wagon and stayed silent all the way to the tomato fields.

"What are we singing today?" Helene asked as she bent to pick her first ripe tomato.

"Maybe later," Peggy replied. She grabbed a tomato too hard and tore off the branch. Stella disliked her for reasons besides her background. And Stella wasn't alone. Other people were more subtle. Conversations that stopped when she came close, the slight currents of mistrust, all hurt. She could buy war savings stamps, hoe vegetables, and pick fruit until her fingers fell off, but she was still the enemy. Would it be like this forever?

She shook her head to get rid of her gloom. What had Binxie told her? No matter what anyone said, she knew she was decent and kind. Her friends trusted her. That had to be enough.

Helene began to sing softly, "There's a bright golden haze in the meadow…" The other farmerettes joined in. At last Peggy did too.

At one o'clock, they returned to Highberry and rinsed off at the pump. Smokey called to them. "Helene, there's a phone call for you."

Helene rushed to the office.

Peggy groaned. Now what?

X

She washed the pungent odor of tomatoes from her hands, though it wouldn't matter. Her work at the farm was finished. It was time.

The other girls jostled to the dining room. After lunch, most of them would shower and get ready for tonight. They would take extra care with their appearance for the last evening at Romeo's. Their last chance to dance with their farm beaus— something she hadn't been able to care about.

From the corner of her eye, she saw Binxie watching her, a small frown on her face. It wasn't the first time. Ignoring Binxie, she headed upstairs for her knapsack. Her sketchbook and private things were tucked safely inside it. She wanted them with her.

Just as she leaned down to pull out her knapsack from under her bed, she noticed the thin red book on her pillow. In spite of herself, she was curious. She flipped open the book. Poetry? She read the poem on the bookmarked page. Hmmm. Who wrote this? Walt Whitman. Who was he? Who left this book here? It didn't matter. She tossed it back onto the bed, shrugged on her knapsack, and went downstairs, outside, to the lake.

Jean

Jean packed the last of Nelly's clothes and things into a box. Reverend Ralston had promised to find families who needed them. She stood up to survey the bedroom. Like the other upstairs rooms, it was scrubbed clean, the floors waxed, windows washed clear. Fran had sewn a red, white, and blue quilt for the bed.

"It's beautiful," said Jean.

"I think Rob will be pleased. I keep him up-to-date on our progress." She paused. "I hope they give him my letters."

"I'm sure he gets them," Jean said with a smile. "They always send a receipt for the packages we send."

"His notes never say much."

"I suspect he's not allowed. Your letters are the important ones—they give him hope and a glimpse of home. And when this war finally ends, he'll come home and see for himself what you've done."

"How I pray for that day," said Fran. "We can finally begin our life together."

"What a wedding that'll be!"

Fran smiled. Then she looked at Jean carefully. "I know I did well. I readied this house. I financed the repairs by renting out the extra fields. I love my position as the mayor's clerk." She paused. "Don't take this wrong...I love Rob with all my heart. But...I don't want to give all that up when we marry."

Jean was startled. Her future sister-in-law had voiced what Jean had been thinking too. She nodded. "I manage our farm as well as a man. My cousin works in a factory in Hamilton. Clara Linton has run her household and the drug store without her husband for three years now, manages it better than he did. What will happen to us when the men come home? Do we all go back to the way it was?"

"The war has changed our world, Jean."

"We've changed even more. I hope the world can keep up with us."

They carried four cartons to the front porch. "Johnny's coming by to pick them up for the church," said Jean, wiping her brow.

"Johnny? You two have been close for so long. Won't you

ever be interested in him as someone more than a pal? He's such a catch."

Jean forced a casual smile. "Maybe, someday. Now let's tackle that parlor."

The girls retrieved their brooms and rags and headed for the parlor—another dusty room overcrowded with heavy furniture.

Fran leaned on her broom. "First let's decide what to keep and what to sell. Maybe I'll earn enough money to buy one of those fancy new refrigerators with a section for freezing food."

"Really! What will they think of next?"

An hour later, they finished cleaning, and packing knick-nacks "My back may never recover," puffed Fran as they half-carried, half-pushed a heavy chair, to the door.

At the sound of footsteps on the veranda, Jean looked up to see Johnny smiling at her. She kept her hello light and cheery.

"Oh good." Fran dropped her end of the chair. "You can take this monster."

Johnny carried the chair to his pickup. After he'd loaded all the cartons, he pointed at an overly ornate broken lamp. "There's room for that too."

"That's so kind of you," gushed Fran.

Jean smiled. Flirting was Fran's way of coping, just as being practical was hers. She no longer questioned Fran's loyalty to Rob. "What about this?" She pointed at a round table covered by a thick blue tablecloth. "One leg is propped up with a book."

"The tablecloth looks new. I'll keep that." Fran grabbed a corner and flipped it off. "Oh my Lord!" she exclaimed.

Jean and Johnny both gasped.

X

Half a mile ahead the lake sparkled clear, clean blue. She would find peace there. The waves washed to shore, then pulled back in invitation. Looking neither right nor left, she kept walking.

But every step she took was set to the beat of those lines from the bookmarked poem: *I remember I saw only that man who passionately clung to me, again we wander, we love…*

She reached the beach and stared at the lake a long time. The water, cool and deep, would solve everything. As soon as she'd made the decision yesterday, she felt calm. This was the right answer. But now something held her back. That poem. She had to read more.

Slowly, she turned toward the farm again. She would return tomorrow.

Binxie

Binxie was heading for bed when the girls clattered home from Romeo's. After yesterday's hard-fought baseball game, this morning's final frantic harvest, and tonight's dancing, they should have been tired. Yet it was their last time together, and they were reluctant to end the day. Tomorrow the exodus would begin.

They collected in the recreation room. Draped over couches and chairs, they laughed over the events of the summer—Hugh's thrilling plane crash, the talent show, baseball, Romeo's, swimming in Lake Ontario, the night they tried smoking behind the barn then threw up, Oslo the farting horse, ice cream at Linton's, the growers' party.

Binxie sat with Isabel, both slightly apart from the others. Each carried one memory of the summer she would never chuckle over or look back at fondly. But they liked the friendship and goodwill around them.

"Anyone hungry?" asked Peggy. "Who's up for a raid on the kitchen?"

They tried their usual outside window but it was locked. "On our last night. You'd think Cookie would have pity on us," sighed Nancy.

But after Myrtle went to use the bathroom, she ran back carrying a large tray. "Look what I found in the dining room." She set down the tray, loaded with little Spam sandwiches, cookies, and apples. "There are two jugs of lemonade in there too. Dear old Cookie."

Helene and Kate ran to fetch them, and the feast began.

"It's been such fun," said Peggy, sipping lemonade. "Let's all come back next year."

"Brilliant idea!" said Rita. Others agreed.

"Yes, we'll ask for Highberry again. I love it here," added Doris.

"Do we have everyone's address?" asked Grace. "Let's keep in touch all winter, sign up together next spring."

Scraps of paper were passed around, and girls scribbled names and addresses.

Binxie knew this summer could never be repeated. Even those who did return would be different. Another year of life, the continued fighting or its end, would change them.

Helene smiled. "I'll be here, but not as a farmerette. When you return, be sure to visit me at Mrs. Fraser's."

"What?" Everyone crowded around Helene to hear her story.

"My mother telephoned today. She accepted Mrs. Fraser's invitation. I'll return to Hamilton tomorrow, work with Mama in the factory until we sell the house, and arrange the move. With luck we'll be back by Christmas. My brothers can start at their new school in January, and I'll finish high school in Winona!"

"It's like a fairy tale...*Cinderella!*" exclaimed Kate.

Helene's entire faced smiled. "We're going to live on Mrs. Fraser's farm. I can hardly believe it."

Peggy hugged her. "You deserve it!"

Isabel touched Binxie's hand and smiled at everyone. "We won't all return, but what matters is, we shared this summer—I couldn't have survived it without you." She dabbed an eye. "Thanks for putting up with my early cooking disasters..."

"And the best desserts in the world," called Helene, as others cheered.

"I'll always be grateful," Isabel finished.

It was a wonderful summer—until August, thought Binxie. *Thank goodness Kathryn made me come.* She frowned. *But it will always bother me that I was enjoying myself while she died. Every birthday from now on will also be the anniversary of her death.* Binxie forced herself not to run to her cot and burrow under the covers.

Peggy looked thoughtful. "We were like travelers on a train. We all came together for awhile, shared everything, and now we go our separate ways."

"Maybe we were more like butterflies," said Helene. "Some dust from our wings rubbed onto others. Changed us."

"You read too much poetry," said Patsy. "But I like it."

Helene stood up and looked at everyone. "I hope I thanked you enough for your generosity about the tractor repairs. It means the world to me." She smiled especially at Isabel, and the girl with the yellow scarf.

"Roll along, farmerettes, roll along. Roll along, farmerettes, roll along," sang Peggy. The others joined in. "Oh, we're here to lend a hand, while working the land. Roll along, farmerettes, roll along."

"I learned so much this summer," Isabel told Binxie quietly. "I can cook healthy meals, pluck chickens, even milk a cow. But I probably won't be allowed to make more than tea and toast at home. I know it's not as important as flying planes, building tanks and bombs—"

"Yes, it is," Binxie interrupted her. "Everyone needs good food, and wants to come home to a clean, comfortable place. A happy home is what makes the fighting and working worthwhile."

"Really?"

"Don't look so surprised. It's an important job, and you do it well. You must tell your family you want to do more."

Isabel looked hopeful, then frowned. "I thought I could attend MacDonald Institute since it's right in Guelph—but now I can't. It's closed for the duration."

Binxie eyed her directly. "Is it important to you?"

Isabel nodded. "Very."

"Find another way. Kathryn always said to follow your star, no matter what."

Isabel sipped her lemonade, then asked, "What about you? Will you really fly an airplane? Go overseas?"

"I'm not sure yet." Binxie realized the irony. Here she was telling Isabel to live her dream, when she still wondered what hers was. Peggy was right. Kathryn hadn't insisted she become a pilot—she encouraged her to do what mattered to her. Well, what mattered to her? Maybe Johnny had known.

Isabel said, "Give yourself time. It's hard to make decisions now."

But Binxie needed something to focus on besides her grief. Something Kathryn would have been proud of.

A few more songs, another story, and slowly the girls drifted off to bed. Binxie headed upstairs beside Helene. "I'm glad you'll return. You belong here."

"Best of all I'll be back at school in January."

"You're really working in a factory until then?" Binxie didn't realize her face showed her disapproval until Helene's gentle answer.

"Lots of girls have to work in factories, Binxie. The pay is better."

"I'm sorry. I wish you all the luck in the world."

"It doesn't feel like it now, but you'll be all right too. Time really will heal," said Helene.

As she put on her nightgown, Binxie realized she'd never sleep next to her friends again. "I'll miss you."

Helene leaned over and hugged Binxie. "I'll always remember you."

"Will you write to me, Helene? I have to find out what happens."

"She's a better writer than I am," Peggy said from her cot. "She still writes every week to three soldiers overseas."

"Two now," Helene said quietly.

"Goodnight," Isabel called from across the aisle. "Sleep tight."

Binxie stretched out her legs—and screamed. Something slimy wiggled on her toes.

At almost the same time, Helene screeched too. "Worms!"

Peggy jumped out of bed. She ripped back the covers. "Wet spaghetti!" she shouted. "Who did that?"

The giggles across the aisle gave them their answer. "Got you! Goodnight, girls." Isabel yanked her blanket over her head just as the soggy pasta flew her way.

SUNDAY, SEPTEMBER 5, 1943

X

The early morning sun warmed her as she watched Isabel cross the yard to the kitchen. Isabel smiled and waved to her. It comforted her. A romance was impossible, but at least they parted as friends.

Binxie was up early too, standing at the pasture fence, quietly patting Cairo. She knew Binxie preferred to grieve alone, but she had to talk to her.

It was that book. Those beautiful, amazing poems. She had taken the book to a secluded spot in the orchard, read the passionate plea in "A Leaf for Hand in Hand" several times. "*You natural persons...You friendly boatmen and mechanics...I wish to infuse myself among you until I see it common for you to walk hand in hand.*" He had called them *natural persons*! She hungrily devoured more, then spent the rest of the day absorbing this major shift in thinking.

Now she stood hesitant, until Binxie stepped aside to let her pat Cairo too. "A horse gives such comfort."

"Did you leave a book on my bed?" she finally asked.

Binxie shrugged. "I thought it was Lucy's bed. We studied Whitman at school last year and she wanted to borrow it."

"I've never read anything like it."

"It's daring and beautiful." Binxie recited,

"From this hour, freedom!
From this hour, I ordain myself loosed of limits and
imaginary lines!
Going where I list—my own master, total and absolute…
I inhale great draughts of air,
The east and the west are mine, and the north and the
south are mine.
I am larger than I thought!
I did not know I held so much goodness!"

Binxie stopped to catch her breath. "We had to memorize our favorite section. This one reminded me of my sister."

"Thank you." Wishing she could say more, she turned to go.

Binxie asked. "What are your plans? Will you go back to Brantford?"

Even the thought of returning to that small town—where everyone knew your business and discussed it with everyone else—made her unsure again. "I guess I have to. What about you?" It felt safer to turn the focus onto Binxie. And she did want to know.

Binxie actually smiled. "It's still a new idea. I have to think it through some more…but maybe…I might train to become a nurse."

"War or peace, they'll need you."

"We have good hospitals in Toronto." Binxie perked up as if the idea had just come to her. "You know, Toronto is a big interesting city. Lots of art galleries, artists, musicians, writers. They appreciate Whitman's poetry. You should visit sometime." With that, Binxie pulled an apple from her pocket and fed Cairo.

"That's something to think about." She watched Binxie and Cairo awhile, then walked away. The air felt fresh, blown clean by the morning breeze. She thought of the forbidden love and the acceptance expressed in that little red book. Someone else felt like her—and embraced it. She wasn't alone. Perhaps it was time she considered her future too.

Isabel

Isabel stacked the last dish onto the shelf, rested the muffin tins in the cupboard, and hung her tea towel to dry. Everything was clean and neat, and the air still carried the aroma of the apple muffins she baked all morning. Her work had officially ended Saturday, but she'd offered to help Cookie with the breakfast today. In exchange, Cookie allowed her to bake the muffins that were now packaged in threes and tied with red wool bows—her parting gift to the farmerettes. They could eat them on their journeys home.

She gazed around the kitchen—at the stove where she'd helped cook over two hundred meals and burned herself six times, at the sink where she'd peeled tons of vegetables, scrubbed thousands of dishes. She had worked harder in this kitchen than anywhere before. She would miss the challenge of adapting a new recipe, the satisfaction of pulling a perfect pie from the oven, the pride when she saw the delight on the girls' faces as they wolfed down her brownies. They had named her the "duchess of desserts." She loved that.

This evening, she'd be home—where the reminders of Billy filled every space. By now the news of his marriage would have seeped through town. She'd hate the looks of pity, the careful words. Would her mother let Itsy run her kitchen? Cookie ranted and shouted, Nanny could be sharp-tongued, but they had let her experiment, fail, clean up her own mess—and succeed.

Would her father allow her the freedom she had enjoyed this summer in Winona? Hitchhiking with local farmers, getting her hands dirty, hadn't hurt her. Helene, Peggy, and Binxie were like sisters. They'd teased and hugged, borrowed clothes and traded secrets, and shared the Niagara Falls adventure. Never once had they rolled their eyes at her like Rosemary, or taken over her work like Gloria.

It would feel good to sleep in her large bed again, in her own pretty room. But she'd grown used to getting up at five o'clock when the day felt fresh, open to possibilities. What would she do with her long days at home?

She sighed and gathered the packets of muffins into baskets to distribute to the girls as they left. Then she carried the pail of apple peels to the pigs. Dan's truck stood in the yard, so when she carried the muffin baskets to the recreation room, she was surprised to see Helene there, helping Peggy and Kate tidy last night's mess. As Helene neatly stacked games and cards into the cupboard, Isabel wondered what the next months would bring.

Peggy picked up the last of her records and eyed the muffins. "Can we have one now? I sure will miss your baking."

Isabel slipped one to her, and to Helene and Kate. "I made extra."

Farmerettes milled around the doors. Packed suitcases lined the entrance. Last-minute items had been located, good-byes said. Now they were anxious to return home and get on with their lives. Helene looked radiant. Even the girl with the yellow scarf looked happy. Everyone seemed eager to go but her.

Helene

Helene watched a bus clank up the lane. An old blue car followed close behind. "I guess that's it," she said to Peggy.

Peggy's eyes were moist. "It's been one heck of a summer."

Helene swallowed and waited to answer. She had gained so much this summer, but she was losing her best friend. "We'll still visit each other."

As girls drifted out to the yard, Isabel waited at the door, handing each one a packet of muffins. Smokey stood beside her, saying good-bye. Many, including Helene, carried baskets of fruit to take home.

Another bus and a small brown car arrived. Several farmers and their families, Reverend Ralston and his wife, the choir ladies, Johnny, and some lovestruck farmboys were there to bid the farmerettes farewell. Dogs darted in and out of the crowd, tails wagging. Where in this chaos was Dan? His truck had stood here almost an hour.

"Good-bye. Thanks for a great summer and the penny-whistle lessons." Kate embraced Peggy, then Helene. "I'll miss you. I hope you'll invite me to your wedding."

Helene blushed. "We haven't planned that far ahead." She turned even deeper red when she saw Dan approach from the direction of the farmhouse. Jean and her parents walked beside him. Jean grinned widely, the happiest she'd looked in days.

Dan faced Helene, his eyes shining green with emotion.

"What's wrong?" Helene asked.

"Everything's better than fine." He paused, then blurted, "Jean found Nelly's fortune."

"Oh." Helene smiled at Jean, but wondered why this mattered to Dan.

"Helene, you can stop worrying," he said.

She stood confused.

"Apparently Nelly didn't trust the bank."

"No wonder she made such a fuss about a new dark table-cloth every year," added Jean.

"Tablecloth?" None of this made sense to Helene.

Dan took a deep breath. "Nelly spread her money flat on the parlor table. Every January, she covered the bills with a new tablecloth and started over again."

"There were twelve layers of money and cloth on that table," said Jean. "Nelly's fortune. According to her will, it belongs to 'Baby James, who should have been mine.' That's Dan."

"But it was in your house," said Dan.

"We've been through this. The will says it's yours. You're kind to share it with us," said Mrs. McDonnell.

"Helene. Do you know what this means?" Dan took both

her hands in his. "I can enroll in Hamilton Normal School. Qualify as a teacher. When this war ends and they finally build farm machinery again, we'll outfit Mrs. Fraser's farm properly. Helene, we can build a future together."

Helene clutched Dan's hands, too overwhelmed to talk.

Peggy, Isabel, and the girls hovering around them made up for her silence. They bubbled over with congratulations, then went back to their farewells and promises to keep in touch.

"Ready!" the first bus driver called. Girls hurried to it, blowing kisses, waving.

Peggy shook Dan's hand, hugged Jean. "Thank you for an amazing summer."

"Thanks for your hard work. I'll never pick another fruit without wanting to sing, 'Hi ho, hi ho.'"

Isabel could only sob. "I'll never forget any of you."

"You have good news too," Helene said to her.

Isabel stood tall. She broke into a proud smile. "I'm going to school to study domestic arts! Doesn't that sound impressive? They closed the classes in Guelph, but this morning Smokey told me they'd moved to Toronto. I'll live with my sister Rosemary during the school term. I can't wait!"

The bus driver started his motor.

"Wait! Where's Binxie?" asked Peggy. Helene pointed to the picnic table where Binxie was talking to the girl with the yellow scarf. The three friends ran to join them.

"Guess what?" Binxie smiled as her friends drew near. "We might be neighbors. She's going to continue working here until November, then come to Toronto, find work in a gallery, maybe attend art school."

"You're so talented. I expect you'll become famous," Isabel said, and the girl blushed with delight.

They all wished her luck and hugged her good-bye.

The second bus driver honked his horn.

Binxie embraced her friends. Peggy and Isabel dashed for the bus. Helene ran back to Dan. It was hard to leave him.

"I'll come see you next weekend," he promised as she pulled herself away and climbed aboard. She sat beside Peggy, and the bus rolled away.

Helene looked back even after the farm was a distant speck. "I'm coming back, Peggy. I'm coming back."

Jean

Jean watched Binxie wave good-bye to her friends on the bus, then turn to Johnny. The two spoke briefly, earnestly. They embraced, not long enough for Jean to feel nervous. With a smile, Binxie headed her way.

The two girls stood quietly together. It felt comfortable, like the walks and rides they had shared this summer. Jean would miss Binxie most of all, even though she was relieved she was leaving.

"Take care of Tinxie for me," Binxie said.

Jean nodded. "And you take care of yourself."

"You'll find a way to see the world," said Binxie. "When you do, send me postcards."

"You will be all right, Binxie. Did you give more thought to becoming a nurse?"

"No. Not a nurse."

Binxie grinned at her. "Me? Clean bedpans? Take orders? Never. I've decided to become a doctor. That'll be a real challenge. Thanks for everything." With that, Binxie hugged Jean good-bye and hurried to the large black car waiting for her.

"She's quite a girl," said Johnny, coming to stand beside Jean. Binxie rolled down her window and waved as the car sped away.

Jean nodded. "She is."

"Much like you." He touched her hand lightly. "Are you up for a horseback ride?"

"May as well enjoy today. The extra work begins tomorrow," she said with a grin.

Along the laneway, car horns tooted good-bye and the buses chimed in. The crowd lining the barnyard waved. The parade of cars and buses rolled onward toward home and the future. With them traveled the memories of a summer spent in sunshine, friendship, fear, laughter, and discovery—memories that would grow both dimmer and more colorful over the years—of the girls who were farmerettes.

ACKNOWLEDGMENTS

Many people helped me write this book. My heartfelt thank you goes to:

Sonja Dunn, who first told me about being a farmerette and started me on this fascinating journey.

The spunky, fascinating, former farmerettes, who described their days on the farms: Budge Wilson, Estelle Salata, Flora Doran, Fran Beaugrand, Iris Berryman, Marion Fuller, Mary Robson, and Ruth Borthwick. And to Lou Puddicombe who married a farmerette and, along with his friend Reg Horrill, shared stories of those days in Winona.

My farm experts, Deborah Kennish McCoubrey, who told me stories and checked the birth scene; Elwyn Tomlinson, John and Ariel Goud, Gene and Pam Bork, and to Cheryl Cooper, who mailed me the book, *Home Farm* by Michael Webster, which provided me with farm life insight and a plot point.

Alice Vandermeer, who showed me around the actual barn where the Larkin farmerettes of Queenston lived and shared her photos, stories, and enthusiasm with me. Also, Annie Gordon,

John Scott, Leah Sheldrick, Lian Goodall, and Jean Covert for their stories.

Bill Tourtel at the Hamilton Warplane Museum, who explained WWII airplanes to me and checked over my crash scene. Diana Barnato Walker from whose book, *Spreading My Wings*, I took much of the information about flying for the ATA.

Leslie Harris—Hamilton Public Library; Lara Andrews—Canadian War Museum, Ottawa; Donna Corewyn—Executive Assistant, Hamilton YWCA; Dorothy Turcotte—Grimsby Historical Society; Sandy Lindsay—Saugeen Times; Louise Caron—Library and Archives Canada (Ottawa).

Sarah Ellis, who encouraged me at the beginning, and Peter Carver who generously read my finished manuscript and urged me to submit it.

Karen Ford, Valerie Parke and Dawna Petsche-Wark, librarians and readers extraordinaire, who read, critiqued, and loved my story.

My writers' group, especially Sylvia McNicoll and Deborah Serravale, whose thoughtful critiques, support, and friendship are dearly appreciated.

My wonderful editors, Kelly Jones and Kathryn Cole, and to Margie Wolfe and the staff of Second Story Press, for their faith and dedication to this book.

And as always, to my family for their continued love and support: my mum, Anneliese Wessberge Tobien, who lived through it all; my children, Becky, Jainna, and Charlie; and especially my husband, Frank.

I also wish to thank the Ontario Arts Council for its support in writing this book.

ABOUT THE AUTHOR

Gisela Sherman grew up surrounded by countryside, books, and her mother's reminiscences, which fed her love of history, the land, and story. Two of her books won the Hamilton and Region Arts Council Best Children's Book of the Year Award, and one was shortlisted as a Manitoba Young Readers' Choice. Gisela taught writing courses at Mohawk College and McMaster University, and enjoys giving book talks and writing workshops. She's a current member and past-president of CANSCAIP (Canadian Society of Children's Authors, Illustrators and Performers) and ACTRA. Her fascination with story and character has also led her to acting in small roles and background in television and movies. She lives in Dundas, Ontario.